THANKS
FUR LAST
NIGHT

THANKS FUR LAST NIGHT

Eve Langlais   Milly Taiden   Kate Baxter

St. Martin's Griffin ⚞ New York

THANKS FUR LAST NIGHT. Copyright © 2018 by St. Martin's Press.
Bearing His Sins. Copyright © 2018 by Eve Langlais.
Bought by the Bear. Copyright © 2018 by Milly Taiden.
The Alpha and I. Copyright © 2018 by Kate Baxter.
All rights reserved. Printed in the United States of America.
For information, address St. Martin's Press,
175 Fifth Avenue, New York, N.Y. 10010.

www.stmartins.com

The Library of Congress Cataloging-in-Publication Data is available upon request.

ISBN 978-1-250-15971-7 (trade paperback)
ISBN 978-1-250-15974-8 (ebook)

Our books may be purchased in bulk for promotional, educational, or business use. Please contact your local bookseller or the Macmillan Corporate and Premium Sales Department at 1-800-221-7945, extension 5442, or by email at MacmillanSpecialMarkets@macmillan.com.

First Edition: January 2018

10 9 8 7 6 5 4 3 2 1

CONTENTS

THANKS FUR LAST NIGHT

BEARING HIS SINS

Eve Langlais

CHAPTER 1

To kill or not to kill. That was the question, the eternal one that seemed so patently obvious.

Kill. Kill. And, yes, kill. Like really. Who pondered this type of shit?

As Cole spied on the happy families cavorting on the neighboring property—swimming and barbecuing and playing fucking tag—*Quick, someone hand me a bag to barf in*—he seriously contemplated what he should do. Logic said Cole should end their domestic misery with the pull of a trigger. Make that three pulls because, to be fair, he should shoot all three guys he spied on.

Imagine the screams. The absolute chaos. What about the fact that he'd probably do the world a favor?

Didn't these men know sinners didn't get to have a happily ever after? These men weren't society's finest. They weren't even human.

Then again, neither am I. Within Cole nestled a bear, hibernating for the moment, his ursine half saving himself in case things got up close and personal. It could happen, especially if Cole chose to leave this tree and opt for something a little more old school. What if he didn't shoot his targets but, instead, adhered to some outdated unwritten law that said fights should be paw to paw. *I wonder how I'd do against those three?*

Win.

His bear's simple answer. Cole's lips stretched, the grin of a true predator.

The squeals of the little boy being tossed in the air by a proud papa yanked his lips straight. Had he grown so cold as to destroy that child's chance of a stable family and future?

Don't forget your own fabulous childhood.

What childhood? He'd never had a chance to be a boy raised by his father. Never got to know the soft touch of his mother. If he couldn't have it, why should anyone else?

The continued domestic happiness grated, nails dragging raggedly across his skin. The laughter pierced his eardrums. And yet, his distraction didn't come from that entirely.

A car rattled and choked as it rolled past on the nearby road, its muffler in dire need of repair. Nothing a roll of duct tape—the good kind bought in a hardware store, not the dollar variety—wouldn't temporarily fix. The acrid smell of fumes, carried to him via a downwind draft, brought back memories of the '69 Chevelle he'd rebuilt in his early twenties.

I loved that car. A shame he had to blow it up. Worth every drop of sweat, though. The insurance money went to good use.

Nowadays, he drove a luxurious, fully loaded Mercedes. Creamy gray leather seats, the supple material cannibalized from real animals, the height of decadence for someone like him. He'd chosen a manual gearshift, wanting the sensation of control. *I am in charge of all this power.* In charge of a mean machine whose powerful engine purred when he shifted those gears.

First . . . Second . . . Third. Yes!

Indeed, that was a boner in his pants. He dared any man not to get one when driving a sweet set of wheels. Wheels that screamed power, and not just because of the hundreds of horses harnessed in its engine. This car said, *I am the man.* Anyone who didn't agree would find himself relocated to an unmarked grave. He didn't like it when people argued with him.

He'd left his sweet ride at a gas station earlier today, about a half mile from the edge of Fabian Garoux's property. A cab had brought him along the public access road that wound through Garoux's property. The mobster had bought all the land he could and then proceeded to protect it. Knowing cameras watched, Cole waited in the backseat of the cab for the precise location to launch the app on his watch that caused a temporary glitch in all wireless signals. In other words, he threw out a bunch of meaningless junk that made a bunch of noise.

While the jamming happened, he paid the driver and hopped out of the taxi within yards of the location he'd scouted. He'd mapped his way well and quickly moved to the cover of the trees, hiking about a hundred yards to his destination. He launched his disruptor app every dozen or so paces, interfering with signals to cameras that might be watching.

But it wasn't the cameras that were the most dangerous. It was the patrols on this property, especially by the nonhuman guards who served Garoux, the city's crime lord. The mobster didn't live in the city. Situated outside of town, he owned enough acreage that a shifter could hunt without worrying about anyone hearing the screams.

No witnesses. No crime. No retaliation.

A good killer did the job without fanfare. Which could get boring. Sometimes being too good at a job led to an itch to try something new.

Maybe after this job, he'd branch out his services, because it sure would beat the boredom that came with sitting in a tree situated on a plot of land, a simple three acres, in the midst of Garoux's territory.

And why had he chosen this particular spot? A search of

the records showed the property deed registered to one Nonna Smith, an elderly lady living here with her spinster grand-daughter. Farmers, as he'd discovered when he'd dug deeper. Holdouts who had refused to sell when Fabian bought the surrounding properties and melded them into one big plot. A big plot with a missing chunk as the women held out against the big bad wolf next door. A perfect spot with a view that sat downwind.

Pow. Pop. The car on the road continued on its way, noxiously belching, soon fading from sight and hearing. Noisy fucker. Smelly too. That was probably why he never heard or smelled her approach, not a single ounce of warning until the distinctive click of a hammer being cocked.

"Care to explain what you're doing in this tree?"

Apparently, I am falling. That was the clever thing Cole wanted to say when he found his nimble grace suddenly gone in the face of her unexpected appearance. How could a man remain stable or even speak when his bear stirred his beastly head and, with great glee, announced, *Mine?*

CHAPTER 2

And Babushka said men didn't grow on trees. A life lesson imparted to Anja, followed by her grandmother lecturing about how Anja was too picky and it shouldn't matter who he was. Status meant nothing. *So long as he can work and doesn't hit you, what more do you want?*

How about a little respect? Someone she could feel equal to. A man who wouldn't be intimidated by her blunt manner of speaking. Who wouldn't find himself put off by her freakish height and wide hips. She gave new meaning to the word "voluptuous." Babushka said she was big boned and perfect.

Anja happened to agree, which was why she wouldn't settle when it came to a man. Then again, saying no to men wasn't that hard. For some reason, she attracted the wrong kind, the kind who wanted to climb her like a tree or lick her big feet. She'd also met clumsy idiots, such as this guy in the tree. Well, more like the guy on the ground. He apparently wasn't the most agile of fellows.

At least he'd managed to recover before hitting the uncompromising earth face-first. This time of the year, the ground around the roots proved unyielding, hard with the first glimmers of frost. A face-plant would have hurt, and she would know. In the past, this particular arboreal specimen had once dumped her harshly too.

I'm pretty sure this oak hates me. Which was really short-sighted of the tree, given she owned an ax.

Eyeing the guy, she had to wonder if a face-plant would have hurt him much. "He's a freaking rock," she muttered aloud, an old habit of hers from tending animals over the years. They at least listened to the farm girl.

Yes, she did something as old-fashioned as farming because her babushka insisted only fresh would do, especially when it came to milk and eggs. "In the old country," she'd say as she started her lecture, "we used to milk the cow every morning to make fresh butter and cheese for dinner that night."

"In the old days, you also married first cousins to keep it in the family."

"Be proud you are descended from an almost pure line."

"I'll be happier when I birth some kids with no horns or tails or three eyes."

Her babushka spat on the floor. "There is nothing wrong with birthing greatness."

"Unless you've watched *The Omen*." The creepy movie had left its mark.

Her grandmother didn't see the world the same way as Anja. In many respects, her babushka had never left the old country. A few decades since she'd come to this country and still her grandmother clung to old ways. Old ways meant sending her granddaughter out with a gun to confront the guy hanging around in their tree. The guy who was about as bright as a rock. In a cave. That was covered by vines.

He didn't have a clue. "Who's a rock?" asked the fellow with the granite-edged face.

"You are."

"I am? Why?"

As if he had to ask. He saw that rocky visage in the mirror every morning. Hard planes set his jaw square. Piercing brown eyes were framed by the darkest lashes, so dark he almost appeared to wear eyeliner. It provided a nice sultriness that went well with his tanned skinned and thick dark hair.

Totally doable. But given his lack of brightness, she worried about him being clingy. Best to pass on this one. "From what I've seen of you, you're either a dumbass or a rock. Take your pick."

He bounded to his feet, a simple leap of his body that appeared deceptively easy. She knew better and remained steady, the barrel of her gun pointed right at him. He might seem benign, but appearances meant nothing.

For example, most people thought she was just a dumb farm girl. They didn't know about her left hook or that she'd won the state spelling bee four years in a row. Funny how the fist left more of an impression with folks.

"What kind of rock do you think I am?" he asked, appearing utterly at ease. His gaze never once strayed to her gun.

She didn't like it. "Does it matter what type?"

"Of course it does. What if I'm a diamond, shiny and hard? Very hard. A diamond you could fondle. Give a gentle roll between your fingers. Perhaps rub me over your lips." The sinfully thick lashes fluttered in a wink.

Dirty talk? The fun didn't stop with this guy. Did he seriously think he could seduce her with those raunchy innuendos? "How about I use your diamonds for target practice?"

"Big words for a little girl."

Little? She could have snorted. She stood six foot, most definitely not petite, and had often been compared to a Viking babe of old during her college years. Actually, she was of Russian descent, which was just as vicious as a Viking maiden. Maybe even more dangerous. Look at her babushka. No one fucked with her. The cable guy brought her coffee when he came to fix the outages. And he'd been five minutes early for the appointment each and every time since the "incident." Then there was the cashier at the grocery store who'd tried to refuse some coupons. Babushka still cackled when the girl made the sign of the cross upon seeing her.

Most people feared Anja's grandmother. *Except me.* Anja lived to bug the woman. Which meant she had brass balls when it came to baiting people, even those who might be dangerous. "Come a little closer and we'll see who's little." She let a grin curl the corner of her lips.

"A challenge? I accept."

Accepted what? What did he mean? A tingling anticipation shimmered through her body, leaving her energized and focused. Not just focused, but intent on him. She couldn't seem to look away, not with so much to catalog—and admire. The stranger bore a neatly trimmed beard, enough to cradle his chin and upper lip with a lush pelt that went on to slash across the bold lines of his cheek.

Soft or bristly?

Would it tickle if he put that head between her legs?

And, most importantly, how long could he go without breathing?

Some women might have been appalled at the direction of her thoughts. Lusting after a perfect stranger, what was wrong with her? And not just any stranger but one hiding in her tree, spying through binoculars and bearing a gun, a weapon currently tucked in its holster.

Dangerous.

And tall. Taller than her.

Panty wetting.

Given my boring life, I don't think there's anything about this scenario that doesn't turn me on.

The man oozed suave confidence. He bore the look of a slick warrior. A gun might be pointed on him, but he exuded cool.

Funny how that very chill made her only hotter.

She never saw him move. One moment, he stood before her, hands spread, attempting to look benign—epic fail—the next, he tried to tear the gun from her hands.

Her fingers curled tight around the stock and barrel, very tight, and she growled through clenched teeth. "You shouldn't have done that."

The old country might be a mythical place that Anja heard about at bedtime or when her babushka hit the homemade potato liquor made in the laundry sink, but her elderly relative had made sure Anja could defend herself and gave her the strength as well.

Farming wasn't gentle work. Just ask her grandmother, who'd done it for the last twenty-five years, taking on double duty when her beloved husband died in the same accident that had taken Anja's mother when she was only months old.

The head-on collision that killed Helga had left Anja alive but parentless, her daddy abandoning her before she was born. The jerk. A good thing she already lived with her babushka full-time. It meant she wasn't alone. Nor was she useless. Once she learned to crawl, her babushka started to teach, her first task being to collect eggs.

Back then, her grandmother didn't yell when her chubby fists crushed the thin shells and spilled yolk. But once she started tossing them at her grandmother for calling her a slow, lazy cow, all of a sudden, her beloved babushka claimed Anja was going to starve them out of house and home.

"I should be so lucky as to move somewhere with a decent signal," she'd yelled back.

Collecting eggs and caring for chickens wasn't all Anja did. Milking the blasted cow was another hated chore. The bovine despised her; she knew it did. She could see it in its giant brown eyes.

The animals were only part of her chores. Anja had built up much of her upper-body strength tossing hay, mucking out stalls, and, in general, doing all kinds of manual labor that left her strong. Stronger than all the other girls she knew, and most of the men.

And why was this important? Because when her tree climber dared to grab her gun, he didn't manage to pluck it from her hands. He barely budged it at all because she tightened her grip along with her determination.

"You don't want to mess with me," she muttered.

"Why?"

"Because." She pressed her lips mulishly together before adding, "Because people who mess with me don't end up in a good place." At least so she assumed. Her grandmother never did say what happened to them.

"Here's the weird thing, though." He stopped pulling and leaned close. "I kind of want to." And then he kissed the tip of her nose before licking it. It startled her, and her trigger finger tightened.

Bang. She fired, the spatter of rock salt and metal filings spraying the air. The recoil shifted them off balance, and their gazes caught. Enjoyment lit his.

Let's see how long that lasts. Her lips curled in mockery as she brought up her knee, and missed, hitting his thigh instead of his jewels. The man had quick reflexes and an odd sense of humor because he laughed.

"A wild one. You can't imagine how much that excites me. And you play dirty. Even more fun. The gun, however, has to go."

A gasp left her when he showed just how little strength he'd applied before. This time, when he exerted himself, he wrenched the gun from her hands with ease. Immediately, it went flying as he tossed it before wrapping his arms around her. For the half second she allowed it, it felt good. Great. Here was a man who had the size she craved. A size to make her feel almost petite.

A size meant to intimidate.

He chose the wrong girl.

He might want to give a hug, but she did not remain still. She pulled away from him, straining against his arms, to no avail. She couldn't budge.

A wave of incredulity arched her body. It did not free her. Her body undulated in a harsh snap, and yet he did not loosen his grip. He reeled her closer.

"Let me go." She cranked her head sharply to the rear and hit him in the lower part of his face, a firm blow to his jaw. She'd sent idiots who got a little handsy to the hospital with broken bones before.

Of course those guys weren't made of stone.

"Fuck me, that was a good shot."

Did he sound . . . impressed?

"Would you like another?" Wouldn't her babushka be proud, showing manners to the enemy?

Her elbow jabbed back and stopped cold when it hit a brick wall. Her foot stamped down onto steel-toe shoes.

It was like fighting a bloody rock. Big, heavy, and unyielding, which meant gravity would love him.

She turned into a limp doll, hanging from his grip with all her weight—a size built on years of Russian cooking, the only kind of cooking that really counted. She let all her muscles relax as she let gravity do the work.

It pulled her down, but was it enough to throw the man off balance?

"If you insist on lying down, then let me oblige you."

"What the fuck!" The curse expelled from her as she found herself hitting the ground, not hard, the man who took her there somehow cushioning the fall. But he did nothing to cushion the hard weight of himself atop her, pinning her with his body. His hands manacled her wrists. He manhandled her as if she were just a girl. And, for once, she was.

"Let me go," she begged like a commoner.

"Later."

"Now." She wiggled underneath him. "Unhand me at once."

He cocked his head and stared. "Why move when I find myself most comfortable?"

"I'm not," she retorted with vehemence even if she lied. Her body very much enjoyed the fact that she lay under him. He provided a solid presence atop her, all male, all delicious. If he didn't hold her hands, she'd probably let them roam his body. Was his ass as taut as the rest of him?

A shiver went through her. She wanted to know. It had been awhile since her body showed an interest in someone. For the past few years, she'd noticed most men left her bored, so bored she'd not been with one in a long time. And longer still since she'd allowed a man to be on top of her.

Usually, Anja sat in the seat of power, riding her way to nirvana, ignoring the, at times, terrified and yet ecstatic looks of her lovers. An ex-boyfriend had likened her passion to watching a storm sweep in, all power and beauty but, at the same time, deadly if not careful.

Boys could be such fragile things. Not so the man atop her. He squirmed. On purpose.

Her eyes narrowed. "That better not be an erection, you bully." Yes, a bully who made her think of a bull who just charged ahead and did as he pleased. With her.

Her panties got a little wetter and, as if sensing it, he shifted his hips, pressing himself even more firmly. And she meant *firm*.

"Yes, that is an erection. For you. Which, I will admit, is really not what I was planning to deal with today. For one thing, it's not been that long ago since my five friends here"—he waggled his fingers—"took care of business.".

"Do you pay them well for servicing you?"

"In a sense." He smiled. "I lotion every day so I don't get too many calluses."

A disparaging noise left her. "A vain man concerned about hiding the proof he works."

"Not vanity. Practicality. If you let them get too rough, it's like jerking off with sandpaper."

She almost laughed. "You speak as if from experience."

"I am a man who is open to new ideas. Especially in the bedroom. You're a farmer. Don't tell me you never tried it with vegetables?" He arched a brow.

"If I said no, is this where you try to convince me I should eat my daily dose of cucumber?" She smirked.

A tilt of his head brought a boyish look to his features. "You are clever."

"For a woman?"

"No, just clever in general. Most people are stupid, no matter their sex."

"On that we agree."

"Don't do that."

"Do what."

He frowned. "Make yourself so likable, which leads to me wanting to fuck you, or at least fuck you more than I want to fuck you already, which is fucked-up because you are not my type. Yet suddenly you are."

The words spewed from him, and despite their roundabout nature, she grasped the gist. "It is not my fault you find my big, ungainly body utterly fascinating. Your body obviously recognizes greatness, whereas your brain is too stupid to see it, probably due to a lack of size on account of your thick skull taking up most of the room."

"Calling the man who has your life in his hands stupid is not very smart. You should be kissing me instead. But not on my lips. I prefer kisses in other places."

"Put that other place anywhere close to my lips, and I will bite. Hard." She smiled. "I will also chew and swallow."

"You have a very bloodthirsty side. I like it."

He what? He said the most deranged things, and yet, the more he opened his mouth, and the more he teased her with his weight, the more attractive he got. So she tried to force herself to dislike him. "I think it's time you got off me."

"I'd like to get off with you. But I really shouldn't. You're a distraction I don't need. A witness I can't afford." His fingers released her wrists, only so they could circle her neck, the tips pressing into her flesh. "Given you caught me, I should choke you and then be on my way. Never leave a witness behind."

She couldn't help but mutter, "Sounds like something my grandmother would say."

"A smart woman, then. So let me ask you, what would she do? I must rid myself of you, and yet, what method should I use? If I choke you to death, it appears as assault, and it might leave DNA. I could toss you from a tree, make it appear an accident."

"There's also a river nearby." If he threw her in, she could swim.

"It might make a good dumping ground because, if I kill you, do I hide the body or leave it to be found? Do you have a preference?"

She rolled her eyes. "Just like a man to prattle on and on instead of getting the job done. Would you get on with the hit already? Kill me. Don't kill me. All I hear is a lot of talk. Do something."

"I will act when I am ready."

"I hope this isn't how you approach sex, because you must

leave a lot of your partners disappointed. Hell, I'm disappointed. A man tackles a woman to the ground with brute force and then"—her lip curled—"he wants to *talk*. Is this how you want to kill me? Are you waiting for me to expire of boredom?"

Both his brows rose in surprise. "I am many things, but I wouldn't say boring is one."

"Apparently you are a man of clichés."

His lips quirked. "Cliché would be me quieting you with a kiss. Or leaping off you and running off, exclaiming, 'We will meet again.' But, instead, I shall—"

"Get off my granddaughter slowly, or I will blow you a new *zalupa*."

CHAPTER 3

Not sure what a zalupa *is, but I probably don't want one.* Something about the heavily accented words left no doubt the woman would do something vile. *But not as vile as what I'm going to have to do.*

This day had gone to shit. He would have to kill not one but two women because Cole didn't want to have to ever admit getting caught unawares not once today but twice, the second time by a garden gnome.

Okay, so the old lady wasn't quite that short. Jumping to his feet, Cole noted he towered a good two feet over the woman—one Nonna Smith, according to his research on the farm. Completely undaunted, she pointed a derringer in his face.

"I've had bee stings that would hurt more than that," he remarked, doing his best to loom over the other woman.

She didn't seem impressed.

"I don't know if I'd bother pricking him, Babushka. He's built like a stone wall. It would be a waste of a good bullet," said the woman his bear wanted to lick head to toe. Personally, he'd prefer to just lick her between the thighs. He did so love honey.

"Letting him go, though, is a waste of good meat." The so-called babushka eyed him up and down. He'd seen butchers do much the same thing. "Italian?"

He shook his head. "Greek origin."

The old woman's eyes lit with joy. "Really? I have a recipe for something Greek."

"What if he's lying and he's not Greek?" asked the woman he wanted to mount—and not as a trophy on his wall, although she'd look good mounted atop his cock. She'd also probably look very pretty on his arm once he put her in a dress.

"It doesn't matter what he is. I'll improvise." The gnome lady bestowed on him the most beauteous and feral smile.

It warmed his hard assassin heart, but not as much as the following words.

"We are not slaughtering him." The woman—*my woman*—rose to her feet and moved around Cole, brushing grass and dirt off her pants.

"We could if you fetched me my good knife."

"I am not getting your knife. Remember what happened the last time you threatened someone with kitchen implements?"

Thin lips pulled tight in the wrinkled face. "I remember. The meddling *politsiya* brought their dogs. But they found nothing. Nothing because I am that good." The evil cackle almost made him smile.

Don't you dare grin. He needed to show them who commanded the situation. Cole plucked the little gun from the old lady. "Let me take that before you shoot someone's eye out." Cole never aspired to the eye patch look. He tossed the weapon to the side opposite the shotgun, then clapped his hands together. "So, who dies first?" In truth, he didn't plan to kill them, but he was kind of nervous. What did a man say to the woman his noisy bear kept insisting was his mate?

Don't talk. Lick. Lick her up and down. That should get the message across that she's ours.

Someone should let her know that, according to his bear, she was fated to be his because he was pretty sure she didn't feel the same connection.

The girl moved fast, pulling the gun from his holster, a first for him. No one had ever disarmed him before.

Click and *click*. It took only a blink to find a pair of revolvers pointed at him. His very own weapon aimed high, face level and no big deal by his Russian lady. *She won't shoot.* It was the one aimed at his man parts that worried him, most especially since he wondered what else the old woman now hid under her shawl.

He cupped his balls. Smiled too. Maybe indulged in a little hip action. He just couldn't help himself. "Whatever you do, don't hit Sally and Joe. They don't deserve to die this young."

"A moment ago you were talking about killing me," said Anja, and, yes, he knew her name. Her social media images might not have done her justice, but there was no mistaking her features.

"Before you fill me with lead, I don't supposed I could make one last request?"

"You're not in the position to make requests, and I think it's time you left," said the woman his bear wanted to dip in honey and lap from head to toe. Especially the soft places in between.

"And here I thought we were having a good time getting to know each other. If this is our first date, just imagine what our second will be like."

"This is not a date."

"Yet, here we are. Together." He smiled, perhaps a touch too wildly. She didn't scream. Good sign.

"I don't date trespassers."

"Neither do I. I prefer to kill them."

"And what about their bodies?" she asked, showing a practical nature that the planner in him drooled over.

"I get creative." He shrugged. "Although I don't get to kill intruders as often as I'd like. Something about my security system being too tight."

"That seems like it would take away all the fun."

"You have a point. Perhaps I shall disarm all my measures and see what happens." *What fun and devious things could happen if someone dared to invade my space?*

"You have a glib tongue. What are you?" Not who, what. In spite of the gun leveled on his jewels, the grandmother examined his face with one eye squinted shut as she tried to peek under his skin.

What am I? A simple question and yet fraught with peril.

Do I tell her I'm a bear? A big one with teeth?

Do I mention that I'm currently employed as a jack-of-all-trades, selling my services to the highest bidder and reaping the rewards? Or should he tell her something more devious, like the truth? "I am Nikolaos Theodoros Arkadios, at your service. My friends call me Cole for short. But you can call me anytime." He winked.

"Flirting with my gram won't get you anywhere," Anja muttered over her shoulder, giving him a glimpse of her flashing blue eyes. "She's got a bullshit meter that detects even the slightest hint."

"I think she will hear my sincerity when I say she is a formidable, dynamic inspiration of life after forty."

"I like him. Bring him to the house." With that, the gnome lady turned around and began strutting through the untouched grass.

What? He blinked, but the view didn't change. Exactly why

was the woman trudging a new trail instead of using the one she'd arrived on? The one that apparently didn't leave a trace. No trace of the grandmother approaching, and no scent to warn him.

How the hell did I miss her coming? His brow knit in a frown, and not because the big blond Valkyrie pushed at his chest.

"Big, stupid, dumb rock." She shoved and heaved two-handed.

He looked down at her. Not far. She truly was a big girl with hips meant for a man to hold as he thrust his way to heaven all night long. "Do you really think you can move me?"

"If I get the right leverage, I can," she snapped, putting her shoulder into him and grunting as she shoved.

He almost made an effort to stay in place. All this manhandling of his body by this particular woman had caused a less-than-subtle rise in his pants. The question was, would she do something about it? Would her annoyance lead to angry sex? Or happy sex? Or makeup sex? He didn't really care so long as it involved sex.

Shifting his grip until his hands spanned her waist, Cole lifted until she was eye level. He didn't lift her far, though, given her height. That didn't stop him from teasing. "I see you trying to get my attention. Did you want something, pipsqueak?"

"Put me down."

"Make me."

"I command you to leave. Now." Said with all the sneering dignity of an empress.

Obedience wasn't in his nature. Obstinacy, though? They were close friends. "I can't leave now. It would be rude, especially since your grandmother seemed adamant I come to your home."

"Because then you'll be closer to her knife collection."

"And her bedroom."

"Why would you say " . . . Her eyes widened, and her mouth rounded into an O. "Oh. Ugh. That is so wrong. My grandmother is like a zillion years old. She is not into that kind of thing."

"I somehow doubt that." But the bedroom antics wouldn't be with her. Cole had eyes for another woman. A woman who tempted him every time she opened her mouth.

I've got something just the right size to stick in there.

"You need to go. Now."

"But I'm not done."

"I don't really care. I don't know why you were on my property perving it out watching the folks next door, but I won't call the cops if you leave now without making a fuss."

"Bah. You won't call them." Stated with calm assurance.

"Are you so sure of that?"

"Very." He leaned close and smiled, inhaling her intoxicating scent. "You won't call because you like me. Like me a lot. A part of you really wants to tear off my pants so we can do it. Right here. Right now."

"With no bed?"

"Who needs a bed? You'll put your hands on that tree." He pointed to a fat one nearby. "I'll enter you from behind and give it to you." He humped his hips and uttered a few moaning noises for effect. "I'm going to ride you like a pony at the races, taking you to the finish line a winner."

Her lips twitched. "So romantic, and yet the reality is you'll spew too quickly because I am too much woman for you, and I will be forced to seek the attention of my vibrator because it at least never lets me down."

With that saucy retort, she tucked his gun in the waistband

of her jeans, bent down to grab her shotgun and her grand-mother's pistol, then strutted away. Oh, yes, she strutted, with those full hips of hers embraced by formfitting, faded jeans tucked into . . . Oh fuck, yeah, cowboy boots. As for her T-shirt, it clung nicely to her upper body and showed the outline of a bra, a sports bra, something sturdy and reliable.

So fucking sexy, especially once it hit the ground and he could see her glorious tits. He wagered they were splendid. Everything about her was fucking magnificent. From her quick and sassy retorts to her lack of fear when it came to violence. She was better than any picnic basket. And she was getting away.

Chase her down.

He shouldn't.

Remember the honey. Ah, yes, the sweet scent of her honey, the arousal she couldn't hide from him. His temptation. His downfall.

Leave now while you can!

His job regarding Fabian was off the table, the offer to kill the people across the street withdrawn months and months ago. He had no cause to be here now. No reason to stay. And yet, he found himself drawn to this place. Drawn by fate, perhaps?

Movement caught his eye. Or should he say a certain ass. *Look away.*

Swish to the left.

He really should go.

Sashay to the right.

If he left now, he could catch the beginning of his favorite fishing show.

She jiggled as she went over a small rain-fed creek in the grass.

The woman wasn't any of his business.

Wiggle. Look at that ass.

My ass.

Fuck me.

He chased it.

CHAPTER 4

He's following.

Anja didn't need to turn and peek to know he shortened the distance between them with his long stride. He didn't have to run to catch her, not like her boyfriend in college. What a whiner Stan turned out to be. How was it her fault his short legs needed to work twice as hard to keep up? Then again, it shouldn't surprise her Stan complained. He was lazy in the bedroom too, always out of breath and asking if they could take a break. Definitely not a bull with stamina.

I wonder if the rock behind me could keep up. It might have added extra swagger to her step. Nothing wrong with giving the guy something to admire.

The house Anja shared with her grandmother wasn't exactly close to the edge of the property. The tree she'd found the trespasser in lay rooted on the far edge of the lot. He'd chosen well, though, given it was the only area to command a partial view of the place next door.

Perhaps she should have left the man to his spying. Perhaps he would do something about the rotten animal who kept trying to buy their land. Gram had told Fabian Garoux, on more than one occasion, where he could put his dirty money—spoken with gusto in half Russian, half English, and a whole hell of what the fuck.

Yet despite the threats to his manhood, Fabian, some kind of crime lord in the area, kept trying.

What a waste of time. Gram was never going to budge. She and Anja's grandfather had bought this place when they emigrated from Russia. It was Anja's inheritance, the one place that held feeble traces of her mother.

As for her father

. . .

She jabbed in the code to the door providing entrance from the back porch, and it beeped before releasing the locks. She stomped into the house very aware *he* was only a few paces behind. An attempted slam of the door was caught as Cole invited himself in.

"Just come on in apparently," she muttered, stalking out of the mudroom of the ranch house into the kitchen, where her babushka stirred a thick stew that Anja would have sworn hadn't been brewing on the stove when she'd left.

When she was a child it never failed to amaze her that her grandmother could, in the blink of an eye, suddenly have a lavish culinary feast ready. As an adult, Anja didn't question; she just ate it.

"I have to come in if I'm going to accept your grandmother's gracious invitation."

She tossed a glare over her shoulder. "I warned you. You shouldn't have come." Who knew why her babushka had invited him. Anja was only half-sure she joked about a recipe. She learned at a young age not to ask what the meat was.

Looking utterly unbothered by her statement, the man made himself comfortable in a wooden kitchen chair, his black athletic pants stretching over thick thighs. He crossed his arms over the wide chest that strained the dark T-shirt with the V-neck from which peeked dark curls. "I came because I was invited. I just wish I'd known ahead of time. I would have brought some wine and flowers for my hostess." He aimed a smile at Anja's babushka, and the old witch smirked in reply.

"Such a good and polite boy," her grandmother cackled. "His mother raised him well."

"His mother raised him to assault women on their own property."

"My mother died when I was young."

If he expected sympathy, wrong house. "So did mine. Cry me a river." She crossed her arms and tossed a challenging stare back.

"My father also died when I was little."

"I never knew mine."

"You live with your grandmother." His eyes glinted, and he leaned forward. "I was shuffled around from home to home. I win."

"That's only because you don't know my grandmother." She couldn't help but roll her eyes and then grin as her babushka screeched.

"Ungrateful child. See if I make you any dessert."

"I don't need your dessert, old woman. I'll just have a treat from my hidden stash. A *processed* treat."

"Garbage!" screeched her old-fashioned babushka.

Score! Anja couldn't help but laugh.

The knife her grandmother tossed flew with precision, but Anja knew to duck. Her guest?

Not so much, but he did have fast reflexes and caught the kitchen utensil by the hilt. He did not even bat an eye as he rotated the blade in his hand. "Nice balance. Thank you for showing it to me. Let me give it back." End over tip, the knife whirled back to thud into the wooden block wall, a mere few inches from her grandmother's head.

Her grandmother, who surely suffered from some form of dementia, smiled. "Aren't you a talented boy? I will feed you."

Not "Are you hungry?" or "Do you want some food?" Her grandmother had suddenly decided Cole was a guest in their home. Which now meant being stuck with him for the next few hours at least. At that, Anja couldn't help but groan and flop into a chair across from him. "Now you've gone and done it. She likes you."

"Yes, I'm just as baffled as you are, yet also oddly delighted. She is a fascinating creature."

"She's a beast, all right. And see if you feel the same way after the sixth course."

"I am wearing stretchy pants." He let his thumb tug the waistband and shot her a mischievous grin. "It's all good."

She shook her head, fighting an urge to smile at the stranger's method of replying. He didn't do or say what she expected. At all. It proved intriguing. Almost as intriguing as the reason for his being in a tree.

"What were you doing when I found you?" she asked as her grandmother whipped a platter of cold cuts in front of the man.

He ate a piece of thick ham before replying. "Sitting in a tree."

"Sitting in it so you could spy. Why?"

He shrugged. "I was hired to kill the folks next door."

"You're a killer?" Anja didn't move, but she knew her grandmother heard.

"I prefer the term 'assassin.' Or, if you really want to make it sound fancy, 'licensed and bonded mammalian exterminator.' A bit of a mouthful, kind of like me. Personally, I like the title 'Reaper's right hand,' except I'm left-handed, and I don't like the idea of that Reaper fellow getting credit for my kills."

"You want people to know you are a murderer?"

"Assassin for hire," he corrected before he shrugged. "A good reputation brings in the big bucks."

"And all you do is kill people?" She could tell he tried to shock her. Not for one instant did she doubt what he said. He bore the arrogance and calmness of a man who knew how to act.

"I don't just kill. I also do other tasks for the right price."

"More illegal acts?"

"Depends on your perspective. I oftentimes do society a favor. They just don't know it."

"Why are you telling me this?"

He drummed his fingers on the table. "Because I am trying to decide what to do with you."

"Do?" She arched a brow. "Exactly what are the options?"

"Either I have to kill you because you know about me, which, I will add, I'm somewhat loath to do. I know. I don't understand it either, and I might have to see a shrink to talk about it. I mean, am I killer or aren't I killer?" He shrugged. "Yesterday my mind-set was all like, shoot the fucker. Today, I'm like, meh, maybe no. Which means if I don't kill you, then I'm going to have to marry you."

Anja couldn't have said what was more explosive. His declaration or the fact that bodies suddenly came crashing against the closed mudroom door leading to the yard. *Bang*. A great big pounding and yet the portal didn't even rattle in its frame.

The sudden attack on the door gave her a moment to digest Cole's words. She peeked at her watch, more than a single glance this time, allowing herself a long look at the digital display flashing between the many well-hidden cameras on the property that stalked every move of the figures who'd just parachuted into her yard.

Parachuted. What the hell? It seemed the opposition grew fiercer and more cunning. She jumped from her chair. "We have company, Babushka. Let me go say hello."

"Sit," her grandmother barked. "You will entertain our guest."

"I'm sure I can wait while you attend to your insistent company," Cole stated loud enough to be heard over the pounding at the door.

"That's not company. They were not invited to dinner," her babushka claimed in a strong Russian accent, despite her decades on American soil. Her grandmother slapped down a bowl of soup in front of Cole, a fragrant cabbage soup with bobbing chunks of carrot and onion. "Eat. It will make you strong. Like my *lapushka*." And, yes, the old bat pinched Anja's arms to show her size.

Anja sighed. "For the last time, not everyone wants linebacker shoulders."

"People don't?" Straightening in his seat, Cole rolled his impressive set. "Everyone wants strength. If they say they don't, then they lie." He bent over the soup, the spoon tiny in his big meaty fist, but he didn't eat like a pig at the trough; he took his time. It was rather fascinating, especially since the pounding continued at the door, along with some muffled shouts.

Another peek at her watch showed the black jumpsuit–clad trio battering at the door with a ram. A useless endeavor. The steel rods that slid into the reinforced concrete walls held fast.

Someone outside tried a different tactic. The glass of the window over the sink didn't spiderweb when someone began to shoot. Her grandmother had renovated this home into a fortress over the years, claiming she did it for the eventual zombie apocalypse. But due to recent events, Anja now understood it was because she suspected this day would happen.

And, of course, it had to happen while they entertained a guest. Then again, their guest didn't seem bothered. Why did he not question more? Surely even a killer like himself had to have some curiosity.

Her turn to lean forward. "Aren't you going to ask who's trying to get in?"

"It's not really any of my business."

"A normal person would still ask."

A wide smile brought forth a dimple in his cheek—a killer look. "I'm not normal."

"Another cliché, but deserved that time." She frowned as she glanced again at her wrist. "Some of the idiots are moving around to the front. They better not trample my flower gardens again. The last time they took out that rosebush I've been cultivating."

"I told you to let me install the land mines," her grandmother muttered as she worked on the next course.

"I think I love your grandmother."

"I am too old to bear you any children, but my Anja, she has good hips," Babushka declared as she slid a plate with a fried lamb chop and sautéed vegetables on it in front of Cole.

"I am not a brood mare," she snapped.

"Or a good cook, but hopefully that won't bring your bride value down too much."

"You are not selling me, old woman."

"You should thank me for ensuring your future with such a fine boy."

"Did it ever occur to you that I can find my own man?"

Her babushka blinked. "No."

Bang. Bang. Bang. The hammering kept on enough that she might have snapped a little. "Would you stop it already out there? I'm having a moment with my senile grandmother."

But the knocking didn't slow down.

A final lick of his fork and Cole set it aside. "Now that I'm finished, I find myself mildly intrigued with knowing why they're knocking so insistently. Even the SWAT teams I've tangled with know when to pull back."

A part of her dearly wanted to hear that story, truly she did, but Anja blinked away her curiosity. "It seems my suitor has not yet taken a hint. Those are more of his mercenaries hired to bring me that I might wed their master."

"What?" The word roared from him, and he stood from the table, seeming suddenly wider than before. More dangerous.

Even more desirable.

"Sit down." Her grandmother, between one blink and the next, swapped the entrée plate for dessert, an apricot torte with the tastiest lemon buttercream frosting. Her babushka shoved a spoonful between his lips.

The mighty assassin fell before the sugary goodness. "Damn. That's good." Cole found himself distracted from the visitors at the door. But it wouldn't last because her visitors wouldn't stop trying to get in.

I should go take care of them. Yet even if she did negate this wave, there would be another. And another.

Anja sighed. Would it never end? Less than two weeks since the last attempt. It seemed her fiancé grew desperate to have her.

Sergei had not yet learned his lesson. Had not clued in on the fact that there was a reason she and her grandmother refused to leave this farm. A reason why none of his soldiers ever returned. There was no better protected place, and the reinforced house had nothing to do with it.

It began with an eerie howl, a ululation joined by a second howling cry. It no sooner faded than the roar of a wild animal sounded. Then all three erupted, vicious predators on the prowl come to protect.

Her superstitious babushka claimed it was the spirits of their ancestor come in animal form to save them from the forces of darkness.

But Anja knew better. She knew of the *oboroten,* a Russian word for legendary shape-shifters. Beings who could live among men but who were also creatures of the fur.

Usually a pragmatic girl, Anja believed in them because she'd seen them, next door, as a matter of fact, and the men who turned into animals were better at protecting the land than any guard dogs. Cheaper too, since they fed themselves.

Bam. She frowned at the back wall. "I think we should request a discount from that security company. Soundproofed doors and windows my ass."

"A delectable ass, I might add," spoken by Cole in between bites of his dessert. "I can't wait to leave teeth marks in it."

Crude and yet still panty wetting. Anja might have frowned at her reaction to his words, but her grandmother slapped him in the head. "No biting until after the wedding with my *lapushka.* She is pure."

Anja rolled her eyes. "For the last time, Babushka, I am not a virgin. I haven't been a virgin in a long time."

The next slap went to Anja. "Idiot. What is wrong with you, advertising your slutty nature to your future husband? Are you trying to sabotage your bride price?"

"You are not selling me to this man." Said through gritted teeth.

"No worries, I won't buy you. That's just wrong. I'm going to take you."

At his imperious claim, she laughed. And laughed. Laughed so hard, she started to cry and snort and hiccup.

A big boom finally hit with enough force that the house

shuddered. A moment later, a puff of fine silt pushed into the kitchen, and yet even the choking dust didn't stem her mirth.

Him standing from the table, every inch of him straining, did. It stole her breath.

He's beautiful. Not that it mattered. He was about to see why she couldn't have a normal girlfriend-boyfriend relationship. *Because nothing in my life is normal.*

CHAPTER 5

Enough was enough. A thin layer of dust covered the last bite of his cake, and Cole eyed it with annoyance. Ruined. It wasn't enough that people kept trying to interrupt his time with Anja. They also had to take from him the last delicious morsel on his plate.

Adding to his annoyance was the fact that those attacking the house—and not very well—were after his woman. *My woman.*

Cole never did share well with others.

Mine. All mine. Perhaps it was time he explained that to them.

"They broke the door. I loved that door," mumbled the old woman. "I special-ordered it to look like the one I had in the old country. And they broke it. Death to them all!" The feisty grandmother headed toward the hazy archway, in her hand a knife pulled from somewhere under her shawl.

As if he'd let her have all the fun. *And, later, I need to find myself a manly version of that shawl.* Because it apparently acted as a pocket dimension that could hold a weapons cache.

He stepped quickly in front of the grandmother. "After such a fine repast, you should rest. I've got this." Gallant? More like selfish. He needed to work off that excellent meal. Then he could justify asking for seconds.

"You're a guest. You should sit. I've got this." His blond temptress hip-checked him and slid through the opening, first tossing him a challenge.

He accepted. A heartbeat later, he dove through the arch. She shot him a sultry look over her shoulder, which could have also been annoyance, given that her lip curled.

"I don't need your help."

"Yes you do." He saw the red dot a moment before she did and propelled her into the wall, his body quickly pressing against hers.

Thwack. The tufted dart wobbled in the plaster not far from her cheek.

Darts, not bullets? Where was the fun? "Don't you have real guns?" he asked as he moved away from the soft cushion of her frame. He stepped in front of his woman. Not usually a protector, and yet, in this instance, it seemed only right.

Acting as her shield also gave him a chance to show off lightning-quick reflexes, meaning he caught the fired darts and dropped them to the floor.

By the fourth failed shot, the attackers realized they needed a better plan. Or so he assumed since they shouted guttural gibberish back and forth, gibberish his lady understood as she yelled back at them, hands planted on her hips.

A Russian hit squad. Things just got even more interesting. Exactly whom did my Russian farm ladies piss off? Did he care? A person should never argue with unexpected fun.

The fellow at the door—the one who would die first—sneered as he put his dart gun away and pulled out something more sinister, with a gleaming black barrel and a long clip underneath.

Not to be outdone, Anja pulled a shotgun from the umbrella stand.

She just pulled out a bigger fucking gun.

He almost came in his pants, especially when, with a cocky Russian accent, she said, "That's not a gun. *This* is a gun." And, yes, she might have winked at him as she declared the biggest cliché of all.

It made him more determined than ever to kill her because she was entirely much too perfect. It couldn't last. She would prove his destruction. He needed to eliminate her before he got in too deep.

The guy with the totally inadequate gun didn't seem to understand just how fucked he was. He shouted something. Something stupid Cole'd wager by his Russian girl's laughter.

She sneered as she pulled the trigger. "Tell your boss it's still no." She dropped to one knee, a good thing since the other fellow fired in a panic, but the bullet went high. Her ammo, on the other hand, didn't. She fired the shotgun at almost point-blank range.

The scattered buckshot hit the fellow in the chest, slugs of hard salt and silver shrapnel. Interesting choice. The intruder screamed like a man having his testicles singed by a lighter. It was a sound that stayed with a guy.

The injured fellow dropped to the ground, wailing and bitching but not dying. She'd get fewer points since it wasn't a kill. And, yes, he totally kept score.

What a shame the fellow wore a bulletproof vest. He also brought attention with his caterwauling. From outside, Cole could hear voices barking in what he now assumed was Russian. More shots were fired, some of them actually making it into the house. Real bullets this time, one close enough to skim past his cheek.

"Finally, a real challenge." He dove forward, away from Anja and yet still managing to shield her, his arms spread wide and his teeth bared. Big bear teeth. He let a little of his feral side push at his face, changing his features, turning him partially into a beast. "Grawr!" Translated, it was something along the lines of, "Hello, I'm going to fuck you up."

Apparently the Russians understood it. With a scream born of terror, and the acrid stench of one pissing himself, the invaders finally turned tail and ran. That was what they got for sending humans.

Cowards. But for humans, they did run pretty fast. Yay. He would chase them down. Swipe at them with his—

"Don't you dare go after them. Let them leave." Fingers grabbed hold of his T-shirt, putting even more stress on the bulging seams. He worried less about his shirt than what she thought to do.

Order me around? Not this man. He yanked away from her, hearing the fabric tearing but not caring as he ran after the fleeing cowards, waiting only until the lights of the house were far behind before kicking off his boots, shoving down his pants, fully shifting shape, and loping on four paws.

The men ran for the perimeter of the property, and Cole wasn't the only one chasing them.

While a crew of invaders might have managed to infiltrate the front of the house, the others at the rear didn't get that far. They couldn't. Not with the pack of wolves, a single tiger among them, haranguing the intruders. The furry critters herded and nipped at the men, sending them fleeing from the house, but the pack of wolves didn't kill them, and they wouldn't let Cole kill them either, one of the wolves slamming into his side as he stood and prepared to swipe his massive bear claws and end a Russian's miserable existence.

The wolves prevented him, pinning his body to the ground so that the human might escape.

Why?

I mean, don't get me wrong, I like to play with my toys too, especially if they squeak, but they're letting the enemy get into their cars. What the fuck?

Only as the taillights winked out of sight did Cole allow himself to change shape. All the animals swapped fur for skin until only men stood.

Slapping hands on his hips, Cole stood there with the same nonchalance as the other naked guys.

"So, nice weather we've been having," he remarked.

The only thing he was allowed to say before Brody—one of Fabian's inner crew—remarked, "That's the bear who's been spying on us," and jumped him.

CHAPTER 6

Anja purposely didn't pay attention to the action on the screens. As far as she was concerned, Cole had left. He was on his own.

On the other hand, her babushka unabashedly watched the drama unfolding on the screen in the kitchen while chewing on a piece of bread slathered with freshly churned butter. "Your man, he's a bear."

"He's not my man." Funny how she didn't bother to refute the bear part. She wasn't blind. She'd seen him change shape. "Are you sure about his beast side? I thought for sure with that hard head of his he was a bull." He certainly had the traits. Headstrong and single-minded about barreling after things.

"Most definitely a bear. A big one too. He will make good babies."

"Not with me he won't."

"Good girl holding him back. No babies until he meets the bride price."

"Which will be never."

"Stubborn *lapushka*. In these matters, you should trust me."

"I do trust you. I trust you to do anything to have me wedded and impregnated so you can have a great-grandchild to corrupt."

"And what is the problem with that plan?"

Anja ignored the innocent blink. "Problem? How about the fact he's a bear?"

"He is strong. Worthy of my *lapushka*. In the old country, a woman chosen by the *oboroten* is considered lucky."

"He is so strong he was taken prisoner." Okay, so she'd peeked and seen him getting jumped by her neighbor and his buddies. She'd noted with way too much interest Cole's limp and nude body—his big, impressively muscled naked body. It did tempt her to go fetch him back—*the things I could do to that body*—but she restrained herself. He'd gotten caught. Not her problem.

"Yes, they took him, and you will save him."

"Oh, no, I won't." Anja plopped on a stool and propped her chin in her hand, thinking about all the damage done during this attack. She found herself at a loss as to how to begin to repair the bombed-out front door. Exactly how to explain that to the handyman. *So our house was attacked by a Russian hit squad.*

As it was, they were lucky they lived in a remote area, or else they'd have to contend with unwanted interest from the police. Again. But Babushka wasn't lying when she boasted she knew how to hide evidence.

"You have a duty to go after your beau," her grandmother insisted.

"He is not my beau, and I am not helping him. I told him not to go after Garoux and his cronies. He chose to not listen, so now he can take care of himself."

"I see your plan now, my *lapushka*. Very smart. I see you were listening all the times I spoke. It is important to set the tone early in a relationship. Next time perhaps your bear won't be so quick to disobey."

"There won't be a next time because we are not getting together."

"Why not? Why must you be so picky?"

"I am not picky. And the why is because I don't even know the guy. What I do know is kind of sketchy. I mean he's claiming he's a killer for hire. Surely you don't want me dating an assassin?"

"No one would ever screw your family over."

She rolled her eyes. "And Daddy could go to jail for being a murderer and only see his family for an hour on weekends."

"See! You do think of him in terms of husband material. The father of your children." Said with utter triumph.

"You are a sick woman, *babulya*." Her term of endearment for the woman who drove her mad. And yet Anja loved the old lady with all her heart. Her grandmother only ever wanted the best for her. Thing was, her idea of the best didn't always mesh with Anja's. Except, in this instance, they both liked what they saw.

Anja could claim disinterest all she wanted, and yet she couldn't help but watch the screen long after the shape-shifters next door disappeared from sight.

Silence fell, broken only by the soft hum of the refrigerator. A faint patina of dust covered the surfaces her grandmother had yet to drag a rag across. The attackers had been bold in their latest attack. Too bold.

The *rat-tat-tat* of Anja's nails on the counter broke the silence. "The attackers carried real guns this time, not just Tasers and tranquilizers."

"Most mercenaries do, *lapushka*. Otherwise, they are just pretenders in uniform."

"I don't think they were trying to just kidnap me this time." She eyed her grandmother and didn't see any surprise in her expression.

"Do not be hasty. They've only ever tried to abduct you before. I think the addition of your beau created a situation."

"I created the situation." She jabbed a thumb into her chest. "Me. Because I exist. How much longer should I put up with this? I don't want to live in a fortress the rest of my life. Now that they've found us, they're never going to stop."

"We'll move."

A frown pulled Anja's brows. "That's a coward's answer. Running won't solve anything."

"It worked for over twenty years."

"And now it's not. Sergei is never going to stop. None of them will. Not until a man claims me. I'm a prize to them. A prize to anyone who wants to try." Anja sighed. "I think it's time," she said softly to her grandmother.

Slam. The small fist hit the countertop. "No. It will never be the time. Ever. I told you before there is nothing for you over there. Nothing for either of us. Nothing but trouble."

"A trouble that won't stop it unless I do something." Her turn to slap the counter. "I'm done hiding. And done having to defend myself. I think it's time I let my *fiancé*"—and, yes, her lip curled at the word—"know that the wedding is off. Permanently. And the best way to do that is in person." With a gun. And a bullet to his head. A knife to his heart would work too. Anja would figure out the details once she got there and could spew her annoyance at the person causing her such grief. "Come with me. Together we shall show them the error of their ways."

"You want us to return to the old country." Her grandmother stilled, her fingers kneading the fluttery fringe of her shawl. "We have enemies in Russia."

"Yes. I've met some of them."

"They will try to kill us."

"They can try. I, for one, don't intend to die. And if you intend to, then know I am going to sell this farm, buy a condo on the beach, and eat processed food every single meal."

"Ungrateful child."

"I love you too."

Her babushka smiled. "What a fine woman you've become. I'll pack our bags."

"I can pack my own."

"Not very well you don't. Besides, you don't have time because you will be busy fetching the bear. We need him."

Need him? It sounded so right, which meant Anja fought against it and, considering it was an argument against her grandmother, meant she really didn't stand a chance from the outset. In the end, Anja didn't pack her own things because she scooted down the road in her truck, taking the proper way around to Fabian's house. She parked her rusted truck right behind a sweet Lamborghini. Before she could change her mind, she'd slammed out of her vehicle and stood on the stoop, knocking at the door.

The last echo had barely faded when it swung open. The stately countenance of a man dressed in dark, pressed slacks, a white linen shirt, and a vest stitched with gray perused her. "Might I help you?"

"I need to speak to your master."

"My lord is abed at this hour. Perhaps if the lady would make an appointment for another time."

"Your lord is not in bed because I just saw him buck-ass naked kidnapping a man, also naked, I might add, from my property. So if you don't want me to post the video, you will let me in and inform him that I want my guest back."

"This isn't how things are done," grumbled the manservant, spinning on a heel and tramping up the hall. "There is a protocol to follow. A certain decorum to be expected."

"Decorum is overrated, and complacency is the enemy." The excuse her grandmother used when she'd randomly toss knives or other sharp objects at Anja without notice.

Grasping a pair of ornate copper-hued knobs, the butler

swung open carved wooden double doors while announcing, "The Russian farm girl from next door is here to see you, milord. She claims you have a guest of hers. She came *alone*." Spoken with a sly glance in her direction.

"Don't you take that tone with me, mister. Or do you seriously want to piss off my babushka? She's made teachers disappear for less than that."

With a pat on his ass, since Anja didn't have money for a tip, she walked in and discovered men in various state of undress. She couldn't help but clap her hands. "Merry Christmas to me."

"What do you want?" asked the silver-templed owner of the house. Fabian Garoux wore loose track pants and nothing else. Of the other fellows in the room, one wore a shirt. That man wasn't Cole.

Cole currently sat tied to a chair. Zip ties, the kind cops used on criminals, bound his wrists to the thick slats on the back. He didn't appear at all perturbed by the situation. He even managed a grin and a wink at her. "Miss me?"

She pointed at Cole. "You have something of mine."

"Are you claiming him?" The very idea seemed to surprise Fabian and the other two.

"She is not claiming me. That would be emasculating," growled Cole. "And I assure you I have my balls. As well as my pride. Neither needs rescuing."

"Yet here I am." She couldn't help but smirk at him. "About to rescue you. Ooh, does that mean the big bad killer is going to owe me?"

"How about the big bad killer tans your ass?"

"How about you both shut the hell up and explain what's going on?" Fabian snapped.

"I am not explaining shit to you." She eyed the supposed criminal lord with disdain. "And, I will add, I expected bigger."

"Hey, hold on a second, are you talking about his dick?

Because I might have a problem with that. If you're mine, that
is. Which you will be if I don't kill you. I'm still working on that
decision. And you coming to rescue me is definitely not weighing in your favor."

She shot Cole a glare. "I am not here because I want to be.
My grandmother wants to hire you."

"Hire him? Didn't he just show up at your property to kill
you?" Fabian asked.

"No, I was supposed to kill you, months ago, as a matter of
fact," Cole interjected. "But then the guy offering the money
pulled the job, and there was no real profit in it. And it bothered me to leave it undone, so I thought, what the hell, maybe
I'll kill you just for fun. At least that was the plan until she
interrupted me."

"I interrupted you because you were in my tree. Which
reminds me, you owe me a discount on your services for the
use of our property."

"How about before we decide a price, you tell me who you
want to kill?"

"My fiancé. Sergei."

"I'll do it for free."

"Free?" Fabian wasn't the only one who snorted.

Anja shook her head. "Oh, no. We will decide on a price.
A price contingent on you actually killing him. However, if I
should happen to get to him first, you get nothing."

"I will kill him. Think of it as a bridal gift."

She couldn't help but roll her eyes. "Are you back to that
again? We are not getting married. I'd rather you killed me."

"I wish I could," he mumbled darkly.

"Don't fucking tell me . . . " Fabian looked from Cole to her
and then back again before laughing. "I see how it is, and nothing I can do will torture you as much as living with her and
the crazy grandmother."

Anja felt compelled to say, "She's not crazy according to the psychiatrists."

"And how many of them still work in this state?"

"None." She smiled. Babushka left a strong impression. "If you are done with the hairy bear, then I am leaving with him."

"I am not hairy."

She arched a brow.

"Well, my back isn't," he added with a shrug.

She shook her head. "I'll bet you clog a lot of drains."

"And that is more than I want to think of. Take him. Go." Fabian waved a hand with the most girly manicured nails. Not a spot of dirt under them. "But when you finish your business and come back to your farm, have him come talk to me about work."

"I don't work for dogs."

"And he'll be too busy farming. The fields need a last till before the frost." If Cole would insist on his foolishness, then she would play along.

"Farming?" Cole repeated the word a few times as they left the house and headed for the truck. The pickup sat where she'd left it, and she could see him eyeing it askance.

"I think we should go grab my car and ditch this rolling hunk of pollution."

"What do you drive?" she asked as she swung into the driver's seat.

"A Mercedes, fully loaded with a V-8 three-liter turbocharged engine."

"Speed brings attention, as do pretty cars. It won't help us go where we need."

"And just where do you plan to take me?"

Lucky for him she actually had a plan. "We need to make it to Russia, which means flying, but the next few flights are booked solid. So, there's a storm drain a mile outside of the airport. It's a tight fit, but will take us right out onto the tarmac. There aren't many flights at this hour, but lucky for us, there is one that is going overnight to Moscow. According to my grandmother"—who stored nuggets of information like a squirrel with nuts—"the baggage guy always goes for a smoke before he does his final check and lockdown."

"You want me to ride in the cargo bay like a commoner?"

"It's a good plan."

"It's an awful plan."

Of course he'd think it was, because he didn't come up with it. However, his disdain went further than that. Cole wasn't just an assassin. He was a snob who liked to travel in style. This pairing of them to collaborate wouldn't work.

She slammed the truck to a stop and leaned across him, tugging at the door handle. "Get out. Your car is one mile south of here."

"Drive us there."

"You can walk there."

"Okay. But you might not like it." He slid out of the passenger seat and stood at the side of the truck. "Let's go."

"There is no let's. This is where we part ways."

"No, this is where I remind you I wear the pants in this relationship."

It was of little satisfaction to her a few minutes later, hanging down over his shoulder staring at his bare ass, that she showed him he wasn't, in fact, wearing pants, not once she demolished his borrowed pair in her fit of rage as he manhandled her. A manhandling that was hot, sweaty, and left her all atingle.

In the end, his brute strength won—he treated her like a girl—and despite the fact that he was bare assed, he upended her over his shoulder and marched off down the road, carrying her as if a sack of potatoes. Except, most people didn't fondle their potatoes.

"You are taking liberties," she noted as his hand brushed over the seam between her legs, the denim she wore not stopping the heat. A shiver she couldn't hide coursed through her frame. "My babushka wouldn't approve."

"I never was good at getting approval. One of my shrinks used to say I had mommy/daddy issues."

"Had?"

"I find I go through psychiatrists a fair bit."

"I doubt not getting a hug as a child is why you're groping me."

"The groping has a purpose. It's getting you ready for later."

"There will be no later."

"Yes there will."

"I didn't take you for a rapist."

"It won't be by force. You'll beg me for it."

She couldn't help but laugh. "I think you're sadly mistaken if you believe that. I don't want you."

He stroked a finger between her clenched thighs, touching her intimately, the fabric of her jeans no barrier. She wondered if he could smell the arousal she couldn't help.

"You can't lie to me."

"You don't know me well enough to tell if I am or not."

"I am a shape-shifter. A bear. I know you saw me. And it didn't frighten you."

"Fear is a waste of emotion."

"You also showed no surprise."

"I've been living beside Garoux and his henchmen all my life. I saw things. Things that couldn't be denied." From cameras no one knew they had. Her grandmother hid them well.

"And you have no questions?"

"Oh, I have questions, and I've read books. I've done my research."

"Yet your research is a garbled mash of the truth. Did you know we are created, not born?"

No she didn't know that and stored that nugget. "So you bite to transfer the virus. Does this mean I need to turn dentist and pull all your teeth?"

He laughed. "They'd grow back. And you needn't fear. The virus that is passed on by our saliva doesn't affect females."

"A chauvinistic affliction?"

"Or a curse for men. Depends on how you look at it."

"Were you bitten by accident?"

"No, it was done quite on purpose by someone well-meaning. And see, you are more curious than you thought."

Dammit, she was. She wasn't lying when she said she'd sought out everything she could on shape-shifters. Yet how to reconcile fact with fiction. Here she finally had a chance to ask a true beast man.

"Do you have superpowers?"

"I can't fly. Nor run faster than a speeding bullet. Which, believe me, I've tried. But I do heal fast. I am strong, even in this shape, and virile. I can show you if you'd like."

"No sex."

"You say that, and yet with my super nose, I can smell your desire. Your need." He purred the words. "Say the word and I will toss you in the grass and give you something hard and long to slather that honey on."

"Not until you put a ring on it." Which made her think of a certain song she liked to blast that drove Babushka nuts. "*Turn off that noise!*"

"I thought you said you weren't virgin."

"I'm not, but I'm also not a whore."

"A ring for sex? You're awfully demanding. Perhaps I should rethink killing you. It might be simpler."

"Perhaps you should kill me if you're too cheap to buy a ring. I won't marry a pauper."

Sharp laughter barked from him. "You are ballsy."

"Practical. And that car isn't," she declared as he plopped her down beside a gorgeous car, the midnight blue of a barely lit sky. "But it sure is pretty." She stroked the smooth paint of this luxury car, left abandoned and alone in a gas station that had closed for the night.

"It's more than just good looks. Get in." With a chirp, the doors unlocked, and she seated herself in the plush interior.

"My grandmother would claim you overpaid for this car."

"She's right. I probably did."

"Expect her to use this against you when she negotiates the bride price. If"—Anja slid him a sly look—"you don't kill me. Then again, perhaps I shall kill you first."

"How about we go out in a blaze of glory together?"

"More clichés?"

He smiled. It was a devastatingly handsome smile. She preferred not to think of the wet spot she might be leaving on his leather. His own fault for flashing her a thousand-watt grin without any warning.

"You're right. Who wants to die when we can live to cause chaos?" The dimple in his cheek deepened. "And let's not forget to eat really good food. When we return from our mission in Russia, I shall show you some of my favorite spots."

"If we make it to Russia. You can't just expect us to board a plane and leave."

Actually, he did. Apparently, he knew people, who knew people who knew how to get people out of the country. It wasn't in the cargo bay, or even something so paltry as coach. They flew first-class. The entire first class, she might add, all to themselves. Even the steward disappeared after Cole slipped him a few hundred dollars.

"Most people pay for service, not to get rid of it."

"I'm not most people." Reclining the seat, he lay back and closed his eyes.

She waited. Tapped her nails. Looked around and sighed, the practical woman raised by a stingy grandmother unable to bear it. "So much wasted space."

"It is. Personally, I prefer to use a private jet and really squander my ill-gotten gains, but when nothing else is available, I have to make do with more public transport. I do find it odd that your grandmother is not joining us. I would have thought for sure she'd want to embark on a murderous adventure."

How well he already knew her grandmother. "She is planning to meet us there." Because her babushka had "things to organize" before she went—uttered by her grandmother with an evil chuckle. But at least she had a plan, and that was more than Anja had. All she knew as she flew over the dark Atlantic Ocean was that she had no idea what she'd do once she got to Russia. Finding Sergei was only part of the problem. If Anja got rid of him, who would come after her next? Babushka had done her best to hide her these last twenty-some years, but the very blood in her veins would always betray her.

There would always be those who sought to take her as if she were some sort of prize. Those same greedy bastards wouldn't let a thing like a man in her life stop them from committing murder. She didn't want to spend her life trying to protect a husband from machinations he couldn't begin to understand.

I wouldn't have to coddle Cole.

The man knew how to protect himself. He wasn't just a killer. He also harbored a wild side, a primal beast that left him completely unbothered by the violence that had erupted at her home. He seemed not the least bit concerned he now flew with her on a plane to Russia to confront a man with enough money to not only track down her whereabouts but also to keep sending mercenary after mercenary in a bid to capture her.

"I can hear you thinking. It's a waste of time."

"Says the man with the small brain because of his boulderlike skull."

"Says the man who will take care of this. Don't worry your pretty little head."

Such a chauvinist thing to say. Everything he did and said was meant to put her in her place. He treated her like a fragile woman. He wanted to protect her. It annoyed mostly because it was so arousing.

She wanted this man. Wanted him with a need she'd never known. It frightened her because she kept having to restrain herself from touching him the way she wanted to.

And why am I restraining myself?

But since when did Anja fear taking what she wanted?

Disposing of the armrest between their wide seats, she straddled Cole and grabbed hold of his button-up shirt, which he'd pulled from the trunk of his car, along with a suitcase of his clothes. As for her, he'd refused to return to her house and, instead, cobbled together a valise for her at the airport from the various duty-free shops. That overpriced suitcase in the plane's hold contained a wardrobe she could use once they landed—if she were a whore.

"I am not a submissive slave you can order around." She leaned close, her lips less than an inch from his.

He peered back at her with calm brown eyes. "I can and will order you when I choose. Especially once you are my wife."

The firm statement brought a shiver that she tried to hide. "You keep claiming you will marry me."

"It will happen."

"If you try to force me, then be warned. I won't be a wife for long. Black looks good on me." She smiled. "And, as your spouse, don't I inherit everything?"

Laughter rumbled from him. "I love how your mind works. We make a fine pair."

Indeed they did. A shame it would never work. But that didn't stop her from kissing him.

CHAPTER 7

The press of Anja's lips against his ignited the fire that simmered in his blood. Something so simple as an embrace shouldn't consume Cole with need. Then again, nothing he'd experienced since meeting Anja was going as it should.

He shouldn't want to rip the clothes from her body and ravish her lush frame.

He shouldn't want to tear the eyes out of every man who set his gaze on her.

He shouldn't be on a plane to fucking Russia about to kill— for free, he might add—the bastard who thought to wed his lady.

Cole shouldn't do a lot of things. It didn't stop him. A sinner took what he could greedily have. And he would have her.

Here. Now. In this fucking first-class seat.

His hands spanned her waist as he opened his mouth to allow her tongue to plunder. Let her think she controlled him for the moment. Her aggression intrigued.

He ground his hips upward, pressing himself against her, the scent of her a sweet halo around him, drugging his senses, driving his need.

She's mine. All mine. I must have her.

Mark her.

Claim her.

He would show the world to whom she belonged.

Sliding his hands past the waistband of her jeans allowed him to cup the full globes of her ass, the worn denim only a thin barrier. She sighed into his mouth as he palpated the flesh. The fact that she straddled him, while a nice thought, did not prove ideal since she did it clothed.

"Sit," he ordered, setting her into the seat beside him. He tried to wedge himself in front of her. The wide legroom of first class wasn't quite enough for him to position himself as he wanted. He growled and pulled at the bolted seats.

The brat laughed. "Oh, Cole. I think I have a solution."

Indeed, Anja did. She reclined her seat back as far as it would go and then perched at the head of it, legs splayed but still wearing her pants.

The cowboy boot, perched on his shoulder, was a nice touch. She still thought to order him around.

And he was obeying but only because it served his purpose. He stripped those sexy boots off her, determined that when they did get a bed, he'd have her wear them . . . and nothing else.

Her jeans went next. It took but a moment for him to strip them from her, baring those long legs with the fine golden hairs at the juncture of her thighs. With her lips curled in a coy smile, she parted her legs.

Pink perfection, glistening with a hint of honey. He almost drooled like the basest of animals.

She shut the doors to heaven. "We shouldn't."

"Oh, we definitely should."

"Aren't you worried someone will interrupt?"

"Only if they want to die. And if that happens, then we'll come up with a story for the corpse. Right now I need you to spread those legs for me."

"Need?"

More than she could imagine. He couldn't help himself. All that sweetness. All that temptation.

The fingers that gripped her knees parted them. He buried himself between her thighs. He licked, his prehensile tongue—a super bear trait—finally getting a chance to show off. It truly had a mind of its own, and that mind was bent on giving her pleasure.

To his surprise, she wasn't a noisy partner. She didn't moan much or cry out. But he knew she derived great pleasure. He had only to feel the sharp tug at the hair on his scalp as she pulled. He could taste the sweetness of her on his tongue, feel the quiver of her flesh at his caresses.

The scent of her surrounded him, a decadent ambrosia made to light all his senses. She brought him to life, made him feel alive, so alive, and focused, only on her. Only on this moment.

It was the ultimate decadence, a letting go of who he usually was. Usually relaxing too much could lead to his death. In this moment, he didn't care. He was already in heaven.

His arms tucked under her thighs anchoring her. His tongue lapped at her honey core, licked and sucked, teased that nub until her breathing stopped.

When she came, she didn't scream, but she did let go of his head with one hand, using it to claw the seat, even as the clench of her other hand tightened its grip on his hair. Her body arched, the taut lines of her skin absolute perfection. So gorgeous, even if her shirt still covered her upper half. The hidden parts of her body added a certain taboo nature to their hasty coupling.

Then again, anything in that moment would have seemed damned sexy, given his cock throbbed and strained, aching behind its prison of fabric.

He stood and unbuckled his slacks, only to be left standing holding his dick quite literally.

"Thanks," Anja exclaimed as she bounded off the chair and

snared her pants. In mere seconds she was shimmying into them. "That was just the kind of tension relief I needed to sleep."

"What about me?" It might have emerged a little more plaintively than he liked.

"What about you?" She blinked those big blue eyes with their fine lashes set in a porcelain face, her Russian heritage clear in her facial features and fine blond hair. She pretended innocence, which served only to heighten her wickedness as she said, "Not until you put a ring on it."

CHAPTER 8

There was a word for what Anja did to Cole.

Smart. Having a touch of selfishness, Anja didn't mind letting him taste the honey, but as for the milking . . . let him work a little harder for it. It might give her time to figure out the strange turmoil he caused in her heart.

Like seriously, what was the matter with her? Why did she find herself so ridiculously attracted to Cole?

The man was a criminal with deadly tendencies, absolutely no remorse, a true badass killer.

Sigh.

Hot didn't come close to describing it. Still, it wasn't just lust for his fine body that drove her to distraction. Cole fascinated her every time he opened his mouth. The man never said the expected. Never behaved as he should.

He was no gentleman, and yet she felt wickedly feminine around him. Her grandmother would probably snort, right after she smacked some sense into Anja and told her to smarten the fuck up in a rapid stream of Russian.

I'll take the slap. Because Anja wasn't sure she wanted to stop feeling this way. There was something delicious about how Cole treated her like a woman. Not a potential brood mare or a workhorse, but an alluring woman.

But did she dare give in? Did she dare give him a chance?

She regarded his profile, his chin a defined square in spite of his short beard. His nose proved jagged, every inch masculine and uncompromising, just like the rest of him.

Hard as a rock and yet I want him.

He, on the other hand, slept. No sudden epiphanies about how he couldn't live without Anja plaguing him. He slept, head leaning back on the seat, lips slightly parted, hands folded on his chest. It made her want to lick a finger and jab it in his ear.

"You can tell a lot about a man by the pitch of his scream when startled," her grandmother often said.

Would he let out a high shriek? A startled and rumbling bellow? Was he worthy of the test?

How unfair he slept while she pondered her future. She glared at him. He didn't fidget in the least. It occurred to her she behaved like a girl, a weak and whiny pining-over-a-man girl.

No more. She turned away from him and extended on her reclined seat—not the same one they'd played in; that one would need some help before it was usable again.

She curled on her side and wrapped the provided blanket around her shoulders. Let him wake and find her ignoring him. Because she didn't need him.

Who cared what he claimed? Who cared if her babushka approved of him?

He's not the man for me.

As she slumbered on that long flight—nine hours in a small space with a big man—she tried not to think of Cole, which led to dreams full of him.

Cole kissing her, their lips meshed and his arms wrapped around her tight.

Pressing against her, the hard length of his shaft a sensory delight.

Fucking her, his hips thrusting as he lay poised above her on those brawny arms, his strokes deep and hard.

She awoke with a gasp, her body trembling, her pulse rapid. And the heat . . . good grief, the heat. It coiled low in her body, her arousal a taut beast ready to spring.

A quick glance showed he still slept, his body completely still. Too still.

Did he feign sleep? She could only hope because, if he awakened, could she resist the temptation he posed, especially now, with her body still afire?

She couldn't help but wonder why he had such a strong effect. Anja wasn't usually overcome by emotion for pretty boys or even handsomer men. Needs were needs. She thought by letting him take care of those carnal needs she could set him out of her mind.

Instead, his touch—oh gods, his touch—served only to make it worse. Now she knew how good it could feel. Now her still throbbing body wanted more.

More.

More!

Yet, she couldn't ask. To ask would show need. It would put him in a position of power. Over her.

No. It's too soon. She wasn't ready for that. She snuggled deep into the blanket, not daring to peek at him, lest she give in to the temptation. She tried to sleep some more. There was nothing else to do during that long flight over the Atlantic. Sleep. Eat. Then sleep some more. The few times she sat upright, they didn't talk much. He seemed caught in his own world, one that didn't involve her.

His aloofness pricked, even as she welcomed it. She didn't mind if her emotions were contrary. However, she would admit to curiosity when he went off, phone pressed to his ear, the rules governing their use in flight seemingly not to apply to him.

Whom did he call? And why wouldn't he let her listen?

Or was he trying to hide Anja's presence from someone?

She'd never asked his marital status. She'd assumed, like the greenest of women, that he was single. *Is he single?*

He better be.

Or else she might want to hunt the other woman down and force a breakup.

Don't give her the stink eye. Her grandmother always said if Anja saw something she wanted, go after it. And if she couldn't get it legally . . . then don't get caught.

In this case, Anja was pretty sure she wanted Cole. Now if only her life weren't so bloody complicated.

He dropped into the seat beside her. "We're about to land in Moscow, where we have a five-hour layover before the flight to Arkhangelsk."

"Five? Ugh. Just long enough to be really uncomfortable. But not as bad as the time I went on the backpacking trip across Europe. They canceled our flight out of Italy, and I thought my grandmother would crawl through that phone when she heard I would not be leaving for another twenty-three hours." Actually, her grandmother was more pissed Anja had gone on the trip. She preferred to keep Anja sequestered on the farm safe and out of sight. Too bad. Anja didn't always pay attention. The farm didn't have warm, sunny beaches, and Anja really liked warm, sunny beaches.

Each time Anja hopped on a plane, she did so without notice, and her babushka always lost her mind whenever Anja called from wherever she'd landed.

"What if I said I could get you a shower?" Cole smiled at her, genuinely genial, with a hint of devious.

"I would blow you for a shower." Like seriously, drop to her knees right now.

His grin widened.

"But don't expect payment until after you shower." She smiled. "I don't do dirty dick."

Guys she'd dated would have cringed at her words. Cole laughed. "Deal. And wash yours nicely as well in case I feel a need for seconds."

"In case?" She arched a brow. "I expect thirds and fourths."

Yes, it was her turn to be cliché, but she couldn't help it. He turned her brain to mush, making thinking hard. Almost as hard as him, and he was pretty hard she noticed when the flight landed and they prepared to disembark. He stood behind her, close, so close her buttocks rubbed against the front of him.

Her poor bear. She truly had teased him awfully earlier. A lot earlier, which meant he was due for another dose of teasing. Emboldened, she whirled and stood on tiptoe, grabbing his cheeks to hold him as she planted a kiss on his lips.

She meant to pull away after a few sucks and tugs of his lower lip, yet he caught her, one arm snaring around her waist while his free hand grabbed her hair in a fist. He drew her close, close enough his next words whispered over her lips. "You are playing a dangerous game inciting me like this. You have no idea of the beast you stir beneath my skin."

Such a serious tone and mien.

"I've seen your beast," she murmured back. "Why do you think you're here?"

"You might think you know what I am, but I'm special. Not quite hockey helmet special but definitely not like the other boys and girls you met growing up. I see the world differently from a human. Feel differently."

"And yet"—she pressed against him—"in some ways, you are very much a man."

"You should stop tempting me. I won't always be able to control myself. Not with the need so strong."

Need? He said it with such hunger. Here was a man who *hungered* for her.

"You're right," she said. "We should stop tempting each other. Getting involved with me is such a bad idea."

"I've been bad my whole life, so you'll fit right in."

Fit in, spoken once again as if he expected her to be with him. He really thought he was going to keep her. He'd soon realize that keeping her was only half the problem. Others would try to take. *He's not the only one who wants me.*

Disgorged from their plane into one of the terminals, she had to follow Cole as he laced his fingers through hers and dragged her through the concourses to the place he knew of to grab a shower.

The first-class lounge they entered had a certain modern luxurious feel with bold colors in the seating area and sedate lighting that gave it a casual, comfortable air.

The room assigned for bathing wasn't big, but it held the basics, the most important thing being the shower. She might have squealed a little when she saw it and barely noticed that he left her alone. She took her sweet time in the shower, luxuriating under the hot, cleansing spray. When she finally emerged, her skin a lovely shade of tomato from the heat, she felt completely refreshed. Standing in front of the mirror, she took a moment to look at herself and blinked for a second look.

Despite the hectic past day, she appeared well rested. Her skin glowed, her lips appeared full, and her eyes shone. Even her hair, hanging in long, wet strands, looked buoyant, hints of the gold catching the light in the room.

Funny how twenty-four hours and the interest of a man could change a look. Who needed makeup when arousal would do the trick?

She made a moue of annoyance. The girlish nature of her emotions irritated. She wasn't usually so impractical. If only she could call her grandmother. Her babushka would reach through the phone line and slap some sense into her.

Grabbing the hair dryer that was bolted to the wall, she turned the noisy unit on and dried her hair into chaffs of pale golden wheat. She didn't find any elastics to bind it and was eyeballing the towel as a possible hair band when there was a knock at the door.

"Who is it?"

"It's a guy with candy looking to ogle your splendid naked body. Then, later, I'll picture it for inspiration when I'm jerking off."

Outrageous didn't even start to describe it. The man was a pig. She wrapped a towel around her upper body and pulled the bolt back so she could open the door.

"You are a crass beast."

"Thank you." He leaned against the opposite wall, and his gaze swept her. "What, not even a peek? And here I brought you a present. Fresh clothes." He held up a plastic bag, the name of a woman's couture on the outside, a pricy brand name.

She held out her hand.

He held the bag out of reach. "First, my peek."

"You saw it earlier on the plane."

"Only half of your body and I was kind of busy at the time." He waggled his tongue.

She almost slammed the door shut, but the idea of fresh clothes . . . "Keep them."

Before she could close the door, he'd grabbed it and pushed it back enough that he could slip in. "You can't stop me from coming in, although I do wish you'd try."

As if she'd wrestle him. She wrapped her arms tight around her upper body, keeping the towel cinched. "Go away. I am getting dressed."

"Don't you need these?" He waved the bag.

"Keep your stuff. I'll wear my own clothes." Which, while a little worse for wear, didn't smell of the barn—much—for once.

She snatched her jeans from the chair she'd tossed them on. She flapped them out in front of her and was about to lift a leg to drag them on when he lunged. He snagged a denim leg and tugged. The automatic reflex was to tug back, and so they both tugged, a tad harder than the well-worn jeans could handle.

Rip.

She stared at the hole running along the seam of the pants. "You wrecked my favorite jeans."

"Wrecked them how?" He held them up and stuck his face under the new hole and wiggled his tongue. "These are perfect now, if you ask me."

"You are disgusting."

"And you are a liar." Cole dropped the pants and grinned at her. "I'm a beast, remember? I smell everything."

"That isn't something I'd brag about." But at least she knew she smelled better.

The pocket at the front of his slacks—that somehow looked fresh once again and neatly pressed—buzzed.

"More phone calls?" she queried, eyeing her torn jeans and wondering how she could fix them.

"I am a man in demand. Kill this. Kill that. I've recently invested in the funeral home business. Not only am I shareholder but I get a referral fee if someone sends them the bodies I leave behind."

"There is something oddly perverse about that."

"More perverse than me being a bear who kills things?"

How to reply? Nothing about him made sense.

The phone in his pocket went silent for a moment before insistently buzzing again.

"I think you should answer that."

"I should." He said it, and yet he waited.

"Well?"

"Well, I can't very well leave without seeing your tits. I came here to see tits, and dammit, I am going to see some tits."

"My tits?"

"Do you see another pair around here?"

She smiled, especially since his pocket buzzed again and he got the most aggrieved look on his face. "I'll show them when you show me a ring."

"You're demanding."

"And you're whining again. Look at me, the big bad killer who is going to sulk because he didn't see boobies." And, yes, she did rub a fist under her eye as part of her mockery.

He didn't seem to appreciate the humor. "I do not whine."

"You complain. Loudly. And often. And I don't believe you're as rich as you claim because a real man of wealth would have no problem getting me a sizable rock to wear."

"Big stones get caught on things."

"Yes, they do, on the sneers of those who would look down on us." She smiled. "Fear not, though. Blood washes off."

"You say the hottest things. But you need to stop distracting me. I've got business to take care of. Catch." Using the oldest ploy in the book, he tossed the shopping bag at her, which meant she had to let go of the towel and raise both her arms if she didn't want to get hit in the face.

The tiny fabric tuck didn't hold. Gravity proved stronger and stripped her.

His low chuckle served as a caress over her skin, giving her an intense shiver of awareness.

"Absolutely delicious. I'll be having those for dessert later." He opened the door and slid out, but not without a parting remark. "I hope you like wearing pearls."

And if you didn't know what that meant, look it up, because the last you thing you needed was your grandmother explaining it in the seventh grade as a dirty, disgusting boy spraying his sticky stuff on a girl's neck thinking free pearls were better than ocean ones.

With Cole gone, she bolted the door again. Too late, though, with his simple incursion, he'd left traces of himself behind. Her body noticed and reacted. Her skin felt sensitized, and her breasts hung heavily, the tips of them rosy.

She should dress instead of noting her different horny body parts. She dumped the bag on the reclining chair, trying to make sense of the stuff.

The fabric caught her eye first. Not denim. Not even cotton. She held up the dress. "He's out of his fucking mind." He couldn't expect her to wear the vivid blue jersey gown. Made of thick knit, the stretchy material would contour every inch of her body, from the tight wrists on the sleeves to the snug bodice to the skirt flowing from her full hips to hang shark-bite style almost at her ankles.

It was a dress meant to show off curves. A dress to seduce. And he'd bought it for her.

I'd prefer my jeans.

She'd also prefer underwear that wouldn't double as dental floss. She held up the scrap of filmy satin. It was only slightly worse than the bra, the cups low cut, the material fine, so fine that when she slid the dress down over her body, it frictioned against her nipples, hardening them into points that showed clearly through the fabric.

A glance in the mirror made her gasp. With her hair blow-dried into disarray, her skin flushed and still dewy, the decadent gown hugging every curve, she no longer looked like a farm girl who worked too hard.

On the contrary, she looked fuckable.

And she couldn't wait to show it off. After slipping on the

cowboy boots because, hell yeah, cowboy boots went with everything, she sauntered from the rented room, noting the hall was empty. Where had he gone?

Since Cole hadn't mentioned he had a room, she didn't bother knocking on any of the doors as she strutted her way to the reception area, the heels of her boots clacking loudly on the floor.

Sauntering into the open public area, she stopped short, especially as she spotted the men in suits at the reception desk. One of them noted her. He pointed.

They always pointed. It was so rude. So obvious. It meant, *Here we go again.*

"There she is," said the one with the wagging stubby finger.

"Grab her before she screams," said his even stupider companion.

"Touch her and die," snapped Cole, the noise of the concourse following him as he stepped through the door into the reception area of the spa.

"Mind your business," snarled the first moron.

Cole's eyes turned flat and cold. "She is my business. I licked her. I own her."

Yes. He said it. The most childish claim ever. Still, it made her smile stupidly, so stupidly her babushka would have slapped her.

"This doesn't concern you. You do not want to mess with us. You don't know who we work for," said one of the idiots in very heavily accented English.

"I really don't care who you are and who pays your bills." Cole took a step forward, his posing seemingly indolent, and yet, the glint in his eye? Anything but. He stood, feet apart, his tan linen slacks loose, his button-down shirt not completely hiding the power coiling within him. "I'm going to show you why you don't touch what's mine."

"Yours? I am not yours," she snapped.

"We can argue about that in a minute. Let me just take care of your visitors first."

"Fine," she huffed. Let him handle the guy who'd pulled a gun. It didn't seem to bother Cole. With a growl, he drove forward, and she leaned back against the wall to watch. It wasn't as if she could do anything else. The formfitting dress wouldn't allow it.

An advantage to being in the audience was she got an excellent vantage point of the fight. While Cole might have growled on attack, he remained a male for the fight, his fists landing with meaty thuds. The gun was knocked early from the guy's hand, just like the moron's companion lost his knife.

They couldn't hope to prevail against Cole. For a big man, he moved with seamless grace. His twists and ducks as he weaved between the two attackers created a beautiful dance that saw him thrusting at the right moment, kicking out the next, pirouetting before doing a leg rotation that knocked the fellow with the stubby fingers out. As for his friend?

He bolted. Coward.

More surprising, no one chased. Cole grabbed hold of her hand and tugged her to the unmarked door behind the reception desk, a desk that had emptied the moment violence erupted.

"Shouldn't we go after him?" she asked, craning to look over her shoulder. "He's getting away."

"Let him. We have no time. Someone will have reported what happened, so unless you'd like to get turned into Swiss cheese or perhaps anally probed without lube for terrorist weapons, I'd suggest we get our asses out of this airport, and I don't suggest we use the front door."

He took her through a room marked STORAGE to another door. It had a touchscreen embedded in the wall beside it. He pulled out his phone and tapped at it, then scrolled a few times before tapping again. Then he held up his device to the waiting scanner.

Beep. The door clicked and opened.

"You are talented." She wouldn't begrudge him a compliment.

He enjoyed it a tad too much, his lips smothering hers, but it was so he could whisper, "Shhhh."

He kissed her to shut her up. She couldn't really deny she enjoyed his methods. He opened the unlocked door, and she went through first. He quickly followed and grabbed her hand before jogging down the long hallway, lined at intervals with other doors marked with company names. He bypassed an elevator, the closed metal door battered, and went for the stairs at the end.

As they clattered down the concrete and metal stair treads, an alarm started.

Whoop. Whoop. Whoop. When it stopped, a robotic female voice began to speak, but, for some reason, she started in French.

Typical. "Any idea what she's saying?" she asked.

"A suave killer and his diabolically attractive companion are in the airport. You are all in epic danger. They are super dangerous. Especially him. Expect to be fucked-up royally if you get in his way."

"That is not what she's saying."

"Think of it as a better translation because that prerecorded version about a possible terrorist attack is boring."

"And you most definitely aren't."

"Boredom is for those who've retired from life."

"And you like this kind of life?" she asked as he did something to the door at the bottom of the stairwell. It popped open, and the fresh air hit her, as did real daylight.

No time to stop and enjoy the feel of the rays on her skin.

Cole still moved, keeping close to the building and yet not slink-ing or slouching. He kept her tucked against him with an arm anchored around her waist.

"We make good targets out here," she remarked.

"We won't be out here for long." A press of his phone against another security device and it took only a second for a beep that meant the door was open.

If asked later, Anja couldn't have said how he did it. The man seemed to know the airport and its failings because, some-how, they went from accosted in the spa on that concourse to the parking garage, where he kept holding down the button on his phone and rotating left to right until a car flashed its lights and beeped.

No way. No one was that prepared.

"Don't tell me you keep a car parked here?" she said as they threaded to the next row over with the vehicle.

"Of course not. My contact in Moscow does, though, and he sent me the car fob signal so I could borrow it."

"You can do that?"

"You wouldn't believe the things I can do. And most of them don't involve handcuffs." He winked at her before opening the door with a flourish.

She sank into the car, another luxury one. As he slid into the driver's seat, she couldn't help but say, "You must have the devil's own luck knowing a friend with this level of car instead of a piece of junk."

"Had I needed something a little more rusty, I had another friend I could call. But, when possible, I like to ride in style. Buckle up. Or don't. But I am going on the record now as saying I doubt this will be a smooth ride." He peeked in the rearview as he started the car, his phone sitting on the dash blinking red and exclaiming, "Start the engine!"

He revved the motor before slamming into reverse. She

might have wondered at his quick movement except she heard the pop then crack as something impacted the car.

"What was that?"

"Gunfire. We're under attack."

"And they're shooting bullets? What happened to trying to capture? That was all they ever attempted before."

Crack. The shattered back window showed that wasn't the case anymore.

"How nice of them to aerate the car."

"They're trying to kill me." She pointed out the obvious.

"You? That seems pretty presumptuous. I am sitting right here, you know. For all you know, it's me they're after. I am wanted by several countries and a few mercenary groups."

The crackle and pop of gunfire made her yell, "Fine, they're trying to kill us both."

"No, they are wasting ammunition."

Screech. He turned a corner, and for a moment, the shooting stopped until they approached the barrier leading from the garage to the city itself. Parked in front of it, a utility truck and, on either side, more gunmen.

Screech. The car skidded in a sudden sharp turn again, whipping around corners until Cole aimed the car at a pair of yellow concrete posts and said, "This might leave a dent."

CHAPTER 9

"Might leave a dent," she muttered in a low tone from the passenger seat of the truck they'd commandeered. "Your little stunt demolished the car, and I got punched in the face by the air bags."

"Don't whine like a girl."

Whack. She punched him. Like a man.

He grinned. "That is more like it."

"You are completely insane. We could have died."

"And yet we didn't. On the contrary, we're alive, and they're not."

Because she and Cole had pretended to be dead. Those who'd come to take a closer look never expected they enjoyed the last moments of their life. Cole didn't waste his movements, quickly disarming the first fellow and snaring his gun, then carefully meting out the bullets. Each one counted, and in short order, he and Anja had left the scene, just moments ahead of arriving sirens.

He'd saved her. That meant she owed him. "I look forward to your thanks."

"Not so fast there, kill-happy boy. Since we don't know who they were after, on account of someone killed them too quick"—the minx shot him a disgruntled look—"don't expect me to pay for those kills."

"Someone has to pay. I don't work for free."

"Then next time leave one of them alive."

"You're being bossy again. I don't suppose you can save a bit of that for later. I know a place that sells leather catsuits that would go perfect with that attitude."

Unlike some women who would slap him, she reached out and placed her hand on his thigh. "No freaky sex until I get my ring."

"Does a cock ring count? I can get one of those too."

The hand left his thigh.

"Where are we going since our flight is canceled?" she asked, peeking out the window, not seeing much. The day was rainy, leaving the world washed in gray and dampness, the moisture beading on the windows and rolling in jagged rivers.

"We are going to hole up at a place I know while I ferret out a few answers."

"Answers to what?" She traced absently on the window, the tip of her finger dragging slowly. It shouldn't have been so distracting, and yet Cole couldn't help but wonder, what if that finger dragged down his body instead?

Focus. He needed to remain focused, given the fact that the attacks kept coming, even though no one knew their plans. Someone had come looking for them, and looking hard. Why?

"You can't tell me all this effort is because you're a runaway bride."

"Is this your way of saying I'm not worth it?" She angled a look at him.

"Angling for compliments? Put your lips down in my lap and you'll see how much I like you."

"I'm saving it for the man who puts a ring on this finger." She waggled her hand. "Which looks like it might be Sergei at this point."

Did she seriously think he'd let her go to another man? Over his dead bear body. "Why does he want to marry you?" Men went to desperate measures only for a few reasons—greed, power, and lust.

"Can't he want to marry me because I have perfect birthing hips?"

Her mere existence was enough reason to marry her, but he might be a tad biased, seeing as how she was his mate. Why this Sergei's interest? "Do you have money?"

"Would I work so hard on a farm if I did?" she replied with a snort.

"Your house was better protected than most military buildings I've infiltrated."

"Babushka and I are lonely women out in the country. We like to feel safe."

"You're playing me." Like a fine fiddle, and he couldn't help but admit that he found her deception kind of sexy. What secrets did she hide? There was something she didn't tell him.

"If I were playing you, I'd be a lot more naughty." She leaned over and put her hand back on his thigh. She slid it upward, stroking the linen, the tips of her fingers just brushing the inner seam.

"It's not attractive to tease."

"Who says I want to be attractive?"

"Are you fishing for more compliments? Because if you're feeling that unattended, we could stop on the side of the road. I got you a dress for a reason. Easy to slip it up and take you with your back pressed against the warm hood of the truck."

"Because fornicating in the street is supposed to tell me I'm hot?"

"Depends on the guy you're with. Trust me when I say any kind of outdoor humping is hot. As is indoor humping. Vehicle fucking is cool, but it can require some finesse with certain steering columns."

"Speaking of vehicles, did we have to take their truck? It reeks of salami."

"It reeks of more than that, and yes, we had to take it, or would you have preferred we remained there longer while I arranged for a new car? Perhaps giving the police a chance to appear and decide we're all criminals?"

"You might be afraid of the police. I, on the other hand, would claim you kidnapped me."

"You would have turned me in?"

She shrugged. "I'm too pretty for prison."

He couldn't help but smile. "Yes, you are." She was also too pretty to die, and way too pretty for him to share with the man who wanted to kidnap her.

Was this Sergei now trying to kill her?

Does this mean he got the memo I sent to every Russian newspaper stating, "She's mine. Get over it"? Addressed to the Douche Nozzle in Russia who got dumped, signed by the man who is going to tap that ass.

Childish? More like a taunt meant to draw out his enemy.

It worked. Cole drew him out all right, with guns blazing and putting Anja at risk. For that, the man would die. He'd also die for a few other reasons, but that one was top of the list at the moment.

Cole parked, and they spilled out of the borrowed truck, hiking over a few blocks until he could hail a taxi. He chatted with the driver as they went, inane stuff to keep him addled while giving him instructions to turn left here, no right there, oops, let's do a U-turn. The fellow did it, and Cole watched for signs of pursuit.

"Paranoid much?" she asked.

"It's what keeps me alive." Said with a wink before he had their driver stop. A trek to a spot two blocks over and they hailed a second taxi, using this one to drop them three blocks from his destination, a condo. His condo, he might add. He actually owned or rented a place in most of the major epicenters of the world. They made good replenishing spots if needed on a job and good hideouts when he wanted to drop out of sight. They also provided a great means of laundering money and making him look like a legit landlord with the governments. Hiding his ill-gotten gains in plain sight. It was poetic.

The condo he owned in Moscow was situated in a low-rise unit with the top level belonging entirely to him, along with the rooftop terrace.

No one knew about it, except for Anja, and she perused it with a haughty air, windblown blond hair a wild nest around her face, her dress somewhat bedraggled and yet clinging to her curves in a way that made him jealous.

I should be the only one allowed to hug that body.

She sighed. "I suppose these accommodations will do."

"It could use a woman's touch," he noted with a smile.

"Could it?" She dropped her hands as she sashayed her way to him. She peeked up at him through fine lashes as she cupped his hardness through his pants. "Is this your less-than-subtle way of saying you want me to touch you?"

"I need you to touch me," he growled. Needed her with a hunger that only grew. A hunger only she could sate.

A hunger she seemed determined to deny. She walked away from him, choosing to go peer out the window. "No balcony," she remarked.

"Less access. Unless you can stick to walls and climb them like a certain superhero."

"A man concerned about safety and yet your door is wooden. Seems rather flimsy for a man whose foes play with guns."

"If they've made it to the door, then that means the systems I have in place failed." He didn't mention exactly how many systems. Automated and easily armed via his phone with the tap of a code, motion sensors went online. Body heat sensors watched who was in the area and if they carried guns. His protocols even monitored the dispatch channels of local authorities to see if any of them were too close to his hideout. All kinds of bells and whistles meant to give him a warning and head start. He'd need them because he planned to get very distracted.

"It's probably not a good idea I stay here. They'll find us."

"I think you overestimate the enemy. I'm good. *Very good.*"

"You're also very cocky." She returned to stand before him.

"It's confidence."

"It's stupidity. My problems shouldn't be yours. You can walk away. You don't have to do this."

"I want you." Not I want to. He said "you" on purpose.

Judging by the slight widening of her eyes, she noticed the slip. She leaned up so that her lips brushed his mouth with her next words. "Being with me is dangerous."

"Being with me is deadly."

"We are too different for this work," she argued, each soft syllable a caress against his lips.

"I want to lick those differences." Lick and fuck and keep. Not kill. Not anymore.

She's mine.

He understood that, but how to convince her she wanted him too?

"I'm a farm girl, up at the crack of dawn feeding hateful chickens and milking a murderous-intentioned cow."

"I sometimes crawl in at dawn and would gladly murder the cow for steak so you could get some more sleep. With me. Naked. I like naked."

"If you want it, then you know what you have to do."

Of course I want it. And you don't yet seem to realize. I licked you. You're all mine.

"Did you just say you licked me, I'm yours? Seriously?"

Um, had he spoken that out loud? Given she'd pulled back and stared at him . . . "You didn't have a problem the first time I said it to the guy."

"I thought you were trying to distract him, not save the last piece of cake."

He couldn't help but grin. "You're better than cake."

"I'm better than a lot of things."

Couldn't argue with that so he shut her up the best way he knew how, with his lips.

She didn't protest unless the stab of her tongue in his mouth was meant to start a fight. Just in case, he sent his own tongue to duel, the wet slide and suck a frenzied descent into the arousal he couldn't help when near her.

All of him ached to have her. His balls hung tight, full and heavy. His cock strained behind the hated barrier of his clothing, ready to sink into her.

She pushed away from him, and he might have protested until she gripped the fabric of her dress and pulled it upward. Up over her firm calves. Over her trim knees. Higher still, revealing those precious thighs.

Then she dropped in a crouch. "Let's see what we have," she purred in the vicinity of his groin.

His slick tongue had no reply as she made quick work of his clothing, soon having his erect shaft springing into the open. It didn't bob for long. She quickly grasped it, stroking her strong hand up and down its length.

"Don't I owe you for that shower at the airport?"

If he were a dog, he might have wagged his tail and lolled a tongue. He was a bear. They had more manners than that. He grunted.

Her hand tugged at his shaft, back and forth, exploring the length of him. "My, what a big dick you have."

"Wrong fairy tale," he managed to mutter, his eyes closed and head leaned back, as he allowed himself to enjoy it.

"That's right. You're not a wolf but a bear. Which means, if I'm lucky, you'll taste just right." She leaned in and let her lips slide over the tip of him. It proved his undoing.

Coherent thought fled, and he barely remained standing. He might have uttered a manly groan. He definitely enjoyed a very masculine shudder.

Crouched before him, Anja paid homage to his member, taking it deep into her mouth on the downward stroke of her hand. Leaving it wet and bereft as she slid past the tip and let it pop free.

Then back into that sweet mouth of hers again for a long suck and pull and more sucking and more . . . Fuck, it felt good.

Sensations bombarded him at her sweet ministrations. His fingers threaded the blond silken strands of her hair, but he let her control the cadence, simply enjoying the oral pleasure. Enjoyed her obvious love of the act. He could smell it, her pheromone perfume surrounding him in a cloud.

His balls tightened, and his cock readied itself. His hips arched and held. She sucked him hard and *yes*

. . .

He spewed his seed hotly into her mouth, marking her with his essence, and she took it. Every last drop.

And then, for the first time during the glow of after-sex, a woman made him laugh as she said, "I licked it. I own it."

In that moment he realized what perfection truly was.

They might have indulged in more coital fun if the grumbling of her hungry belly hadn't taken them from the moment. "Is this a hint I should feed you?"

She snickered. "I thought you just did."

"Apparently, that wasn't enough, so I'd better get you something you can chew because we all know you have swallowing down pat."

"I can hold on awhile longer if you want to show me the ceiling in your bedroom."

The hint almost swayed him. After all, he had the coolest ceiling and the best mattress; however, once they got in there, they might not leave for hours. "If you faint during the marathon sex I have planned, I'm going to be emasculated. So food first. Then sex. Then maybe more food with sex."

Of course that plan would have worked better if, the moment he went to check the kitchen for something, the door to his place hadn't been kicked open and men dressed in dark suits and sporting guns hadn't barreled in.

All of them leveled on him. They looked at him and saw a threat.

Wow, were they wrong.

Hands planted on her hips, looking every inch an avenging blond goddess, Anja spat, "I see you hiding behind your goons. I should have known you were responsible for my problems."

"That's Sergei?" Cole asked, eyeing the elderly man dressed in an impeccable suit and smelling of pussy. The big cat variety, not the between-the-thigh kind.

"No, that's not Sergei. That's my grandfather. Matvei Tygrov."

The fucking Russian mobster king himself. Holy shit. Cole stuck out his hand. "An honor, sir, to meet a legend."

A legend who wasn't impressed that Cole's pants were still undone because his granddaughter had blown him.

"Bring the bear. And don't be gentle."

CHAPTER 10

"Don't you dare harm him," was her imperious command. Anja stood in front of Cole as she faced her grandfather, acting as a shield. But the dumb man just had to talk.

"That's your grandfather? The renowned Russian mobster? Why didn't you tell me?"

"It never came up." Because, really, how was that conversation supposed to go? *Hi, my name is Anja Helga Tygrov, and I'm a Russian mob princess who is in hiding from my family because if they knew I was alive they'd kill me.* Or someone not of the family would try to marry her and become part of the family. The name Sergei came to mind. A previous attempt by another suitor had failed. Antov died during his courtship. A mishap with her grandmother's cooking. The cops could never prove how the poisoned mushroom ended up in the benign batch her babushka had bought from the grocery store.

"It never came up? That's bullshit," Cole hissed at her a moment before they got into the backseat of her grandfather's limo parked in front of a hydrant at the curb. "Maybe you could have tried, like, 'Hey, Cole, I'm the granddaughter of the biggest criminal gang in Russia.' Do you have any idea of how sexy that is? I mean, I am hooking up with fucking royalty."

"Shoot him," stated the man whom she'd refused to see since he started contacting her months ago.

"Don't you dare harm a single hair on his head," she threatened, narrowing her gaze.

"This common ruffian is not a proper consort for a princess."

"I'm a farmer."

"Only because you refuse to take your rightful place here." The patriarch of the Tygrov family, a family that had abandoned her, glared at her from under bushy white brows. Not much of a change from pictures she'd seen of him when he was younger. The males in the Tygrov line tended toward platinum locks. She knew this from all her online stalking. What they didn't mention was how hard it would be to contain her curiosity now that she was face-to-face with her grandfather.

"Maybe I would have taken my rightful place if your son hadn't dumped my mother."

"He didn't have a choice. Your father was betrothed to another and chose to honor that promise out of respect for our family name. But had he known of your existence, we would have taken steps."

"To what? Kill me?"

"Of course not!"

"Then what would you have done?" Her lip curled. "Torn me from my mother? Ripped me from my grandmother?"

"You are a Tygrov. You belong with us."

"That will never happen. As far as I am concerned, my grandmother is my only family."

"She can't protect you."

"I can." Cole finally tossed in his two cents. It earned him a dual stare. "What? I am just saying I can."

"Says the man taken unawares." Her grandfather sneered.

"Is that what you think?" Cole's lips pulled into a smile, and he appeared utterly at ease. "Sometimes the spider has to leave the web wide open to trap a fly."

"And sometimes a lighter sets the strands on fire and they

all die." Two sets of eyes turned on Anja. She shrugged. "I can't stand spiders, and my grandmother won't waste money on bug spray."

"Your grandmother is a meddlesome hag," grumbled her grandfather. No, he'd not earned that title. He was nobody.

"You're a kidnapper."

"It's not the worst thing I've done in my life. Not even close." The old man couldn't help a note of pride.

"The worst I ever did involved cheese, a goat, and some pictures. There is still a bounty on my head in Utah because of that stunt. Speaking of stunts, you never did say where you were taking us."

"I am taking my granddaughter home."

She crossed her arms over her chest. "My home is an ocean away."

"Only because you were stolen from me. Now be quiet while I speak to the assassin."

"Why? Are you going to try and hire him to kill me? Afraid to get your hands dirty?"

"I don't kill family," growled the senior Tygrov.

"No, you just cast them off when they don't mesh with your plans."

"For the last time, it's not my fault your father chose to abandon your mother."

"Did you threaten to cut him off from the money tit?" Cole fixed the old man with a stare. "Did Daddy Dear tell the little teat sucker to dump the peasant girl?"

"I didn't know she was pregnant."

"And he obviously never loved my mother enough to find out what happened to her." Anja's stark observation sat in the air and killed all conversation.

It lasted a fair moment. It resumed eventually with Cole baiting the older man and tossing out impossible antics. If Anja had been less annoyed, she might have enjoyed it more. As it was, the closer the car drew to the airport and the next flight out, the more she tensed.

Why was she nervous? It made no sense. She'd known she'd have to confront the Tygrovs at one point. She couldn't move forward unless she dealt with her family name. Perhaps she could ditch it. Have herself disowned.

Maybe I can finally have a future. One that didn't involve hiding—both herself and bodies.

The attempts to see the positive didn't ease the tension. Neither did the private jet with its luxurious interior. Although her stomach did stop grumbling, as her grandfather had a meal served as soon as the plane left the ground.

"My *babulya*'s is better," she confided to Cole as she took a bite of the lox provided with the cold cuts.

"Don't speak of that old crone," her grandfather grumbled. "It's her fault I didn't know about you for so long."

"No, it's your fault for being a stuck-up ass who wouldn't let my mom and dad marry."

"And apparently you've not learned your lesson." Cole speared a piece of meat and observed it. "Anja tells me she's supposed to marry some Russian dude she's never met. Your doing, I assume?"

"Not entirely. When my son died, without a known heir, it was assumed my brother's son would succeed me. That changed the day I found out about Anja."

"And it's my fault you found me." She grimaced. "Turns out my babushka had us well hidden. I messed that up when I decided to go on a school trip to London. Babushka said I couldn't go. I did anyway, except, while they let me into London easily, getting back to U.S. soil proved more difficult. The person I bought the forgery from was using stolen identification. I got pinged and detained."

"Not detained for long." Spoken with a harrumph from Tygrov. "By the time my men arrived, you'd vanished again."

"My *babulya* pulled some strings. She pulled some for years while reinforcing our home. She told me it was for the day the dead rose. I think she meant you, though."

"She is a meddlesome old woman who did a finer job than I would have expected keeping you hidden. And yet you left the safety of your home with her to come back here."

"I didn't have a choice. It wasn't safe anymore." Not for her babushka, who might deny it but who was getting older. Her grandmother deserved some peaceful years.

Her grandfather leaned forward, and Cole finally showed a dark hint of the assassin. "Come no closer." So softly spoken, yet the threat of it hung in the air.

"You will not threaten me."

"I don't threaten. I promise."

She placed a hand on Cole's arm. "I'm not afraid of him. Let him speak."

"When I announced you as my heir to the clan, I never thought things would escalate."

"Escalate seems a little mild for guys parachuting out of helicopters and blowing up my door. They even attacked us in an airport. I could have been killed."

"But killing you makes no sense." Her grandfather frowned as he leaned back in his seat. "Why shoot the main heir to my fortune? It gains my enemies nothing."

"Thanks for your concern."

Tygrov's brows beetled. "Don't fish for false reassurances and platitudes. It's unbecoming of a princess. And, keep in mind, your very existence is your safety. In order to gain access to my riches, they must marry you."

"Do they need her alive?"

"It tends to work better that way," was her sarcastic retort.

"But what if they decided it didn't?" Cole prodded. "What if, say, this Sergei fellow decided to kill you and keep you on ice while his goons drum up some stuff to make it look as if you were married. Pluck a few hairs and leave them on pillowcases. Rub some DNA on the toothbrush just in case the cops went looking."

"You are talking about extreme lengths," she retorted.

"People will do almost anything to get their hands on the kind of money your granddaddy over there"—he jerked a thumb—"has amassed. Killing a woman who won't cooperate and then forging shit is nothing to these guys. Staking a claim works best if Sergei or whoever can build a chain of evidence, which includes planting DNA in the obvious places. Show a few doctored images. Hell, if he's really good, he'll even have a sex tape."

"I would never have sex with him."

"You won't be able to admit that if you're dead." He leaned close to murmur, "And if you do have sex with Sergei, or anyone, for that matter, I will kill them. I don't share."

The possessive heat in his eyes shot warmth to the very heart of her.

So, of course, the old man just had to ruin it for her. Just like he'd ruined her life. "Ahem."

She aimed a hot glare at him.

He didn't turn into a pile of ash.

Pity.

Her grandfather cleared his throat again. "While your theory is sound, there is one major point you didn't take into consideration. Even if I die, no husband of hers would inherit my fortune. The assets amassed over the decades are tightly bound to the original family. The fortune, the companies, everything can be passed on only to a direct descendent. A spouse doesn't count. If she should die, without progeny, the riches revert to the next in line."

"So who's next in line?" Cole asked. "The son of your brother that you mentioned before?"

"Not quite. He had an unfortunate incident. My other brother's daughter's son—"

"Sounds like the start to a hillbilly skit," she muttered.

"—is next. But he is an imbecile, by choice, I might add, because of alcohol. Given his addiction issues, I've left strict orders to kill him before anyone lets him take over."

"What if they don't?" she challenged.

"Don't talk me into killing him early. My brother would be most displeased with me."

"Why can't you just rewrite the way the family fortune is set up? Create a trust for direct descendants so that all of them can share? Share." Cole snickered as he repeated the word. "What am I saying? Greed is the number one reason for bad mistakes. Like the first time you covet that freshly baked pie and you know if you take the whole thing, it's going to taste so good." He rolled his eyes heavenward and moaned as he sucked his finger. He sat up straight. "But if you take it, you'll get into so much trouble. The people I lived with didn't spare the rod. Do you know how many times I asked myself, as I stared at that still steaming fruit pie, is it worth the price?

For some reason she wanted to know, were danger and possible pain worth the price of pleasure? "And?"

"I took the pie every single time. And I'll tell you, it was the best damned pie."

Except stealing pie only ever got him beaten. Being with her could put him six feet under.

CHAPTER 11

The flight to Arkhangelsk didn't take long, and in a few hours, they were driving into the city, the weight of its age visible in the layout and the structures themselves. In other words, old, and also the seat of power for the Tygrov family.

"You are entering the city of the archangels," Matvei claimed. "In times past, we used to have the most beautiful churches. Including a fantastic basilica."

"What happened to them?" Anja asked, peeking at the passing scenery.

"What happens to all things that people don't understand or tolerate: destruction. During Stalin's reign, he ensured the removal of most of them."

"The churches were destroyed. However, he did leave the city intact. He had to, as it serves as a major Russian seaport and has for centuries." Cole had done his homework once he knew their destination. This would be a first for him. He'd avoided Arkhangelsk in the past. Most shifters without invitation did. Some places even bears did not trespass. Until now.

And the old man hasn't killed me for it yet. It made him wary. What game did Tygrov play?

A disarming one, apparently, as Matvei, with a nod of acknowledgment, complimented him. "The boy knows his history."

As if he needed the old man's approval. Okay, so he did kind of enjoy it. It also roused his suspicion, and he waited for the knife to come out of hiding. Or the drug to hit. Something. What he knew of the Tygrov patriarch didn't have him affable, and yet the old man sat calmly across from him.

"In my line of work, it's best to be prepared. I know history. Cultures. Languages. I'm very good at *French*." He didn't look at Anja but felt her stiffen beside him. About time she was rigid instead of him. His cock knew to behave at the moment. Somehow he didn't think an erection in front of her grandfather would pass muster, and he preferred not to be neutered.

"More clichés, assassin," she murmured softly.

"It's not cliché if it makes me good at my job and, even better, keeps me alive. Killing isn't just about the fun parts where you see your target's eyes go wide as he reaches for a gun a moment before you pounce him and show him why he shouldn't fuck with you. You have to be smart if you don't want someone to shoot your fat ass so they can stuff and mount it. I might have started out small and petty, but a few close calls told me I needed to educate myself. Not just with books and articles, but with people and actual experience. I've traveled to every continent. I've visited so many places that my air miles get air miles."

"I wouldn't mind seeing more of the world." She loved the farm, but sometimes an escape was needed.

"You should go with someone who can show you the best places to eat and play." Not exactly a subtle hint. Then again, he wasn't a man for subtlety.

"And do you mix work with play?" she queried.

"Sometimes."

"You should always combine the two," Matvei advised. "Then your accountant can write it off as an expense."

More friendly advice? Cole eyed Tygrov, yet it was Anja who

spoke. "You called Cole an assassin earlier. You've heard of him?"

"Indeed, your killer has quite the name for himself. One that claims he always gets the job done. Except for recently. I hear he missed his last target."

"Not exactly. I had Fabian Garoux in my sights." Cole raised his hand and aimed it gun-style at Matvei. "However, the one putting out the hit became unable to provide payment. I wouldn't want to get a reputation I work for free."

She arched a brow. "You don't always kill for payment. You've been claiming you're going to kill me since we met, and yet no one's offering to pay you."

Actually, he would never kill her, but Cole wasn't about to admit that in front of the old man. "Killing to protect myself is allowed without payment, but in your case, I've decided to hold off. For now."

"And how long is for now?"

Forever? Probably too soon to admit. "I probably won't end your existence today or tomorrow."

"What about the weekend?"

Her insistence on a time frame made his lips twitch. "I'll reevaluate."

Hers quirked right back. "If I don't kill you first."

"Ahem." This time the old man received an annoyed look from both of them, but his interruption served to stifle further conversation.

In silence they weaved through the streets of the town. Daylight had long since faded, and only the yellow glow of streetlamps and windows shuttered by blinds or curtains served to illuminate their path.

A part of Cole expected they would head to the marina, because surely a family as rich and prestigious as the Tygrovs would live on one of the islands dotting the bay. Yet, instead, they went past the city, past the edges of civilization, following a road that twined and wound around a forested mountain. When they emerged at the top, the headlights illuminated the oddest structure, precariously balanced, a series of additions, layered around and on each other haphazardly. The uppermost part rose like a spire.

"Was the architect related to Picasso?" because tall and seemingly created of wood, the planks not entirely straight, the entire home appeared slightly off-kilter, as if the slightest push would send it toppling like a domino.

"It is a replica of the famous Sutyagin House, the tallest wooden house in Russia, with thirteen stories, or at least the tallest home until they tore it down for being unsafe."

"And you felt a need to recreate it?" Cole cocked his head, unable to deny the appeal of the precariously balanced structure. "I have to admit to house envy. It is unique. I could see why someone would want to inherit. Maybe I should kill you."

"Even if Anja is my most direct heir, you still wouldn't get your hands on it."

"I would have my hands on her." He waggled his fingers and smiled. It earned him a jab to the ribs. He glanced over and noted Anja bit her lip, trying not to laugh. So he winked, and she snickered.

"You speak rather possessively about the girl. Is it your intention to marry my granddaughter?" Matvei fixed Cole with a calculating stare.

Anja leaned forward. "If you say, 'I forbid it,' I will declare him my husband so fast your head will explode." She eyed her grandfather. "Actually, on second thought, say it. I want to see what happens. Maybe if I'm lucky, you'll keel over at the thought of an assassin as your grandson-in-law."

"He's more likely to keel at the thought of my white ass pumping as I do debauched things to your body." That was a touch crass even for him but totally worth the ruddy color in Tygrov's face.

"He's an ignorant killer."

"And you're a pompous jerk," was her retort.

"He's a bear."

Anja recoiled. "How do you know that?"

"Because I am a tiger."

"So where's the lion?" she retorted. "Isn't that how the rhyme goes?"

"This is no joke. Marrying him would cause no end of problems. Tigers and bears do not get along."

Her chin tilted. "Good thing I'm not a tiger. And, even more to the point, I don't take orders from you. I'll do whatever I damned well please whether you like it or not."

The old guy's lips pulled into a flat line. "Rebelling against me is a futile waste of time."

"Says the guy handing out rules like candy. Don't you know they teach us at a young age to never take the candy. And the second lesson is don't ever follow me home in a white van. It makes Babushka really mad. But I wish she'd at least kept the candy instead of dumping it with the truck."

"Once we inherit this house, she should come live with us." And, yes, Cole spoke as if it were a done deal. Not really. A part of him hyperventilated. The thought of tying himself to one stupendous woman terrified him more than death.

But the thing scarier still?

What if she walked away?

When Cole had first encountered Anja—was it only a few days ago?—he'd been simply a hired killer, doing a job, a job he found himself reluctant to complete. Working for money was fun, until he'd realized money didn't buy happiness.

All his life he'd scoffed at the idea of a true mate. How could there be one woman, one being, who was awesome enough he'd want to keep her forever? Impossible to imagine. Wouldn't it get boring? Then again

. . .

I eat peanut butter on toast almost every single day and love it still.

The feel of a thundershower on my skin never fails to delight.

And that cracking of a can of fresh soda where the popping bubbles get up your nose and that first sip makes your eyes water. He still loved that feeling.

Why couldn't he have it for a woman, especially since what he felt toward Anja was so much more than anything he'd ever experienced before? She consumed his thoughts. Stimulated his mind. Ignited his lust. She was a part of him now. He'd licked her. She'd licked him back. They owned each other— body, spit, and soul.

"I don't know if I would want to live here. It's not very inviting." Anja wrinkled her nose. "And it's old. Like probably missing-basic-conveniences old."

"We could tear the shack down and build something modern."

"Keep speaking, boy. It is obvious you do not want to live until morning," Matvei remarked as he headed up the grand porch steps composed of layered stone slabs leading to the door. It swung open at his approach.

"I heard that, Matty! Do not threaten my future grandson-in-law." Blocking the entrance was Anja's grandmother, wearing another voluminous black dress, arms crossed over her chest, a thick woven shawl around her shoulders. He wondered what the woolen covering hid today. A flamethrower, perhaps?

"You!" Matvei spat. "What are you doing in my house? You have a lot of nerve coming here after what you did."

"After what I did?" Her voice rose in pitch. "You are the reason I had to leave. I wasn't about to see my granddaughter's life put in danger because you couldn't let two lovers be together."

"Are you still harping on that, woman? Pyotr made a promise to another woman. A promise he chose to honor."

"A promise that should have never happened," Nonna spat. "Helga deserved better than that."

"Perhaps she did, and perhaps things might have been different if you'd not taken Helga and the unborn child away."

"What else could I do to ensure no one would use Anja as a pawn? We both know Pyotr's fiancée and her family would have never let the child live."

"She is my granddaughter. I would have protected her!" Matvei's face turned a mottled red as he yelled, and Cole found it interesting how one little old woman with simple words could reduce him to a spitting rage.

"Protect her how?" Nonna's lips pulled into a sneer. "You are the problem. The fact she's related to you is why these attempts would keep happening. It's why I took her away, and would have stayed away if you hadn't found us. You should have left us alone."

"What did you expect me to do? She's my blood."

"Everyone is allowed a fault." Nonna leaned forward and, despite her shorter stature, oozed more menace than a rabid bear on 'shrooms. "My fault was in letting you live."

"Maybe you should have killed me, because you certainly fucked me over when you left . . . wife."

Everyone could see the shock on Anja's face as the realization that the man she'd heard about her entire life, her perfect *dedushka,* her supposed dead grandfather, was standing in front of her. Very much alive.

Her shock was the only thing that kept Cole from clapping his hands at the shocking twist.

Anja spun on her heel, ignoring her grandmother's cried, "*Lapushka,* my sweet. Stop. Let me explain to you."

"Fuck you," she yelled over her shoulder as she marched off down the drive. "Fuck you. Fuck off. Fuck me. Argh."

When Matvei and Nonna started to go after her, Cole stopped them. "Don't." In her state of mind, no good could come of it. Cole would know. Betrayals by those closest to a person hurt the most.

"I need to explain—" the old woman stuttered, looking all of her frail years for once.

Cole interrupted. "Explain what? That you lied to her? That you both majorly fucked up with no regard to her feelings and needs? I thought I had a messed-up childhood, but congrats, I think you made an even bigger mess of Anja's."

"I did what I had to," the old woman said, anguish pulling her lips down at the corners.

"You were selfish keeping her from her family," snapped Matvei.

There was blame to share for everyone. "And you were an asshole for pushing Anja's dad to be with another woman. She is right. You both fucked up. You both meddled when you should have left Anja's parents to work things out on their own. Perhaps they would have stayed together, or perhaps not, but neither of you gave them a choice, and that girl"—he pointed in the direction she'd gone, the woods having swallowed her form as she stalked off in anger—"was deprived because of it. Now the question is: What will you do to fix it?"

"Buy her something expensive," Matvei suggested, only to spit out a curse as Nonna slapped him in the head.

"Buy things. It's always buying things with you. Jewelry and cars can't fix feelings. Not everything is about money."

"You liked my money well enough when you were spending it," snapped the elder Tygrov.

"While you both hash out your obvious issues as a couple, I'm going to go find Anja before someone else does."

"What are you implying?" barked Matvei, his brows beetling. "She is safe here. She is on Tygrov land."

"Yeah, that doesn't mean shit to me. So I am going to hunt my woman down, and while I'm gone, smarten the fuck up, or I will kill both of you. For free."

A suave killer never allowed himself to run when in pursuit. A certain decorum was to be expected; however, within minutes of entering the forest, the almost barren branches creaking overhead, the air crisp, his gut clenched and his bear whispered, *Danger.* He couldn't say why. There was no scent but that lingering behind of Anja's passage. The leaves underfoot proved noisy when he stepped on their crisp carcasses, and yet his were the only steps he heard. It was if Anja had disappeared into thin air, and when he came to the stream, he realized what she'd done. Clever girl, using the water to mask her scent.

She was good.

He was better.

She had a killer on her trail. Given her skill at hiding her tracks, he'd need to pull the big bear out. Cole took a moment to strip and folded his clothes in a pile that he placed on a rock. The brisk air pimpled his skin, but excitement kept him warm.

We're going on a hunt.

It took him only a moment to coax his inner bear forth. The shaggy beast never hesitated at a chance to drive their body, and Cole had long ago gotten used to the pain of change. Every time, as his skin grew fur and his limbs reshaped, the agony reached a purity that stole the breath and then faded abruptly. Faded and was forgotten until the next time he swapped skin.

Giving his big shoulders a roll, he lumbered into the chilly stream, the fur on his paws instantly soaked, but he wouldn't have to stay in for long. Only long enough for him to catch his mate's trail again. Despite her tricks, the faintest hint of her hung in the air, and he followed it.

His mate had moved quickly, hopping out of the stream less than a quarter mile down onto some rocks, then climbing through some fragrant brush that did much to mask her scent. But he didn't give up. He watched the ground, seeking the faint scuffs and bent foliage that would show her passage.

During his pursuit, he found several bodies, their eyes staring sightlessly, their throats cut, but these were not dead by her hand. Someone with claws had killed the sentinels in these woods.

The woods were compromised, and Anja was in danger.

A copper scent brought him to another body, not a guard this time, he'd wager, given the camouflage clothing. He found traces of Anja here, a few strands of hair, a sharp burst of fear and anger still perfuming the air. A bloody blow to the head had downed the fellow on the ground, but she'd left him breathing.

Sloppy.

Cole fixed her mistake before moving on, her trail now easier to follow. But she'd moved fast, faster than he would have expected.

Cole quickened his own pace, but he wasn't quick enough. He burst from the woods and found a section of the road that wound into the property. The scuffing of the ground on the shoulder showed a struggle. He also found a body that he'd wager belonged to Anja's enemies, yes, enemies, because, make no doubt, more than one had come to brazenly fetch her. He could tell by the scents and markings that she'd fought hard, but they were too many—*and I wasn't there to protect her.*

His first real job as a protector, and he'd failed. The enemy had carted her off through a short section of woods to a road bisecting it. They'd left in a car, the faint traces of exhaust still lingering in the air. She was gone, and Cole had no idea where they'd taken her.

But I will find her. As soon as he got his hands on his phone. The dress Anja wore wasn't just sexy. He'd installed a tracker inside.

Time to go hunting. And kill, because Cole was done playing nice.

CHAPTER 12

In the movies, the heroine usually woke in a cell and could wail about her fate while gripping the bars of her window.

In reality, Anja woke tied to a chair, needing to pee, with something cottony stuffed in her mouth. The gag wasn't as disturbing as the white gown billowing around her legs, legs she could only kick. A futile gesture since all it did was cause a ruffling wave effect in the crinoline.

Who the hell wore crinoline? Add to that the horrendous gown had an awful fit that strained over her breasts and gaped at the back—not by design, she'd wager. The dress appeared made for someone smaller. More disturbing than the wearing of someone else's clothes, though?

Someone dressed me. Not just any dress. They had the nerve to put her in taffeta.

What was the problem with denim? Did no one believe in letting a woman wear comfortable jeans?

Then again, this was her wedding day, or so the man in the tuxedo seemed to indicate as he stopped in front of her. Tall and reed thin, with a hairline that had receded past the point of return, she recognized his hawkish nose. The ever-annoying Sergei. Just the man she was looking for. Of course, when she'd imagined this moment, she was usually straddling him with a knife at his throat and a knee in his man parts.

But the day was young. Or was it late? She had no idea how long she'd spent knocked out after those thugs accosted her in the woods.

"About time you woke." He had the nerve to look annoyed that his drugs had worked. "We can begin."

Begin? The thought didn't even fully percolate before hands gripped her chair on either side and lifted, carrying them both to the front of the church, past wood pews, their empty rows polished and lacquered a dark gleaming brown. Stained-glass windows filtered in daylight, illuminating the space in a rainbow.

They'd brought her to a church. A holy place, and despite apparently being descended from the disciples of Satan—both her grandparents deserving of an award for their subterfuge—Anja didn't burst into flame. Neither did the guy waiting impatiently at the altar.

Personally, if Sergei was in a rush, he should have chosen someone other than the decrepit old man in the cassock who wavered on his feet behind the altar. She was pretty sure the priest was almost asleep, hard to tell with those bushy white brows.

If Anja were naïve, she'd expect this man of God to show some concern that the blushing bride was bound and gagged, but without even the slightest glance in her direction, he instead made the sign of the cross and began the marriage ceremony in Russian, using the slowest cadence she'd ever heard.

And she meant slow, enough that she glanced around and cataloged the old church. It was empty if she discounted Sergei and his two men. Given he'd sent more guards than this to kidnap her, she surmised he had more of them stationed outside.

How brazen of him to kidnap her from her grandfather's property. Her own fault for stalking off alone after finding out about her grandmother and the lies.

So many lies.

Did the fact that babushka was a Tygrov mean she had more family on her mother's side? Her grandmother had always claimed she was the only family Anja had left, but it turned out her word was worth shit.

People all around her lied. *Cole doesn't.* He had a bluntness to him that she appreciated. He didn't hide what he thought. Or felt.

And he feels something for me. He wouldn't allow her to remain a prisoner of this asshat.

At any moment she expected Cole to come riding to the rescue. No, he wouldn't ride in like a hero. He'd find that emasculating. He'd come in guns blazing. Except, he didn't have a gun on him that she knew of. But he could probably get one.

Then again, why get a gun when he could turn into a bear and maul anyone in his way? Such a big, shaggy beast with thick, lush fur, impressive strength, and—

"Are we boring you?" Fingers snapped in front of her eyes.

She cocked her head and tried to tell Sergei an eloquent fuck-off with her eyes. Apparently he'd prefer to hear it, as he tugged the gag from her mouth.

If he expected her to beg or plead, he'd wait a long time. "Untie me."

"Later. First, you will say 'I do.' Make it loud and clear. It's being recorded."

"Bite me."

"Oh, I will bite you, among other things. A bitch like you must be put in her place. And I will record it so that I have all my proof the marriage was consummated. But first, you will say 'I do.'"

She leaned forward. "Fuck." She smiled. "You."

"I've had enough of your antics." Sergei's lips peeled back over his teeth, teeth sharper than they should be. His arm reeled back, and she noted his nails elongating into claws. Another shape-shifter? What the hell? First her neighbors, then Cole, and supposedly her grandpa. Now this twerp?

His hand turned furry, not that the soft layer would matter since the claws on his mutant hand would probably cause some damage. He started to bring his arm forward, except his hand never connected because it developed a perfect coin-sized hole. It took only a moment before the blood began to stream and the screaming started. Not by her, of course. She laughed.

Her bear had arrived. With a gun. She was only a little disappointed he hadn't brought out the bear.

"Who dares?" Sergei yelled, spittle flying as he held his wounded hand to his chest.

"I dare." Cole vaulted down from the balcony on the upper level, landing with knees bent, his eyes never leaving them. "You know, I was willing to let you marry her, but I have to draw the line at hitting."

"You meddle with things you shouldn't."

"No, you touched someone you shouldn't have. She's mine."

"I am," she confided to Sergei. "He licked me."

"My men will kill you," shouted the other man as he backed away.

"Yeah, about your guards." Cole shrugged. "They're kind of dead, which you really should thank me for because they sucked at their jobs. I mean, none of them even saw me coming. Then again, few people ever know I'm there. Just like you never knew I was watching almost right overhead."

She blinked as his words filtered. "If you killed them all, then what were you waiting for to rescue me? I was like only an 'I do' away from marrying him."

"I know. I was watching the whole thing and then Ser-dick had to pull a dumb move and try to slap you. He just couldn't wait until the priest was done."

Her gaze narrowed. "You were going to let me marry him?"

Cole rolled his eyes. "Well, yeah, I was going to. Unlike your crafty grandpa, douche bag over here doesn't have a will. He's a straight inheritance case, enough for an island I've been eyeing."

"Hold on. Let me see if I understand. You were going to let me wed him and then what, kill him and marry me?"

"I see you understand the brilliance of my plan."

"I can't believe you would let me marry someone else."

"For money."

"That does not improve my state of mind."

"How about the fact I gave up the money so he wouldn't slap you?"

"Poor financial decision. He was too weak to really hurt me."

His brows rose to an impressive height. "Are you now berating me for not letting you be slapped? Should I perhaps, next time, just stand by and allow him a few little taps? Maybe give him some pointers?"

"How about you stick to your original plan. There's still time for us to get married and widowed. Grab him before he escapes."

Perhaps another girl would have wasted time asking Cole how he'd found her, or was he serious about marrying her? Except . . . none of those things mattered.

He'd come, ergo he wanted her. He also left her tied to a chair as he took off after Sergei. Since being a damsel who waited for rescue didn't appeal, Anja wobbled in the chair, tilted it right over until it fell and hit the stone floor.

The sturdy chair didn't break. Her arm, on the other hand, would sport a lovely bruise.

Uttering a frustrated growl, she thrust with her legs, seesawing and thrashing, trying to loosen her ropes.

She finally managed and stood with a triumphant, "Aha."

Only to find a gun jammed in her face.

CHAPTER 13

The tiger slammed into Cole's side as he went out the door, but he didn't mind. He kind of wanted to slap the little prick a few times before dragging him back inside to lay at the feet of his woman.

Having already shifted once today, Cole wasn't replenished enough to do it again, but that didn't mean he was useless. He grabbed the tiger around the neck and kept away from those jaws. But the claws were also a problem.

He flipped himself so he straddled the tiger's back, still holding it in a choke hold. He rammed the tiger's head into the ground a few times, dazing it for the few seconds he needed to spring to his feet and bring his gun to a spot between its eyes. "The wedding is off, asshole." Cole pulled back the hammer and was ready to fire, only someone else pressed a barrel against the base of his spine. Someone short, with no warning scent.

He glared over his shoulder at Nonna. "I'm a little busy here avenging your granddaughter."

"I'll handle the vengeance," Matvei declared as he appeared from around the side of the church.

"The same way you handled it before when you let him go after Anja?"

"The boy served a purpose. I knew that eventually, if he

bothered them enough, my granddaughter and wayward wife would come back to me."

"More games?" Cole shook his head. "You want him. You have him." He drew back his gun, but Nonna didn't remove hers from his back.

"Back inside," she ordered.

Since Anja was in there, he didn't argue. He also didn't kill Anja's grandmother. He knew his woman was fond of the old lady. Hell, he was kind of fond of her too. Especially her cooking.

As soon as he stepped into the church vestibule, Cole found himself surrounded by Tygrov men—more tigers wearing a veneer of humanity—as they marched back in, Matvei leading the way. Nonna kept the pistol tight to his spine.

"Is this any way to treat a future family member?"

"You will not join this family. Anja needs a tiger," growled the patriarch of the family, stepping through the doors into the church proper.

"What she needs is someone to take the gun out of her face," snapped Anja, who stood, arms raised and glaring down the barrel of a revolver.

Cole groaned as he saw who held her hostage. "What are you doing here?"

"You know that man?" she asked, not sparing him a glance.

"He's my uncle." His uncle Barnabas to be exact, a big, burly bear of a fellow with a thick dark beard. And a gun. On his woman. This wouldn't go well.

"I thought you were an orphan." Anja's words held an accusatory note.

"I am. My parents died when I was young, and then my aunts and uncles took turns raising me." All nine of them. And only one had a job approaching legal, although some would say his uncle Abraam's profession as a lawyer was the most crooked profession of all.

"He enjoyed his time spent with me best," boasted his uncle Barnabas.

"Bullshit." A figure dressed in a pale lilac pantsuit stepped out from behind a statue, another gun in hand. His aunt Dareia had also come. Cole had expected her, since he'd called her on the flight over to Russia. "I taught the boy what he needed to know to survive. Without me, he would have died on his first job."

"The only reason he didn't die was that I dragged his ass to safety." The newest voice appeared a moment before in the slim form of yet another uncle, his emergence from under a pew in the front row a credit to his ability to hide.

Cole sighed. "Uncle Abrax, for the last time, the job was done, and all you did was save me from scoring with the redhead that night."

"Cockblocker." His uncle Barnabas coughed.

"Filthy Greek bears. Unhand my granddaughter," Matvei ordered. "And get off Tygrov land. You have no sanction to come here."

"He's here." Cole's aunt jerked a thumb in his direction. "That's all the sanction we need."

"The last time bears came to Russia, it was war," Matvei declared, his skin rippling. "Remember who won?"

"Perhaps it's time for a rematch," snarled his uncle Abrax, tearing at his shirt.

"I might be a heathen, but I draw the line at people stripping in church," Anja yelled.

"No shedding blood in the house of God," declared the meek priest.

But no one paid him any heed.

"This is how we fight our battles," stated Anja's grandfather, also pulling off his shirt and handing it to Nonna. Cole had to wonder if the old lady noticed that the gun drooped in her grip.

"More shape-shifters. Is the entire world an animal except for me?" Anja planted her hands on her hips, which drew attention to what she wore.

A wedding gown. How propitious. It gave Cole an idea. "I know how we can stop a war between our families. Marry me, now." Not exactly the most romantic of declarations.

"I will not have you marry me because these guys can't behave like men and would instead prefer to brawl like wild animals." She crossed her arms over her chest, which only served to yank at the ill-fitting gown.

"Nothing wrong with a good brawl," announced his uncle Barnabas. "It's not a party until blood is shed."

"Fighting saves verbal misunderstandings," Matvei muttered.

"And spares us the smell of piss," added his aunt. "I swear, get a bunch of men posturing and all they want to do is drink and mark territory."

"What your aunt is trying to say, Nikolaos, is no need to marry the girl. You can do better," said his uncle Abrax.

"He could not," sputtered Matvei. "She is a princess."

"With good birthing hips," interjected Nonna. "It is he who is not good enough for her. Related to a family with ties to crime in Greece."

A sneer pulled Barnabas's lips. "Says the woman married to the big pussy running the Russian black market."

And it went on and on, back and forth, but the good news was no one turned furry and attacked. The bad news was no one turned furry and attacked. It meant Cole couldn't avoid what he had to do.

He was nervous for the first time since his initial kill as a boy.

Suck it up and get it done.

"Aunt Dareia, did you bring it?" His aunt didn't even look

his way as she tossed him the small package. He caught it one-handed and then strode toward Anja, who currently scowled down at her dress.

It was hideous beyond belief, but to him, she appeared beautiful.

Because she's mine. That certainty meant ignoring the arguing of the families as Cole did something he thought he'd never do. Something he'd always mocked other men for doing. He dropped to a knee in front of Anja.

That drew a startled glance from her. "What are you doing?"

"So, I know both our families are extremely annoying."

"Understatement," she muttered.

"And that I am perhaps not the ideal male, given I like to kill people for a living."

"At least you're employed."

"But I need you, Anja. You are my true mate."

"Does this mean you don't want to kill me anymore?"

"I never did. Although I had difficulties perhaps expressing that. But if you want the truth, here it is. Unvarnished. You are the one I wish to spend my life with, however short it might be. It's why I had my aunt bring this." "This" being the ring that used to belong to his mother. It wasn't a big ring, the band of gold simple, the ruby inset within bordered by the tiniest diamonds, and yet Anja's eyes rounded.

"Oh, Cole." She sighed his name.

"It was my mother's, so you can blame my father for its small size. Which, I assure you, is the only small thing you'll ever get from me." Wink.

"It's perfect." She held out her hand, and he slid it on, realizing as he did that everyone present had fallen silent, so of course, the priest chose that moment to wake up and shout, "Did the girl say 'I do'?"

"I do."

"And the boy?"

"I fucking well do."

"Then, by the power vested in me, and the gun at my head by this very short woman, I declare you man and wife. You may kiss the bride."

Cole did, vigorously and thoroughly, as their families continued to bicker in the background. Who cared? He'd claimed his mate.

His bear was content. Now to please the man. But for that, he'd require some privacy.

Tossing Anja over his shoulder, he strode from the church, not even pausing when Matvei shouted, "Where are you taking my granddaughter?"

"For some well-deserved debauching." And licking.

CHAPTER 14

I'm married.

The realization stunned her as she stared at her pale features in the mirror. Cole had come to her rescue, and she didn't mean just from Sergei.

He'd rescued her from a future of loneliness. No longer would she have to settle when it came to affection. She didn't have to hide who she was, or feel oversized, or too anything, because Cole had chosen her.

But does he love me?

She emerged from the bathroom into the room he'd rented in town after getting them away from that church. As soon as she noted the washroom, she'd claimed it so she could shed the hideous dress. She also bathed and, yes, peed. Now, dressed in only a towel, she stepped into the room to find Cole lying atop the four-poster bed, his hands laced behind his head.

"Do you love me?" she asked. A blunt question and yet that was who she was.

"I married you, didn't I?"

"Sergei wanted to marry me. It didn't mean he loved me."

He bounded off the bed, tall and domineering. He stood before her, a man of imposing size, a man who could kill with his bare hands.

Yet he touched her gently, his knuckles brushing the skin of her cheek. "Are the words that important?"

"No." It wasn't the words that mattered but rather how he made her feel. How he treated her. His soft caress turned into a rub of her lower lip with his thumb. Her lips parted, and he slid a finger in. She sucked the tip, watching his face. His eyes locked with hers, the expression intent.

"Show me your tits." Trust him to lighten the heavy moment with his words.

"Tell me you love me," she teased.

"Why don't you tell me first?" he retorted.

So she did. "I love you. *Husband.*"

His nostrils flared, but instead of a reply, he crushed her to him, smashing his mouth against hers. Instant arousal swept through her, a wave of sensation that deluged her senses. Need hit her, fast and hard, along with a hunger for more of his touch. She wanted his hands on her. His tongue. She wanted him inside her.

I want him.

The hair on his head proved perfect to grab as she devoured his mouth. As always, a simple touch from him ignited her.

A soft sound came from him as she accidentally nipped his lip. So she bit him again, and this time he growled as he crushed her closer.

Their kiss slowed from frantic to caressing, the lingering sucks and strokes of his mouth and tongue fanning the flames of her passion. Her open mouth allowed his tongue easy access, and she trapped it with her teeth, sucking on him and knowing when he groaned again that he remembered the last time she'd closed her lips around a part of him.

Cool air hit her backside as he tugged the towel free, baring her body to him. Lifting her off the ground, his hands at her waist, he carried her to the bed, laying her upon the fabric duvet. He broke away from her lips, and she opened her eyes to protest, only to have her breath hitch when she saw him stripping his shirt, baring his torso.

What a view. She couldn't help but admire Cole's wide shoulders. His arms bulged with muscle, and his chest held a slight fur. He drew near, and she reached up to drag her fingers through his soft pelt. She couldn't wait to feel the friction on her skin.

She pressed her palms flat on his chest, feeling the hard muscles tense beneath them. Her fingers tweaked his nipples, loving how they reacted to her touch.

He unbuttoned the top of his slacks, revealing the black briefs that contained him. Barely contained. His erection strained, and the sight of it brought even more moisture to the throbbing spot between her legs.

"Keep looking at me like that and you'll be wearing pearls."

"Maybe later. Come here." She gripped his upper arms and pulled at him until he dipped his head. His lips found hers for a torrid kiss as his body pressed against hers.

She was right. The fur on his chest did tickle and tease as he lay against her. But more interesting still was the hot and hard heat of him pressing against her.

And then he pulled away, taking his delicious weight with him, but only so his hands could roam her skin, touching her, cupping her breasts, his thumbs swiping over her erect buds.

She caught her breath and then arched off the bed as his tongue flicked against her nipple. Using his lower body, he pinned her to the bed while he teased her nipples one by one with his mouth. Every time he sucked her breast into his mouth, his teeth applying pressure, she felt a zing of pleasure shoot through her. She began to gyrate her lower half against him, the ache in her sex a throbbing demand for more.

And Cole wanted to give her more. He moved down her body,

letting his lips lead the way, peppering kisses and licks over her belly and down through her trimmed mound.

"Yes!" was the only coherent word she managed before his tongue lapped her.

So intense.

So good.

And he seemed to enjoy it just as much as she did, his soft grunts of pleasure a sweet vibration on her flesh. And when he thrust two fingers into her, adding them to the bliss?

She came. Came hard. Came with a body-bucking intensity that almost broke the creaking bed.

He wasn't done. Tremors still racked her as he moved back up her body, kissing and mumbling against her skin. "You're mine. All mine."

"Yes, yours," she whispered against his lips, tasting herself on him but not caring because the tip of his shaft pressed against her.

Her thighs fell open, wide and welcoming, as he poised himself at the entrance to her sex.

"I love you," was his soft whisper before he drove himself in.

She cried out, her sheath still rippling and clenching. It gripped at his cock and held him tight as he thrust, short strokes meant to simply push himself deeper, deep enough to hit her sweet spot.

They fell into a rhythm, their bodies rocking in time, his hardness throbbing and thick inside her, triggering a second climax. This time she screamed. And he yelled with her as he pumped, his hips pistoning until he thrust one last, deep time and went rigid.

Heat bathed her womb and her heart as he, once again, whispered against her lips. "I love you, Anja. I will love you forever."

She just hoped that forever would last a long time, even if their families seemed determined to make him snap.

The whispers a few hours later woke her, and yet she kept her eyes closed.

"Staying at a hotel." Utter disgust by her grandfather. "Unacceptable. I shall have the master bedroom in the west wing renovated for them."

A snort from a woman. "Now that he is married, he will return to Greece and take his place in the family business."

"Like hell. He is married to my only granddaughter. He stays here. It's not as if you bears"—said with such disdain—"need another heir."

"Would you both shut up?" Cole grumbled. "There is only one person who gets to say where I'm going, and I'm going to bet she tells me to get under these covers to show her once again why she's mine."

He was right. Anja wouldn't mind Cole paying a visit down there, but "Not while they're here," she whispered. "I don't need our families giving us pointers."

"As if the boy needs pointers. He's a bear."

"No, he's annoyed." The gun came out from under the pillow and pointed at the group huddled at the foot of the bed. "Leave. Now. Or I will start shooting."

"Ungrateful cub," grumbled his uncle Barnabas.

"Disrespected in my own city," lamented Matvei.

"He will make strong babies," cackled Nonna.

"Very strong," agreed his aunt.

And then they left. She waited a moment before venturing to say, "Is this the wrong time to say I love you?"

"Of course you do. It's only natural, given my awesome nature and good looks. Just like it's inevitable I love you."

"Because I'm your mate."

"Because you are the most incredible." Kiss. "Exciting." Nibble. "Sexy." Lick. "Woman to ever walk the face of this earth, and just so you know, I'd eradicate both our families if they ever tried to keep us apart."

"Oh, Cole." A phrase repeated later when he licked her, then again when he found her fresh pastries, and one last time when he smuggled them out of the city and out of Russia under both their families' noses and took her on a honeymoon around the world.

EPILOGUE

A few weeks later, when the shine of travel wore off, Cole took Anja home, and she'd never been happier to see the cow that hated her—cared for by Garoux's men during their absence—and those damnable chickens, who showed more respect after Cole wandered into their coop as a bear.

Traveling was nice, but there was truly no place like home, especially since they had the place to themselves. Her nonna had elected to stay behind in Arkhangelsk for the moment in order to slap some sense into her grandfather. But given the number of times Anja called via video chat and caught her nonna looking disheveled, her grandfather usually close by and shirtless, more than talking was happening.

Shudder.

During the past few weeks, Anja had learned that her mother had been an only child, raised by a distant cousin who worked for the Tygrov family. It was how her parents met. So cliché, the maid and the lord's son. And it seemed Nonna truly was right to fear for Anja's life because the woman who should have married her father went on to marry another after his death and then proceeded to kill all his brothers and their children, that her husband might inherit. It seemed Cole knew all about her father's old betrothed, given he was hired to kill the woman.

Anja called him an avenging hero. He'd spanked her in reply. She spanked him back, and a good time was had by all.

Speaking of a good time, she knew someone who liked to wake up frisky. She pressed closer to her husband, loving the feel of their naked limbs entwined, the moment delightfully languorous. Decadent, she might even say.

"I have a meeting later today with the dog next door to discuss his needs," he murmured.

Anja tickled fingers across Cole's bare chest. "Are you sure you wish to work for *that man*?" That man being Fabian Garoux, not a bad sort as it turned out, but she wasn't about to relinquish the feud so easily.

"Working for him means coming home to you every night, which is a big bonus."

"Won't you get bored?"

"I was getting bored in my old job, so I'm open to try something new. If I don't like it, or he looks at me funny, I can always kill him." Cole grinned as he lobbed his most oft-used solution to every problem.

"You can't kill everything," she noted as she rolled herself atop him. "Some annoying things must be tolerated."

"Annoying things should die."

"If you harm our baby because it cries and wakes you, then I will have to eviscerate you," she whispered against his lips. "Slowly and painfully."

"What did you just say?"

"I am going to kill you."

"Before that?"

"Oh, the baby. The one I'm carrying." Because, as soon as she'd missed her period, she'd peed on a stick to be sure. "The next Tygrov princess. Your daughter."

Before she could blink, Cole dumped her on the mattress and bolted from the bed to snare his pants, hopping into them on his way to the door.

Surprised at his reaction, she sat up, hair a tousled mess around her bare shoulders. "Are you abandoning me, you coward? I shall hunt you down like a dog and skin you," she yelled.

He whirled, his craggy features set in shock. "Leave you? Never. I go to make ready. We only have months to prepare. Mere months to protect the biggest treasure this sinner has ever coveted. I can't believe you're bearing my child." He shook his head before ducking out into the hall.

"More like bearing sin." She rolled the word sin around her tongue. "Sinthea. A worthy name for a princess."

"You should call the baby lazy, like her mother," her babushka yelled before stomping into the room. "Lying abed at this hour."

"It's not even seven A.M."

"Lazy wench. Shirking her duties. Thinking she's a princess."

"I am a princess. Remember? And what are you doing here? I thought I left you in Russia."

"Saucy wench. As if I would abandon my *lapushka* during her time of need."

"I don't need you, old woman," she said with a soft smile. She didn't question how her beloved *babulya* knew she was with child. Some things her grandmother just knew.

Her babushka sniffed. "Ha. Impertinent chit thinks she's better than her grandmother. I am the grand tsarina once again of the Tygrov clan. And yet I shall lower myself to making you breakfast since you are obviously incapable and the baby is hungry. The things I must do for a lazy, ungrateful brat."

Which translated from Russian meant: I love you.

Meanwhile, a few states away, a certain Greek bear was minding his own business when the letter arrived in the mail, mail as in an envelope with a stamp and an address, his address, handwritten in block letters. Strange, but the oddity paled compared to the card inside.

On the front, a blue background with a stork carrying a swaddled child in its beak.

Inside

. . .

Congrats, Asshole.
It's a boy.
The woman you never called back

BOUGHT BY THE BEAR

Milly Taiden

CHAPTER 1

Josilyn Martinez blew out a breath and glanced at the stack of bills staring at her from the coffee table. She knew two things. One: she had to pay all of them. Two: she didn't have the money in her negative-forty-three-cent bank account.

"Josie?" Nick called from his bedroom. "Could I have cereal for dinner?"

She thought back to the cereal he'd had for lunch and winced. She'd never met a boy who could eat so much Froot Loops. "You sure you don't want some of the chicken I baked?"

"Nah," he said, rushing by her, wearing a Superman cape and Batman boxers. Clinking noises came from the kitchen, dishes and cutlery being moved.

"Be careful," she said automatically and thought about getting up at the same moment Nick walked in front of her, his socks sliding on the wood floors, picking at the cereal loops at the top of his bowl without stopping.

He lifted his head and crunched on a red Froot Loop. "I'll be careful."

"Don't worry about washing that bowl when you're done." She glanced at the clock on the wall in the shape of a tree trunk Nick had picked out from the local thrift shop. "I'll come and get it. Just brush your teeth and get your butt to bed, mister. You're off to Grandma's in the morning."

"Okay." There was a pause, then Nick came out of his room, threw his arms around her neck, and kissed her cheek. "Good night, Aunt Josie."

"Good night, baby bear." She cuddled him for a moment and sent him off. She went back to staring at the unopened bills. Frustration and anger ate at her chest. How she wished she could do more than she was for Nick, but her ex had gotten his best friend and asshole of a lawyer to get her for every dollar she'd ever worked for in their divorce.

She groaned and stood. Sharp needles of pain shot through her back muscles from being on her knees scrubbing toilets all day. She'd lost everything thanks to Michael. No reputable company wanted to hire her. Not with what Michael did.

She'd gone from having a great job and extra money in the bank to having nothing in less time than it took for him to pack his shit and leave her for Miss Double-D from the car wash down the street. While Josie had big boobs—all right, she had big everything—she couldn't compete with those puppies.

She grabbed a cup to fill with water and stopped. She hadn't had wine since the night she found out she was beyond broke. She went from getting her hair and nails done weekly to getting rid of everything of value to scrape up money for food.

The divorce hadn't been the worst of it. Her sister Lucy and brother-in-law Frank had died in a car accident, leaving Josie with the added responsibility of a new child to take care of. While Frank's mother could easily take care of Nick, it was clearly stated in the couple's will they wanted Nick raised by Josie.

Mildred, Frank's mother, used money to get her way and had tried many times to bribe Josie to let Nick live with her. None of her efforts had worked.

Josie eyed the bottle of wine her neighbor Shawna had given her. Shawna was the closest thing to family Josie had. She'd given her a shoulder to cry on and listened even when Josie herself had no idea what she was saying. Having someone she could vent to kept Josie from losing her mind.

She grabbed the bottle of wine and a glass and carried them back to the coffee table. Then she went around the apartment, shutting off lights and finally checking on Nick. He'd inhaled the cereal and she hoped he'd followed through and brushed his teeth. She turned off his lamp, and his nightlight automatically turned on. His cape hung on a chair while he lay sprawled on his back, soft snoring sounds coming from him.

She leaned down, kissed him on the head, and brought the covers up to his neck. She picked up the dirty dishes, turned on his fan, and closed the door. At the sofa, she poured a glass of wine.

When she smelled the alcohol, that one night from her childhood, the one that changed her life, played through her mind.

Her father had smelled the same as the wine, except much stronger. They had been at the family Christmas Eve party for hours. It was late and her mom wanted to go home, but Dad told her to relax and he shoved a short glass with amber liquid into her hand—the same thing he'd been drinking and refilling his own glass with all night.

Josie knew her father was drunk. Being the head of a big corporation made him high-profile, which meant he never did anything in public to embarrass himself or the company. So his drinking tonight in the comfort of friends and family took away his ability to reason.

Mom finally talked him into going home. Like usual, Josie and Lucy sat in the backseat of the car. They had unwrapped boxes around them that Santa had dropped off at their aunt Lucy's home earlier. The Barbie she had wanted for so long lay beside her. Being late at night, she let the smooth ride of the

Mercedes lull her to sleep as they drove past houses and lawns covered in snow.

Suddenly, she woke when her body was thrown forward and a loud noise hurt her ears. The seat belt around her waist kept her from hitting the front seat with her face. She looked around, trying to figure out what had happened. Why she was awakened.

Through the spider-webbed windshield, she saw the front of the car was crumpled back. That was all she could see in the darkness, except for another car sitting upside down in the road not too far away with its headlights shining. The driver's side of the other car looked smashed in, but she wasn't sure.

Her mom hollered out her and her sister's names and pivoted in the front seat to look back at them. Josie took in her mom's wide, fear-filled eyes and knew something bad had just happened.

Thinking back to those times made her miss Lucy. Lucy with her bubbling personality and never-ending positive comments could make anyone feel like they were on top of the world. At this moment, she felt she was drowning. It didn't help that Mildred would get Nick for a full week on this visit. Her high-priced lawyer got a judge to allow grandparent visits that were longer than an overnight stay.

If she were honest with herself, Josie would admit she worried Mildred would go for full custody again, and this time Josie couldn't fight her. Not without money. Hell, as it was, she could barely feed the boy. But Frank and Lucy had been adamant about keeping Nick away from Frank's mother and, dammit, Josie would do whatever she could to follow their wishes.

She lifted the wineglass to her lips, took a sip, and rubbed her temple. She needed to figure out how to make more money. Unfortunately, she didn't qualify for any loans and her credit was so bad she'd stopped getting junk mail asking her to open an account. She'd have to take on a second job. It wasn't ideal, but maybe she could beg Shawna to watch Nick when she was off at work and trade it for the Spanish lessons her friend had been wanting to take.

A soft knock sounded at her door. She put the half-empty glass down and didn't bother worrying over how quickly she'd guzzled that wine. She opened the door to Shawna. At five foot four, she considered herself short, but Shawna beat her by about two inches. With short dark hair and a curvy physique that had a lot more toning than Josie's, Shawna slid her yoga-attired body into the apartment like a breath of fresh air.

"I have good news!" Shawna exclaimed, her melodious voice a lot more excited than Josie had been in too long.

"Great," she said, grinning. "I already opened the wine. We can celebrate your good news in style."

Shawna snorted a giggle and sat, her pink-and-blue trainers tapping at the edge of the chair she'd swung her legs over when she sat. "Not for me, silly."

Josie brought a second wineglass from the kitchen and filled it. With raised brows, she handed it to Shawna. "Then who are we celebrating for?" She sat again and shrugged. "What the hell, maybe it doesn't matter. At this point I'd celebrate the fact I still have frozen vegetables in the freezer."

Shawna sipped her wine, her smile widening. "You look so beat." Her smile dimmed and she shook her head, making her short locks whip around her chin. "I'm sorry you're so stressed, girl."

She shrugged again. "I'm getting used to being stressed. I'm just worried about Nick. I don't want to have to fight Mildred in court for him. I keep thinking no judge would let me keep him with how bad my finances are."

"I told you I had good news!" Shawna dug into her pocket, pulled out a folded piece of paper, and thrust it at Josie. "Here."

Josie took the paper and unfolded it. "'Mate for hire'?" She frowned and read the ad.

Wanted: *Single female.*
Description: *Opportunity for short-term assignment. Female to pose as mate. Must be available for functions and gatherings. Perks included. Half paycheck upon first week of work and half upon completion. Serious inquiries only.*

"I don't understand what this means. Some guy is looking for a friend?"

Shawna grinned and sipped her wine. "No. This is a new website my boss has me working on." She rolled her eyes. "Apparently, his boss thinks he's the one running it, but the reality is the dick has me doing all the work. Anyway, so our clients want to hire a mate for whatever reason. The women sign up to be hired as a mate because they need the money, and a lot of them are hoping the man will want to keep them. Mate for hire." Shawna blew out a breath. "My program browses through the candidates and chooses the right person for each client."

Josie frowned. "Okay?"

"The program chose you for this client. I put your information in and the system spit you out," she squealed.

"You what?"

Shawna bit her lip and pouted. "I'm sorry, but I wanted to try and help you. I know you need money. These women went through a rigorous screening to get in there. I want to take stress from you."

She glanced down at the paper. "Shawna, it doesn't even say how much—" She gasped. "Holy shit! Is that the pay?" She glanced farther down the page.

"Yeah. That's just half."

Holy fucking shit, she was going to start stripping if this was the kind of money available out there. "You mean to tell me I get hired by some guy and I get this?" she choked out. "Two times?"

Shawna nodded vigorously. "And the best part? No sex."

She tore her gaze from the sheet to look at her friend. "Say what?"

"No sex. I mean," she said, grinning sheepishly, "not unless you want to. The rules are very specific. Someone needs a mate for whatever reason and he's willing to pay to fake it."

"Isn't a mate a friend? I don't get it, though. Why would a man pay for a friend?"

Shawna shook her head, leaning forward excitedly. "Not a friend. These are shifters. They're hiring you to fake being in a relationship. Like a girlfriend."

Shifters. Deadly. Badasses. Super sexy. "A shifter wants to hire me to be his fake girlfriend?"

"Technically, he wants to hire any female to be his fake girl-friend. The point is the program picked you for him, and this is your chance to make enough money to pay your bills, *chica!*"

Josie glanced at the paper again. The amount of money listed was a lot more than her bills totaled and that was only half the amount offered. "No sex, you say?"

Shawna grinned. "None. The guy is pretty specific about having to hire someone urgently. Most women need a few days' notice. He wants someone tomorrow. That narrowed down the list a lot. And since Nick will be with Mildred, that gives you a few days to get this done." She stood and sat next to Josie on the couch. "Come on, Josie. This is what you've been waiting for. A legal way to make money and not have to sell your ass."

Josie snorted. "That's yet to be seen."

"Trust me. My company is huge. The owner would never do

anything as stupid as get caught up in some escort service when his mother is very much involved in all aspects of our day-to-day operations." Shawna grasped Josie's hands in hers and squeezed. "Do it. What's the worst that can happen? You decide his offer isn't for you and say no."

She gulped. It wasn't like her to be so indecisive. But after Michael and the downward spiral her life had taken in the past year, she had no idea what else could be looming in the distance. "Okay. I'll do it. What do I have to do?"

"Don't worry, girl. I will tell you everything you need to know to make sure this is a hit." Shawna jumped to her feet. "Let me go to my apartment and grab the papers I brought home. Pizza should be here shortly. We can eat and discuss this."

Man, if Shawna got pizza, that meant she was serious. She never broke her Pizza Friday rule. It was only Thursday. Josie glanced at the amount again. If she got that much money, she could be clear of debt and put Nick in that martial arts class he'd been asking about.

Heck, she might even be able to rent the space and equipment to open that bakery she'd been considering with her other neighbor, Tiana. Though Tiana was traveling, it was something they could discuss if the money thing happened. It was a lot of money at stake. Nick's future was at stake. She wouldn't—couldn't—let him down.

CHAPTER 2

Xander Ursi tugged at his tie. He hated the damn thing. He couldn't wait to be out of it every day after his meetings and undo most of the buttons on his shirt so he could feel less like he was being choked to death. He stomped down the long hallway that led from the office building to a private gym he and his employees used to de-stress. He'd rather go off and run the forest in his bear form, but he didn't have enough time for that right now.

"What's up, bro?" Keir, his close friend and head of marketing, greeted him. "Are you hitting the bags or running?"

"Hitting the bags." Xander headed straight for the changing room with Keir by his side.

Keir glanced around the empty locker room before speaking. "Did that ad work out?"

"They sent me an email saying they're sending the person their system feels would work best for this job." He switched out of his suit into a pair of workout shorts and a tank top. He grabbed his wrist wraps and gloves and headed to the main gym.

"This is good, isn't it?" Keir got on a treadmill next to his and proceeded to start warming up. "You asked me to find you a way to solve your problem, and I did. Now you use the girl, let your grandmother think she's your mate, and your troubles go away."

Right. Then why did it feel like shit was only going to get worse? His human grandmother made it a point to let him know in no uncertain terms that the only way she'd give him the controlling portion of XJ Financial was when he mated and showed her he was ready to settle down.

"She's got a good heart, but trying to get me to mate is not like getting a human to marry," Xander growled. He hopped off the treadmill and wrapped his wrists. He was too antsy to wait any longer to hit the bags. Once his gloves were on, he started with straight one-two punches and continued talking. "A bear can't mate any female just because she's hot."

"Well, my father did. Granted, he's not a bear." Keir laughed. "Didn't work out as well as he would have wanted." He strapped on his gloves and hit the bag next to Xander's. "Try this new place. I know this is weird, but you need to do something to get her off your back and finally take control of XJ." He took jabs at the bag. "Julia is a lovely woman, but just because she is loaded with dough does not mean she knows anything about shifter love lives."

That was the truth. His mother had been human. That didn't stop Xander from taking after his father and picking up the shifter gene. He'd been a bear and had bear needs. One of them was a mate. Unfortunately, he hadn't met the right woman. His grandmother felt that dangling the majority share of the company she owned would somehow make Xander go out there and magically find a mate. If it were that easy, he'd have done it a while back. At almost forty, he was yearning for cubs.

"Grandmother feels it's time she had some great-grandkids. She misses my parents and I'm the only one she can really bug about it. No other grandkids to go harass and all that." He ignored the burn in his muscles and the sweat dripping down his temples.

His grandmother was a great woman. But she assumed because she'd read up on shifters and had a few years knowing Xander's father before his parents had died that she was a shifter encyclopedia.

"When do you meet your new employee?"

"Later today. I have a dinner meeting at Ricardo's. Maxton's sister Ally is in town, and she's demanded I make time for dinner. I figured I could kill two birds with one stone and set up for Josilyn to meet me there so we can discuss the arrangement."

"Ally." Keir frowned. "I don't remember an Ally being Maxton's sister. I remember a Sara."

Xander chuckled at Keir's intense frown. "Yeah. Maxton has two sisters. Ally was younger, so unless you visited his house, you wouldn't have met her. They sent her away to boarding school when she was young."

"Ah. Well. That explains it." Keir hugged the giant punching bag and huffed out a breath. "Let me know how that works out with . . . did you say her name is Josilyn?"

Xander stopped punching and started throwing high kicks at the bag. "Yeah. Ms. Josilyn Martinez. There was a photo included, but it wasn't a close-up so I'll have to figure it out when I see her. Thankfully, the staff at Ricardo's knows me well enough to send her straight to my table when she arrives."

Keir glanced at the clock on the wall. "Good luck. I think it would be a great idea to use their services. Especially since I might be needing to hire my own mate in the near future."

"Your dad still giving you trouble?"

Keir growled and hit his bag again. "Yeah. For a lion, he's being a real pussy. Ever since he lost his sense of smell, he's freaking out over someone taking advantage of him and wants me to take over the operations at the bank."

"What's the problem? You know you can do it." Xander punched and kicked the bag with his left arm and leg, staying on his toes, and then did the same with his right.

"I don't want to mate. I'm fine as I am." Keir started kicking his bag in full earnest.

"You mean having meaningless sex with women you'll never see again?" Xander asked.

"Yeah! Let me tell you something: meaningless sex is very underrated. You don't have to call, and everybody knows where they stand. I don't have to worry about some woman getting her feelings hurt. It's great."

"Only you, bro." Xander laughed outright, his arms starting to tire from the grueling exercise.

"Don't give me that. You've had enough sex-only dates that you can appreciate how well it works."

That was true. He had enjoyed it at one point. Not any longer. "There comes a time in a person's life where you want more. You want to have that link to someone and feel like there is another person who wants to be with you just as much."

Keir stopped and stared at him with raised brows. "You need to get laid, man."

Xander shook his head and tugged the gloves off to grab one of the towels on a shelf. "Sex is easy. What I need is a lot more complicated."

He needed a fake mate, but if he had his wish, he'd finally find the right woman for his bear. His animal was growing antsy and needy. It wasn't natural to go this long without a life partner. Xander's bear reminded him daily that he needed offspring and a mate. A real one.

CHAPTER 3

Josilyn smoothed her hands down the sides of her leggings and long top. She had paired the outfit with nice sandals and simple makeup so she wouldn't look too outdated. The reality was she'd gone from a huge closet full of things to a handful of items she could work with. This was one of the only outfits she'd refused to part with. The top had been a honeymoon gift from Lucy.

She stared at the usually busy main street, which happened to be deserted at that moment, and stopped when she reached Ricardo's. This was a top-of-the-line restaurant. She'd loved coming here in the past. The food was delicious and their caramel bomb lava cake did things to her no man ever had.

The restaurant was never empty. She glanced in the window to see tables filled with couples on dates. Nerves made her belly quake and she rethought the plan. What was she doing there? She was going to work as some guy's fake girlfriend. No, not some guy. Some shifter. Even worse.

She paced outside the restaurant, her mind trying to come up with a plausible excuse to call off the meeting, but all she could think of was the money she'd be giving up. Money she needed more than another sleepless night.

Someone grabbed her arm, and she whipped her head to look into a pair of angry, glowing gold eyes. "You're mine."

"Excuse me? What the hell do you think you're doing, ass-hole. Let me go." She tugged on his hold but to no avail.

He started pulling her away from the restaurant toward a dark alley around the corner. "I said, you're mine."

"And I said to let me go, asshole," she yelled.

He backhanded her with his other hand and scratched her shoulder with his long dirty claws. "I'm taking what's mine."

What the fuck? Fear and anger sprouted wings in her chest. Her blood boiled with rage that a stranger put his hands on her. She dropped her bag and started hitting the guy with the cell phone she had in her hand. The sound of the phone hitting the guy's face made her wince. Still, he wouldn't stop. A man coming down the road stopped and frowned at them. "Help me! I don't know this guy!"

She tugged the other way while the man continued to pull her to the alley. The stranger pulled out his phone and started recording a video instead. She wished she could toss something at him. Meanwhile the man was almost dragging her as she strained in the other direction. Pain shot up her arm, but she ignored it and continued fighting. Her heart raced.

Finally, the phone she'd been hitting the guy with cracked. The glass screen broke on the side of his face. He wasn't fazed. She really started to worry at that point and screamed at the top of her lungs. "Help! Somebody help me!"

It had been too good to be true for her to come here and get paid so much money for a job. Something had to go wrong. Her luck lately had been that bad. It seemed something was always happening. Her crappy car had two flat tires in one month. Her one credit card was over its limit and denied at the grocery store. And someone stole her few remaining clothes from the Laundromat when she stepped into the bathroom. The world was out to get her.

She glanced around, but there wasn't a body in sight. Even

the guy with the camera had run off when the man tugging her let out a loud growl.

She screamed again and then remembered that during these types of situations people might assume it was a domestic dispute and not get involved. "Somebody help me! I don't know this man!" She slammed her fist on the guy's shoulder, but it didn't stop him. He growled again and kept fighting her. He was winning. "Let me go, you piece of shit!"

"Fire!" she yelled, hoping to grab someone's attention. Nothing. Then she heard a couple talking behind her on the sidewalk and knew someone had left the restaurant. "Help me!"

Her plea came at the right moment. The man hauling her yanked harder and was about to pull her into the mouth of the darkened alley when a mountain of a man showed up out of nowhere and punched the guy on the side of his face.

The hit was hard enough for the guy to let her go. She fell on her ass, pain thumping on her backside and legs. The man who had been hauling her turned to her rescuer, bared his fangs, and started to shift. *Oh, shit!* The guy was a shifter. She glanced wildly around. There was a beautiful woman watching the whole thing. She must have come out with the guy who'd hit the freak. The woman didn't appear concerned over the insanity. She watched her boyfriend toss the lunatic to the ground.

Josie glanced up and met the gaze of the man who came to her rescue. His eyes appeared to glow a deep gold and a furious frown that would scare anyone was etched on his forehead. He was big and didn't seem bothered by the other man's body ripping through his clothes.

"Wait, stop, please," a voice hollered out as another man rounded the corner at a dead run and wedged in between her rescuer and the shifting man on the ground. "He's my brother. Let me calm him and we can fix this," the frazzled man said as he turned to face the shifting angry freak.

"Trey, stop. Don't shift, return to your body now." The seconds ticked by as Josilyn stared at the men and the insanity before her. "Trey, now. I'm not going to tell you again," the man barked out in sharp command. Slowly, the shifting man's features returned to the look of the psychotic man who had dragged her into the alley.

The stranger turned and faced her rescuer again. "I'm sorry. It was a misunderstanding. He wasn't supposed to be away from us; he slipped by."

Josie had heard enough. This was the kind of shit she tried to stay away from. She had somewhere to be, and as much as she wanted to thank her knight in shining Armani suit, she needed to meet her new boss.

No matter the circumstances, being late was not a good idea. Especially if she wanted to ensure this job and the money she so desperately needed. She climbed to her feet and quickly walked to the woman at the entrance to the alley while the men's attention was turned from her.

"Can you tell your husband I said thank you. I don't know what would have happened if he hadn't intervened." The woman opened her mouth to respond, but Josie didn't have time to talk. "I have to go. I'm late. Thank you again," Josilyn said as she hurried to the entrance of Ricardo's. With one final glance at the man who had saved her, she entered the restaurant and left thoughts of his intense golden eyes behind.

Ricardo's hadn't changed much since the last time she had been there. The hostess looked up with a smile as Josie approached. "I'm meeting someone, but I'm not sure if he's here yet."

"Of course, no problem." The hostess frowned while staring at Josie's face. "I don't mean to be rude, but are you okay? You have a nasty red mark on your face that looks like it's starting to bruise."

Josie tenderly touched her swollen cheek and winced. "It's nothing, but thank you."

The hostess gave her an unconvinced nod. "May I ask the gentleman's name?"

"Xander Ursi." It was easy to recall such a manly name. Different. For some reason, saying it gave her goose bumps.

"Oh, yes, he said he was expecting someone. He stepped out to handle something a little while ago, but said he'd be back. I can show you to his table."

Josie sighed in relief that she hadn't left him waiting. She needed this job too much to screw things up thanks to some deranged shifter lunatic. She thanked the hostess, sat, and waited for her fake mate to show up. With any luck, he would be as mouthwateringly gorgeous as the man who had come to her aid in the alley.

A tiny sigh escaped her throat. Damn, good time to think of that man's good looks. She could sit and stare at him for hours and never get tired of it. What a shame a man like that wasn't the one needing to hire her. His girlfriend was proof of that.

She had been sophisticated and beautiful, and curvy. That at least gave Josie hope she would find a man to look at her the way her rescuer had for that brief moment.

CHAPTER 4

Xander frowned as the man attempted to explain the actions of the shifter on the ground. Did he really think he could say something that would make dragging a woman into an alley against her will okay?

"My name's Dominick, this is my brother Trey. If you can give me one minute to have my men pick up my brother, I will explain in full." He wasn't given a chance to reply before the man pulled out his phone and gave directions to his location, listened for a moment, and then hung up with a sigh.

"My brother is not okay. His actions today prove that, but he is closely guarded at all times. I will speak to my men and find out who allowed him to sneak off and will make sure it doesn't happen again."

"You do realize your brother was dragging a woman against her will into this alley, and if the bruise on her face is any indication, he hit her as well. I'm not sure what you're used to, but I don't condone violence against women."

Dominick shook his head wearily. "We don't, either. My brother's mate was killed a few months ago when they got into a fight and she was attacked. Since then, he's been slowly losing touch with reality. Your mate looks similar to her, and I can only assume that set him off. I'm sorry; I promise we will keep a better eye on him from now on."

Xander didn't bother correcting his assumption about the woman. The minute he looked into her eyes, he'd known. The connection was there. Palpable. Like nothing he had ever experienced. He watched as Dominick's men came up and dragged off Trey. Dominick nodded and turned to where the woman had fallen, and frowned.

"Where did she go? I wanted to apologize and assure her he wouldn't be a threat to her again."

"She ran off a few minutes ago. Said to say thank you for rescuing her, but she couldn't be late," Ally called out from the sidewalk.

Xander nodded in understanding and turned back to Dominick. "Just keep an eye on your brother. The last thing we need is shifters going crazy and assaulting females. We have enough problems with humans as it is."

"I assure you," Dominick said with a steely edge to his voice, "he will be guarded at all times. I have my own issues in my pack, and allowing him to cause problems won't be good for me."

Xander nodded. A frown still playing his forehead. Everyone had issues with their people, it seemed. "Good luck with him."

He turned away after Dominick nodded, dismissed both men from his mind, and approached Ally. "Sorry about that." Xander frowned and looked up and down the street for the first woman in his life to make his bear wake in raging lust.

"Really, Xander. What you did was truly nice. And don't apologize. After all these years, I'm used to your knight in shining suit act." Ally winked.

"You haven't changed a bit, have you? Still an incorrigible little brat, but it's why we always let you tag along when you were home."

Ally laughed good-naturedly. "I forgot how much fun you are to be around. Good news, maybe I can tag along again and you can introduce me to some of your single eligible friends."

"Like I would let you near them, or them near you, for that matter," Xander said with a grin and pulled her into a hug. "I'm running late, brat. I'll see you Saturday and we can catch up more."

"It's a date, of sorts."

Xander smiled and watched Ally cross the street to the valet area where she'd parked. The same valet who had taken Xander's car rushed from the parking area to meet her. When he finally saw the guy escort Ally to her car, he felt confident enough to turn back to the restaurant. She had grown up a lot in the years since he saw her last. It was going to be nice having her around again. But now it was time to meet his hired mate.

He looked around for any sign of the mysterious woman, but knew it was a lost cause. She was long gone at this point. Fucking hell! The one woman to stir both his interest and his bear's, and she disappeared.

With a sigh of regret, he turned and headed back to Ricardo's and his pretend mate for the next couple of weeks.

"Mr. Ursi, your friend arrived. We seated her at your table a few minutes ago," the hostess announced as Xander walked in the restaurant.

He nodded his thanks and made his way to the table. His pseudomate had her back to him, but he liked what he could see so far. She had long curly light brown hair that cascaded down her back and curves that made his mouth water. He wanted nothing more than to get closer to her. The thought stopped him cold. He hadn't been this attracted to a female from behind in a long time.

"Hello, you must be Josilyn Martinez," Xander said, and moved to sit in the chair opposite his hired date. The idea alone made him almost laugh out loud. A soft gasp of surprise brought his eyes up to the woman. He grinned in absolute pleasure—

sometimes the stars aligned in his favor, after all. "We meet again."

"You're my . . . rescuer," she said in a soft husky voice that made his cock jerk.

He loved the way her voice trembled slightly, and she gave him a wide-eyed stare. "I was lucky enough to be in the right place at the right time." Then he noticed her face and the bruises forming. The bear inside him roared to life and wanted to find that moron who touched her. "Are you okay? Your face is bruising already. Let's get you some ice to keep the swelling to a minimum."

She waved his concern away. "No, it's all right. He didn't really hurt me, well, not badly. He scared me. He was a lot stronger than I am, and I couldn't get away."

"I'm really happy to hear that you weren't seriously hurt. Let me formally introduce myself. I'm Xander Ursi and it is without a doubt a pleasure to meet you." He paused as he watched the smile brighten her glowing caramel skin. He longed to kiss the dimple on her right cheek. She was gorgeous in a way he hadn't been expecting; the small picture he had did not do her justice in the least.

"It's a pleasure to meet you. Please call me Josie," she said with a bashful smile, and brought one hand up and brushed the lock of hair off her face. With shaky fingers, she tucked it behind her ear.

"Only if you call me Xander."

Xander was intrigued even more now by this beautiful woman. Her light hazel eyes lit up and the dimple flashed again. His cock hardened and he had to shift slightly to relieve some of the pressure. He felt like a teenage boy in the throes of his first crush. Who was he kidding? It was so much more than that. His bear was clawing to come out and mark her as his. Josilyn, hired mate, was, in fact, his one true mate.

CHAPTER 5

Sex on a stick. That's all she could come up with about the man across from her. Her gaze slowly trailed up his suited body. She couldn't see muscles, but she could tell he was damn big and had this whole powerful personality thing going. When she got to his face, she gasped in recognition and shock. Her knight in shining armor was her date. Who would have thought the handsome man from the alley, who had so helpfully jumped in to save her from a shifter, was the same man she had come here to meet.

Wait, that didn't make sense. Why would he need a fake mate if he had that beautiful woman he was with in the mouth of the alley?

She frowned. "Xander, I'm confused. Why would you need a mate for hire, when you had that beautiful woman with you earlier?"

He gave a slow grin that made her panties shrivel into nothing. "That wasn't my date." He continued to hold her gaze hostage. "Or my girlfriend, if you thought she was. She's an old friend who's moving to town and she wanted to catch up. Her older brother's a very close friend. She's practically my sister. Besides that, the reason I need you is to get my grandmother off my back. She knows Ally, so it wouldn't have worked."

Josie was strangely pleased to hear that woman wasn't

his mate. She berated herself for the tingles of excitement at knowing he was single. Not going there. Nope. Not even if her hormones debated with her. She had so little luck in love. Besides, it didn't make sense considering she just met the man and was only here as his hired mate.

Besides, he was a shifter. Dangerous. Alpha. She glanced up, saw his intense, hungry stare, and had to squeeze her legs together. Great time for her lack of sex to make itself known. She was in trouble if a single look made her wet and ready to beg.

"What made you hire a mate, exactly? I'm afraid I don't know any details other than you needed someone as soon as possible."

Xander cocked his head to the side, his brows rising and confusion clear on his face. "You weren't told the details? I made everything clear when I applied."

"No, they didn't tell me much. Just the duration, the fee, and when I was to meet you." Josilyn couldn't help the blush that flamed when she thought about what else her friend had told her. No sex. *Unless you want to.*

Now the words kept running circles in her head. She would love nothing more than to ride this man until they both passed out from exhaustion.

"My grandmother is coming to town. I need to show her that I've found my mate and I'm ready to settle down."

It was Josie's turn to be confused. "I don't know much about shifters, but won't she wonder later why I'm suddenly gone from your life? I was under the impression shifters mated for life."

Xander nodded and smiled. "You're really smart. That's correct. My grandmother isn't a shifter, though. She's human. She believes it's more of just finding the right person and that I'm being too picky."

They were interrupted by the server standing beside their

table, "Hello, my name is Julian and I'll be your server today. Can I get you something to drink?"

"Wine okay with you, Josie?" Xander asked politely. She nodded her agreement. She had walked to the restaurant so didn't need to worry about driving under the influence. He turned to the waiting server. "Hi, Julian, can we get a bottle of your house red, please."

"Of course, Mr. Ursi. Do you need a few minutes to look over the menu, or would you like to order now?"

Xander winked at Josie. "A few minutes, please. My lovely date has not looked at a menu yet."

"Oh, that's okay. I haven't been here in a while, but I still remember my favorites." Too bad he wasn't on the menu.

There she went again. This was dangerous. What if after one glass of wine she flung herself at him? She really needed to get laid and stop mentally stripping this poor man.

They ordered their meals and Julian left them to finish their conversation.

"What's next, then? I mean, did my showing up here help you decide if I'm filling that role for you? What if your grandmother takes one look at me and says, 'Nope, not good enough,' or something, and you did this all for nothing?" She folded her fingers on her lap and tried to stop wringing her hands together. Stupid nerves.

"Honestly, yes, you're it for me. My grandmother will be here in a few days. I just need you to spend time with me so we can get to know each other. When she gets here, it will look like a real relationship because we know each other's quirks." He smiled as he spoke, and the way he said the word "quirks" made her shudder. She was reading something dirty into everything.

"How much time are we talking here?" Because he was really close to being in need of saving from her if it was a long time. "I don't see how a few 'dates' are going to accomplish all that." Plus, what she really wanted was to ask if they could reconsider the no-sex clause. She *really* wanted him to reconsider.

"Of course not. You have to move in with me for the next week," Xander said with a sinful grin that sent tingles through her already aroused body.

Close quarters with this man. Well, she might as well go buy a new set of batteries. She was going to need new toys too. Shit! Him and her together and no sex? That had to be considered cruel and unusual punishment in some states. How was she supposed to be around him all the time and not beg him to fuck her senseless?

She was turning into a sex maniac. This had to be what happened when you hadn't gotten any in over a year. It was either that or something else was going on. Why did this guy affect her to the point she would drag him to the bathroom, have a quickie right now, and not think twice about it? Ah, fuck! A quickie sounded good.

Josie did another quick glance over his body, what she could see of it, and choked back a whimper. Fuck quickie. She wanted to climb him like a maypole. The things she would do to him would get her arrested. Well, probably not in private, but she'd definitely end up in a messed-up version of a *Cops* public sex video.

Xander cleared his throat, and Josie blushed at the train of thought she'd been following. Shit, hadn't she heard shifters could smell when someone was aroused. She met his gaze and had her answer. Oh, hell to the yeah. The way he inhaled like someone just baked a pie made her squeeze her legs tight.

Words weren't necessary. They stared into each other's eyes and she knew she wasn't imagining the promise in his gaze of really dirty things to come. Well, maybe she imagined it, but she was okay with that. They were jolted back to the present when the server Julian returned and placed their wine and food on the table and left without a word.

Josie blushed, picked up her wine, and tugged at the neckline to her top. She was feeling all kinds of hot. Food was the last thing on her mind. "You said move in with you for the next week. Doesn't that seem a bit extreme?"

"Normally, yes, but I don't have time to for us to do this any other way. Is there any issue about staying with me?" The way he raised his brows told her he was expecting her to have a man issue. "I guess we could stay at your place for part of the week too, unless there's a reason you can't . . ."

She grinned at his obvious insinuation. She should let him believe she had a man, but she wanted the job, and him too, for that matter. "Um."

She was struggling to get past the living-with-him part, to formulate a logical plan to stick to not jumping him in the middle of the night. Nick was with his grandmother. That was one less complication, at least. Wait, what was she saying? She'd just met this guy. Yeah, he saved her life, but that didn't entitle him to anything. Josie needed some answers, and she knew just the person to call. "Excuse me for a moment. I need to use the ladies' room."

As soon as she was out of sight, she went back to the hostess who had been nice to her.

"Hi, could I possibly use a phone for a second?"

The hostess smiled and nodded. "We have one in the manager's office right around the corner. Just follow me."

Once she was alone in the office, she pulled her planner out of her bag. People always told her nobody carried written phone numbers anymore because everything was saved on cell phones. Well, she had a broken phone and still had all the important contact information she needed. She called her best friend. Shawna was the person who had gotten her into this in the first place. She paced, as she waited for the call to go through.

"Shawna, I swear I'm going to shave you bald and throw you in front of your yoga class naked."

Shawna laughed that cute giggle that usually made Josie burst into laughter too. "Well, hello to you too, darling. What crawled up your sphincter and rotted?"

She huffed out a breath. "You didn't tell me I'd have to stay with him night and day for a week! That is something kind of important to know ahead of time, don't you think?"

Shawna gasped. "I didn't know that part. The arrangements are between you. All I did was input your data and the computer matched you to him."

Great. Where did that leave her? Back to square one.

"I don't know the first thing about him and neither do you, it sounds like." Not that her body cared. Her girl bits had decided he could show her how much bears liked to lick on honey. Her honey. Lord, she needed to stop the insane sexual thoughts.

"That's not entirely true. I know of him. He is a loyal client to my company, and on top of that, everyone has to go through a rigid background screening. He is safe, gorgeous, and relatively harmless. You're in great hands." The cheerful note in Shawna's words almost did her in.

"Oh, so that means it's safe to send your best friend off with him for the week? This doesn't cause you any sort of concern in the least bit? What if he turns out to be a cannibal? And wants to eat me for dinner!"

Shawna laughed. "If he wants to eat you for dinner, I suggest you enjoy every second of it."

"Shawna!" she grumbled. "This is serious."

"Orgasms usually are. If he's as good as most other bear shifters, he's gonna have your knees buckling and your legs shaking for hours."

Just great. She so did not need that visual . . . or expectation.

"You're not a very good friend."

Shawna giggled again. "The way I see it, you can sit home and be depressed that Nick is with his grandmother while you stress over money, or you can spend a fabulous week with a walking wet dream. Maybe finally get all the sex you haven't gotten for years."

Josie laughed at that; leave it to Shawna to put things into perspective. "I still don't know about this. Are you sure it's safe?"

Shawna sighed. "Woman, I swear to you on the threat of no more Pizza Fridays that you're safe with him. Well, as safe as you want to be, that is."

"Sometimes I really wonder why I'm friends with your crazy ass."

"That's simple. Because you love me, and I spice up your life. Now stop hiding and get back to eye fucking that hunk of a man and remember to live a little." She ended the sentence with a loud meow.

Josie smiled and said good-bye before slowly making her way to her table and the enticing man sitting there. She might be a fool, but she trusted Shawna.

"Where were we?"

Xander winked and lifted his glass of wine. Lord, those eyes were doing some crazy things to her heart. "You were getting ready to say yes to my proposal."

He'd already eaten most of his food, so she had to sit down and pick at hers quickly while trying to think of what to say. Every few seconds, she'd take a tiny bite and try to decide how to answer him. After she'd made an attempt at eating some of the meal, she sighed and met his gaze.

"You sure are confident, aren't you?" She couldn't help but

laugh at his self-assured demeanor. The man knew he was hot and was using it to get his way.

"Not at all, but I know what I want and I don't give up easily. The only question now is, are we staying at your place, my place, or back and forth?"

Josie put her hand up in a slowdown gesture. "You don't even know me. How can you trust me to be in your house, around your stuff, and not be even the slightest worried?"

"I know the hoops I had to jump through to be included in the mate program. That leaves me fairly confident you did the same. Besides, I know the owner of the company and I trust him." Xander waited with raised brows, almost daring her to come up with another reason he could shoot down.

Well, hell. She might regret this later, but at least she'd regret it with her bills paid. "Fine. I agree . . . for now. Don't make me change my mind."

Xander beamed in satisfaction as he waved the waiter over. "Can we get the check, please?"

"We're leaving now?" Josie squeaked in evident surprise and alarm. Damn, she'd barely had enough wine to blame for throwing herself at him if she happened to go that route.

"Yes, it'll be easier to get to know each other in a more relaxed environment. This restaurant is wonderful, but it's hard to talk freely when you're constantly aware of eyes and ears of those around you listening in on every word." He stood, his massive body making her feel small and dainty.

"Where are we going? I walked here from my apartment. Are we staying at my place or yours?" Why was she suddenly thinking about the fact she hadn't shaved her legs. Or wasn't wearing matching underwear.

"Do you have a preference? I want you to be comfortable and at ease. I understand this was sprung on you last minute and I apologize for that," Xander said. He handed Julian his card. Julian was back within thirty seconds. Xander smiled and signed the check. Then he offered her his hand. "My place, or yours?"

Josie opened and closed her mouth a few times trying to figure out a response. She hadn't shaved her legs! "I . . . um . . . Do . . ."

Xander laughed. She knew why. She probably had that fish-out-of-water look. "Calm down, sweetheart. How about this, you run home and get what you need for tonight and tomorrow. I will give you my address and phone number and you can meet me at my house as soon as you're done. This way you have your car and can leave if at any point you don't feel safe or if you're overwhelmed or whatever."

Josie nodded in agreement and stood to follow Xander from the restaurant. Things were happening so quickly and she couldn't process any of them. It was one thing to do a job for some guy. Quite another to be this attracted to the man hiring her. She was having trouble processing the fact he was going to pay her to be his fake girlfriend and all her mind was focused on was getting him naked. She needed some alone time.

"Let me call you a cab or drop you off. I don't like the idea of you walking after what happened earlier."

In all the excitement, she had completely forgotten about her near miss earlier in the night. "A cab would be appreciated," she said with a shiver as she searched the shadows around her.

Xander placed his arm around her shoulders and pulled her close. "Don't worry. I won't let anything happen to you."

Josie couldn't concentrate on a word he said, her head was filled with the musky man scent that was all Xander. A mixture of woods, man, and something she couldn't quite identify, but it left her hungering for a taste of him.

CHAPTER 6

Xander filled his coffee mug and sat down in his home office with a frown. He leaned back on his leather chair, trying to control his bear and the need to go looking for his mate. He doubted Josie would appreciate being stalked while still trying to make up her mind about him.

What in the hell had come over him to say that? A week together nonstop was going to be pure torture. He wanted to kick his own ass for the self-imposed agony. All those days with his mate so close. Well, he'd have to convince her he was the right man for her before he died of blue balls. He had to. There was no way he'd be able to refrain from taking his mate and fucking her senseless ten times a day.

Fucking great. He hadn't been thinking with anything other than his dick. Then again, his bear was roaring "mine" in his head repeatedly. He'd been lucky he hadn't taken her on the table and witnesses be damned. He found his mate and he wasn't letting her go, no matter what he had to do.

His ringing phone startled him out of his stupor. Shit, just what he needed. Keir.

"Keir, you're not going to believe this," Xander said in lieu of a greeting as he answered the phone.

Keir groaned. "Was it that bad?"

"Just the opposite. She's my mate. My hired mate is in

actuality my mate. Can you believe that?" He sure as hell still couldn't.

"Seriously?" Keir said, surprise evident in his voice. "What are the chances of that happening? So tell me about her. Wait, why are you on the phone with me if you found your mate. Go claim her and fill me in later."

"It's not that simple. You know how humans are. They don't get the whole 'you're mine' thing. They need more than that." And he planned to give it to her. His highest priority now was getting to know her and allowing her the chance to see him as a real mate, not just some guy hiring her to fake being his girlfriend.

"Does anything ever go easy? What's your plan?" Keir sighed.

"I improvised and convinced her we needed to be together twenty-four seven for the next week to convince my grand-mother we're mates. She agreed after a small bit of persuasion." All he could hope for now was that his charm and personality kept her going through with the agreement. That and her clear desire for him. There was the fact she'd been paid for the job. She didn't seem like the type of person to flake out.

"Seriously? She bought that?" Keir laughed. "No offense, but you aren't that good a liar, so why did she agree?"

Xander had a feeling her needs had taken over her ability to say no. He'd seen the open desire in her eyes. All he needed was for her to give him the green light and he'd prove to her they could be fucking amazing together. "She did take off to the bathroom shortly after, I half expected her to run. She must have done some thinking in my benefit because she came back and agreed. She's at her apartment getting some things to-gether and coming to my place after."

"She's coming to your place . . . Is that wise?" Keir asked hesitantly.

Hell, yes! The closer he had her, the easier it would be to convince her she was truly his. "Why wouldn't it be?"

"You're mates, I get that, but your house isn't exactly family oriented, if you know what I mean. It's like a bachelor pad on steroids. She might be a tad overwhelmed and run. Plus, if she finds out how much you're worth, she might freak even worse. Women either fuck you, hoping to get a piece of your money, or they run in intimidation."

He thought about the number of times women had thrown themselves at him for his money. Then about the times they'd decided he was an immature teenager with raging hormones. Neither way looked good. "Shit, I didn't think of that. What do I do?"

"How in the hell would I know?" Keir roared with a laugh. "I just fuck them and leave them. You're the one who wanted a mate."

Xander growled in frustration, "After this is settled and she is mine, remember this, it will be your turn soon enough. And I'm going to sit back and laugh. Watching your mate make you suffer will be the highlight of my year."

"I'm just going to hire my own if I need one. And trust me, they're not likely to send me Ms. Perfect Mate." Keir laughed.

It was Xander's turn to laugh. He had a feeling Keir was going to be falling sooner rather than later. "Eventually you'll meet the one. And she'll turn you upside down with frustration."

"You keep thinking that, buttercup. I'm not cut out for the mate life. Eat, sleep, and screw—that's about as much as I need out of life." Keir sighed. "Okay, fine, why don't you call her and give her a heads-up. Just put her at ease so she doesn't freak when she sees it all."

"Good idea. I'll do that. By the way, when you do meet your mate, I'm going to laugh my ass off as you flounder and try to change years of womanizing ways in the span of minutes."

Xander hung up with his friend's curses ringing in his ear. His instinct told him that Josie wasn't a gold-digging whore. Even his bear rumbled in disagreement. She was more likely the type to hate him for having money. He pulled out the paper he wrote her information on from the mate service and called. Two, three, four rings and the voicemail picked up.

"Hey, it's Xander. I just wanted to give you a heads-up before you showed up and freaked out on me. My place isn't . . . I'm not sure how to put this, so I'm just going to say it and hope you don't get the wrong impression. I've lived here since college. I haven't redecorated since then, so you could say it's in a classic college frat boy décor." His animal pushed for control. A clear indicator that he felt Xander was fucking things up.

"I swear next week I'm having it all ripped out and redone to fit my lifestyle. I just didn't think about it and I don't want you to get the wrong impression." He mentally groaned as he tried to figure out what else to say without sounding like a complete and utter loser. "So, anyway. I'll see you soon." He hung up, leaned back in his chair, and groaned. Fucking awesome.

He decided to get out of his home office and look over his home with the eyes of a stranger coming in for the first time. He wanted to make the best impression possible. He blanched. He saw what she would and knew it was a lost cause. Josie would take one glance, flee in terror, and probably take out a restraining order on him at the same time.

How could he have been so fucking stupid? Fifteen years he had lived in this place, and it still looked like a playboy den. His phone rang again, startling him out of his thoughts. He groaned when he saw it was his grandmother.

"To what do I owe this great pleasure?" he asked with real enthusiasm. He loved his grandmother, even if she did drive him crazy.

"Can it, boy." She laughed. "That charm won't work on me,

and you know it. Is this a bad time? I was calling to give you the details of when I'll be in town."

By the time he got his grandmother off the phone, he knew it was too late. There was nothing to be done but face the music and hope for the best. The doorbell rang. Shit, she was already there. He hesitated with another quick glance around before gathering his courage and opening the door.

She could see the headlines in tomorrow's paper: "Woman Killed Playing the Role of Fake Girlfriend. No Sex was Involved. That's Right. None. Not Even a Little." What was she thinking agreeing to this? A quick look around at the rapidly emptying cabinets and she mentally fortified herself to do what was necessary for Nick and to keep the promise she had made.

"It won't be so bad. Think of it as a minivacation. Except you still have to work, and pretend to be in love with a stranger. Lust is easy and close enough." Well, it was official, she had lost her damn mind. It was bad when she resorted to talking to herself aloud in her empty apartment.

She missed having Nick around. The quiet unnerved her and made her jump at the slightest sound. Tonight's incident notwithstanding, she was tired of being on guard all the time. Maybe a few days away would get whoever was playing pranks on her to back off.

Between the hang-up phone calls, the trash left outside her door, and the messages on her car window, it was getting harder and harder to hide it from Nick and her neighbors. If only she caught someone doing it, then she'd give that lowlife a piece of her mind. But as it was, she was clueless.

If the jackass would just say something, or give some clue as to why he was doing this, it would help. Even the notes on her car were only crude drawings of a stick person with red puddles around her and the word BITCH in bold block letters. Clearly whoever was playing the pranks wasn't very artistic, but he got his point across.

She had toyed with calling the police, but felt stupid. There weren't any direct threats, nothing had been damaged, and no one had seen anything. For all she knew, it was some bored kid playing a prank. It was better to believe that than thinking someone was out to hurt her in this weird childish way.

Josie quickly finished packing her bag. Now that it was time to go, she was nervous and, if she was truthful, excited too. She had never met a man who captured all her senses as he did.

She was lucky she kept her old cell phones after she upgraded and had been able to switch SIM cards and get it working again. Now she could communicate with Nick if she needed to.

The ringing of her phone startled her a few minutes later. Unfortunately, she had a tendency to put her phone down and forget where she left it. Thankfully, the ringer was on and she was able to hear it down the hall. She found the phone in a kitchen cabinet. She hadn't even remembered opening that one.

It was a good thing she agreed to this. She was in desperate need of money. She dialed her voicemail and played the message on speaker. Oh, boy. Xander's sexy tones filled her apartment. How could only the sound of his voice make her tingle? His words worried her, though. Just what was she going to see when she got to his place?

"Come on, girl. You can do this. Put on your big-girl panties and do what you have to do." Josie continued the pep talk as she carried her bag to her car. She took care of her older model because it was the only one she had. She half wanted to run back to the safety her little place offered, but common sense won out again. Nick was her priority.

Once she had this money she'd be able to provide better for

him. She just had to keep that in mind, and she would get through this, hopefully without embarrassing herself with Mr. Tall, Sexy, and Lickable.

The drive wasn't long enough to completely convince herself this was a good idea. She circled the building a few times before she found a spot and, with reluctance, parked. The minutes ticked by. Her hands shook on the steering wheel. This went against everything she stood for, but Xander wasn't putting pressure on her. He needed her and she was going to do a job. It's a job. Just a job.

Then why did it scare her to go up to his place so much? Maybe because she lusted for the man like she hadn't for anyone before. The fact that he seemed to be interested in her as well made this harder. Her heart flipped. She didn't do sex without commitment. Not that he was asking her to. For cripes sakes, he wasn't asking her to do anything but the job he hired her for.

She knew why she was scared. The longer she spoke to Xander, the more her emotions got that electrical charge as if she was feeling more than lust. That was dangerous. She didn't normally believe in love at first sight, but these feelings weren't normal. It had to stay lust, or this whole operation was in danger. She stared up at the building and her new home for the next few days. A tap on the window startled her and she jumped and let out a yell.

Josie quickly rolled the window down and peered at the stranger standing there in a security uniform.

"Miss, are you okay? You've been sitting here for about fifteen minutes. You look so worried I couldn't help but check on you." He motioned to his badge and the security patrol car parked behind her own vehicle. "I'm the security guard for the place, and I just wanted to check in before I moved along on my patrol."

"I'm sorry, yes, I'm okay. I got lost in thought and didn't realize how much time had passed. I'm here to stay with a friend for a few days." Keeping the tremble from her voice was not an easy task. Talk about needing to get her shit together.

"As long as you're sure, I'll be on my way. Have a good night." The guard walked back to his car, and Josie felt her face flame in embarrassment. It was now or never. She climbed out of the car, grabbed her bag, and started walking to her next adventure with the prime morsel that was her employer. Yes, that's what she had to keep in mind: she wasn't a paid escort, and she wouldn't sleep with him for money. No matter how enticing he was.

Xander opened the door with a hesitant smile, and she was hard-pressed not to drop to her knees and worship at his feet. Yes, he was that gorgeous. It was that tall, broad shoulder size combined with those eyes that spoke of pure sin. And that tempting smile. Oh, let's not forget his beard. She had never wanted to lick a man's face like she did at that moment.

"Hi." Xander smiled sheepishly. He stepped back and made room for her to enter his apartment. Josie came to an abrupt halt. What the hell? She saw the living room for the first time. No wonder he was worried. Was that a blush on his chiseled features?

A pool table, a dartboard, a bar that took up one whole wall, a giant-screen TV mounted on the wall with tons of gaming consoles below it. The centerpiece, a massive black leather couch that looked more like a bed that would hold six people on it. That thing was a monster.

The walls were a deep shade of red that made the room darker. "Can I turn on a light?" Josie asked. Nerves made her reach for the switches on the wall next to her. Xander reached out to stop her, but it was too late. The light switch flipped on, and the room came to life with mood lighting, soft romantic music, and the fireplace turned on. She gaped at Xander in fascinated horror and amusement. Holy crap. She was in the Playboy Mansion!

He cleared his throat. "I don't even know what to say."

Josie nodded and moved into the room farther. She took two steps and then burst into hysterical laughter. "Do you really have a disco ball lamp on that end table?"

"It doesn't work anymore," Xander replied with an almost defensive tone.

"But you have one. That's what counts." Josie moved on, taking in all the fascinating details of Xander's life, even if it was a holdover from his college days.

"Why don't we head over to the spare room so you can get settled in?" Xander motioned for her to follow him down a short hallway. "This is the main bathroom, towels and anything you need are in the closet here," he said, pointing to a small door beside where they stood. "And this will be your room. It's safe." He met her gaze. "The door has a lock. Everything was replaced once my roommate moved out years ago. I'm the next door down if you need anything. Feel free to make yourself at home. The kitchen is stocked too." He gave her a soul-deep stare. "That's your space. I won't go in there . . . unless you ask me to."

Josie nodded in appreciation that he'd known she was concerned. His taking time to explain she was safe in her room meant more than he knew. "Thank you. I would love to get cleaned up and settled in. It's somewhat late and a lot has happened. Is it okay if we call it a night?"

"Of course. Do you have to work tomorrow?" Xander leaned against the doorway waiting for her response. His eyes darted around the room.

She bit her lip and wanted to ask if there was a blow-up doll that would pop down from the ceiling but decided against it. "Yes, till five. What about you?"

He shoved his hands into his pockets, stretching the material of his slacks across his hips. Oh, damn. "Same. I'll meet you here and we can talk and get to know each other. I'll leave you a key on the counter in case I don't see you in the morning."

"I broke my phone earlier, when I used it to hit that guy. I have an old one that still works but sometimes freezes up."

Xander frowned, clenched his jaw, and a brightness lit in his eyes. The bear. She'd heard enough about them to know their animals made themselves known in the eyes first. "I understand. I'm sorry about that. You should never have been in harm's way."

She nodded. "It's not your fault."

"Have a good night, Josie." His churned-gravel voice warmed her to the core.

"Good night," Josie replied softly, watching him stroll away. She took her sweet time staring after him before she finally shut the door and slumped against it. When had her life become this weird, and exhilarating? Her heart pounded hard. Seeing Xander so insecure and embarrassed made the butterflies in her stomach take flight and dance in a flutter of excitement. It was going to be a long night. Thank heavens she brought her best friend for the past year, her rabbit vibrator.

CHAPTER 7

Josie woke up with a groan. She swore she'd just hit the pillow when her alarm went off. Stupid fantasies making it harder for her to rest. The dreams that followed left her restless and needy. Just being in the same house with Xander made her hormones go into hyperdrive. She needed a shower and an orgasm. If it was a choice between an orgasm and a shower, she didn't know which one would win out.

She slipped into her robe, grabbed her toiletry bag, and ventured to the door, listening intently. She couldn't hear anything. Did that mean Xander was still asleep, or had he already gone to work? She opened her door as quietly as possible and peeked around up and down the hallway. The last thing she wanted was to get caught with bed hair and morning breath. So far so good.

She dashed into the bathroom and shut the door quickly. Once she turned around, she blinked in confusion. Was she dreaming, or was she really staring at a shower with the Twister game all over the walls and floor. She didn't even want to know what had transpired in this bathroom.

Good God. Xander was such a man-whore. She was going to castrate him if she got anything from his guest shower. The cold tiled floor made her curl her toes in. She tentatively stepped into the shower and turned on the water. The warmth seeped all the way to her bones. It was glorious to have all that hot water pouring down her body and for once not having to worry about using too much.

She took much longer than planned, but it'd been so decadent, she didn't have it in her to care. Only the thought of how much trouble she would get into if she were late to work made her jump out and get dressed. Stupid real life had to intrude in everything good.

Please don't let him be out there. Josie wasn't ready to face him in her work clothes. Her company required her to wear a modern-day version of a maid's outfit, and the catcalls and whistles grew quite tiresome. Add in curves and it was a recipe for disaster, usually leaving her ready to knock a few teeth out of some rude man's mouth.

On the kitchen counter was a note with a key on top of it. The writing was immaculate and neat for a man. For crying out loud. She needed to get her shit together. She had it bad to be admiring his handwriting.

> *Josie,*
> *I will be home about 5:30. If you get here before I do,*
> *here is a key. I'll see you in a few hours. I swear this*
> *apartment isn't me. Give me a chance to show you the*
> *guy I am, not the boy I was.*
> *X*

She couldn't help the smile. He was so cute in a little boy sort of way. A kid caught with his hand in the cookie jar explanations. He was an odd mix of feral man and gentleman that drew her in like no one else ever had. If she were truthful, she wouldn't mind trying that shower with Xander. Maybe not to play naked Twister. She didn't think she had the flexibility needed for it. But she could sure think of some fun stuff they could do instead.

With a wistful sigh, she headed to work and the grueling day she knew was ahead of her. Snarky comments, bitchy bosses, and dirty toilets. She really hated her ex for putting her in this position.

Standing in the front office after checking in for the morning, she looked at her schedule for the day hanging on the bulletin board. It showed she had a two-hour break between jobs midafternoon. That would be the perfect time to see Nick for a bit.

She hurried to the employees' lunchroom and dialed Mildred's number. As normal, the old lady answered with a haughty voice that so disgusted her. But to her surprise, the woman readily agreed to the visit, and Josie was off to her first assignment, happy to get the day going.

Time dragged so slowly that morning, Josie wanted to scream at the clock and call it a lying piece of shit. But she doubted the lady owner of the house would appreciate that.

When she finally parked in front of the Mildred's house, she stared at the Gothic-looking house with its gargoyle roof ornaments and high peaks. She shuddered. No wonder her sister and brother-in-law didn't want Nick living here. It scared the crap out of her being so close to it. Not because she didn't appreciate that décor in the right environment, but in this house, it was creepy.

The front door opened and Nick came running out. Energy filled her and she hurried from the car and scooped up his scrawny eight-year-old body. She squeezed him tightly.

"How are you, little bear? I've missed you so much." She put him on his feet and held him at arm's length. "I think you've grown ten inches since I saw you last."

Nick rolled his eyes. "Aunt Josie, if I was ten inches bigger, I'd be taller than you."

She looked incredulous. "You don't think I could've grown ten inches too, so we'd be the same still?"

Mildred stepped onto the front porch. "Nicholas, bring your aunt inside." She waved him in. "Quickly, now, boy. I don't want anyone seeing her kind as a guest in my home."

Josie stopped dead in front of the old woman, Nick continuing into the house. "What *kind* is my kind? The nice kind? Hardworking kind? Caring kind?"

Mildred's eyes were hard. "No, dear. The poor and pathetic kind."

Oh, yes. That pissed her off royally. If the bitch wanted to get personal, then bring it on, mama. She was ready to rumble.

Josie walked through the doorway, making sure the old bat was a step behind her, then slammed the door shut. Something banged against it, a knee or foot, perhaps. She then threw the door open just as quickly.

"Oh, I'm so sorry, Mildred. It's just such a habit to close the door behind myself. I forgot you were behind me." The woman said nothing; her wretched scowl said it all. She limped through the house. Josie followed, gawking at the tremendous amount of crap stuffed into the place. She felt like she was in an episode of *Hoarders*.

The walls were lined with artwork that looked like a two-year-old's barf of peas and carrots. She figured they cost fifty times her annual wages. So many strange knickknacks filled shelves and niches.

The heavy curtains were closed, keeping the space dark and cold. And holy shit. She'd heard about people like this, but she'd never witnessed it in person. Each piece of grand, luxurious furniture—"You have plastic covering your furniture? Seriously?"

Mildred stopped and slowly turned to her. "I understand how dirty and unsanitary you people can be. But in my home, that is not the case."

Josie bit her lip to keep from spewing venom at the woman. Casually, she stepped closer to Nick's grandmother—right into her face, actually. "Tell me, Mildred, what makes you so much better than me?"

The old woman straightened. "At least, you know proper grammar. But the answer is easy. I have money, and you don't." Josie inwardly cringed at the truth in her words. "I can give Nicolas the best of everything: private schools, Ivy League status, proper clothing and manners, high-society living, a chance for success in life. What can you offer?"

Josie nodded. "I do offer the most important thing, which wasn't on your list: love."

Mildred stepped back and sputtered. "Of course, it's on the list. That's a given. He's my grandson."

"No, Mildred, it isn't a given. Based on what I know of you, I'm surprised my brother-in-law was such a nice person. My sister wouldn't have married him if he wasn't."

"Yes, well, obviously, we should have stayed on top of him better," she said, disgust clear in her tone. "Letting him marry a commoner."

"What the hell is wrong with you, lady?" Josie exploded. "We aren't living in an aristocratic society. We live in a world where children are snatched off the street and murdered. Terrorists can walk into any grocery store or bus and blow it up, killing hundreds of people. Whether or not he has the perfect clothes and manners isn't going to do him shit if he's miserable with his life."

Mildred spun and walked away. "I'll show you to the kitchen." She stopped and turned to face Josie. Gave her body a scathing look. "Try not to knock over anything. It is all very expensive." She continued on her way.

Christ, Josie had never been this tempted to hit an old woman with her own crap at that. She wanted to throw up. Walking behind the biddy, she pulled her chin in and raised her brows, mocking under her breath, "It is all very expens—" Josie jerked to the side, losing her balance. She'd stepped on her untied shoestring. She crashed against a shelf holding fancy dishes.

She heard the grandmother screech as she picked herself up off the floor. "That was an ancient teacup set from the Qin Dynasty."

Josie dusted her hands off. "Sorry, it's now a lovely mosaic set." She picked up a few pieces and placed them against the wall. "You could do something really cool here." She scooted the pieces around.

"You know, these are pretty dusty," she said with fake surprise in her tone. "I know a cleaning company who'd come in and get rid of all this crap for you. Might cost a shiny penny, though. There's *a lot* of crap here."

From the corner of her eye, she noted Mildred shaking and her hands had fisted. Maybe it was time to find Nick.

"Grandmother, Aunt Josie, is everything okay down there?" Nick's angelic voice floated into the room. She followed the sound through a doorway to a set of dark-stained majestic stairs. Damn, she'd always wanted one of these. She pictured herself coming down the steps, elegant in her white wedding dress and glass slippers. The image of some sinfully handsome man like Xander waiting for her at the bottom took center stage in her mind. Great. Just want she needed, to think of the *fur*-bidden fruit.

"Aunt Josie, come up to my room," Nick called from the second floor, bending over the railing. She tied her shoe, then hurried up to see him sitting on his bed, waiting for her.

The first thing she did after entering his room was throw open the heavy, velvet curtains. "Let's let the sun shine in. Whaddya say?" Nick hopped off the bed and repeated her action with the other windows. "And what the hell? The weather is beautiful today. This room needs some airing out." She rotated the window's lock and pushed the frame fully open.

A shrill screech blasted downstairs. Josie looked at Nick. He shrugged. "I think it's the alarm."

Josie was impressed the woman was advanced thinking enough to have one. Another scream erupted, more humanlike, though. They heard mumbled words along the lines of "I don't remember the code."

They both laughed. Nick shut the door to block the irritating whine and together they plopped back on the queen-size bed. Staring at the ceiling, they both sighed at the same time. They looked at each other and laughed again.

Josie returned her look to the ceiling. She didn't want him to see her face if he gave her an answer she couldn't handle. "So, you liking it here?"

He snorted. "Are you kidding? I swear it's haunted. And did you notice the funny smell?" She did, thought it was mothballs or something. She didn't realize people still used those things. Well, it was the grandmother they were talking about here.

"There aren't any kids here my age, and Grandmother won't let me ride my bike in the cul-del-sac. She doesn't have any video games, or TVs, for that matter." He sighed. "She doesn't even want me playing with my toys by the stairs. She said she could trip and fall."

Josie sighed, feeling bad for him. "Well, you know when your grandmother was born, back before the dinosaurs roamed the earth, there were no TVs."

His giggles made her heart smile. "I know Grandmother isn't *that* old. She doesn't run very fast and would've been eaten pretty quick."

She burst into laughter, not expecting that to come out of his young mouth. His smiling face turned serious. "Aunt Josie, why does Grandmother want me to stay with her? I don't like it here." She rolled toward him and scooted him into a spoon hug and kissed the crown of his head.

"I don't know why. Maybe she's lonely by herself." She thought she knew why too. Who the hell wants to sit on plastic during a tea party? Someone would say please pass the sugar. Then someone would stand, and the plastic would stick to the back of the legs, below the skirt line. The whole piece would slide forward and fall into the seat, making a huge pile of crispy-sounding stuff that would keep them from sitting back down. How FUBAR was that?

"If Grandmother is lonely, why doesn't she play with me or talk to me? She says good morning and good night, then only speaks when I do something wrong. I miss Mom and Dad." He sniffed. Her heart broke all over again for her nephew.

It seemed like yesterday when Lucy and her husband were taken from Josie's and Nick's lives, though it had been much longer. Lucy had asked if she could borrow Josie's car to pick up a Christmas tree. Josie's vehicle at the time had rails on the hood they could tie the tree to. She handed over the keys gladly. She began to worry, when hours later, they hadn't returned and weren't answering their phones.

Later that evening, a policeman stood on her doorstep with Lucy's son staring up at her. The accident had been bad. A driver in a stolen truck T-boned the driver's side and pushed it into oncoming traffic where the passenger side was then bashed in. Both front seat occupants were killed almost instantly. Nick had been in the middle of the backseat and escaped injury.

The driver of the truck fled. In fact, no one was ever caught. Their deaths went unavenged. That's what hurt the most. There was no person she could vent her anger on. No one to blame such a senseless act on. But she had to get over that to take care of her nephew. She would be the best substitute mother she could.

"Tell ya what," she started, "how about I come back later in the week and we'll go for ice cream."

He rolled and looked at her with big shiny eyes. "Can I have two scoops?"

"Yes, you can have two scoops." She laughed. Outside, sirens approached the house. "Well, I think it's time for me to go. I have another job before I can call it a night."

He threw an arm over her ribs and hugged her tightly. "Okay, Aunt Josie." She blew him a kiss when leaving his room, then hurried out of the house before she broke down in tears.

CHAPTER 8

Keir was waiting for Xander when he finally made it into work. "Dude, you're never here this late. Did you have trouble leaving your bed this morning?"

"Yes, as a matter of fact, I did, but not from what you're thinking. Get your mind out of the gutter."

Keir frowned, confused. Join the crowd, buddy. He turned to follow Xander. "So what's got your balls wrapped so tightly they're past blue and in the purple stage? I thought since you found your true mate, you would be in a much better mood than this."

"It's not that. My mate is a goddess in every way." She was an absolute beauty, and he could tell she was even lovelier from her personality thus far. "I'm irritable because I knew she was down the hall. I could smell her arousal and hear the moans and whimpers she let out as she slept." He grumbled. "I wanted so damn bad to run in there and take care of her myself."

Keir's eyes twinkled in amusement. "Are you sure she was asleep?"

He groaned and sat down with a sigh. "Don't go there. I can't even think that. My bear wants her too badly to make jokes about it."

"Just your bear?" Keir laughed.

Xander growled. "No, of course not. I can control myself, but I'm quickly losing control of him. Part of me wants to give in and tell her she is mine and damn the consequences."

"But?" Keir waited patiently for Xander to finish his sentence.

"I can't handle it if she leaves or rejects me. I've never felt like this before. It's like suddenly my whole life has meaning, and I haven't even kissed her yet. I'm not the kind to worry about that shit. I'm an alpha bear. I get what I want. But when it comes to Josie . . . I'm lost."

Keir frowned and shook his head. "The more I hear you talk, the less and less I want a mate."

Xander chuckled. "When you find her, you won't think that way, I guarantee it. All of a sudden, she'll be there in front of you when you least expect it, and your world will never be the same."

He picked up a stack of papers and glanced through his messages. "By the way, my grandmother is coming to town earlier than planned. She'll be here tomorrow. Also, Ally came to town to finalize some things. It would seem she is moving here to run a branch of her family's business." He crumpled up some papers and tossed them in the garbage. "Though I'd really like her to come work for us instead."

"Tomorrow? No offense, but are you sure your mate is ready to meet her that quickly?"

Xander rolled his eyes at Keir's question. "What would you have me do? Tell my grandmother to wait, that my hired mate hasn't learned enough yet?"

"Sarcasm really doesn't become you. I still don't get why I never knew about Ally, either." Keir flopped onto the couch in Xander's office and gave him an arched stare.

"I told you, she was away at school. It's not like she was a secret or anything." He raised a brow at Keir's frown. "I did not date her, if that's where your mind is going. She was a good friend. Stop distracting me, that's not the point. As I was trying to say before you so childishly interrupted to complain is that she is moving to town in a couple days, she wants to meet for dinner this Saturday. I would like you to attend as well. We will be doing business with her company, so it's a good idea for you two to meet and be on friendly terms."

"A business meeting, then?" Keir questioned with a lopsided grin.

"No, this is informal, so the company won't be paying, you cheap ass, besides, you're loaded. You're going to have to be on your best behavior, though. I'm bringing Josie, as well."

Keir sat up and looked gravely at Xander. "I have one question before I have to get to a meeting."

Xander quirked an eyebrow and waited with a scowl on his face. Knowing his friend as well as he did, the question would be one of snark and sarcasm.

"Did she see your guest bathroom?" Keir chuckled as Xander's face paled at his words.

Ah, shit. He didn't even think of that. Bringing Josie to his place might have been the biggest mistake of his life.

The next few hours dragged on. What he really wanted was to call her and make sure she hadn't been scarred for life by the bathroom. He counted the ticks of the clock as each second went by. At one point, it really looked like the minutes were playing jokes on him and going backward.

His thoughts centered on nothing but seeing Josie when he got home. He wanted to look into her beautiful eyes again. Each minute felt like an eternity, and he was slowly going insane.

Keir stormed into the office and slammed the door shut. "Bro, go home. I swear if one more employee comes out of here crying because of something you said or threw at them, I'm going to kick your ass. I don't have time for this shit."

The tension in the room slowly escalated as Xander rotated his chair from his position staring out the office window. He cocked one eyebrow. "What did you say to me? Have you forgotten I'm your boss while in this building?"

"You can take your job and shove it up your growly ass. I'm coming to you as your friend to warn you. Your secretary, you know, the one who has been here from day one and dotes on you and treats you like her grandson, she's ready to stage a mutiny, and if that doesn't scare you, she threatened to call Julia on you.

"As your friend and closest thing you have to a brother, I offered to come in here and save you that fate." Keir paced, shooting Xander glares as he raked him over the coals verbally. "Now you have two choices. You can pack your shit and go home and fix whatever has you so out of it, or you can deal with your grandmother. Which is it going to be?"

Xander sighed and leaned back in his chair. "I didn't really throw the balled-up paper at her. I merely passed it to her."

"Right. From way over there, while she was way over here," Keir said with a raised brow. "You're lucky it was your secretary and not one of the other employees. She knows you well enough to let it slide this time. What has gotten into you? I have never in all these years seen you so unglued and disheveled."

He didn't know what to say for himself; he had never felt like this either. His whole body was on fire, and all he could think about was Josie. How to make her his, what her luscious body would feel like under his.

He wanted to know everything, her dreams and fears, her favorite color and scent. Hell, even how she liked her coffee. There wasn't a thing about her he didn't crave to discover, and it was driving him mad to sit here and hope she would be at his place tonight.

"It's Josie. I can't get her out of my mind. What self-respecting woman would want a man with an apartment like mine at my age? I barely know anything about her, I don't even know where she lives. All I have is her name and phone number, but even that is useless. How desperate would I look calling her in the middle of her workday?"

Keir stared at him wide-eyed. "Bro, get it together. The more I see of you acting like this, the more convinced I am that my life is perfect the way it is. A nice warm willing body in my bed and no complications. You, my friend, are a serious wreck, and as you said, you haven't even kissed her."

The idea of Josie's lips on his drove his bear wild. He wanted his mate. Mating heat. He groaned and slapped a hand over his head. Of course. Now that his bear knew she was his mate, he wanted her as soon as possible.

Keir frowned. "You better get straightened out before Julia arrives tomorrow. She sees you like this and it's going to raise questions you may not be ready for."

Xander groaned in frustration. "Don't remind me. The last thing I need is her figuring out that I'm a lost cause."

Keir sighed. "Just go home, fix dinner. Have flowers and music playing. Sit down and talk to the woman, get to know her and, if at all possible, try to make it to second base if not a full home run." He gave him a sad shake of the head. "Trust me, you both will feel better tomorrow if you do."

"You really are like a preadolescent boy, aren't you? Bases, home runs? No wonder you only have one-night stands." Xander stood and grabbed his briefcase. Not that he minded hitting a few home runs tonight. Maybe it would help the bear calm down. "I'm leaving, hold down the fort and apologize for me, please. I'll see you later and thank you for this."

Keir smiled. "That's what brothers are for. Now, get some of that hot mate of yours."

He had a few hours before Josilyn was due to return to his apartment. It was time to make a good impression. Hopefully, he could still do that without screwing anything up. A few phone calls, a couple pit stops, and he should be set to go.

CHAPTER 9

Josie groaned. Throbbing pain on her lower back made her wince with every step. Physical and mental exhaustion had her worn out mentally and physically.

For so long she'd had a nice job in a cushy office. Until her divorce, she'd never known what it was really like to work so physically hard and earn so little, and with people who did nothing but disrespect you. They took one look at her curves and judged her. All her life, she had dealt with people who thought because she was bigger she had no feelings.

She was in better health than ninety-five percent of them, too. She just had her physical and the doctor confirmed it; she was in fantastic shape. That didn't make her a bad person, and she was tired of anorexic housewives looking down their noses at her.

Josie pulled her car to a stop outside Xander's apartment and waited, debating what to do. Part of her wanted to run and never look back. The sane part reminded her how much she needed that money. She could do this.

She had survived the slander and abuse her ex dealt out, so surely, she could handle one panty-dropping man for a few nights. Right. Maybe if she had enough wine in her. Who was she kidding? Wine would probably make her panties drop even faster.

This was for Nick. What made things harder was that she couldn't figure out why she couldn't get Xander out of her mind. All day she'd done nothing but imagine his sexy eyes, that gorgeous smile, and his voice. His voice had sent shivers racing down her back.

She barely knew the man, but he was going to drive her to drinking at this rate. Her heart told her he was the one. That alone was enough to send her running for the hills. How could she feel anything for a guy she'd barely spent a few hours with? All because he'd come to her rescue. She needed to stop the whole Cinderella mentality and get her shit together.

She climbed out of the car and marched toward his door with determined strides. She debated about knocking or just entering. He'd given her a key, but was that too presumptuous? Josie hesitated and glanced around, trying to decide what to do. She smoothed down her skirt and pushed the loose strands of hair behind her ear.

She was glad she had brought a change of clothes, but now all she wanted was to take a shower, minus the Twister game, and go to bed. She knocked twice and then opened the door and stepped inside hesitantly.

Surprise stopped her in her tracks. What the hell? Was she in the wrong place? The apartment had been transformed. The dartboard had been replaced by a scenic painting of bears playing in a stream surrounded by the forest.

The disco ball was gone and replaced with two elegant lamps, one on each side of the still very large couch. The pool table had a covering on it that transformed it into a table and it even had chairs around it. The table was set and had candles and flowers in the middle.

Xander stepped out of the kitchen with a bottle of wine and smiled. "Hey, sweetheart. Welcome home."

Josie floundered for a response, her mouth dry at the sexy

vision he made standing before her. Did he just call her sweetheart? Great. That's all she needed, pet names.

He wore a formfitting old T-shirt. She could tell it was a favorite from how worn-out it was. Jeans that rode low on his sexy hips and had faded patches from too many washings. Bare feet and the sexiest grin she could ever recall seeing on a man.

"I hope you're not offended when I say that outfit on you is giving me some very interesting ideas, and none of them have to do with cleaning."

She blushed and laughed at his words. He was sincere, if the clear lust on his face was any indication. She licked her lips and looked up at him from beneath her lowered lashes. "You have a thing for curvy maids, do you?"

Xander cleared his throat and set the wine bottle down. "I have a thing for you, and now after seeing you dressed like that, I have to admit I just might have a thing for your curves in that."

Josie's blood heated. He slowly stalked closer, the heat in his eyes threatening to burn her alive. "I need to take a shower. I'm all gross and dirty from working." She turned and fled to the safety of her room. A low growl sounded behind her. She didn't dare stop to look. She was too close to throwing caution to the wind, and for once giving in to her hormones for melt-your-batteries-hot-loving time. Of course, that could only happen once she did take a shower. Not now. No way.

A soft knock at the door made Josie jump. She leaned her head against the door and whispered past the dryness in her throat. "Yes?"

"Dinner will be ready in fifteen minutes. Unless you want to try out the Twister shower with me, and in that case, I can put the food to warm so we have time."

It didn't matter that she heard the humor in his voice. She

was so very tempted and almost groaned aloud at his words. The images that suggestion created in her mind were positively decadent. "Fifteen minutes is perfect. I will be out in ten, no problem."

She waited with her ear pressed to the door for his footsteps to move down the hall. If she saw him right now, she'd be in trouble. Oh, such trouble. There was no doubt she would jump him and ride him all night long. Her hands trembled at how badly she wanted to open the door and invite him in. It took all her might to hold her ground.

She quickly gathered a change of clothes and headed into the shower. This was going to be torture. Her body hummed. Her skin felt hot, tight, and so sensitive. She was sure she could come from just the slightest touch.

Thirteen minutes later, Josie hesitantly entered the kitchen to offer her help. She burst into laughter as she came around the corner and found Xander with his head in the freezer. "What are you doing?"

Xander jumped back with a curse. "Shit, I didn't hear you come in. I, um, was um . . ." He sighed and blushed. "I was cooling off. To be honest, knowing you were in the shower after seeing you in that outfit, I got a little overheated, I guess you could say."

She bit her lip, heat crowding her cheeks. To know he wanted her that much made her ache. She moved to sit so it wouldn't be obvious that she was soaking through her panties. She was glad she had put one of her nicer bras on. This one helped hide the fact that her nipples were at attention and begging for his mouth.

"Would you like a glass of wine? I wasn't sure what you liked, so I went with something simple. It's an old family recipe, honey-basil chicken. I also have fresh green beans and new potatoes, and for dessert a three-layer chocolate fudge cake."

"You cooked all that? When did you have time?"

Xander looked sheepish as he placed the food on the table. "My best friend, Keir, sent me home from work. He said if I didn't leave, I was going to have to hire new employees as half of them were threatening to quit. I might have been a bit anxious to come home and see you and get to know you better."

"I'm flattered, and a bit intimidated." She glanced around the kitchen. "You went to so much work. It smells amazing."

"Good, all I wanted was to make you smile." He passed her the dishes one by one and urged her to eat as much as she wanted. "Don't be embarrassed to eat around me. I appreciate a woman who doesn't hold back."

"I was surprised to see the changes in the apartment today," she said hesitantly, curious as to what he would say about it.

"I should have done it years ago. I just got complacent and didn't think about it. No one ever comes here, and I spend too many hours at the office out of boredom. I can't tell you how embarrassed I was when I realized what you were going to walk into. I wasn't able to do much on short notice, but I tried."

She grinned at how quickly he went from big tough man to slightly embarrassed. "It looks wonderful, Xander, but you didn't have to worry. I wasn't judging you by this apartment. I could tell what type of man you were from the minute I met you in that alley."

"Speaking of that, how is the bruise today? The colors are definitely coming out quite nicely. Did you have any problems at work over it?"

Josie frowned slightly at his words. "Actually, I did. My boss isn't happy. She is making me take the next few days off. Something about giving the clients a bad impression."

"Seriously?" he spat, his tone deeper into a rough growl. "Did you tell her how it happened? That it wasn't your fault. You were attacked."

Josie reached out and placed her hand on top of his and squeezed gently. "It's okay. I knew that was a possibility when I went in this morning. These people are rich, snotty housewives who already think we're trash. I really don't mind taking a few days away from the nasty remarks and veiled criticisms of my body."

Xander's face grew red, and for a second, she was mesmerized watching him sprout a beard out of nowhere. "That's not a way to handle this kind of situation. Clearly your company needs to be advised of proper employee human resources management."

They lapsed into silence after that, both eating their meals very aware of the other's stolen glances. The tension continued to rise as they made small talk about their days and what they liked to do.

CHAPTER 10

Josie made sure to keep things light and superficial. Once he relaxed, his features returned to panty-soaking gorgeous and the facial hair receded. After this week, she would never see this man again and she didn't want or need to burden him with her problems.

"Dinner was wonderful. You're an amazing cook."

"Thank you. My grandmother believes that everyone should learn, so she made me take lessons. By the way, she is coming in tomorrow instead of this weekend like originally planned. I'm not too worried, though. From what I saw tonight, we get along fantastically and can muddle our way through any issues that arise." Xander stood to clear the dishes. Josie jumped up to help, and together they quickly put the kitchen back to rights.

"Do you have a landline I can use? I need to make a phone call. I have an older cell but it died on me earlier."

"No, but feel free to use my cell. It's on the counter over there." He pointed to a spot over her shoulder. "While you do that, I will get dessert ready. Would you like coffee to go with it, or maybe some milk?"

"Milk would be wonderful; there is just something about chocolate cake and milk together that reminds me of childhood."

Josie grabbed the phone and moved back to her room for privacy. She wanted to check in on Nick before he went to bed. She missed having him around. The phone rang a few times before Mildred finally picked up.

"Hello, Mildred, it's Josilyn. I was hoping to speak to Nick for a minute, if you don't mind."

"Of course, he just had his bath and is getting ready for bed. Hold on, please."

The minutes ticked by as she waited patiently for her little bear to come to the phone, finally after what seemed like an eternity, his young voice came on the line.

"Hi, Aunt Josie."

"Hey, baby bear, how are you? You having fun with your grandmother?"

"I'm holding on. But it's weird being here so long. I miss you."

"I miss you, too. I just wanted to say good night and sweet dreams."

"Will you come and see me the day after tomorrow?"

Josie bit her lip, unsure what Xander had planned. But this was her baby, her priority. "Of course, sweetie. I'll come get you and we can grab that ice cream I promised you. Sound good?"

"Yes!" he yelped excitedly. "Aunt Josie?"

"Yes, baby?"

"I still get to live with you, right? Grandmother said something that worried me."

She clenched her teeth to keep from growling. "You will live with me as long as you want, honey. Nobody but a judge can change that. Now get some sleep, baby. I love you."

"I love you too, Aunt Josie. Don't forget to come."

Her heart did a downward thump at that moment. "Never. I'll see you soon, baby bear."

Mildred took the phone back and politely but coldly said

good night and hung up without giving Josie a chance to say anything.

It took Josilyn another ten minutes before she could calm herself enough to face Xander. God! It hurt to breathe. Her throat felt closed from the lump there. She missed Nick more and more. Each time he went with his grandmother, it became a little harder for her. She couldn't help but worry that Mildred would find out something that would give her the edge to take Nick's custody from her. He was too important to her to ever let that happen. He was all she had left of her sister.

A light tap came from the door. "Josie, everything okay?"

She quickly stood and wiped the tears from her face, pasted on a too-wide smile, and opened the door. "All good. Ready for that cake."

"You've been crying. Who upset you? Tell me," Xander said as he wiped a stray tear from her cheek.

"No, it's okay. Don't worry. I promise there isn't anyone you can hurt for this." She could tell he didn't like her answer, but there wasn't much he could say. They moved back to the kitchen and sat down to dessert.

Xander brushed his fingers down her damp cheek. "Talk to me, sweetheart. Let me share the burden with you."

She sighed, then bit down on the inside of her cheek to keep the tears back. "I have a nephew named Nick who is a beautiful eight-year-old full of life and love, just like his mom. At least he was. Not too long ago, Nick's mother, my sister, died in a car accident with Nick's dad.

"His parents' will said they wanted me to have custody of Nick if something happened. They didn't want him raised by his grandmother. And now I know why. She's a coldhearted bitch who thinks money will buy her everything."

Xander stiffened for a second, then relaxed. He probably took it as an offense against rich people. Well, it was. So there.

She continued. "Anyway, she's been fighting for custody of Nick since then. The courts have abided by his parents' will so far. But I don't know how much longer they will think I can provide for him. It's a struggle to buy enough food sometimes."

She bit her tongue to give her pain to stave off tears. God, she hated being so fragile. She needed to talk about something else. "So tell me, Xander, you haven't mentioned your parents. Just your grandmother. Why is that?"

"My parents died a while back. It's just been my grandmother and me since then. She is a wonderful woman but a bit set in her ways. She wants me mated and settled down. Julia wants grandkids, and that's all there is to it, in her mind."

Josie smiled at the love she heard in his voice when he spoke about her. "She sounds like a handful."

Xander let out a bark of laughter. "Oh, you have no idea. She is one in a million. When she gets an idea in her head, forget everything else until it's done. It's what has made her so successful in business."

"I still don't get how she isn't a shifter but you are."

"My father was the shifter. My mother was human. An offspring can go either way. Julia, as much as I love her, hasn't quite grasped the concept of shifter mates."

Josie frowned in confusion. "What exactly does that mean? I have to admit I'm unfamiliar with shifters myself. You're the first I have ever met and spent any time with."

"We each have a mate out in the world. A single person who was made specifically for us. When we meet that person, we know instantly. There are no questions or doubts. We will never want another once we have our mate." Xander smiled when she blinked in surprise. "Our mate . . ."

"You say 'our,' what does that mean?"

"It's almost like a split personality, you could say. There is me, but there is also my bear spirit in this body. We inhabit the same space. When we find our mate, both my bear and I feel the connection and longing to be with her."

"This might be a stupid question, but that guy in the alley was starting to shift into an animal, wasn't he? How did that guy get him to stop like that?"

"The shifter who attacked you is a wolf shifter. His mate died and he has gone mad from the loss. The guy who showed up and interrupted was his brother and the alpha of their pack. When the alpha commands you to shift, you must obey."

"I think I understand. What about you?"

Xander looked at her questioningly. "What do you mean?"

"Do you have to obey him, too?"

"No, definitely not. For one, I'm more powerful than he is. Also, I'm not of their pack."

"Pack? Like a family or group or something?"

"Yes, basically. I don't have a pack in that regard. I'm not what you would call a rogue either, though." Xander raised one hand forestalling her next questions. "A rogue is a shifter with no allegiance to anyone else. You see, after my parents died, I left the pack we belonged to and chose to live with my grandmother. That isn't normal for shifters, but I knew how much she needed me. She was struggling with their deaths, and I was afraid I would lose her as well."

She understood that struggle too well. After that night of the accident, her father was a different man. More quiet and withdrawn from the world. Years later, Mom told her he blamed himself. They both knew the truth while the police report and newspapers said the mishap was weather related. Snow on the road made it slick, causing the collision. Just a tragic accident.

There never were any accusations, any inquiries about the woman's death. Josie tried to remember the woman's name. Debra or Debbie something.

Her father didn't stand trial in front a group of his peers

nor did he serve community time for his sins. But the self-inflicted suffering he went through for years was worse than any jail sentence could be.

Eventually, the company moved him to Connecticut where she lived now and had met the most incredible man she had to be careful not to fall in love with. Especially since he was a different species.

She asked, "If you aren't a rogue or part of a pack, what are you?"

"Misfits? I don't know what you would call us. At XJ Financial, there are a bunch of us shifters with no allegiance to a pack, pride, or group of shifters. We have kind of banded together to become our own group. We have all types of shifters and live in peace and help each other as a normal pack would. We just don't live in one area together. For one reason or another, we need to be around our own kind to have that sense of belonging, but we also crave our own space, and Willowbend, Connecticut, works for us perfectly."

"I get what you're saying. Besides shifting into animals, what else do you have that is different from humans?"

He glanced at her lips. "The main thing is our sense of smell. For instance, I know you're aroused and wet for me."

She sucked a breath in.

"Don't be embarrassed. I want you, too. I'd like nothing better than to lay you over this table and devour you, to fuck you until you can't walk. To hear your whimpers as I plunge my cock in deeply, until you're begging for release."

Josie didn't know how to respond to his words; all she did know was how she felt. Her body was on fire. She wanted this man more than anything she had ever wanted, and that scared her more than she could possibly admit.

"I . . . I think it's time for me to go to bed," she said as she stood and raced out of the room. Josie slammed her door shut and leaned against it, panting from adrenaline and excitement, and from need.

"Good night, sweetheart. I promise you're safe here. I won't touch you until you say it's okay. I'll see you in the morning. Sweet dreams. I know mine will be full of you."

"Night, Xander," she squeaked out before she collapsed on top of her bed. She lay there debating the sanity of pulling out her toy, knowing he was just down the hall. Shifters had a heightened sense of smell, he said, but what about hearing? Could she pleasure herself knowing he would know what she was doing?

She groaned in anticipation. Fuck, yes, she could. The thought made her tingle and burn even more. One orgasm coming up. Now if only she could loosen up enough to let him play more than in just her imagination.

CHAPTER 11

It was going to be a long day. He'd barely gotten to sleep when his phone rang and woke him. His grandmother had wonderful timing as usual. It was all Josilyn's fault. Soft sighs and moans of pleasure combined with that low humming sound let him know what she was doing behind closed doors. Even after she'd drifted into a contented sleep, all he could hear were her breathy groans of ecstasy. She was going to be the death of him.

Xander climbed out of bed and made his way to the kitchen for much-needed coffee. Between the lack of sleep and the tongue-lashing from his grandmother for still being in bed at this late hour, he was done. The rich scent of freshly brewed strong Colombian coffee hit him as he came down the hallway. He rounded the corner and stopped dead in his tracks.

She stood facing the coffee machine, her head dropped forward as if inhaling the coffee scent. Fuck she was sexy leaning against the counter like that.

He moved up behind her and trapped her there between his hard body and the cold counter. "Morning, sexy," he whispered as he nuzzled against her neck. "Sleep well?"

She tensed for a second before sighing and pressing back against him, letting her body relax.

"Morning," she said as her voice quavered slightly. "I did, very well, actually. How about you?"

He pushed his erection into her delectable ass. "Barely slept a wink." He rubbed his lips over her ear. "I'm being patient, Josie, but it's hard. I want to dive balls deep into you." He nibbled on her lobe. "Thinking of how hot and slick you're going to be is making me hurt."

She gave a soft moan. "I'm sorry."

"Not as sorry as my hand is. I've never had this much solo action. You're driving me crazy. I want to hear those moans in my ear tonight, and not from down the hall."

She stiffened and turned to face him. His cock pressed at the juncture of her thighs. "You could hear . . . I didn't . . . I'm . . . oh, my gosh," she stammered as her face turned bright red.

"Don't be ashamed, baby girl." Xander smiled and leaned in so his lips were millimeters from hers. "You will be in my bed. It's only a matter of time. I'm warning you now. Make a choice, but if you come back here, I will fuck you. I won't say when, but I will. You can be sure of that. I will fuck you within an inch of your life. Then just when you think you can't handle it, I will do it again. Just when you think your body has given all, you'll tense up and fly when I remind it you're mine. You will never want one of your toys again. Not unless I'm the one using it on you."

She gasped, and he took advantage to slam his mouth on hers. His tongue invaded and stroked hers with masterful swipes. He nipped at her lips and pulled her tightly against his aching cock. The taste of her was addictive. He'd fucking known she would be.

He'd never get enough. Not now that he had. Not when all he wanted was to have her warm body curled up around him as he pounded deep into her, taking her over and over again.

Reminding each of them this was where they both belonged. He slowly pulled back and leaned his forehead to hers.

"If we don't stop now, I'm going to set you on the counter and bury my head between your legs. The next time I stand, my face will be coated in your honey and your legs will be shaking for hours."

He smirked in self-satisfied delight as she reached for the counter to hold herself steady. "Are you hungry?"

Her eyes shot up to his. She cleared her throat and her tiny pink tongue roamed over her lips. "You could say that."

"Get dressed. My grandmother is here early and would like to meet us at a café."

Xander turned and headed to his room for a highly needed cold shower. That kiss left him throbbing, and if he didn't get relief soon, he was going to explode. Touching himself was nothing when it was her hands he wanted on him. Her body he wanted pressed up against him. Fucking hell! It was her mouth he wanted wrapped around his cock. This was going to be the longest day of his life.

Forty-five minutes later, they were walking into the little café Julia preferred on her rare trips to town. Xander grabbed Josilyn's hand and gave a gentle squeeze. "Calm down, sweetheart. She is going to love you. There is no doubt in my mind."

"How can you possibly know that? You have only known me a couple of days yourself. What if I ruin this for you? What happens if she asks me something I don't know the answer to? What if she tries to trick me to catch me lying?"

Xander laughed and pulled her to a stop outside the café doors. He turned her so she could look into his eyes. "Baby, stop. I promise, you're reading into this way too much. If you get freaked, just take a sip of water, and I will jump in. You have nothing in the world to worry about."

"If you say so. I just don't want to disappoint you."

"You could never do that. You have already exceeded all my expectations. Now come on, let's show my grandmother what an amazing mate I have been gifted."

Xander didn't give her time to fret or argue. He pulled the door open and guided her through with a gentle hand on her back. As soon as they walked in, he spotted Julia sitting in her favorite booth in the corner. She narrowed her eyes and gave him a glare. Xander chuckled and gave Josilyn a slight push to get her moving again. They stopped next to the table, and Xander leaned over and kissed his grandmother's weathered cheek.

"Stop scowling at me, you old bat. I'm on time and you know it." Xander gestured for Josie to slide into the booth and he scooted in beside her. "Grandmother, this is Josilyn. Josie, this is my grandmother, Julia."

Xander watched as the two most important people in his life sized each other up. Josilyn was nervous, and that was obvious. His grandmother had that evil gleam in her eyes he'd come to know so well. He scowled at her and shook his head in warning, but she ignored him.

"So, Josilyn, you're my boy's mate, he tells me."

He wanted to groan in frustration; this was going to be a long lunch. He slipped his hand under the table and placed it on Josie's leg and gave a slight squeeze of reassurance.

"Yes, ma'am. You raised quite a gentleman." Xander preened at her words and had to hide a smile as his grandmother grinned broadly at her words. He wanted to hug Josie for that brilliant remark. His mate was smooth.

"How did you two meet?" Julia asked as she cocked an eyebrow at Xander and glanced at his missing hand.

He winked in reply and waited to see what Josie would say. They hadn't discussed this part. Stupid on their parts, it was a logical question, after all.

Josie frowned in concentration. "It was outside my favorite restaurant. I was being attacked."

"Oh my God!" Julia gasped.

"It's okay. Xander rescued me. It was like a fairy tale, the way he swooped in and saved me."

Xander could barely hold in his laughter as his grandmother's mouth gaped in surprise.

"Too bad she ran from me before I could learn her name."

Julia leaned forward intent on their story. "Ran? Then how . . ."

"I had a reservation and I was late. I didn't want them to give up my table. I told the lady Xander was with to thank him, and I ran into the restaurant while he was dealing with this shifter issue in the alley."

"You were with another lady? Shifter issue? I'm so confused," Julia said as she stared back and forth between the two of them. "Are you two making fun of me?"

"No, I'm deadly serious, Grandmother. This actually happened. I was with Ally. She is moving to town and we were discussing business. I was outside saying good-bye when I saw Josilyn being dragged off by this half-crazed shifter. I was dealing with that, and when I turned around, she had disappeared. Luckily, Ally had seen her go into Ricardo's, and I went in after her."

Julia's eyes bugged at his words. "You went in after her? What if she had been on a date?"

Xander was having trouble keeping his laughter contained.

"He marched right up to my table and sat down. The rest, as they say, is history."

He caught his breath as Josie placed her hand on top of his on her leg. He flipped his hand and twined their fingers. This shit was surreal. He'd never felt this connected to another person, human or shifter, before.

"It was fate. There is no other explanation for it," Julia said in an awed whisper.

"As soon as I looked into her eyes," Xander said in a soft tone as he met Josie's eyes, "I felt the connection, the instant pull. My bear and I knew it immediately. She was the only one for us."

Xander lifted their joined hands and kissed the back of her knuckles.

CHAPTER 12

Josie was going to burn in hell for this—the seventh ring, at that. There was no doubt in her mind. This woman was eating up every word they said, and here they were lying their asses off to her. Well, not completely. They did meet like that, and he did follow her into the restaurant. But they weren't really mates, and she hated lying to the sweet older woman.

"I can see how much you care for each other already." Julia reached for both their hands and gave them a squeeze. "It does wonders for my sanity to know you have found each other."

That just skyrocketed her guilt level to epic proportions. How was he supposed to continue lying to his own grandmother? It was Xander's fault, may he burn in hell for deceiving the nice lady. God. Her stomach burned with nerves. She should have never taken this job. Lying wasn't her thing. She sucked at it. Most times people knew she lied because she stammered so much. Poor Julia was going to see her in such a bad light after this.

A waitress stopped by their table and placed three glasses of water down. "Welcome back. I haven't seen you two in a while. I assume you to want the usual?" Xander and Julia both nodded, and the waitress turned to Josie. "Welcome to the café. We don't have menus, but if it's for breakfast or lunch, we have it and it's amazing. What can I get for you?"

Josie wasn't sure what to say; she hadn't expected no menus. What had they ordered? She didn't want to order something that made her look like a glutton, but she also didn't want to order something that was going to leave her starving in a couple of hours.

"Just give her the same as me." Xander spoke up, saving her from deciding. She sighed in relief and gave him a gentle nudge to say thanks.

The seconds ticked by in companionable silence. Josie took a moment to study the small café and was surprised by the homey atmosphere. It seemed more like a family's kitchen than a public restaurant.

"Josie, tell me, what do you do for a living?" Julia interrupted her thoughts to ask.

"I work for a cleaning service." Josie waited for the condemnation she normally got when she said that. She wasn't ashamed. It was an honest living, and she worked hard, but people always looked down on her as if cleaning wasn't good enough.

"That must be hard, exhausting work," Julia said, surprising her with the kindness in her words.

"It is. I was fortunate to get the job, though. I won't look a gift horse in the mouth. It pays the bills for the most part and keeps my head above water."

Xander and Julia shared a puzzled look at her words. "What do you mean you were fortunate to get the job? Did you have trouble?"

Josie blushed, she hadn't meant for them to pick up on that. She cleared her throat and prayed the waitress would come back so she could change the subject. No such luck, though.

"I was married before. My ex, Michael, took me for every dime I had in the divorce. To make it worse, he and his friends spread horrible lies about my bad business sense and inability to handle the accounts I had at my previous job, and I quickly became someone no one wanted to hire in my field."

Julia raised her brows high. "It couldn't have been that bad?"

"Oh, it was worse. He took accounts I normally handled to supposedly do random checks and balances. This was right before we broke up. He messed them up so much that I would need a lot of time to fix them but wasn't given the opportunity because nobody trusted me at that point. He was my boss, so people believed him. I mean, he told them he divorced me because I had made so many people lose money and he couldn't be with someone like that."

"I'm guessing that wasn't true?" Julia asked.

"No. I divorced him after I realized he was having an affair."

"Oh my God!" Julia shook her head in disbelief.

"The only job I could get was cleaning houses, and then only because he hadn't gotten to them yet."

Julia scowled. "I don't understand. Why would he do that?"

Josie shrugged. She really didn't know why. She could only come up with guesses. "He was jealous. I was the breadwinner. He was my boss in the business, but I brought in the accounts. People trusted me. He had a handful of clients. None were multimillion-dollar companies like mine. I brought in three times as much money as he did. We both have college degrees, but he struggled to get clients. He found some bimbo to shack up with and got his buddies from school to pull strings and complain over my bad business practices. They smeared my name all over. I was fired, but he stayed and took everything I had ever worked for. He moved in with Miss Double-D and I got a small apartment."

Xander growled and squeezed her hand to get her attention. "What is his name? Where can I find him?"

She grinned but shook her head. "Karma will come back and get him. I have to believe everything happens for a reason. It did, actually. If all of that hadn't happened, I wouldn't have met you that day."

Xander grunted and kissed her knuckles again. "That's true, but I don't like that he got away with pulling that crap."

"Out of curiosity, what field where you in?" Julia asked with a kind smile.

"I'm an accountant. I graduated with full honors and had the pick of jobs out of school. I stupidly moved here because I thought I was in love. I took a job at a small firm we both worked at, and I was happy. I quickly become their top accountant, above Michael, who was my supervisor, and that's when things went downhill. He couldn't handle being second to a woman."

"An accountant?" Xander and Julia said in unison before they looked at each other and chuckled.

She was confused. What was so funny about that? What did she miss? Most people didn't have that type of response to a regular bean counter.

Julia cleared her throat. "Has Xander told you what he does for a living? Who we are exactly?"

Josie felt like she was missing something important. What were they? Minor royalty or famous or something? "No, it never came up. Why?"

Xander blushed. "Have you ever heard of XJ Financial?"

She didn't live under a rock. Everyone who was anyone in the accounting field knew of the company. "Of course, I've heard of it."

Julia's eyes twinkled in merriment. "Do you know what the XJ stands for, by any chance?"

No, there was no way they were implying what she thought they were. She shook her head in disbelief and embarrassment.

"Yes, you got it. Xander and Julia Financial. It's our company. That also brings me to why I came down for the day."

"You came down to meet my mate. That's what you told me."

"I did, and if you recall, I told you I was coming down, and then you told me you wanted me to meet her. I had already planned on it. It just worked out that I accomplished two goals at once."

Josie could feel the tension that filled Xander at his grandmother's words. Was she sick and that's what had worried him? She looked well and seemed lucid and in control of her mental facilities. Josie reached over and leaned into his side to offer what comfort she could. It was odd, but she felt perfectly comfortable doing this even though she had met the guy barely forty-eight hours ago. It was almost as if she were his mate, that they did share that connection.

"Don't look so dire, boy. It's nothing that bad. You're going to give yourself a heart attack always jumping to the worst conclusions. Josie, make sure you help him lighten up. He always has too much self-imposed stress."

Josilyn smiled and nodded her agreement. She could think of a few ways to help this gorgeous man de-stress. She almost purred, thinking about all the fun they could have while making him relax.

"I want you to give up that wretched apartment of yours and move into the house. I've decided it's too big for me, and since I'm not here much, it's sitting empty. You have a mate now. Fill it with the sound of kids, and give me a reason to come visit."

Xander's jaw dropped. "It's been your home all my life. How can you walk away?"

"Stupid boy, I'm not walking away. You will keep a room for me, of course, but I'm being practical. The house needs a family." Julia winked at Josie before continuing. "Give in graciously. I won't be changing my mind."

Josie felt guilt overtake her, and she wanted to cry in frustration. They were deceiving this poor woman and here she was offering them a house to raise their nonexistent family in. She was going to hell. There was no longer a doubt in her mind. She might as well buy prime real estate in front of the pit now.

Their conversation turned to lighthearted banter, and Josie slowly fell in love with Julia. She had a sarcastic tongue that left her laughing more often than not. This woman was one hell of a businesswoman and a devoted grandmother. Josie hoped she could be half the woman Julia was one day.

After brunch, Xander offered his car to Josie so she could run errands while he rode with his grandmother to the office to catch up with some of the staff and she could read through some papers he held for her visit. He really didn't trust Josie's car and would make it a point to try and get her to use his until he could get her a new one.

Julia signaled to change lanes in the heavy traffic heading toward the office. "Tell me, Xander. I know you had someone check into that man who attacked your mate."

"Of course, I did. His name is Trey Randulf. His brother Dominick is alpha of their wolf pack. Trey recently lost his mate in a fight which, according to my sources, was suspicious. Trey was badly wounded but survived. Grief and the attack have left him with limited capabilities mentally. He is under constant supervision while off their lands. Dominick is well respected and is fighting a battle to keep his lands from some outside interest trying to run them off."

"You think it was a random attack, then?" Julia questioned.

Xander paused to think over his words before replying. "I

could find no evidence of Josilyn and the Randulf pack having any connection. For the life of me, I can't figure out what motivation there would have been for Trey to take her. It has to be random, wrong place, wrong time type of thing. It makes no sense any other way."

Julia nodded and stared out the window. Xander smiled and let his mind wander to his mate. She had been fantastic at brunch with Julia. The two most important women in his life seemed to like each other, and that gave him hope. Now all he had to do was convince her she was his mate.

"I like your . . . mate," Julia said with a quirk of her eyebrow.

Xander groaned. "How?"

"Nothing obvious. You both did well hiding it, but I have my own sources, and they informed me of how you met her and when." Julia smiled. "I also know that from what I saw today, she is your true mate, and that makes me very happy. I like her, son. She is a good woman with a pure heart."

"Yes, she is. Please don't tell her you know the truth. I have to get her to stick around so I can convince her. She doesn't understand shifters and how we operate. I need to ease her into our lifestyle and ways."

"I think I can help there, my boy. Don't you worry. You don't get to be my age without cooking up a few schemes. Now, let's get to work so you can pick up your mate."

Xander chuckled and climbed out of the car. There wasn't a day that passed he didn't think how lucky he was to have this woman in his life. He was hard-pressed to think of a shifter he knew who was stronger willed than his grandmother.

"Time's a-wastin', boy, let's go. I have a lot of people to catch up with and things to do. That secretary of yours always has the best gossip."

He almost froze in his tracks when he realized just what gossip his grandmother was going to find out, his throwing stuff in the office due to lack of sex. They'd have no sympathy for his sexual frustration to forgive him for his office outbursts. His fake mate was causing him so much more trouble than he could ever have imagined. He shuddered to think what would happen when they were finally mated for real.

CHAPTER 13

That night, Josie waited anxiously in her room. She didn't know how to do this. Wearing the guest robe, with nothing under it, she ambled back and forth in front of the bed. Would he come? Should she go to him? What the fuck was she doing to herself? All this crazy thinking was going to make her lose her mind. She didn't have it in her to go chasing after him. No matter how much she wanted him.

She turned to her bag and took out her pocket rocket. Maybe she could take the edge off in case nothing happened with him tonight.

She slipped open the robe and lay in the middle of the bed. Her thoughts centered around Xander and his gorgeous smile, beautiful eyes, and that body she imagined riding every time she looked at him.

Her breaths came in short spurts, she turned the toy to a low buzz, running it over her nipples and gasping at the way it shot pleasure to her clit. God, she wanted Xander so fucking bad. This is what she got for not getting that man out of her mind. She kept the toy on her nipple and slipped a hand down between her legs. She was hot, wet, and aching. With a quick switch, she had the toy gliding between her legs and her other hand tugging at the hard points of her nipples.

"God!"

She squirmed on the bed, lifting her hips and wiggling them at the same time she did the vibrator. The closer she got to her body reaching the edge of that pleasure she wanted so badly, the harder it became to breathe.

Thump! Thump! Thump!

Loud knocking pulled her out of the moment and she growled in frustration. Slamming the toy down on the mattress, she slid into her robe again, her frustration making it almost impossible to tie the damn thing around her waist.

She yanked the door open and glared at the object of her aggravation. "What?"

His eyes were a bright gold and his lips were pressed into a thin line. The muscle at the side of his neck worked to the point she almost forgot he'd stopped her mid-self-gratification.

"You can't fucking do that," he growled, storming inside the room. He wore pajama bottoms and nothing else. Fucking hell, he looked so delicious. All those muscles tense. Every time he took a breath, she wanted to slide her hands up and down his abs and thank every deity who created the V that went from his waist directly to his crotch.

She blinked. "What?"

He pushed toward her, wrapping his hands around her head and pressing his lips hard on hers. Need soared to a new delectable ache inside her. She kissed him back with every drop of desire she clung to, finally giving in to the lust roaring at her veins.

She gripped his shoulders and continued kissing him. They staggered back until the back of her legs hit the bed and both fell on it with a thud. His hands were all over her, touching, squeezing, driving her fucking insane.

She gasped a breath the moment he pulled back. Her body thrummed with need. She needed to come so badly. There was that desperate hungry look in his eyes that made her slicker.

"You can't play with yourself and make my cock so fucking hard I'm seeing double. I want to be the one playing."

She cleared her throat but didn't know what to say. He was rougher and growlier than she'd seen so far. It was intimidating and so damn hot she almost melted into the bed.

He grabbed the toy off the bed and brought it to his lips. She gaped as he licked it, the glint of fire in his golden eyes burning brighter.

"Let me be the one to make you come."

She nodded. Her robe slipped open and he sucked one of her nipples into his mouth. Good God, that was amazing. The feel of his cool tongue flicking around her aching point had her grasping the sheets hard.

The toy buzzed on her belly, then at her mound, and finally at her entrance.

"Oh, God!"

He sucked her other nipple into his mouth and bit down, giving it that small painful torture she had come to love. She spread her legs wide, every tremor making it harder to control her own body. It was as though he were the one pulling her strings, and her responses were his, all his.

He licked his way down to her belly, dipping his tongue into her belly button and gliding farther down. Then he was there, replacing the toy at her clit. His tongue flicked back and forth over her aching point at the same time he pressed the buzzing rod into her. Her hip shot off the bed and she screeched.

Tension wound inside her. With a few licks and sucks of her clit she readied to let pleasure take over. She tugged at his hair, pulling him into her crotch. She didn't even remember letting go of the bedding and grabbing him instead.

"Fuck! Oh, my goodness!"

She lost her breath at the moment he pushed the toy in farther and sucked on her clit hard. Colors burst behind her lids and for a moment she felt like she was floating. Waves of bliss took over her bloodstream. She choked on air, sucking breath after breath into her lungs while her body continued to feel the aftermath of the biggest orgasm of her life.

She blinked her eyes open and inhaled harshly. He lifted his head off her crotch, his face soaked with her scent. Fucking hell, that was one of the sexiest things she'd ever seen. She pulled him into her and kissed his wet face, tasting herself on him.

His pants came off in a rush. They were once again both on the bed, and she pushed him to lie down, straddling him. His cock was hot, hard, and filled her hand in seconds. She pressed him into her entrance, moaning and gasping at how big he felt.

Their gazes met and held. She wanted him so badly.

"Do it," he growled, his voice a breathy whisper. His raised his hands up to her chest and palmed her heavy breasts. She ached all over. "Slide down and take my cock. Take it all."

Slowly, she glided down and he filled her body with his length. She gasped at the fullness and how amazing he felt. He gripped her hips and helped her ride him. Up and down. Her body curved forward, and his fingers dug into her ass the faster she went.

"Xander," she moaned.

"Fuck, baby. You feel so good. So tight."

He started lifting and dropping her, harder and harder. She couldn't keep up with his pace. Her control snapped and her pussy gripped hard at his cock. She squeezed her eyes shut, a loud scream tearing from her throat.

Her body shuddered and pleasure cascaded through her like warm lava. He continued dropping her on his cock, pressing her all the way down so her pelvis rubbed on his. Then he slowed until he finally stopped. He grunted and bit his fingers harder into her flesh.

"Mine!" he growled. His cock pulsed inside her, filling her with his seed and making her light-headed and her pussy suck at his dick all over again.

CHAPTER 14

Josie wasn't sure what to do with herself now. If it hadn't been for urgent business, Xander would have been in bed with her still. Instead, he was in his home office and she was alone until he finished with his business call.

She hadn't had a day off during the week in forever, and without Nick at home, she was at loose ends. She thought about calling Shawna, but a quick check of her pockets and she remembered her oldie phone she'd been working with had died on her the previous night.

She hadn't managed to get it to turn on yet. Her thoughts ran back to the sensual promise Xander had made and she smiled. She knew just what to do to pass the time until she could see him again. Last night had been amazing, and she wanted to be in his arms again. Then she'd call Nick in a few hours for more dessert.

After hanging up with Nick, having made their plans, she waited for Xander to emerge from his office. It didn't take much to convince him to join her and her nephew for a couple hours at the fair.

She hadn't been at the fair in years. She'd forgotten how people packed in to buy cotton candy, take a try throwing a ring around a bottle, getting in line for the biggest, baddest roller coaster for miles. Cheery carnival music piped through old beat-up speakers, adding to the charm.

Josie rested her hand on Nick's back. "Okay, Nick, what do you want first?"

He jumped up and down. "I want ice cream, two scoops. And a funnel cake and a fried Twinkie."

"Nice." Josie rolled her eyes. "You're going to throw up all that on the first ride. You know that, right?"

"No, I won't. I promise." He looked to Xander on the other side of his aunt. "Do you like roller coasters? They have one here that does three loops in a row, then dives fifty feet in two point three seconds."

He shook his head. "That is Puke-town, all the way." He paused. "I'm in." Nick hollered out and they high-fived. They were off to find ice cream.

With funnel cake and ice cream in hand, they sat at a weathered picnic table. They people-watched and laughed at the outlandish outfits the clowns and character animals walking around wore. Nick even got to shake hands with Batman.

"Aunt Josie, we didn't get anything to drink." She looked at the table and noticed no cups.

"I'll get something," Xander said as he pulled one leg over the picnic bench. He'd already paid for entrance tickets and the snacks here, lending her the nice car. Her pride was a bit bruised, but her morals were still strong.

"No." The word came out harsher than she intended, but she wasn't setting a precedent of somebody else buying everything for her. Both guys looked at her with concern. "What I mean is, I'll get a drink for us on my way from the restroom. Be right back."

Nick and Xander looked at each other with a WTF expression.

Nick swallowed his bite of funnel cake. "Does Aunt Josie do strange things around you, too?"

Xander cocked his head. "Strange how?"

The one young shrugged. "I don't know. Sometimes I hear her crying in the bathroom, but she says nothing is wrong." He gazed into the milling crowd.

Xander knew his words could change the tone of the relationship between the woman he loved and the child who needed her. Should he bring Nick into the adult world of bills, money, evil people, or should he allow the worry-free childhood to last?

"I think your aunt misses her sister, your mom, a lot. Sometimes when you miss someone, it hurts enough to cry." Nick dropped his chin to his chest. He pushed his ice cream around the bowl.

Great job, dipshit. *You reminded him about his dead parents.* "Then again, she's a girl. And girls do strange things because they're girls."

Nick's head popped up. "I know. There's this girl in my class who tried to kiss me. That's gross. That's how you get cooties. From girls. Eww."

"My man," Xander raised his hand for a high five, "girls are eww. Don't let them ever kiss you. 'Cause weird things start happening. You get stomachaches, all the time. You suddenly don't know what you're doing or why. You get pains in your butt, and you can't concentrate."

Nick nodded and sighed. "Brain damage. I knew it. Cooties."

"We men have to stick together to get through these things." He held out a hand to the boy. Nick stared at it, not moving.

"I'm guessing you're my aunt's boyfriend. Are you going to marry her?"

"As soon as she says yes, the deal will be done."

"Are you going to make her sad like Uncle Michael did?"

"I will do my best to never make her sad. I only want to see a smile on her face." Xander realized how much this child loved his aunt. If the boy was worried about her well-being, then Josie was a wonderful mother. Just like he knew she would be.

A huge smile came to Nick's face, and he slapped his smaller hand into Xander's. "Then, yeah. We men have to stick together."

Josie stepped out of the bathroom stall, still chastising herself for acting so dumb in front of Xander and Nick. Yes, her pride at being a strong, independent woman was in danger. Xander had been the most awesomesauce man she'd ever been with. He wanted to take care of her and just because he had money—lots of it—didn't mean she wanted him to pay for everything.

She wasn't a leech, but this was a new feeling for her. Depending on someone else meant putting yourself in their debt. She didn't feel comfortable there. What if she couldn't repay the debt? What if she didn't have enough or wasn't good enough?

A bimbo-looking woman pulled brown paper towels from the dispenser. Normally, Josie wouldn't notice others, but this woman blatantly stared at her. Chills raced down her back. Josie soaped her hands twice, waiting for the woman to move on.

"Excuse me," the woman said to her. "Have we met before?"

Josie very seriously doubted she shared commonalities with this woman. But it was possible.

Josie said, "You could work for one of my past company's clients?" Though, for the life of her, Josie wouldn't know which one.

The woman flashed a toothy smile that was pretty except for the one missing canine. Elly May Clampett came to mind, but not so innocent. "Yes," the lady said, "you're the accountant." She clasped her hands. "You've got to meet my husband," she said, grabbing Josie's hand and dragging her out of the restroom.

Josie tried to jerk her hand away, but the bitch had a clamp for a grip. "I don't work for the company anymore," Josie said. The blonde led her around the backside of the food court. People working the food stands paid no attention to them.

"Hold on a minute," Josie said through clenched teeth. She dug in her heels, stopping the woman. "Look, ma'am. I'm sure your husband is a nice man—"

That was all Josie got out when the woman spun around and swung her arm at Josie's head. For once, being short had its advantages. Josie ducked and shoved at the woman in her four-inch heels. Both ladies went down, Josie landing on her knees.

"Let go of me, bitch." With Josie's new job, the physical work had shaped and strengthened her muscles. With her free hand, Josie balled her fist and sent an upper cut to the over-made-up, heart-shaped face.

Freeing her arm, Josie climbed to her feet and ran back the way they had come. She came around the end of the restroom facilities and slammed into a human brick wall. Josie bounced backward and Xander grabbed her shoulders.

"Whoa, there," he said.

Josie sucked wind, trying to pretend everything was all right. Nick stood next to Xander and she didn't want to scare him with her story of almost being kidnapped or robbed. And both ideas sounded dumb now. She was a client who was overly happy with Josie's past work.

"You okay, sweetheart?" Xander asked. "Where were you?"

"I'm good," she replied. "I just made a wrong turn and rushed to get back here." She ruffled Nick's hair. "I know this little guy needs a drink really bad."

Xander drew his brows down at her. She played it off as nothing, which it was.

CHAPTER 15

The next two days passed in a blur of agitation and embarrassment as Xander followed the trail to his grandmother. She always seemed to stay one step ahead of him, and the employees in her wake chuckled as he searched her out. He couldn't even begin to guess what stories she had been telling and what questions she had been asking. Some of these people were actually blushing.

"Dude, just give up. She is running you in circles, and you know it," Keir called out with laughter filling his voice.

"You wouldn't believe the things I've heard. That woman is a menace," Xander growled in frustration.

"Come on, she'll eventually turn up at your office or more likely your secretary's desk. We can hide and wait for the perfect time to trap her."

"It's my grandmother, remember," Xander groused in sullen reply.

Keir frowned. "Oh, yeah. We never did get away with that. Did we ever figure out how she already knew?"

"Hell, no, but I want to learn that trick before I have kids."

The two men headed back to Xander's office laughing and reminiscing about their adventures and the times Julia had figured them out and chased them with the water hose, brooms, or whatever else was handy.

"There you are. I was beginning to think you had gotten lost," Julia called out from her perch on the outer office desk.

Xander and Keir shared a quick glance and sighed in resignation. This woman always knew exactly what was going on and how to foil their fun and games.

"And, Keir, it's about time you showed yourself. You're looking well, but I hear you haven't changed a bit. Still up to your whoring ways. Not ready to settle down yet, you big pussy?"

Keir's face flamed and he stuttered in an attempt to reply. Xander couldn't help but laugh at his friend's reaction.

"Why are you laughing? I heard what you've been like. Throwing things, growling, and just being an ass."

It was Xander's turn to sputter and blush in reaction to her words.

"All right, that's enough foolishness. Give me those papers we never got around to signing after breakfast the other day and go get your mate. Keir, I expect you to meet us for dinner tonight, as well. Also, while I was waiting here, a call came in from Ally. What a sweet girl she is. Anyway, she will be joining us as well. I made reservations at Ricardo's for all of us."

Keir and Xander smiled sheepishly, said yes, ma'am, and quickly left the office and the line of fire. Julia's quiet chuckle trailed after them.

"What are you doing for the rest of the day?" Xander inquired with a twinkle in his eye.

"Not much. Why?"

"I let Josie use my car again. I really don't trust hers. Not that she cares. Took a lot of convincing to get her to use mine. I'd buy her another, but with her reaction to just borrowing mine, I am guessing she'd flip if I got her a new one. Want to give me a ride to her? I'll even let you meet her, but you better be on your best behavior, or I will hurt you so badly your dates will be canceled for the next six months."

Keir's eyes widened and a slow smile spread over his face. "Oh, I can't wait to meet her now. She's got you this possessive after only a few days, then she must be something."

Xander rolled his eyes. "You'll understand when you find your mate."

"Whatever. Just tell me where to take you so we can get away from Julia and those all-knowing eyes of hers."

"I don't know yet. I have to check the GPS tracker on the car."

"You're stalking your mate? Seriously?"

Xander scowled. "No, of course not. My car's a new model, so of course, you can track it. It's just I'm worried about her and want to make sure she is okay. She was attacked, remember."

"Are you trying to convince me of that, or yourself? Because it's pretty thin, my friend."

"Just shut up. I want to see her okay."

Xander grumbled under his breath as he opened the app and located his car. "She's at her apartment. I recognize the address from her file the service gave me."

"Then by all means, let's rescue your mate from her scary kitchen appliances. Who knows what they will do to her."

"You're such a smart-ass. Why am I friends with you?"

"Because you're a sarcastic ass too, and we work well together."

"Oh, yeah, I keep forgetting. Lead the way. I have a damsel to rescue from her lonely time away from me. She must be counting the minutes until I'm with her again."

"Dude, it's getting really deep in here now." Keir snorted. "I think I'm gonna need a paddle to wade my way out of all the emotion."

"Dick."

CHAPTER 16

She couldn't remember the last time she had time to relax in a hot bubble bath. Josie laid her head back and let the heat soothe her stress-filled body. She needed this after the past few days.

That story they'd fed Julia was so wrong on so many levels. Then to come home to more hate-fueled messages and even a dead rat on her doorstep.

Maybe it was time to call the police; for the first time, the messages actually scared her. They were becoming more and more violent. This person was psychotic and had left five messages over the last twenty-four hours, each one a little angrier than the last.

Josilyn stayed in the bath until her hands were like prunes and the water was growing cold. She sighed and stood to dry off. She felt like a wet noodle, pliant and soft from the hot water relaxing her to the point she was dozing. It took almost too much energy to get dressed in her old sweats and tank.

She padded into her bedroom and came to an abrupt stop. A tall, well-endowed woman sat on the end of her bed with a look of utter hatred on her familiar face. "You're finally here, you pathetic bitch."

"You again," Josie said, staring at the bimbo who dragged her away at the fair not too long ago. "How did you get into my apartment?" Josie's voice was high and threaded with anger. She'd had enough crap for someone to yell at her in her own goddamned apartment.

The big woman jumped to her feet and snarled, "I told you to stay away, but you wouldn't listen. Now I'm here to make sure you do."

"Are you the asshole leaving me messages, putting trash on my doorstep, and just plain harassing me for weeks now?" Josie asked in bewilderment. "I don't know you and I don't work for the company anymore. What in the hell is your problem?"

The woman stomped on the wooden floor like a five-year-old ready to throw a tantrum. "Don't play stupid with me. I know what your family did to my husband. It's the only reason he married someone like you."

Josie laughed as she suddenly caught on to who this woman was. "You're Miss Double-D from the car wash down the street. The one my dipshit ex, Michael, cheated on me with? You were the cause of our divorce!" She laughed. "I would thank you, but you don't seem like the reasonable type."

Josie wondered what the woman meant by what her family did to Michael. Josie's family hadn't done anything to Michael except take him in as a son-in-law. She thought Michael married her for love, but now that she thought about it, he hadn't been a fraction as loving as Xander.

Josie had never seen an adult act so childish before. "What are you going to do, try to kidnap me again? You don't really think I'm going to sit here, do you?"

Miss Double-D gave an evil smirk. "Oh, no, honey, that would be too easy, and I won't be the one doing anything. But I will help my husband get his revenge and he will come back to me." She glanced to the doorway behind Josie and smiled. "Have you met Trey yet? He says you belong to him, and he isn't happy that you've been hiding from him."

Josie's eyes widened as she slowly turned to face the freak from the alley. His eyes were glowing as he prowled closer.

"Mine, you belong to me. You're my mate. How could you leave me to go to another man?" He stalked closer and closer. "Mine, I won't let you forget it this time."

Josie screamed and hurled herself across the bed and away from the freak shifter, but she hadn't taken into consideration the woman who sat there in her frightened fight-or-flight response. Miss Double-D jumped on top of her and held her down as the freak came closer.

"Stop fighting me. This will be easier that way," the deranged woman gritted out as she fought to subdue Josie.

Josie clawed and kicked. "Get off me, you crazy bitch." She heard a slap, then the weight on her back was suddenly gone. Trey grabbed the woman around the neck and lifted her off the floor. He slammed her against the wall, denting the surface.

"Don't hurt my mate. No one touches her but me."

Josie gathered enough of her senses to scramble across the bed, headed for the door. Hopefully, that monster would take care of Miss Double-D so she'd never be a problem again. Not that Josie wanted her killed; she just didn't want notes or dead animals left at her front door.

She made it to the far side of the bed, ready to swing her feet to the floor. A rough hand grabbed her foot and yanked her backward. She rolled over and kicked her heel at his nose. A crunch against her skin felt good.

Her other foot was released, but she fell off the bed from being dragged. The beast roared and fell against the wall, stumbling over Double-D's body. Josie was up and around the bed in a blink. As soon as she stepped out, a heavy weight slammed into her back. She crashed on top of the secondhand coffee table, knocking out her breath as it crumbled beneath them.

The squeeze of his arms was suffocating her, not letting her take the breath she needed. She felt her consciousness slipping away. Her tank top was ripped away as her body was rolled face-up. She heard a huge crash and the floor shook under her.

The beast's face was in hers. His breath was rotting decay. If she was going to pass out, now would be a good time. She didn't want to live through this experience. If she lived.

The face was suddenly gone, and the last thing she heard was her window shattering.

CHAPTER 17

Xander stared at Dominick, debating whether or not to trust him. "You said you were keeping him under guard."

"I was, am." Dominick ran a hand through his tousled brown hair and gave a weary sigh. "He incapacitated two of the guards and nearly killed a third. That woman had been planting ideas in his head after she saw him accost her on the street. I've been away dealing with pack business and didn't become aware of it until I returned about an hour ago to find the men laid out."

Xander studied the man in front of him and wanted to believe him, but something just didn't seem right. Almost as if he was holding something back. "I want to believe you aren't involved, but it just seems a bit too coincidental for my tastes."

"You'd be right. I, too, thought it was odd that my brother randomly found your mate to attack. It would seem the people trying to take my land by force and your mate's ex-husband are in cahoots. That's where I was since I left you the other day."

"What a fucking mess."

"You can say that again. I don't know how Michael got caught up with that group, or why he targeted my brother onto Josilyn. These people want me thrown out of my leadership role so they can railroad my pack. If my brother caused enough harm, then it would be likely they could succeed."

"What convoluted chaos. Thank you for what you did today. I'm sorry about your brother. I wish there had been another way."

"My brother died that day along with his mate. That man lying on the asphalt thirty feet below is what was left after his psyche broke from their connection shattering. I had never seen two people more in love than those two. My only solace is they're together again now."

Xander nodded. There was nothing he could say to that.

"Dude, I think there is something you need to see," Keir called out as he came to a stop in front of a door.

Xander gave him a questioning look and moved to his side. It was a child's room, sparsely furnished and decorated but definitely a child's room.

"She has a kid?" Keir asked quietly.

"She's taking care of her nephew who lost his parents in an accident," Xander replied just as quietly.

"This place is neat and clean, you can tell she works hard at it, but it's also old, used furniture. Almost as if she got everything from a secondhand store. I even looked in the cabinets and fridge. They're all empty or close to empty." Keir glanced around to make sure Josie wasn't around. "I think she is really hurting."

Xander sighed and rubbed at his temples. It hurt to see his mate struggling with so much. She was tough, there was no doubt of that. "Josie?" Xander called out as he moved to the kitchen where she sat on a stool looking dazed.

"Yes?"

"Was Nick here?" Xander asked gently.

"He is with his grandmother for the week." She trailed off

as a tear slipped down her cheek. "After this, she will probably push for custody. I promised I would keep him and raise him. I'm so afraid I'm failing him." She glanced at him. "I don't care about myself, Xander. Nick"—she gulped—"he's my life."

Xander slipped his arms around her and pulled her into his side. He didn't think she was even aware of the people in the room with her. She'd hit her breaking point and needed a few minutes to pull herself together.

Keir nodded and gestured for Dominick to follow him to the back of the small apartment. With their shifter hearing, they would still hear everything, but it would give Josie a semblance of privacy.

"Why will she take custody of Nick?" Xander asked quietly as he pulled Josie into his lap.

"His grandmother wants him, but I promised I'd raise him. Michael took everything, literally everything, including most of my clothes during the divorce. Though I handled accounts, he was the face of the firm. I mean he wined and dined people. It's how he made so many high-profile friends. This? Nick? It's a battle I'm losing, and if his grandmother finds out about this, she will use it to take him away."

"It's not going to happen. You're the most amazing, strongest woman I have ever met. This place may not be high priced, but the love and comfort are obvious for anyone to see. You have options, we were going to talk to you about a few of them at dinner tonight, as matter of fact. Just trust me that things are turning around. I promise."

"You know, I came here to take a bath and soak in some bath oils so I could rock your world tonight." Her laugh sounded hollow to him. "After the other day, I wanted something special again. Now here you are seeing me a crying mess. This wasn't supposed to happen this way. I was planning on us making memories I could carry with me after I was no longer your employee."

Xander cleared his suddenly dry throat. "We can still make it all happen."

She sighed. "Let's get through dinner and we can go from there. How much time do we have? I have only one nice outfit, and it needs to be cleaned after that night in the alley."

"Don't worry. We will get it taken care of. Keir, Dominick," Xander called out with a wink to Josie.

"Josie, are you here? What's going on? Josie?" A frantic voice called from the living room.

"Shawna, I'm in the kitchen. It's fine. Come in," Josilyn called out and slumped against Xander.

Xander's body slowly relaxed as he heard the familiarity in Josie's tone as she called out. "Friend?"

"Yes, she is my best friend and neighbor. She keeps me sane most days. I don't know what I would do without her."

"Hey, baby girl, what happened to your door and who is this sexy thing you're drooling all over? Girl, you been holding out on me or something?" Shawna catcalled as she strolled into the kitchen.

"Shawna, this is my fake mate, Xander." Josie turned and looked into Xander's eyes. "She is the one who set me up with you."

Xander's smile widened. "I owe you a debt I can't repay. Thank you for bringing this feisty hellion into my life."

Shawna giggled and winked at Josie. "I like him."

Xander shook his head at her antics and placed Josie on her chair. "Shawna, I'd like to introduce you to my best friend, Keir. Just be warned, stay away from him. He is a bit of a womanizer and I'd hate to have to hurt him for making Josie cry with his mistreatment of you."

Keir frowned but nodded a hello to Shawna before moving

off to scowl at Xander from outside the kitchen. "Ass," he mumbled as he went by.

"And this is Dominick, a new acquaintance of ours," Xander added, introducing the wolf.

"How do you both do? It's a pleasure to meet you." Shawna grinned.

Xander smiled and moved to stand next to Dominick and Keir. "Dominick, you okay?"

"Yeah, I'm fine. It's been a shitty day," Dominick grunted.

Xander and Keir watched Shawna and Josie catch up on what had happened.

"Why don't you come to dinner with us tonight, and I'll see if I can convince Shawna to come as well?"

"Thank you, but I can't. There are things I have to handle." Dominick waited a beat before growling, "Life's unfair."

"Things will work out well, I hope." Xander frowned.

"I hope so. I must make arrangements for my brother."

Xander watched the alpha walk off, his posture ramrod straight. He knew how hard it was to have to handle a family or, in Dominick's case, a pack depending on him.

"Bro, do me a favor. Can you order a dress for Josie and have it delivered ASAP to my apartment? Shoes and all that necessary stuff too, please."

"Done, don't even think twice about it. I'll have it there in an hour, tops. What time is dinner, by the way?"

"Eight. I'll see you there?"

"Of course. Later, bro," Keir said as he tossed a jaunty salute and headed out the door.

"Sweetheart, we have got to go so we won't be late for dinner. Shawna, would you be interested in joining a few of us at Ricardo's for dinner tonight at eight? My treat, of course."

Xander chuckled quietly as Shawna's eyes widened and

mouthed to Josie, *sweetheart.* He would never understand women.

"I don't know. I don't want to be a third wheel or anything," Shawna said as she bit her lip in indecision.

"Decision has been made. You will meet us. There will be six or seven of us, at least, so don't worry about feeling uncomfortable," Xander said with a wink as he grabbed Josie's hand and dragged her to her feet.

"Come on. We need to go."

Josie frowned. "But it's barely five now. We have plenty of time."

Xander smiled devilishly and leaned down to whisper in her ear. "Not if you're going to make me scream like you promised."

He couldn't help the chuckle when Josilyn's face flushed a deep scarlet. He took a deep breath and bit his lip to hold back his groan. She was hot and wet. Fucking hell, he was dying already. It wouldn't take much to make him lose control at this point.

CHAPTER 18

Xander wasn't sure where to wait for her. He'd planned this shit out to the smallest detail. There were flowers all over the goddamned room. That's what Julia said women liked. He'd gotten enough candles in the bedroom that it looked like an altar. He was worried the whole room would catch fire.

Of course, Julia decided to tell him now that she meant for him to get the flameless candles. Like he was supposed to know that somehow.

A bottle of champagne sat chilling in an ice bucket along with chocolate-covered strawberries. He'd done everything. Even went as far as getting the weird elevator music Keir suggested. He'd never heard of any instrumental stuff before. He kept waiting for someone to start singing, but it didn't happen.

She finally walked into the bedroom from the bath she'd been taking and stopped in her tracks. The softness that entered her eyes when she glanced around the room and the smile on her lips made him feel like a fucking superhero. All he'd done was toss some flowers around and this was her reaction? He'd have to remember to do that shit more often.

"What is all this?" Josie asked softly. Her gaze trailed around the room, going from the flowers to the bed to the candles.

Yeah, he'd done a great job. Maybe Julia was onto something. He marched toward her, ready to rip the towel off and touch her curves with his tongue.

"For you. Just something to show you the bathroom game is not the man I am anymore."

She licked her lips and raised a hand up to his jaw. He should've shaved, but he'd showered quickly and insisted she take her bubble bath while he set up the room in secret. Her hand rubbed the day-old beard, her nails scraping lightly over his hair.

"Every time I think I have you figured out, you do something to make the walls around my heart disappear."

He grinned. "Then I'm doing something right."

She dropped the towel and pressed her naked body to him. "I want you."

He opened his mouth to ask her more about that since she'd been pretty hesitant about things after the last time they'd been together. There wasn't a chance to ask anything. She curled a hand around his head and pulled him down, pressing her lips to his. The kiss was harder and deeper than any other. It was as if she were finally opening herself fully to him. Mind, body, and soul.

She shoved his pants down, her hands immediately caressing his erection, and he fucking loved it.

He pulled back from their kiss and met her gaze. "Do you know what you're doing?"

She licked her lips and kissed his chest. "I think I can figure it out."

He groaned and closed his eyes, filling his hands with her hair and gripping the strands tightly. She continued her trek down. Every breath he drew, her lips were there to place another soft kiss on his body and make it harder for him to think straight. The kisses continued. On his abs, his belly button, his hip and, finally, he glanced down and saw her open her lips and take his cock into her mouth. His heartbeat pounded in his ears like ocean waves crashing over him.

She curled her sexy tongue over his cock, flicking it back and forth, making him ache from how badly he wanted to shove it straight down her throat.

"Fuck, baby," he grunted.

She took him deep, her hot mouth sucking tightly and enveloping him in heat and wetness.

He gripped her hair, guiding her as he thrust into her mouth and pulled back. Fire shot down his back and he readied to come, but he didn't want to. Not in her mouth. He wanted in her body. In her tight little pussy where he could bite and claim her. Scratch her and make her his.

He propelled back and growled. She blinked and gave him a smile so seductive it made his balls tighten.

"I want you now, baby. Not after you have my cum crawling down your lips. I want inside you," he growled and hefted her up and tossed her on the bed. She squealed as she landed on her belly, her head twisting so she could glance over her shoulder at him. "I want to slide in your hot pussy and fill it. Take it. Make it mine. Make you mine."

He crawled up her back, placing his legs to either side of hers and lowering to put his body flush over hers. She was hot, soft, and coated in perspiration.

"Xander . . ." There was a hitch in her voice he found sexy as fuck.

"Lift your sexy ass up for me, sweetheart."

She wiggled up and widened her legs enough for him to be able to rock into her from behind, pushing his cock straight into the center of heat.

"God," she moaned, dropping her head forward on the bed and clutching a pillow.

He slid his hand under her to hold her upper body tightly

to his. Then he pulled back and pressed forward. He drove deep into her, grunting as the wet suctioned from her sheath.

"Fuck, you're wet. So slick and hot."

She pushed her ass up. He plunged deeper, giving her more of what he knew she wanted. Going deeper. Harder. Longer. Faster. He increased his speed and held on to her, their bodies slipping due to the perspiration coating their skin. The heat in her channel increased to a fiery inferno.

He thrust faster and faster. Harder and rougher. Every slap of skin making her moan and pulling a loud grunt from him. He couldn't stop. He needed to brand her. To own her. She was his and nobody else's.

He moved one hand down to her hip, holding her, and allowing the bear to come through. His hand changed, fingers shifting into claws digging deep into her flesh. Deep enough to create puncture wounds that would forever mark her as his.

She tensed. Her pussy squeezed harder at his dick. She was close.

"Come, baby girl." He licked her shoulder and pressed hot kisses on the back of her neck. "Come on my dick. Soak it with your cream so I can fill you with my cum."

She gasped, choked out a scream, and her body softened at the same time her pussy gripped tightly at his cock.

The feel of her channel sucking hard at his length pushed him over the edge. He growled, bit down at the back of her shoulder, and drove deep, taking everything she gave. His cock pulsed and filled her heat with his cum. Electrical currents shot down his back with every spurt of semen spilling from his dick into her.

He never wanted to move. This was where they both belonged. Him inside her, making her his. Her taking everything he gave her. Loving every bit.

He switched them so she lay draped over him after a

moment. The scent of his seed inside her made the bear finally quiet down. She was his. Theirs. Nothing and no one would change that.

"You're mine."

She snuggled into him and sighed. "You're bossy and demanding."

He growled and slapped a hand over her ass, grasping a cheek and pulling her to lie right above his once again erect cock.

"I am both, but it changes nothing. You're mine."

She laughed and sat up, grasping his length in her hand and giving him a wicked smile. "Forget me belonging to anyone. How about we figure out how many times you can go, bear?"

He raised his brows. "I'm a shifter. We can go all night. Many nights in a row."

She blinked and licked her lips. "Many nights?"

He palmed her tits and loved how big and heavy they were. All her fucking curves drove him and his animal insane with need. "That's right. We can do this until you can't walk."

She snorted. "Doubtful."

"How much I can fuck you won't change the fact you're mine."

She rolled her eyes and lifted enough to take him into her wet heat. Fuck! He grunted and dug his fingers into her wide hips, groaning when she slid down until he was fully inside her. "I haven't agreed to be yours."

He chuckled and drove his fingers into her hair, yanking her head down to take her lips. She was his. He didn't give a fuck if she believed it yet or not. Eventually, she'd get the picture. By then, he'd have her barefoot and pregnant with his babies.

CHAPTER 19

"Josie, we have to get ready or we're going to be late. You don't want to make my grandmother wait, do you? I can guarantee she will question and weasel out of you why we're late."

Josie jumped up, frantically searching for clothes and her shoes. She slowly became aware of Xander standing in the doorway staring at her in stupefaction. "What are you doing? Don't just stand there, get ready. There is no way in hell I'm telling that woman anything about what transpired over the last couple of hours. I'm already going to hell for lying to her and I'm not compounding my sins."

Xander chuckled and walked closer. "Sweetheart, it's okay. You have plenty of time. The restaurant is only fifteen minutes away and we have forty-five minutes before we have to leave. Take a deep breath and go take a shower. I'll have something for you when you get out."

Josie glared at him. "I was going to see if you wanted to join me in the guest bathroom shower for a round of Twister, too. Now, I don't think we have time."

"Oh, hell, yes we do. *I'll* explain it to her," Xander growled as he started to pick Josie up to carry her for a game of Twister sex.

"Save it for dessert, big boy. I need to look pretty for tonight, and that isn't going to happen if we spend the next thirty minutes rocking my world."

Xander lowered her to her feet and pouted. "Okay, but only because you said I rocked your world."

Josie smiled. "You rocked my world the minute I looked into your gorgeous eyes from the ground of that dirty alley."

"I need to tell you something, sweetheart. It's—" Xander was interrupted by the ringing of the doorbell. "Fuck, I'll be right back."

Josie smiled and moved to the master bathroom to take her shower. If she waited for him, they would never make it to dinner. He made her legs weak with a glance, let alone in the shower with water streaming over his hard body.

The hot water felt amazing as it hit her sore, overworked muscles. Not that she was complaining. If you were going to be sore, there weren't many better reasons for it.

"Let's go, slowpoke. Get out here and get dressed. Twenty minutes till we have to walk out the door," Xander hollered from the doorway.

Damn, she'd let the time get away from her again. She quickly washed up and climbed out of the shower into one of the softest towels she had ever held against her naked body. This might be what a cloud feels like, she thought.

"Sweetheart, come on. I have a surprise for you," Xander called out, impatience clear in his voice.

Josie rolled her eyes and took her time coming out of the bathroom to see her gorgeous fake mate standing next to the bed in the most gorgeous outfit she had ever seen him wear. Her mouth drooled and she whimpered in delight.

"You keep looking like that and we will not be making it to dinner," Xander ground out in a harsh voice filled with suppressed need.

Her mind was having trouble coming up with more than

one word at a time: suit, tie, molded, tight, sexy, mouthwatering, mine is all she could think.

"On the bed is a dress. Put it on and meet me in the living room. I can't stay in here. I need you too much," Xander growled as he fled the room, taking deep breaths to get himself under control.

Josie slowly shook herself out of her daze and moved to the bed. She gasped in shock at the most gorgeous dress she had ever seen. She picked it up and sighed at the texture, soft and filmy, almost like silk. She stepped into it and pulled it up over her curvy hips and round stomach. Under the dress on the bed, she noticed the silky undergarments and smiled. The underwear was going in her purse for a special surprise later.

She finished getting dressed and turned to view herself in the mirror. She felt like a Queen of the Damned in this sexy outfit. The long black material fitted her body like a second skin until it flared slightly at the knees. A slit on one side showed off a good portion of her leg and upper thigh. The top was black strips crisscrossing strategically over her large breasts and wrapped around her neck. Her back was open and bare for the world to see. She slipped into the heels that were provided and smiled. Xander was going to die tonight. She was going to fuck him into oblivion after this meal was done.

"Sweetheart, you ready? The car is out front," Xander called out as he stopped in the doorway and gaped in amazement.

Josie turned and smiled. "Well, how do I look?"

Xander swallowed and stalked closer, his eyes glowing a feral heat that made her squeeze her legs together.

"Don't touch me, Xander. I mean it. If you rumple me, I will shank your ass and then tell Julia what you did."

He burst into laughter at her threat. "You'd tell on me. Damn, woman, that's harsh."

"That was a look that said this dress was getting ripped off, and I'm sorry, but as much as I want your face between my thighs, I'm not ruining this decadent piece of clothing."

"Get in the car before I show you how easily that dress would accommodate my face." Xander panted as his eyes smoldered in need and desire.

Josie didn't have to be told twice. She bolted out of the room, a soft chuckle floating back to the barely controlled man she left behind. She waited at the door as he came up to her. "You forgot your purse." A hot breath of air puffed over her ear as Xander pressed close and whispered.

She could feel his erection pressing against her and she whimpered and faltered for a moment. "It's going to be a long night, isn't it?" she whispered.

"It's only the start, baby. By the time we get home, you're going to be begging for my touch."

Josie smiled and threw a glance over her shoulder to Xander. "Look in the purse for me, and then say it again." He slowly opened the purse and looked inside, half admitting he was afraid of what she might have concealed in there. To his surprise, he found a tube of lipstick, her ID, and some cash, and his thoughts shut down as he discovered what he was supposed to see. Black lacy panties that should be on under the dress right this moment.

He conceded defeat. He already wanted to drop to her feet and beg for mercy. How in the hell was he supposed to sit through dinner knowing what was right beside him? And with Keir knowing exactly what the two of them were feeling?

Xander raced toward the car to catch up with Josie. He slid into the driver's seat, giving her a sly smile. He pulled onto the street and stopped at the first light. Traffic was sparse at the moment, everyone just returning home from work and getting ready to go out. He took the momentary reprieve to move his hand under the slit in the dress and caress Josie's firm thigh.

Xander smothered a chuckle and moved his hand farther up Josie's thigh. He had to know if she was playing with him or if she really was bare under the dress. Another inch and he could feel the heat radiating from her. He wanted to see her luscious skin.

From the corner of his eyes, he saw the light change from red to green. He released the brake and rolled into the intersection. The last thing he saw was Josie's eyes widen and heard her scream.

CHAPTER 20

Electric chills ran up and down her leg from Xander's calloused hand rubbing her sensitive flesh. It was going to be a long night, indeed. Maybe they could have a quickie in the restroom stall.

She watched him stare at her thigh as he inched his fingers closer to her mound. Movement over his shoulder of the cross traffic caught her eye. A large, cargo-sized truck pulled into the other lane, passing cars that were slowing for the light to change.

Xander let off the brake and the car rolled forward as the truck sped into the intersection. She saw the inevitable conclusion to the situation. There was no way anyone would survive a direct T-bone hit from a vehicle that big, going as fast as it was.

Next she knew, she felt her body being moved. Whoever was helping her cussed up a storm. In fact, it sounded a lot like her ex. Josie forced her eyes open, hoping she was in a dream and would wake up.

The first thing she noted was that Xander was draped over the center console, leaning his head on her shoulder. The driver's side door crushed him toward her. He couldn't possibly be alive in such a narrow space.

Next thing she noted was hands under her arms, dragging

her out. Josie wanted to beg the person to leave her and get to Xander. He'd need help; she was fine.

Her legs gave out when her rescuer set her on the pavement. A voice growled in her ear and she turned to look at the face belonging to her ex-husband. What the fuck? What was he doing here?

"Come on, bitch. Get your fat ass up." He lifted her to her feet and forced her down the sidewalk. Her mouth didn't seem to coordinate with her brain.

On this side of the intersection, no cars were waiting on the light. All the action was behind them. She couldn't help her feet from dragging, slowing progress. A sting zipped up the same side of her face as the bruise from her attack outside the restaurant. That seemed like forever ago.

"Goddammit, bitch. Hurry up," Michael snapped and tightened his grip around her shoulders.

She heard voices hollering far behind them. Hopefully, someone was helping the man she loved from the wreck. The thought he wasn't alive refused to take root in her brain. He wasn't dead. Couldn't be.

Michael opened a car door and shoved her inside. She rolled from the seat to the floorboard. Her body arched over the hump in the middle. The car started and they were moving.

How weird was it that she'd met her ex's new lay and now here he was? She tried to remember what happened to the big-boobed woman when Trey attacked the second time. The blonde was thrown against the wall and that's all she knew. There wasn't a body in her room when she packed her stuff to go to Xander's home.

"How's your new wife?" she asked. Josie almost laughed at herself. Here she was lying on the floorboard of a car, kidnapped by her bastard of an ex-hubby, and the first thing she asked was about his significant other.

He didn't answer. Did he not want to answer or did he not hear her? She sucked in a deep breath and asked louder. Her body pressed against the front seats as the car came to a skidding stop. They couldn't have been a block away from where they had been.

Michael got out of the front and threw open the back car door. He grabbed her feet and raked her along the seats, pulling her out. Before she was completely out of the car, he dropped her legs then gripped the material of her dress.

Fabric tore as he yanked her up and pushed her ass to the ground. There was no softness in his actions. No care in his glare. The opposite, actually. The hate and fury she saw was nothing new. During their marriage, it showed up a few times. Curiosity finally got the best of her.

"Michael, why in the hell do you hate me so much? What did I do to you to earn your wrath to totally fuck up my life?" she asked.

Her answer was a swift kick in the side. Air rushed from her lungs, not coming back in. She slumped to the side, leaning against the open door. The pain went away quickly. Her body and mind were in shock.

"What did you do?" he asked, bending down to get in her face. "What the fuck did you do?" Spittle landed on her lips and nose. Her chin tilted down, trying to get out of the line of fire.

A streak of pain shot through her neck and scalp. He'd snatched a fistful of her hair and yanked her head back.

"You and your family ruined my life." Michael hit her temple with the heel of his hand. "Because of you, I had to dig through Dumpsters to feed myself as a child. I lived in cardboard boxes until I was put into child services where my life became one day of hell after another. Because of YOU!"

Never in her life had she been so clueless to what someone

was saying. "Michael, I never met you until we dated. I'm sorry about your childhood, but I didn't have anything to do with it." She now understood why he never talked about his past. She figured it was unhappy, but she had no idea he was on the streets.

His fists gripped the front of her dress and he dragged her to the side, then slammed her back on the car. Her head bounced off the polymer material. Why the fuck was he hurting her? She gritted her teeth against the pain.

"Does the name Debra Collins sound familiar?" he asked. Yes, the name was familiar, but from where? She thought back, racking her brain for the connection to the person. Then it hit her. Oh my God.

"She's the woman who died when my dad hit her car one Christmas," she whispered. What did he have to do with her? His last name was Strobel.

"My mother and father were divorced. She took back her maiden name. Wanna guess what it was?" Holy fuck. It couldn't be. Her family was responsible for his terrible life. Her heart hurt for him, for what he lost, for what he never had.

His eyes were wild, unfocused. Drool ran down his chin. Even though he'd barely moved, he panted like he'd run a mile.

So much made sense now. He hadn't married her for love, but for revenge. He wanted to ruin her life like she ruined his so long ago. Tears flowed from her eyes. Sorrow for all the pain and hurt crushed her heart. The blond bimbo's words came back. She wanted revenge for her husband. He must've told her.

"Why did you have to hurt Xander?" she asked. "He is a kind and generous man," she asked.

Michael laughed. "So was my mother, bitch." He backhanded her, knocking her toward the wheel well. A tangy copper taste filled her mouth. "I thought ending your loved one's life like the way my loved one died was quite poetic, don't you think?" He squatted in front of her. "Yes, poetic justice, indeed. You don't deserve to be happy. Your father got away with murder because he was a powerful person while my mom was only a hardworking single parent."

He opened the passenger-side door and pulled something from the glove box. "Now the tide has turned, cunt. I'm a high-powered man and you're the hardworking single mother."

Josie's breath caught in her throat. *Single mother.* Nick.

"Did you cause the car accident that killed my sister?" she asked. A grin spread across his face. Fury swirled in her chest. Her heart pumped lava through her veins. She'd kill him if he was responsible. Didn't matter how bad his past sucked. His future wouldn't exist.

"Forgot about that," he said with the grin.

"You son of a fucking bitch," she roared. Energy like she'd never felt fueled her limbs, giving her strength and speed she'd not had before.

Her hands were around his neck before her brain registered she had moved. Her thumb dug into his throat. His hand swung up and smashed into the side of her head. What he held in his grip, crashed into her skull. Pain shot through her brain.

Her strange strength gone, she stumbled back and fell to her knees. Her vision blurred, not able to focus on the ground. Nausea racked her stomach as her world spun. But her hearing was fine. The sound of a gun cocking came from where Michael stood.

"Good bye, Josilyn. Say hi to my mom and tell her you're *sorry.*"

Josie bent forward, putting her palms on the ground, readying for the bullet. The only regret she had was that she let Nick down. His grandmother would gain custody and Nick would become a wealthy, stuck-up snob.

Well, there was one other thing she regretted—never telling Xander that she loved him. Everything had gone so fast, her mind was in a constant whirlwind. And of course, she'd lied to Xander's grandmother about everything.

A roar scared her half to death, and she felt like she was already halfway there. Josie sat back on her heels, making her head spin. Her eyeballs whipped side to side, unable to stop. She tilted and fell flat on her face.

The ground shook in a steady rhythm, like a huge monster stomped toward her. She had no idea what was going on.

Gunshots rang out, but they were not directed at her. Another roar, this one filled with anger. The pistol clicked several times, telling her the ammunition had run out. Michael threw it to the ground and ran.

The growly creature followed him and she heard a male's scream cut short. What happened? Was he okay? She may have hated him, but she didn't wish him dead. Well . . .

Strong arms wrapped around her and pulled her against a hot body. Her hands met smooth flesh and her nose told her who held her. She collapsed into Xander, letting him hold her, keep her safe.

"I-I thought you were—" she couldn't bring herself to say the word *dead*.

"Josie. I have to tell you something. Please hear me out, okay?" Xander waited for her nod.

This sounded important. "Now?" she asked.

"Yes, now. I won't wait any longer. I almost lost you." He squeezed her to him. "The jig is up, sweetheart. Julia knows. She knew from the start. You don't know something, though."

"Love, it may have been fake in the beginning, but one look

at you and I knew it was true. You're my real mate in every sense of the word. My bear wants you forever. I want you forever. Please stay with me, you and Nick. I love you, and I will love Nick, too."

"What?" Josie stuttered in shock. "Are you serious? We're true mates?" She opened her eyes and looked at him, her vision had returned to normal. No doubt she had a concussion, but that could seriously wait a minute.

"Yes, love. It's why you feel that connection to me. The minute I looked into your eyes, I felt it snap into place. I crave you, body, mind, and soul. Being away from you even for a few minutes hurts us. My bear is fighting me. You belong to us. I've marked you, mated with you. We're one."

She gulped. "I don't understand. I've just met you." She cleared her throat and lowered her voice. "That was just sex. Great sex, but just sex."

He barked a laugh and heat flamed her face.

"Sweetheart, nothing that we do is just sex. You're mine now. All mine. Tell me, do you love me?"

"I think so. I can't explain it." She stopped for a second and took a deep breath. "Yes, I do. I know I do. When I saw you standing above me in the alley, it was like something felt right inside my soul. The sun was suddenly shining a little bit brighter. When I'm near you, it's all I can do not to touch you and hold you close."

Xander's eyes sparkled that gold she knew belonged to his animal. "That's our mates' connection. Your heart and soul know we belong together. Give me a chance to prove it to you. Be mine forever."

"I thought you said you mated with me already?"

"I did, but if you wanted me to leave you to have your own life without me, I would find a way to give that to you. Your desires are all I want to make happen now. Your happiness"—

he cupped her cheek in his hand and stared deeply into her eyes—"is my happiness. Will you take a chance and choose to be mine?"

Josie's cheeks hurt from how wide she smiled. She couldn't help it. This was the best moment of her life. "Yes, Xander. I'll be yours. Forever." Her hands slid around his neck. She whispered in his ear. "Um, you know we're in public and you're completely naked, right?"

Just how she wanted him every night they would spend together.

EPILOGUE

Josie glanced at the test with a smile. She and Xander hadn't seen each other in almost two weeks. He'd gone to the other side of the world to set up a new location for the business. Not that she minded. She'd been busy getting Nick established in the new house and all their possessions moved over. As well as meeting with a caseworker assigned to Nick once Mildred filed for full custody.

"Aunt Josie?" Nick called from the door.

She twirled to find her boy in a little tuxedo she absolutely adored. He looked like a little man. "Hi, baby! You look so handsome."

"You look really pretty, Aunt Josie. That's a big dress. It's so fluffy," he said, and pushed at the champagne organza skirt. Can we go now?"

"In a second, baby. Are Ally and Keir still arguing?"

Nick bounced on his black sneakers. "Yes. He keeps growling and she keeps rolling her eyes. I don't think they like each other."

Josie chuckled. "Oh, honey, I think they like each other a lot."

She slipped the pregnancy test in her drawer. She wouldn't need it. The moment Xander got a whiff of her, he'd know that their quickie before he left for the airport had gotten her pregnant. It was a good thing he hadn't seen her since he arrived that morning. He'd told her in no uncertain terms he'd make his damn wedding even if he had to fly the damn jet himself.

"Are you happy here?" she asked Nick.

He giggled and nodded. "Yes! I love it here. I love you. You are a lot more fun than Grandmom."

"Oh, sweetie, I love you so much! I never ever want you to feel I don't want you to live with me. I will always do whatever is necessary to keep you by my side."

Josie still couldn't believe Nick's pleading to the caseworker assigned to handle the visits with Mildred. The woman felt Nick knew who he wanted to live with, and his and his parents' wishes needed to be respected. The caseworker had given Mildred the chance to stop the custody request she'd filed and let Josie have Nick like his parents intended. Shockingly, Mildred conceded as long as she could still visit with Nick, something Josie had never thought to stop.

"I love you, baby bear. Now, let's go get me married."

Nick grabbed her hand with his little one and squeezed. "Then can we have cake?"

She laughed and walked beside him to the door. "Then we can have cake."

THE
ALPHA
AND I

Kate Baxter

CHAPTER 1

Fat, wet snowflakes flew toward the windshield like tiny white missiles in the glow of the headlights. Highway 21 wasn't a picnic to drive when the weather was good, but tonight's blizzard was enough to make Devon Kincaid wish she'd slept on the cot she kept in the storage closet at the bar. Her Jeep's windshield wipers were working overtime to keep the window clear, and the fan blasted hot air throughout the tiny cab to keep the chill of the wind at bay. Buying a soft-top might have been one of the worst decisions of her life. Okay, maybe not the worst, but it was definitely up there in the top ten.

The storm made it tough to make out anything in her periphery, but Devon kept her eyes peeled for any sign of wildlife. Deer and elk usually littered the sides of the highway, and even though she was certain any herds in the area would be hunkered down to wait out the storm, she wasn't taking any chances. The Jeep's boxy frame made it squirrely as hell on the snow-covered road. If she had to swerve to miss a doe darting across, she'd be toast. She kept a death grip on the steering wheel as she counted down the miles to home.

Why in God's name had she thought it was a good idea to buy a bar and move a million miles away from civilization? Oh, right, because her piece-of-shit ex didn't know the meaning of a restraining order and he thought it was totally acceptable to stalk her until she'd had no choice but to move two states away.

A flash of motion in her headlights caught Devon's attention and even though she knew better, she slammed her foot down on the brake pedal. The Jeep fishtailed and adrenaline dumped into her system as she steered into the skid to keep from sliding off the road. She eased her foot off the brake and pumped the pedal rather than applying constant pressure. The four inches of wet snow on the unplowed highway sucked her tires to the right but she managed to keep the Jeep upright and on the road. Her limbs quaked with unspent energy and her heart hammered against her rib cage. Stars swam in Devon's vision as she tried to slow her rapid breaths and brought the Jeep to a stop on the side of the highway.

"Damn," she said on a shaky exhale. Had it been her imagination or had something seriously just flown across the road in front of her? *What in hell was that thing?*

Devon put the Jeep in park and dug a flashlight out of the emergency roadside box she kept in the back. Apparently, tonight was a night for bad decisions because against her better judgment, she turned on the emergency flashers, pulled on her gloves, and climbed out of the Jeep. The wind whipped the strands of her hair not held in place by her beanie around her face and shoulders. Snow pricked her cheeks like tiny needles and she turned away to let her back take the brunt of the storm.

Midnight. In the middle of a blizzard. With nothing more than a flashlight and looking for something that could very well have been a figment of her imagination. Devon gave a shake of her head. What she needed to do was get her butt back in the Jeep and get out of this damn storm. The beam of the flashlight cut a bright swath through the nearly impenetrable barrage of snowflakes. The slightest movement at the end of the flashlight's reach caught Devon's attention. Definitely *not* her imagination. No four-legged animal would cast that sort of shadow. Wolves were common in this part of the state, but in the course of the year she'd lived in Lowman, Idaho, Devon had yet to see one. Still, the outline she could barely make out was much too tall to be a wolf. It looked more like . . . "Holy shit!"

Devon waded through the deep snow, off the highway and down a small embankment to where the ground leveled off onto a flat space that bordered the river. Her teeth chattered and her muscles grew taut from the blast of freezing wind and wet snow that peppered her. The flashlight shook in her grasp as she made out the form of a man, huddled over in the snow. The snow melted as it hit his bare and bloodied skin and rivulets of pink-tinged water ran down the muscles of his chest and over the ridges of his abs. His shoulders were hunched and dark hair cascaded over his bowed head. His chest rose and fell with heavy breaths that sent great clouds of steam into the cold night air.

A naked and bleeding man, out in the middle of nowhere, at midnight, smack dab in the center of one of the worst blizzards of the year. Nothing out of the ordinary about *that*.

Jesus, Devon. What if he's a serial killer? Or worse?

She guessed she'd find out soon enough. "Hey!" Her voice barely carried over the din of the blizzard. "Are you okay?"

Of course he wasn't okay. What in the hell kind of a question was that? She waded out farther into the open field toward him, the flashlight trained on his wide chest. Whoever he was, he was built like a professional athlete, every inch of him corded with muscle. He definitely wasn't local. During the time she'd lived in Lowman, Devon had gotten to know all of the permanent residents and most of the seasonal ones. She'd never seen this guy before.

A warning shiver raced up her spine. Devon sensed the weight of eyes watching her. She swiveled to the left and the right, shining her flashlight up one side of the field and down the other. Nothing. There was no one else around. In fact, how in the hell had this guy gotten here in the first place? No wrecked car. No disabled snowmobile. And not a stitch of clothing anywhere on the ground. It was like the guy just popped out of thin air.

He took a stumbling step and sank to his knees before face-planting in the snow. His body went still. He didn't even try to push himself upright, and Devon lurched toward him with a gasp. A gust of icy wind stole her breath and she explained away the mad rush of her heartbeat and the worry that welled up within her to the unspent adrenaline that coursed through her veins.

Was he dead?

Devon waded through the thigh-deep snow to where he lay unmoving. The flashlight roamed over his body and though he was covered in blood, she couldn't find a single injury, not even a scratch. Her hands shook as she removed one glove and reached to his throat to feel for a pulse. She pulled back with a jerk. His skin was on freaking fire! The wind died down long enough for her to hear his low groan of pain. The nearest hospital was at least two hours away and with no cell service for miles, calling an ambulance wasn't even an option. She grabbed onto his massive shoulders and tried to haul him upright only to struggle with the bulk of his weight. Devon lost her grip and fell backward into the snow. She let out a frustrated grunt. How in the hell was she going to get him to the Jeep if she couldn't even move him?

She cast a furtive glance back toward the highway. It wasn't going to be the most pleasant experience for him but she didn't think he could feel much worse than he already did. Her teeth chattered as she shucked her puffy down coat and draped it over his shoulders before wading through the snow back to the

Jeep. Her limbs were numb by the time she climbed back into the cab, and Devon took a minute to warm up her hands, holding them up to the blast of hot air coming from the vents in an effort to regain a little sensation. She wouldn't be worth a damn to either of them hypothermic.

When she finally felt like she wouldn't shiver her skin right off her bones, Devon put the Jeep in gear and maneuvered it so the front end pointed toward the open field, headlights trained on her mystery man. A slow breath compressed her lungs as she pulled her gloves back on and left the warmth of the cab to face the blizzard again. The wind whipped at her and snow peppered her face as she rounded the blunt nose of the Jeep and shone her flashlight on the winch attached to the brush guard. She flipped the switch to let out the length of cable and threaded it through the cab of the Jeep before she towed it down into the field, back to Mr. Tall, Dark, and Unconscious.

"Hope you've got an even temper," she remarked as she looped the cable around his torso. "Because you're going to feel this when you come to."

Every inch of Liam Murphy's body ached. He came slowly awake and braced his left arm on the mattress beneath him as he tried to clear the fog from his mind and the haze of pain from his vision. The room swam in and out of focus, the smell of wood smoke carried to his nose from somewhere close. He choked on an intake of breath. Gods. Even his lungs ached. He tested the skin beneath his pecs with his fingertips and hissed. The skin was raw and welted. Had someone dragged him behind a bullet train sometime in the middle of the night? His body was beat up enough to have bounced around on the tracks for a few hours . . .

He racked his brain for some scratch of memory. The last

thing he remembered, he'd been running with the pack out-side of Stanley on a full-moon hunt when something had jumped them. But as evidenced by his very human form—and the fact that his wolf had grown quiet in his mind—it was obvious that night had passed and the moon had begun to wane. How many hours was he missing? And what had happened during that lost time?

The loud clank of a pot drew Liam's attention and he sat up straight on the bed. His surroundings were unfamiliar. Rough-hewn log walls boxed him into the room and the single window was covered by a heavy curtain that closed off his view from the outside. He stretched his neck from side to side and the box springs of the log-frame bed creaked beneath him. The scent of an animal tickled his senses and the wolf that had gone nearly dormant in the depths of his psyche stirred with curiosity. Dog. Domestic. Not a threat.

The chocolate lab poked its nose past the door that stood ajar and peered inside before giving an anxious whimper and taking a tentative step back. The lab sensed the more danger-ous predator and knew better than to go inside. Not much of a guard dog. Then again, not many canines were interested in going toe-to-toe with a werewolf whether he was in his human form or not.

"Mac? Come here, boy."

Liam's ears perked at the sound of the sultry, feminine voice. His wolf stirred once again. Curious. So much for being dor-mant. Nothing about this place smelled familiar. Where was the rest of the pack? Who did that tantalizing, smoky voice be-long to? And what in the hell had he fought in the forest that had managed to kick his ass to the point that he was sore from head to toe?

As he stretched, the aches in Liam's muscles faded by small degrees. One of the benefits of quick healing. He swung his legs over the bed and the blanket fell away. Naked. *Huh.* He'd obviously transitioned sometime during the night before he wound up here. Was it too much to hope that whatever had happened last night, it had been a good time? A warning shiver raced down his spine. Nothing about this screamed wild night. He brought his nose up and inhaled. Aside from the dog whose scent lingered everywhere, there was no sign any member of his pack had been here.

Not good.

A door swung open and then closed, leaving a still silence in its wake. The sound of the dog's footfalls outside accompanied a human set. Liam's ears perked as he listened to the light steps crunch into the snow outside. Curiosity got the better of him and he decided if a doofy chocolate lab was his greatest threat, he could probably further investigate this unfamiliar place.

Liam's feet came down to the floor without a sound as he pushed himself off the mattress to stand. Supernatural healing allowed for him to take quite a bit of damage and bounce back quickly. That he was still sore from his encounter in the woods spoke volumes. Someone—or something—had handed his ass to him and it rankled. He eased open the door to find himself on a second-story landing of a small loft. The cabin couldn't have been more than eight hundred square feet and looked to be for the most part, unfinished.

The sturdy log frame made for a sound structure with plywood subfloors that had yet to be covered. The ground level of the cabin appeared to be nothing more than a tiny kitchen-slash-living room with another doorway that he assumed led to a bathroom. Every curtain in the place was drawn, shutting out the early morning light. A tingle of night air still vibrated along his skin, which meant dawn had barely broken. He let out a slow breath. Chances were good he'd lost less time than he'd thought. Hopefully. The details of his misplaced memories rested solely with his wolf. It would be nice if the bastard let him in on the secret.

The front door swung open, letting in a gust of chilly winter wind. With it, came a scent that washed over Liam's senses and settled in his gut like a stone. His muscles grew taut and his jaw clenched. His wolf came to full attention in his mind, zeroing in on the source of that delicious smell. The animal's attention was held rapt by the woman who waited for the lab to skitter into the house before she kicked the door closed behind her, her arms wrapped around a small stack of firewood.

Deep mahogany shoulder-length hair framed the delicate features of her face. Her cheeks and the tip of her upturned nose were tinged pink from the cold. Dark lashes fringed her bright eyes and her full lips were pursed in a determined set, accentuating the sharp lines of her delicate jaw. Her frame was lean, solid, and the thick cable-knit sweater she wore barely hid the swell of her breasts and the taper of her waist. Her jeans hugged the curve of her hips and her slender thighs, disappearing into the snow boots that laced up to her knees. She embodied the forest in autumn and her scent reminded him of warm days and crisp cool nights.

Mine.

The thought resounded loud and clear in the depths of Liam's mind and vibrated through every inch of him. *Oh, hell.*

What were the damn odds? The mating instinct seized him, a desire to rush down the stairs and rub his nose, face, and body over every inch of her almost too strong to resist. Her attention wandered to the landing where he stood, watching her. Her bright hazel eyes went wide and her mouth formed a silent O as the firewood tumbled from her arms to the floor. Liam looked down the length of his naked body before his gaze found hers again. He wondered at her shocked expression. The gods only knew how long he'd been naked. Had she not been the one to put him in the bed? His appearance couldn't be that much of a shock.

Liam scented the air. He couldn't discern the presence of another male, but that didn't mean one hadn't been here. His wolf grew agitated in his mind. It would do him no good to get riled before he exchanged a single word with her, but his wolf was ready to fight anyone or anything that might've already laid claim to her. The animal had no fucks to give about common courtesy or decorum. Not when her scent called to them with such visceral intensity. Not when instinct screamed that she already belonged to him.

"Um . . . you're naked."

The sultry tenor of her voice rippled over him as chills broke out on his skin. A low rumble gathered in his chest as the wolf echoed its approval. Her statement coaxed a smile to his lips as Liam once again took stock of his body. "Looks like it." His own voice rasped in this throat as though it had gone days without use.

Her cheeks flushed—not from the cold this time—and the rich perfume of her scent spiked with her embarrassment. Liam stamped down the smug satisfaction that rose within him. His wolf was a cocky bastard and liked to get a rise out of her it seemed. Liam didn't have any qualms about presenting himself for her inspection, either. He displayed his body proudly, his blood heating from the spark of interest in her eyes.

The dog gave a nervous whine. Obviously on edge with a larger, more aggressive predator so close to his owner. Her brow furrowed and she leaned down to scratch behind his ear. "It's okay, Mac. Go lie down." He did as he was told and trotted over to the fireplace to curl up on a large pillow there. His gaze was mournful as he rested his chin on his paws and watched his owner. She turned her attention back to Liam and said, "Want to fill me in on how you got that way?"

He could, but he doubted she'd believe him. He shrugged his shoulders. His wolf recognized this woman as their mate. There was one sure way to know for sure. It was impossible for a werewolf to speak any untruth to its mate. A lie would confirm it. "Haven't got a clue."

Liam's jaw clamped down as a bolt of sharp pain stabbed through his chest. He swallowed down a grunt and reached out to the banister for support. The lie burned through him in hot waves that scalded his internal organs and left a bitter tang on his tongue. He breathed through the discomfort, nostrils flared, as he waited for the effects of the lie to pass. *Gods.* He let out a gust of breath. It was true. This woman—whoever she was—belonged to him.

"Seriously, I can't talk to you while you're standing there like that."

A smile tugged at Liam's lips. Modesty meant little to a werewolf. "Like what?"

She waved her hand up and down. "Like that!"

Liam folded his arms across his wide chest. He didn't even know her and he already knew that he liked to see her flustered. "You mean naked?"

Her eyes went wide again. "Yes! I mean, doesn't it bother you?"

Liam shrugged a casual shoulder. "Not really. If it would make you feel more comfortable, you can join me."

She drew in a sharp breath. "Not a chance in hell, buddy!" She stepped over the pile of discarded wood and stomped toward the kitchen. "I've got a Beretta in the drawer and I'm not afraid to use it. Cover yourself up or you can take your ass back outside where I found you."

She jerked open the drawer and pulled out the handgun.

Her hand shook as she pointed it at him but her jaw squared stubbornly, telling him she'd have absolutely no problem pulling the trigger if need be. Good. He liked that she had backbone.

"What's your name?"

Her jaw hung slack as though she couldn't believe he would ask her that while she had a gun trained on him. "What?"

"You know, your name? That thing people call you when they want your attention."

She let out an exasperated huff. "My name's Devon Kincaid. Now how about getting some damn clothes on."

Snarky. He liked that, too. His wolf purred with approval in the recess of his mind. If the damn animal had his way, they'd have her on her back before they even had a chance to break the ice. *Down boy.* Liam gave the wolf a mental shove. The mating instinct was intense and if Liam didn't force himself to ignore it, it would land him in trouble. A bullet wouldn't kill him, but it would sure as hell sting.

"I'd be more than happy to oblige you if I had any clothes to throw on. Care to give me a hand with that?"

"I don't have anything you can wear and I have no idea where your clothes are." Devon's arm relaxed and the gun dipped toward the floor. "You weren't wearing anything when I found you. But the least you can do is throw a sheet around your waist."

The last thing Liam wanted to do was piss her off. Especially since her trigger finger looked a little shaky. He walked back into the bedroom and jerked the sheet from the bed, flinging it loosely around his waist. He stepped back out onto the landing to find her leaning against the kitchen counter. She let out a shaky breath and when she caught him in her peripheral vision she pushed herself away from the counter to face him, back straight and shoulders squared.

She cast a sidelong glance his way. "Thanks." Liam moved to come down the stairs and she brought the gun back up, the palm of her free hand facing out to stop him. "If you don't mind, I'd rather you stayed put."

He liked that she was cautious. Only a fool would invite close contact with a perfect stranger who could easily overpower her. Devon had a good head on her shoulders and obviously knew how to handle herself in a potentially dangerous situation. Which made him wonder how she'd learned that lesson. His wolf stirred once again. Whether he posed a threat to her or not, Liam was one hundred percent predator. Some part of her must have sensed it. Must have feared it. But he vowed that after today, she would never be afraid of anything ever again.

CHAPTER 2

Devon hadn't been kidding when she'd said she'd shoot. Dazzling good looks aside, she didn't know anything about this guy. She'd found him naked and bloody in the middle of a blizzard for Christ's sake. Not exactly something that would bolster her confidence in thinking he was a good guy. She looked him over from head to toe, amazed he didn't have a single visible injury. The guy had been bloodied like someone had given him a severe ass kicking. It made absolutely no sense.

"I can stay right here. No problem."

The timbre of his voice was warm and decadent with the slightest rasp. It reminded her of a burning fire on a chilly night and it heated her blood. *Stop it, Devon.* So what if he was good-looking? So what if his voice made her want to moan and the sight of him made her breath catch? She'd known plenty of guys who had charm and good looks in excess. It didn't mean anything. It didn't mean he'd earned her compassion.

"Okay, I gave you my name, now how about yours."

A wry grin spread across his sensual lips. Devon cleared her throat and pulled her focus from the intensity of his dark brown eyes. His stare swallowed her whole. Made her feel as though she were about to be devoured. That intensity didn't frighten her, though. Instead, it made her blood quicken and her heart race.

"I'm Liam Murphy," he said.

"You're not local."

His brow furrowed as he studied her. "Not really. I moved into Stanley a few months ago."

Stanley was at least fifty miles away. Devon hadn't seen any sign of a car, snowmobile, or any other means of transportation for that matter when she'd found him on the side of the road. She dropped her arm and let the gun hang at her side. "Is that where you were headed when you crashed?"

Liam studied her for quiet moment. He took a deep breath that expanded his wide chest and Devon stared, rapt, at the play of muscles from the simple act. "I wasn't in a wreck. I know that much."

His expression was guileless. "Then how did you get here?"

A corner of Liam's mouth quirked in a half smile. "I don't suppose you could tell me where 'here' is?"

Maybe he'd suffered a concussion. It would definitely account for his confusion. "Lowman," Devon said. "I found you last night in a field off Highway 21 bleeding and naked in the middle of a blizzard."

His expression turned contemplative. His fist tightened around the length of sheet wrapped around his waist showcasing the tendons in his arm. "Was I alone?" His brows came down sharply over his dark eyes and his jaw squared. "Did you see anyone else?"

Fear trickled into Devon's bloodstream. She'd never forgive herself if she'd inadvertently left someone out in that blizzard to die. "I-I didn't," she stammered. "It was dark and snowing really hard. I had a flashlight and I looked around as best I could. As far as I could tell you were alone."

Liam let out an audible sigh. The tension in his shoulders relaxed a small degree and he cupped the back of his neck as though to massage a knot away. "Lowman," he repeated. "How many miles from Stanley are we?"

He wasn't kidding when he said he was a recent transplant. "A good hour away," Devon replied. "And that's when the roads are bare. Honestly, with the storm as bad as it is I'm surprised they haven't shut the highway down." It wasn't uncommon for the stretch of Highway 21 between Lowman and Stanley to be closed in the winter. Avalanches were common and with a warm front moving in, it could get bad really fast. Hell, the road department might've already shut the highway down which meant she was stuck with Liam, at least for the time being.

"I need a phone," Liam said.

"Don't have one."

He cocked a brow. "You don't have a phone? How is that even possible?"

An indignant fire kindled in Devon's gut. "What's that supposed to mean?" He must've been a transplant from L.A. or some shit. Only a guy from the city would feel entitled to technology. "Lots of people don't have phones."

"You don't own a cell?"

"I do, but there's no service here. We're sort of in a black hole."

Liam let out a frustrated breath. "No landline?"

"There was no phone when I moved in." Good Lord, why did she even feel the need to justify herself to him? "And I don't really have much need for one." Liam muttered something under his breath that Devon was pretty sure she didn't want him to repeat. At least, not if she wanted to keep her temper in check. "There's a phone at the bar. As soon as the road's plowed we can drive up there and you can use it." The sooner the better. Though she had no idea how she was going to explain Mr. Toga Party to some of her regulars.

"Thanks." Liam's gaze softened, and Devon swore for the barest moment the color of his eyes lightened from a deep chocolate brown to gold. "And thanks for not pointing the gun at me anymore."

Devon looked down at the Beretta still clutched in her fist. She let out a measured breath that did a little to release the tension still pulling her own muscles taut. She might not have been afraid of Liam, but there was something about him that unsettled her. Not in a bad way, just . . . different. She set the gun back in the drawer and pushed it closed. It took actual effort to turn her back to him but she forced herself to do it anyway. "You want some coffee?"

"Hell yes," Liam said.

A smile curved Devon's lips but she quickly tucked her amusement away. "Well I'm not delivering it to you up there, so you'd better come down and get it yourself."

Liam chuckled and the sound vibrated over her skin. "Yes ma'am."

"And tighten that sheet." She forced her own tone to remain stern. "I've got nosy neighbors."

"Oh yeah? Are you sure you don't want to give them something to talk about?"

"God, no!" Heat rose to Devon's cheeks at his flirtatious tone. It was bad enough she was about to take a half-naked man up to the bar. "Just sit down and try to be inconspicuous."

"I can do that. But I've gotta say, this place looks pretty nosy-neighbor-proof."

The stairs creaked under Liam's footsteps. Devon's heart inched its way up into her throat and she fought to remain calm despite the fact she felt like prey. This had to be up in the top ten of the worst decisions she'd ever made. She just hoped that being a Good Samaritan wouldn't end up biting her in the ass.

———————

It was pretty tough to look like a badass while trying not to trip over a sheet, but Liam gave it his best shot. He hit the bottom stair and strode past the tiny potbelly stove into the kitchen and dining area. Devon's posture stiffened as though she sensed him behind her. The tang of her fear soured the air, and Liam cleared a breath through his nostrils in order to banish the offending scent. He didn't want her to be afraid of him, but he'd be damned if he knew what he did want. His wolf seemed more than ready to answer that question for him, but Liam wasn't ready to listen. Not when there were still so many unanswered questions.

"Until you mentioned neighbors, I was working under the assumption that we were living in a cave," Liam said with a chuckle. "You have something against sunlight? Are you some sort of vampire?" Had Devon actually been a vampire, she would've identified Liam by his scent and she more than likely would've left him to die out in the storm. Lucky for him she was merely human. Or maybe not so lucky, since his wolf was drawn to her like he was starving and she was a big juicy steak.

Devon gave a nervous laugh as she reached for the coffeepot. She poured two cups and turned toward the two-seater dining table. "I don't have anything against sunlight." Her lips drew into a petulant pucker that damn near made Liam's mouth water. "Keeping the curtains closed retains heat."

Liam considered Stanley a rustic community. Apparently, it had nothing on Lowman. He took a quick look around. No vents meant no forced-air heating. The little stove in the center of the cabin was her only means of heat. Devon set the two cups of coffee down on the table and went to the fridge. She grabbed a tiny container of cream and reached for the sugar on the counter beside her before setting them both down on the table.

"Gotcha. Heat retention—good." Devon handed him a spoon and he added some sugar to his cup and a splash of cream before mixing it all together. She added a little sugar and cream to her own cup before cradling it in her hands and taking several steps back. Rather than sit down at the table with him, she leaned against the counter near the kitchen sink, her gaze trained warily on him.

"You still didn't tell me how you wound up in that field."

"Believe me, if I knew I'd tell you."

"Where's your car?"

Her scent soured once again, but Liam didn't need his keen senses to know she was suspicious of him. He didn't blame her. His circumstances were sketchy as fuck. Really, what in the gods' names had possessed her to save him in the first place? His wolf gave an agitated growl in the recess of his psyche, obviously displeased that she hadn't been more cautious. He could've been anyone, and Liam knew from experience that there were things in the world more dangerous than a werewolf.

"Would you hold it against me if I told you I'm not sure?" It wasn't a lie. Any member of the pack could have his pickup right now, out looking for him.

Devon's eyes narrowed. "Would you hold it against me if I call bullshit on that?"

Liam chuckled. He liked her sass. "Not at all. In fact, I'd be worried if you were so eager to trust a perfect stranger."

"Trusting, I'm not. But you were in trouble, and I was raised not to turn my back on someone who needs help."

Liam gave her a gentle smile before he sipped from the lip of his mug. The smooth taste of coffee rolled over his tongue, just sweet enough with the right hint of cream and not even a little bitter. Delicious. He was certainly thankful Devon had pulled him out of that storm, but not for the reason she thought.

The blizzard wouldn't have killed him. Exposure wouldn't have killed him. But something had laid the smack down on him and whatever it was, it had packed a punch. "For what it's worth, I appreciate it."

"I just did what was right," Devon replied before sipping from her own mug.

Liam needed answers, the memories his wolf kept from him, to help shed some light on his current situation. But he needed to be careful of what he asked and how he asked it. The supernatural world kept their secrets well and he wasn't about to be the one to spill the beans. At least, not until he knew he could trust her as well. "You didn't see any animal tracks where you found me?"

"Nothing." Devon's gaze met his. The color of her eyes fascinated him. A mosaic of green, brown, and blue. Turbulent like the sea. "Then again, it was snowing so hard any tracks in the area would've been covered up within minutes."

True. Liam cradled the warm mug in his palms and stared into the creamy coffee as though he'd find last night's memories in its depths. "How long till the roads are plowed?"

"It's hard to say." Devon traced the lip of her mug with her forefinger. Liam found himself drawn to that simple act and he shivered thinking about what it would be like to have her touch him in the same way. "The road department is pretty good about getting the snow cleared. I'll run up to the highway and check in a few minutes."

"Couldn't I use one of your neighbors' phones?" Liam didn't want to wait on a snowplow. He needed answers now.

Devon gave him an incredulous look. "Trying to keep a low profile here, remember?"

Liam grinned. "It's the sheet, isn't it?"

Devon let out a snort. "Buddy, the sheet's only half of it."

Being patient wasn't one of Liam's strong suits. He wasn't

interested in fueling the fire of Devon's suspicions, however. He had no choice but to play it cool. That didn't mean he had to like it.

"So, Lowman. Must be pretty small if you can identify a local on sight."

Devon flashed a wide smile. It was the first truly genuine expression he'd seen from her and it was blinding in its brilliance. "I'm being generous in saying that there *might* be seventy-five full-time residents. Maybe another fifty or so that are part-timers and seasonal."

"What do people do for work?" Liam knew he had it easy. One of the benefits of being long-lived was the ability to amass a fortune over centuries. He could live practically anywhere without having to worry about how he was going to pay for his next meal.

"A lot of the locals are retired," Devon said. "One of my neighbors is a long-haul trucker, and another is a teacher in Garden Valley which is only about twenty minutes away. I know a guy who's a hunting guide and there's a couple that owns a rafting company."

"And you?" Liam asked.

Devon's eyes sparked with mischief. "I own the only bar in town."

Liam couldn't think of much else to do in the winter but drink in a town the size of Lowman. "Sounds like a sweet gig."

Devon gave him a sad smile that didn't quite reach her eyes. "Finish your coffee," she said. She went to the door and grabbed her coat from the hook before sliding it on. "I'm going to run up to the highway and see if the road's been plowed."

Looked like Liam wasn't the only one with secrets. And he was determined to learn Devon's.

CHAPTER 3

Devon had to get the hell out of there. And how messed up was it that she'd been driven out of her own house? It wasn't that Liam made her uncomfortable; in fact it was the complete opposite. She felt too at ease with him, as though it would be no big deal to sit and cozy up with him by the fire. She wasn't even that comfortable around people she'd known for years.

Only a complete basket case wouldn't see something wrong with that.

In the time it would take to warm up the Jeep and thaw out the windows, Devon could walk to the highway and back, so that's what she did. Mac scurried up from his post on his bed by the fireplace, no longer pouting that he'd been sent there in the first place and followed her out the door, ready for a quick frolic in the snow. The lane that led from her tiny subdivision to the highway wasn't more than two hundred yards. Besides, she needed the cold air to clear her head.

One of the things she liked about living in Lowman was the low probability of running into someone in her own age demographic that she might find datable. Some of the river guides who lived there in the summer were definitely eye candy, but they were more hookups than boyfriend material. So what did that make Liam? He was way too stunning to meet the typically low standard of guy she'd dated in the past and he sure as hell wasn't a hookup. When you found a guy like that, you dug your claws in and didn't let go. He was the guy you brought home to your parents. The guy you showed off to your friends. Maybe even the guy you walked down the aisle with.

What are you basing that opinion on? His rugged good looks? Or his rugged good looks?

Devon looked around for the nearest tree so she could bang her head against it. Superficial much? She reminded herself for the hundredth time that good looks did not equal a good person. Still, she couldn't shake the feeling that she knew Liam on more than just a superficial level. Cliché? Probably. But that didn't make it any less true.

Little clouds of steam puffed into the cold air with each of Devon's breaths by the time she made it to the end of the lane. Mac leapt through the deep snow at the edge of the road, nose down and sniffing as though he wasn't already familiar with every inch of property from here to the bar. Last night's storm had passed, but it looked as though another was brewing. Clouds gathered in the north and the wind swept them quickly across the patches of blue sky. The sound of metal scraping against pavement drew her attention, and she looked up the highway to see the snowplow headed her way. Perfect. The quicker she could get Liam to a phone—and off her hands—the better.

"Let's go, Mac!" The dog changed course and fell into step behind Devon as she hustled back to the cabin. He gave an anxious bark as she kicked the snow from her boots and went inside. Mac let out a chuff of breath, avoiding the kitchen as he circled the far edge of the living room and plopped back down on his bed. Devon found Liam standing at the kitchen sink rinsing out his mug and washing the dishes she'd left from the night before. "You don't have to do that." The words left her lips with more force than she'd intended. "I'll just wash them when I get home later tonight."

Liam's answering grin turned her bones to mush. It should've been illegal for a man to look so downright mouthwatering while dressed like a drunken frat boy. "I don't mind," he said. "You did save my life. It's the least I can do."

Heat flushed Devon's cheeks. She hated that a perfect stranger could affect her so easily.

"I've been meaning to ask you though, if I was unconscious, how'd you get me into your car?"

Devon cringed. "I sort of hooked you up to my winch and pulled you into my Jeep."

Liam's mouth softened and his eyes widened a fraction of an inch. He dried his hands off on the sheet wrapped around his waist and reached up to feel the skin just below his pecs. "Here?"

Devon looked away, guilty. "Yep."

His good-natured chuckle stunned her. "Good thinking," he said as he grabbed a sponge and dove back into the dishes. "I was wondering how you'd managed. There's no way you could have carried me on your own."

Despite him being absolutely right, Devon couldn't help but feel a little insulted. "I'm stronger than I look, you know. I could have totally carried you."

Liam cocked a challenging brow.

"I probably could have," Devon amended. "You don't know."

Liam laughed as he continued to wash and rinse the dishes. Devon was struck by the peaceful domesticity of the moment and it sent an anxious jolt through her system. She didn't want to feel anything for this mysterious stranger. She didn't want to feel anything for anyone. All love managed to get her was hurt. She'd never known it to be any other way.

"I don't know what we're going to do about shoes for you."
She needed to keep this all business. No more small talk. She
looked down at his feet. That old adage about a man's feet re-
lating to other parts of his body was certainly true. She'd seen
proof enough of that last night.

Devon looked up to find Liam studying her. "You're blushing," he remarked. "What are you thinking about?"

She didn't like the mischievous glint in his dark gaze. His
eyes raked her from head to toe and she swore the heat he
threw off was enough to make her sweat. "I'm not blushing."
Okay, that might've come across as a little too defensive. "I
just came in from the freezing cold, of course my cheeks are a
little red."

His grin widened. "If you say so."

An indignant fire burned in Devon's chest. How dare he in-
sinuate she'd been having salacious thoughts! Whether or not
that had actually been the case was immaterial. "I do say so."

"Like I said," Liam replied. "If you say so."

Devon had the feeling he liked to push her buttons. She
wouldn't deny she didn't like a little teasing, though. Especially
when it came from someone who looked like Liam. "The road's
plowed. As soon as I can figure out how to make you present-
able, we'll go." She might've liked his teasing, but he didn't need
to know that.

Liam rinsed off the last plate and stuck it in the dish caddy
to dry. He grabbed the sheet once again and rubbed it over
his dripping hands. "I can go as I am," he said. "I don't have a
problem with it."

"I have a problem with it." If anyone got a glimpse of Liam,
she'd never live it down. Besides, it was twenty degrees outside. He'd freeze to death. "You can't just walk around in the
middle of winter, naked and barefoot, with a sheet tied around
your waist."

A corner of his mouth hitched into a wry half smile. "Worried about what people will think?"

"No." *Yes!* Of course she was worried about what people would think.

"Liar."

Devon was taken aback by the certainty in his tone. As though he had some sort of built-in lie detector and had caught her. "Would you be worried about what people thought if you'd found me naked in the middle of a field and paraded me through your place of business wearing nothing more than a sheet?"

His heated gaze burned through her. "Absolutely not," he said without an ounce of humor. "I'd be one proud, cocky son of a bitch."

Devon wanted to be scandalized by the admission but she couldn't help but find it a little flattering. And maybe, had her place of business been a women's dorm, she might have paraded him down the hallway with an equally smug smile plastered on her face.

"You can't go out like that." She turned and headed for the staircase that led to her loft. "Give me a few minutes and I'll find you something to wear. Then we'll leave."

She walked up the stairs without another word, and though Liam didn't respond, she felt the weight of his gaze follow her. Who in the hell was this guy? And what sort of mojo was he working to make her feel this way?

The sway of Devon's hips hypnotized Liam as she made her way up the stairs. It had been a long damn time since a woman could hold his attention with an act as simple as walking. She wasn't an ordinary woman, though. She was human, but not mundane. Centuries of instinct coupled with a healthy dose of magic made sure that Liam would know that. Devon was special. She was *his*.

A mate bond. Holy hell.

He still couldn't believe it. Liam had found his mate in a tiny wilderness town in the middle of nowhere. Had he not been attacked and dragged miles from his territory, he never would have found her. Knowing that shook him to his core. Mate bonds with humans weren't unheard of, though they were unusual. A human life span was like a flash of lightning in comparison to that of a supernatural creature. The logistics of any relationship with Devon were problematic at best.

Relationship? He didn't know the first thing about her aside from the fact that she owned a bar and had winched him out of a snowbank last night. Not exactly the foundation for a strong partnership. His wolf didn't care about such trivialities, though. The mating instinct that rose up inside of him didn't give a single shit if she was a human, a werewolf, or a kelpie straight out of the swamp. The wolf recognized only one thing: she belonged to him. Nothing else mattered.

"Okay, I think I've got something that'll work."

Devon came downstairs with an armful of clothes and a pair of old black boots. Liam let out a snort. If she thought he was going to squeeze his feet into those tiny things, she had another think coming. "I'd rather wear a sheet than a toddler-sized T-shirt if it's all the same to you."

Devon's lips formed a petulant pucker. Gods, he wanted to kiss her when she did that with her mouth. "They're not toddler-sized." Her pouty tone was almost as sexy as her lips. "This T-shirt is an extra large."

Liam's wolf gave a warning growl in the back of his mind. Devon was a tiny slip of a woman, a little over five feet tall and probably about a buck-ten soaking wet. If she tried to make him put on a shirt that smelled like another male, he'd go out of his fucking mind. He couldn't do a damned thing about the hardness in his tone when he asked, "You keep a stockpile of men's clothes for emergency situations?"

Her adorable pucker made a downturn that caused Liam's gut to bottom out. He filled his lungs with breath and let it all out in a forceful gust.

"Not that it's any of your business, but I like to sleep in big T-shirts. Plus, they're great as a cover-up when I don't want to get dirty."

The scent of her anger was like sulfur. It burned Liam's nostrils and left a tang on his tongue. She held the T-shirt out to him and he took in the image of a unicorn leaping over a rainbow. Oh, hell no. He'd rather wear the sheet. Liam raised a dubious brow as he brought his eyes up to meet Devon's. A smug smile played on her lips. She obviously loved every minute of this. Sadistic. And sort of a turn-on.

"I'm not wearing that," he said.

She shoved the T-shirt into his arms. "If you want to use the phone you are."

His lip curled in distaste. "It's got a rainbow on it."

Devon didn't even bother to hide her amusement. "Uh-huh."

"And a unicorn."

She kept her expression level. "Yep."

For a long moment they simply stared at each other. A battle of wills that Liam was determined to win. Stanley was only fifty or so miles away. It wouldn't be long before his pack members found him. He'd rather live in isolation for a year than wear that fucking T-shirt.

"What's the matter?" Devon asked sweetly. "Not man enough to rock the unicorn?"

Oh, she was good. There was no way he could back down from the challenge now. Without a word in response he pulled the T-shirt over his head and jabbed his arms through the sleeves before smoothing the soft fabric down his torso. He gave her a defiant look, daring her to utter a single word.

"It's a little tight." Her admiration manifested as a rich bloom of scent that drove Liam wild. "But you can totally pull it off."

He'd endure the humiliation if it pleased her. He looked down at the pair of sweatpants she still held in her grip. His thighs were like tree trunks in comparison to hers. "I'll wear the T-shirt," he said. "But I'm drawing the line at those sweats."

"They're extra—"

"Not gonna happen." She might have managed to shame him into wearing the T-shirt, but those pants were going back to where they came from. "I don't care if they're double extra large. They're not going to fit me and I'm not even going to try."

"Okay, fine." At least she wasn't going to fight him on it. "Try the boots, though. They were here when I moved in. They might fit."

The cold wouldn't harm his preternatural skin but it would be nice to not have to go barefoot. He might not get frostbite, but the chill might become a little annoying. He took the neoprene Muck boots from her opposite hand and turned them over to check the size. Eleven-and-a-half. They'd be snug, but they'd work.

"Thanks." There was no way he'd leave this house not looking like a fool. Seriously, the pack really needed to do something about leaving changes of clothes at checkpoints or some shit. Of course, when some son of a bitch jumps him and drags him miles from his territory, a clothing cache wasn't going to do him much good.

Liam slipped on the boots. His toes reached the end but they weren't too uncomfortable. He looked down at the sheet still wrapped around his waist and brought his gaze up to Devon's to find her fighting her amusement. "Are you sure you don't want to try the sweats?"

The sheet might have been embarrassing, but those tiny pants would have been absolutely asinine. "I'm positive."

Liam untied the sheet from around his waist and spread the two halves wide to readjust. From the corner of his eye, he caught Devon's gaze dip below his torso. Her mouth softened and her tongue flicked out at her bottom lip as she stared. Liam forced his thoughts to the most *unsexy* things he could conjure: old wrinkled grandpas in Speedos, a plate of barbecued cockroaches, a broken nose. . . . If he didn't distract himself from the way Devon looked at him right now, his cock would betray his thoughts in a single stiff second.

Before he was tempted to throw the sheet aside and answer his desires, Liam bent over and grabbed the length of fabric that rested between his feet. He pulled it up between his legs and tied it loosely with the other two ends forming some very functional, though hideous, harem pants.

Beside him, Devon broke out into robust laughter. Gods, it was the most beautiful sound he'd ever heard. "You look ridiculous," she said through spluttering giggles. The dog's ears perked as Devon headed to the door and she gave him a shake of her head. "Nope. You stay home, boy. I'll be back soon." He responded with a sigh as though he knew the routine and settled back down on his pillow.

"They're still better than those toddler sweats you offered me." He headed toward the door, more than ready to take a little action. "Come on, let's get to that phone." He was in deep shit, that was for sure. And the least of his problems was whatever had jumped his pack and left him for dead.

CHAPTER 4

"That's where I found you." Devon eased her foot off the gas pedal and pointed to the open field to her left. Last night's blizzard had covered up any trace of Liam's presence. Wisps of white swirled over the smooth surface of snow, stirred by the wind of another oncoming storm.

Liam's gaze stayed glued to the field, neck craning as they drove slowly past. His expression was contemplative, his dark brows drawn sharply over his eyes. He remained silent for a long moment and Devon couldn't shake the feeling that he knew more than he let on. Anxiety unfurled in her stomach and her grip tightened on the steering wheel. Whatever his secrets and his reasons for keeping them, she hoped to God they wouldn't make her regret her decision to help him.

"Do you see many bears around here?"

The question seemed to come out of left field and threw Devon for a loop. She assumed he'd ask for details about last night, not the local wildlife. "Not really." She kept her eyes on the road as she spoke. "I've seen a couple of black bears in the spring and fall, but they tend to stay up high on the ridges. They really don't have a reason to come down because there's not much of a food source here. Berries grow on the ridges and the bears love them. The deer and elk are pretty thick in the spring and summer, though. In the winter, they move on to the lower valleys for the most part."

"What about wolves?"

Devon caught a glimpse of Liam's grim expression from the corner of her eye. His jaw was squared and his lips thinned. This conversation made her more anxious by the second. "A lot of locals say they see wolves all the time. Big ones. Timber wolves. I've lived here almost a year and I've never seen one. I've heard them, though. Some nights it seems like they're everywhere."

Liam turned to look at her. He didn't say a word but the worry was plain on his face. After a moment, he turned to stare out the window. The rest of the drive passed in silence and Devon's unease grew with every mile. By the time they made it to the bar, the cab of the Jeep felt even smaller than usual. They might as well have been driving in a tiny cardboard box. The air was too warm, nearly unbreathable, and Liam was much too close.

The Jeep's tires spun out in the deep snow as the four-wheel drive engaged. Devon would have to break out the snowblower later this morning and clear out the parking lot. Otherwise, she'd have an even bigger mess with vehicles stuck everywhere. She loved living here. Loved the isolation, the gorgeous views, and the river that wound lazily through the canyon along the highway and in front of the bar. She could do without the hassle of the snow, though. Luckily, it wouldn't last long. A couple of months, maybe three, before the snow line rose to higher elevations.

Liam climbed out of the Jeep and stared up at the sign that read LOWMAN INN mounted on a long post at the edge of the property. "It's a little misleading since there isn't actually lodging here," Devon remarked. "But as soon as I'm a little closer to being in the black, I plan on adding a few tiny cabins or maybe some camping sites."

"This place is pretty far from your home," Liam said.

Devon dug the bar keys out of her pocket and headed for the door. "Yeah, eight or nine miles, or something close to that. When I first moved here, the drive felt like forever but now I barely notice it."

She turned the key in the lock and pushed open the door. She glanced back over her shoulder to find the same concerned expression on Liam's face. Warm emotion blossomed in her chest at the thought that he might be worried for her driving back and forth on the highway. But that was silly, wasn't it? They didn't even know each other. There was no reason for him to be worried about her.

"Well, this is it." Devon held out her arm and swept it wide. The place was small. It could barely accommodate a hundred people. But it was hers and she was proud of it.

The previous owner had completely remodeled the space. It was the perfect blend of shabby chic and rustic farmhouse with all of the pieces of Americana you'd expect to decorate the walls and shelves. A large mirror covered the entire wall behind the bar and the four flat-screen TVs throughout the space were a huge draw for locals who wanted a place to hang out and watch whatever sporting events were broadcast on any given weekend.

"It's nice." Liam wandered the thousand square feet or so of space. He was distracted to the point that Devon wondered if he was aware of his surroundings at all. They could've been standing in the middle of the county dump and he might have said the exact same thing.

"The phone's back here." Devon pointed to the counter behind her. "Go ahead and grab it. I'm going to start some coffee."

Liam turned to look at her as though only now realizing

they'd come here for a specific reason. "Right. Thanks." He rounded the bar and grabbed the cordless from the cradle. He stared at the phone in his palm as if he had no idea how to use the damn thing before glancing Devon's way. "Would you mind if I took this outside?"

"Oh, no. Sure. Go ahead." Liam's demeanor had done a complete one-eighty since they left her cabin, and Devon couldn't shake the feeling that something was up. It shouldn't have bothered her that he wanted a little privacy for his phone call. There was nothing sketchy about that. But it made her wonder who he was calling. Did he have a wife? A girlfriend? If so, why would it even matter? *Maybe because you haven't had a date in over a year and you've been eyeballing the guy like he's a juicy steak ever since he walked out of your bedroom naked this morning.*

Devon's cheeks heated at the memory. His body was a work of art and the way he strode out onto the landing, completely shameless, had only served to intensify her admiration, no matter how scandalized she'd pretended to be. It had taken an actual physical effort to tear her gaze away. Hands down, the past twenty-four hours had been the most exciting—not to mention rewarding—of her entire year.

Liam pulled open the door and stepped outside, letting in a draft of chilly air with his passage. Devon figured she might as well make herself useful while he was on the phone. Otherwise her curiosity over who he was talking to and what he was saying would eat at her. It was cold enough inside that her breath fogged the air. If it wouldn't cost her an arm and a leg, she'd do something about having a central heating system installed. But until Lowman had a population explosion, or she hit the lotto—which seemed a hell of a lot more likely—she'd have to settle for good old-fashioned woodstove heat.

Devon crossed to the far end of the bar and threw some

kindling and wadded up newspaper into the stove before adding a few large pieces of wood. The deep rumble of Liam's voice
carried to her from outside and she strained to hear his words.
No such luck. She struck a match and held the flame to the
newspaper until it caught fire. She eased the door to the woodstove almost closed, leaving just enough of a crack to allow the
fire the oxygen it needed to grow. Once she was back behind
the bar, Devon turned on the Bluetooth speaker she kept near
the phone and opened a Spotify playlist on the iPad that also
served as her cash register. A moment later, the quiet gave way
to One Republic's "I Lived," and she let out a slow breath. She
didn't know why it mattered so much who Liam talked to or
why he needed privacy. But it did, and that bothered Devon
more than anything.

"Jesus, Liam, where the hell are you? We've been looking for
you since last night!"

The worry in Owen's tone did little to put Liam at ease. He
pinched the bridge of his nose between his thumb and forefinger and filled his lungs with the chilly morning air.

"I'm in Lowman. Is everyone okay?"

"Lowman? Isn't that the tiny town north of us? How in the
hell did you get that far away?"

Liam blew out a breath. How he'd gotten where he ended
up was the least of his concerns. "Was anyone else hurt?" he
asked. "And what in the hell ambushed us?"

"Everyone's fine," Owen replied. "We can't be certain, but
we think it was a shifter. Bear. And the bastard was *huge*."

That Owen and the others remembered details that Liam
couldn't recall indicated he'd taken the brunt of the attack. His
wolf retained the memories that Liam forgot. A defense mech-
anism meant to protect him. Which only meant he was lucky

to be alive right now. If their attacker had in fact been a shifter, it would've only been a matter of time before he'd found Liam and finished him off. He truly did owe his life to Devon. A rush of nervous energy entered Liam's bloodstream. Owen's concerned tone echoed Liam's thoughts. A bear shifter. It wasn't a coincidence. Couldn't be. *Fuck.* He'd thought they'd left their problems behind in Colorado but they'd obviously followed them to Idaho. He had no doubt the shifter was still in the area. In fact, the son of a bitch had probably settled down somewhere close.

"Did you check the registry for bear shifters in the area?" The supernatural community followed a strict set of rules. Each territory had its own governing body and the residents therein were required to register before they moved into any territory. It helped to maintain order and squashed territorial disputes before they had a chance to crop up. Liam said a silent prayer that there was, in fact, a shifter registered in the area and last night's attack had simply been a misunderstanding.

"We did." Owen's tone was grim. "But we came up empty-handed. Not a single bear shifter in at least a two-hundred-mile radius. Sort of weird considering the terrain, don't you think?"

Very weird. *Damn it.* Every new detail seemed to confirm a truth that Liam didn't want to face. Remote wilderness areas like this were prime real estate for shifters and werewolves alike. In fact, Liam had been surprised to find the Stanley area didn't already have a pack in residence when he moved his own group there. Devon had referred to the area as a dead zone. Liam was beginning to think that applied to more than just cell phone service. But why? His unanswered questions were beginning to pile up and that made him twitchy as hell.

"It's definitely strange," Liam said. "I hope you've told everyone to stay on their toes." In Liam's absence, it was Owen's job as the Beta to keep the pack in line. Either some unregistered shifter wasn't happy a werewolf pack had moved into the area and was bound and determined to scare them off, or an enemy of the pack had managed to track them down. The first option was bad but could be managed. The second option could be disastrous.

"We've been on guard and then some. Especially with you missing. It's going to help with the tension around here once everyone knows you're okay."

The order within the pack depended on the Alpha. Without that order there was chaos. Knowing everyone was all right did wonders for Liam's own unease. If anything had happened to any member of his pack, he never would've forgiven himself for his inability to protect them.

"The sooner you get home the better," Owen said.

Liam's wolf gave an anxious whine at the back of his mind. Going back to Stanley meant leaving Devon here, and his wolf rejected the prospect of that separation. Especially with the likelihood of a road closure if they were to get another bad storm. "I'm concerned with how a bear shifter managed to get me fifty miles out of our territory," Liam said.

"What exactly happened to you?"

"I don't know." And gods, did that ever burn. His wolf knew and was, for some reason, protecting Liam from it.

Owen let out a frustrated gust of breath. "Shit." Liam appreciated that he didn't have to explain the gap in his memory to him. Owen knew the logistics of their dual nature and knew why Liam couldn't remember. "Are you at least somewhere you can make a stand from if you have to?"

Liam turned and glanced through the window of the bar into the building and watched as Devon wiped down one of the counters with a rag. Her brow furrowed and she worried her bottom lip between her teeth. She was lost in thought and Liam wished he could crawl inside her brain and see what she was thinking. How could he go back to Stanley and leave her unprotected, knowing there was a potentially dangerous shifter in the area? His scent was everywhere: at her cabin, in her Jeep, and now here. It wouldn't be hard for a shifter to pick up on it and assume that Devon was a friend of the pack—or even something more.

Because of him, she was no longer safe.

"More or less," Liam said. Really, if he ran into the shifter again, odds were good he wouldn't survive the fight. Liam was strong, fast, and agile. The only thing save a silver bullet that could kill him would be to take his head from his shoulders. Not many shifters could accomplish that feat except for one. And odds were good that particular shifter had tracked them all the way from Colorado.

"I'm sending someone to pick you up. What's the address?"

"No." Until Liam confirmed the identity of the shifter that was after their pack, he couldn't leave Devon unprotected. "Not yet."

"Not yet?" Owen's incredulous tone would've been funny under different circumstances. "You need to get home so we can figure out our next move."

It was true the pack needed Liam to make any firm decisions about anything. Pack hierarchy was serious business and the buck stopped with the Alpha, plain and simple. "Whatever jumped us last night managed to drag me a good fifty miles from our territory." If Liam reasoned with Owen, he could justify staying in Lowman for a while longer. At least long enough to try and explain the situation to Devon. "I'm willing to bet I'm smack dab in the middle of the shifter's territory. It's a good idea to do a little reconnaissance while I'm here. I don't think it's a good idea to waste an opportunity to have the upper hand."

Owen remained silent on the other end of the line, obviously weighing the advantages to having Liam so far from the pack. His second-in-command was more than competent enough to manage the pack in the Alpha's absence. "Come on, Liam. You don't believe this was a random attack any more than I do."

A nervous tremor raced through him. Owen didn't believe in coincidences and neither did Liam. "No," he said. "I don't. But until I know for sure, there's still a chance this could be random. I trust you to manage the pack until I get back," Liam added. "We'll work both ends to the middle until we ferret him out. He can't hide from us for long."

"It's a sound idea . . ." Owen began. "But not having you here is bound to cause tension."

"That you're more than capable of handling." Ultimately, Liam's word was law and the others would have no choice but to obey. That's not how Liam wanted it to go down, though. He didn't think of the pack as a monarchy. He wasn't any more a king than Owen was a prince. The pack simply relied on structure. For the pack dynamic to function properly, everyone needed to know their place. That was Liam's job. And until he returned home, it would be Owen's.

"I just need a couple of days," Liam said. "Let me do a little digging. You hold down the fort until I get home."

"All right." Owen's response came across as though he were giving Liam permission when in fact he needed none. But that's how Liam wanted it. He wanted Owen to feel some measure of responsibility. He'd need it in order to keep the pack in line for the next couple of days. And if Liam ran into any trouble between now and then, Owen might be taking on that responsibility permanently.

Liam cast a furtive glance through the window to find Devon had moved on to washing glasses. There was so much more than the pack's safety at stake. Because now, Liam had to protect his mate.

CHAPTER 5

Devon forced her attention away from the door as Liam came back inside. He set the cordless back on the bar and took a seat on one of the high stools. She brought her head up, and in the large mirror that lined the wall, Liam's eyes met hers. He held her gaze for a long silent moment that she swore lasted years. It made absolutely no sense that she didn't feel even a little nervous under the weight of his stare.

"Did you get ahold of someone?" She didn't want to pry, but curiosity ate at her. Who had he called? And why was she saying a silent prayer that whoever it was *hadn't* been a wife or girlfriend?

Liam nodded and Devon turned to face him. "I did. My cousin."

There were more like him? Devon's knees went a little weak as she imagined what that gene pool must look like. "Is he coming to get you?" Disappointment soured her tone. *Ugh. Not at all needy, or overeager, Devon.*

The door swung wide to let in a draft of icy wind. Kelly Hartsock, one of Devon's regulars who happened to work for the road department strode in. He was decked out in his usual work attire: heavy-duty Carhartt insulated overalls and coat, Sorel boots, ski gloves, and stocking hat. He shucked his coat and gloves and pulled the beanie from his head to reveal the flattened-down mass of his dark brown hair. He threw a friendly nod Liam's way and paused as he looked him up and down, his expression perplexed. Devon swallowed down a groan. She could only imagine what Kelly thought about Liam's outfit. Thankfully, Liam was confident enough to own it without looking a bit embarrassed. Kelly threw a grin Liam's way and said, "Looks like someone had a wild night," before bellying up to the bar to take a seat on one of the stools. "Got any coffee, Devon?"

She grinned and winked at Kelly. "When have you known me to *not* have coffee?" Her conversation with Liam would have to be put on hold. She grabbed a mug from beneath the bar and poured Kelly a cup. "How's your day so far?"

Kelly's eyes lit with the sort of excitement that indicated he was about to share some juicy gossip. "Did you hear someone found a body up by Kirkham hot springs yesterday afternoon?"

Devon snapped to attention. Her eyes went wide as they met Liam's and an anxious tremor vibrated through her. He didn't give anything away. His expression remained inscrutable, which didn't do anything to assuage her blossoming fear.

"N-no." She cleared her throat and willed her tone to remain conversational. Liam turned his attention to Kelly and Devon followed suit. "Where did you hear that?"

Kelly leaned in as though about to confide a secret. "Ted Davis."

Ted Davis worked as a deputy for the Boise County Sheriff's Department. If anyone was a credible source, he was. "Was it a car accident?" *Please, please let it be a car accident.* Liam's appearance last night couldn't be a coincidence. He'd been bloodied as though he'd taken a pretty good beating, but last night, as well as this morning, Devon hadn't seen a single scratch on his perfect body. No bruises, either. She'd thought it was a little weird, but now, she couldn't help but feel unnerved.

Had someone else's blood been all over Liam when she'd found him last night?

"Not as far as Ted thought. The guy's car was in the parking lot. Some folks driving through to Sun Valley stopped there to soak yesterday before the storm hit and found the body on an outcropping of rocks a few feet away from the top pool. Ted said it looked like maybe the guy's neck had been broken."

Devon swallowed against the lump that rose in her throat. "He could have slipped?" The rocks surrounding the hot springs were slippery in the summer. Covered with ice, it wouldn't be tough for someone to lose his footing and fall.

Kelly shook his head. "He was beat to shit. It's not official, but Ted said they're calling in the state police to investigate it as a murder."

Liam sat, calm and collected as a saint in church. Not exactly what Devon would expect from someone who might've committed a murder. Then again, if he was some sort of sociopath, he probably wouldn't have any qualms at all about his victim being found. Jesus. Was she seriously contemplating the possibility that Liam was some sort of serial killer? It would be just her luck that the first guy she'd met in months who managed to get her attention would be on some sort of Idaho backwoods killing spree.

"Animal tracks?" The words left Devon's mouth in a garbled rush. She'd remembered Liam asking her if there had been any animal tracks in the snow where she'd found him. Why was she grasping at straws in order to defend someone she wasn't even sure needed defending?

Kelly's brow pinched. "What?"

Devon took a deep breath, which only served to make her chest feel tighter. "Were there any animal tracks near the body? It could have been a wolf. Or a cougar."

Kelly shrugged. "Don't know. Ted didn't mention anything

about an animal attack. I guess we'll find out what he has to say after the state troopers get up here and start poking around." With his epic gossip delivered, Kelly turned his attention to the steaming mug of coffee in front of him.

Devon stared at nothing as she tried to gather her jumbled thoughts. She didn't make eye contact with Liam. Couldn't. She knew there would be an accusation in her gaze whether intentional or not. She'd never had much of a poker face.

"I don't suppose the police identified the victim?"

Devon and Kelly turned simultaneously to look at Liam. The rumble of his deep voice resonated through her in a way that shook Devon to her foundation. All signs pointed to him being some sort of psycho killer and still, she found herself drawn to him in a way that she couldn't explain or understand. *You sure know how to pick 'em, Devon. Jesus.*

"All I know is Ted said the guy wasn't local," Kelly replied. Lots of people traveled through Lowman on their way to Stanley, Sun Valley, and countless other places. People came from all over to get a glimpse of the Sawtooth Mountains. Highway 21 was a favorite for road-trippers and motorcyclists. Though the latter didn't usually travel through until the snow had melted for the year. The guy could have been from anywhere and his murderer could've been anyone . . . "The car had Colorado plates."

Against her will, her eyes found Liam's. His expression remained impassive, but serious with the penetrating intensity that never seemed to waver. For the second time, she noticed the color of his eyes lightened from a rich, deep brown to a honeyed hue. Was it the play of light or a figment of her imagination? She looked away before her own expression gave her doubts away.

It was obvious Liam Murphy was a dangerous man. But was he a murderer?

More disconcerting than the bomb that had just been dropped, or even Liam's own doubts and worries, was Devon's reaction to it all. Liam could still taste the bitter tang of her fear on the back of his tongue. Kelly might have been oblivious to Devon's unease, but Liam's senses were much sharper. It wasn't only her scent, but the slight shift of her body that became more defensive. Her pupils dilated and her muscles tensed. Not enough for anyone but perhaps a werewolf to notice. Devon thought Liam had murdered someone at the hot springs. And why shouldn't she?

Colorado plates. Again, Liam knew it couldn't be a coincidence. The last thing he needed was for local law enforcement to get involved in pack business. The supernatural community had policed itself for thousands of years without the interference of humanity. Granted, Liam didn't know if the dead man had been human or not but considering the circumstances, it was likely a supernatural. Perhaps another shifter, or a rogue werewolf. Liam had told Owen to sit tight, but now he was wondering if it wouldn't be better to have Owen and a few others drive down from Stanley. The pack dynamic guaranteed they were more effective as a group. Alone, Liam could only do so much.

"You still have that forty-five under the counter, Devon?"

Liam's eyes slid to Kelly. It was obvious he wanted Liam—a perfect stranger—to know Devon had the means to protect herself. In a town that was literally a bathroom break on the way to somewhere else, anyone who wasn't a local would be under suspicion. Liam's wolf let loose a warning growl. Devon didn't need anyone but him to protect her.

"I do," Devon replied. "Hopefully I won't have to use it, though."

"If push comes to shove," Kelly said, "don't even think about it. Just pull the trigger."

Liam needed to get to the bottom of whatever the hell was going on. Before this area drew the attention of more than the local sheriff and state police. Secrecy was key. The isolation of these small mountain towns—not to mention acres of wilderness—were what drew packs like Liam's and kept their secrets protected. It was essential they keep a low profile.

"I've taken self-defense." Devon grabbed the coffeepot from the warmer and refreshed Kelly's cup. Liam wanted the human out of here so he could have a private word with Devon. But it seemed she wanted him here for as long as possible. "I know what to do."

Liam scoffed. Lots of people thought they could handle themselves in a hostile situation. Thinking you could and following through were two completely different things.

"What?" Devon turned her attention to Liam. Finally. He was sick and tired of her dealing with her nerves by pretending he wasn't there. "You don't think I can handle myself?"

He fought the urge not to crack a grin at her agitated expression. Anything was better than her fear, however. She cocked a challenging brow and Liam was sorely tempted to push himself off the stool and teach her a lesson. Maybe later. When they were alone and curious eyes didn't watch, he'd make sure she was properly educated on how to defend herself.

"I'm sure you know what to do," Liam replied. "But like your friend just said, you can't hesitate. That's the first mistake people make in an attack situation."

Devon let out an indignant huff of breath. "What makes you think I'd hesitate?"

He gave a casual shrug. "It's human nature."

Her beautiful hazel eyes narrowed. "So is survival instinct."

She wasn't going to win this argument. "So is compassion."

Supernatural creatures were much closer to their animal natures than humans. Especially those who dealt with duality like werewolves and shifters. Animal instinct was wired into their psyches. Hell, their very souls. Compassion didn't always play into the equation. At least, not right away. Devon needed to realize that and quiet the part of her brain that would second-guess her gut.

"You're saying I'd have compassion for someone who was about to attack me?"

Kelly swiveled in his seat to face Liam. His expression was pleasant as though he enjoyed the exchange. Likewise, it was apparent he'd seen Devon in similar verbal sparring matches in the past. It seemed he was settling in for the show, anxious to see who would come out on top.

"I'm saying, you'd consider whether or not an attacker was truly a threat before deciding if you should protect yourself or not."

Devon's mouth formed a petulant pucker and Liam's eyes focused on the petal-soft flesh he was dying to kiss. "Try me."

Dear gods. He could read so much into those two simple words. She had no idea how much he wanted to try. Her lips, her soft skin, her mouth, and the wet tight heat of . . . *Whoa*. Liam shifted in his seat. The last thing he needed was for Devon—and the guy sitting next to him—to see the evidence of his lascivious thoughts.

He'd try her and then some. Later. When she had a chance to settle into the reality of what she was to him. Until then, he'd settle for teaching her a quick lesson about the misguidedness of human ego.

Without a word, Liam hopped down from the bar stool. He held out his arms, inviting her to give it her best shot. Devon cast a superior glance Kelly's way and the two exchanged smiles that stirred Liam's wolf to thoughts of violence. The wolf didn't like that they were friendly. The wolf was too damned territorial for his own good.

Devon rounded the bar. She threw her shoulders back as she approached Liam, a sexy smirk curving her full lips. Her hand came up to brush the length of her dark hair off her shoulder as she shifted her weight from one foot to the other.

"Okay," she said. "I'm ready. Attack me."

Liam gave a sad shake of his head. "See, that's your first mistake. No one is going to give you a warning before they jump you."

She cut him a look. "There's not exactly an opportunity for spontaneity when you practically called me out."

Liam let out a chuff of laughter. "Called you out?"

"Yeah." Her indignant tone only served to further fuel his amusement. "You basically said I couldn't handle myself. All I want is the opportunity to prove you wrong."

His wolf was more than ready to rise to the challenge. To teach her a lesson and put her in her place. For no other reason than to prove to her that she needed them to protect her. Completely juvenile. And yet, Liam wasn't about to change his course.

Rather than lunge at her, he dug his bare feet into the soles of the rubber and neoprene boots and kept himself rooted in place.

A mischievous glint shone in Devon's eyes. "Nice outfit."

Antagonistic. He liked it. With every passing moment, Liam became more enamored with her. "Thanks," he replied. "It's a Liam Murphy original."

Her mouth twitched as though fighting a smile. "Don't you mean it's a Devon Kincaid original?"

He kept his eyes glued to hers. "Whatever."

"I gave you a chance to prove your point. But if you don't have the balls . . ." She let out an exasperated huff of breath before turning on a heel. The second she turned her back on him, Liam's wolf surged to the forefront of his psyche. He was a predator, after all. And Devon had just made herself prey.

CHAPTER 6

Apparently, Liam Murphy was all talk. When push came to shove, he wasn't ready to put his money where his mouth was. Or maybe, he was playing it cool so Kelly wouldn't see there was more to him than the goofy stranded motorist he'd painted himself to be.

A shiver of anxiety rippled down Devon's spine. Maybe it wasn't such a good idea to call him out. She refused to let him see her nervous and off-kilter, though. Through with playing games, with male ego and posturing, she turned to head back behind the bar.

Before she could register what had happened, her right wrist was seized in an iron grip. She let out a surprised yip a split second before Liam spun her around and grabbed her left wrist as well. It was a classic hold. One of the first things she'd been taught in self-defense to free herself from. All she had to do was twist her wrists and bring her hands around the outside of his forearms and she'd be clear.

It should have been so easy. Instead, Devon's mind went blank. *Shit!* She knew what to do, damn it! She'd done it a hundred times with her instructor. Liam's grip tightened, his fingers closing together around her wrists.

She knew where she stood now as well. His grip was solid.

The man was freaking strong! It wouldn't simply be difficult to get free. It would be damn-near impossible.

"Come on, then," Liam goaded. "Free yourself."

Arrogant bastard. Devon was dying to smack that smug expression from his finely chiseled face. A little tough to accomplish when he had her hands trapped in what might as well have been vises. A shred of much needed common sense returned to her brain and she pulled back her right leg, prepared to catch him in the knee.

He anticipated her body language and spun her, crossing her arms in front of her in the process so that her back was molded to his chest and his arms caged her in, using her own arms to restrain her like a straightjacket.

"Now what, Devon?" Liam's warm breath in her ear made her shiver with pleasant anticipation.

She couldn't let him show her up. Her pride refused to take that sort of hit. On impulse, Devon brought her head back sharply and connected the back of her skull with Liam's face. His body jerked backward and he let out a grunt of pain. A shocked gasp escaped from between Devon's lips as he released her. She turned to face him and her eyes went wide at the damage she'd done. Blood trickled from his nose and a wide split she'd made in the skin that covered his left cheekbone. Devon's shock turned to astonishment as the split skin seemed to heal right before her eyes. It sealed as though by magic, leaving only a rivulet of crimson to betray its presence.

"Holy shit," she said on a breath.

"Devon." Liam's warning tone told her it would be in her best interest not to say another word.

It wasn't possible. . . . No one could heal that fast. Devon's jaw went slack. Her gaze remained locked with Liam's. Her heart raced in her chest and her mouth went bone-dry. Her brain tried to reconcile what her eyes told her, but getting from point A to point B without short-circuiting might not be achievable.

"Damn, Devon!" Kelly gave a robust chuckle that helped to pull her from her shock. "Remind me not to ever piss you off." She glanced over Liam's shoulder at Kelly. He tipped back the mug and finished off his coffee before setting it back on the bar. "I've gotta get back to it, but I'll stop by on my way through this evening if you're still here. There's another storm front moving in, so be careful tonight."

"Yeah." She watched as he pulled on his coat, hat, and gloves. "You too."

Liam didn't move. Didn't speak. Didn't so much as blink. Devon stayed rooted to her spot on the floor, unable to do much more than force a smile to her face and offer Kelly a friendly wave on his way out. On the inside, she was about to melt down.

A blast of icy wind hit her in the face as the door opened and closed with Kelly's passage. Silence descended like the blanket of snow outside. Was it too late to run after him and ask Kelly to stay? Because Devon was pretty sure he'd left her alone with a murderer. Or worse.

She jumped as Kelly's plow truck roared to life outside. Snow crunched below the big tires, the sound echoing in her ears, and she watched through the window at what might be her only lifeline.

Liam's brow furrowed. His lips formed a hard line and his jaw squared as though he knew exactly what Devon was thinking and he didn't like it one bit. She took a tentative step backward and he shadowed her movement, taking a step forward. His eyes sparked with bright gold and she realized it wasn't a play of light or her imagination. His eyes had actually changed color. What in the hell was going on?

"Devon. . . ."

"Don't come any closer." Her heart beat a wild rhythm in

her chest as she took two stumbling steps away. She drew in a sharp breath when her back met the bar. The knotted wood of the handcrafted countertop jammed uncomfortably into her spine and she braced her arms behind her as though it would help her to be strong in the face of the impending attack.

"I'm not going to hurt you." Liam actually looked pained at her severe reaction. His nostrils flared with an intake of breath and a deep crease cut into the skin above the bridge of his nose. A low rumble reverberated in his chest, so much like the growl of an animal that it left her shaken.

Devon bucked her chin in the air. She doubted he bought the act of bravado, but it was worth a shot. "That's exactly what a psychopath says before he's going to do exactly that."

Hurt sliced through his expression and a pang of regret tugged at Devon's chest. Liam had said it himself, though. Compassion was the enemy in a situation like this. She couldn't afford to feel compassion. She couldn't afford to feel anything for him.

"You don't believe I could hurt you." Liam's confident tone gave her pause. She puffed out her chest, kept her posture defensive, as her hand wandered behind her for a glass, a bottle, anything she might be able to bash him over the head with. Her fingers brushed the cool wooden handle of the knife she'd used to cut limes with last night and she paused. All she needed was a couple more inches and she'd have it.

"You have no idea what I do or don't believe."

Liam leaned in closer. His woodsy, masculine scent washed over her and Devon's eyelids drooped for the barest moment. She didn't know what she believed. Her gut told her she'd be safer with Liam than anyone else in the world. A slight shift to her right gave her the extra reach she needed to wrap her fingers around the knife. Without thinking about her actions, her arm whipped around in a downward stabbing motion. Her gut might have trusted him, but her brain wasn't on the same the page yet.

Liam could've blocked Devon's blow. He could have plucked the tiny paring knife from her hand before she could even track his movement. But if he was going to go all in with her, she needed to see. She needed to *believe*. It was the only way she'd accept the situation.

The blade ripped through the fabric of the T-shirt she'd lent him and sank into the flesh above his left pec. Devon hadn't put much force behind the blow. It was more of a superficial wound than anything. Liam gritted his teeth against the slight bite of pain—it had all of the impact of a wasp sting—and when Devon pulled the knife away, shocked at her own actions, he peeled the T-shirt off and discarded it on the floor beside him.

Devon's eyes went wide as the knife slipped from her grasp and landed on the floor with a muted *thunk*. Liam's skin tightened as the wound began to heal and her eyes slid from his shoulder to his face. Her voice escalated with every word that left her lips. "What in the hell is going on?"

"Devon." Liam kept his voice low and level. "I need you to stay calm."

"Calm?" Her own reaction was the opposite of level. Her eyes bulged and her jaw went slack. "I hit you hard enough to break your nose, cut your cheek, and stabbed you! Your skin closed up and healed instantaneously! That's not even *possible*!"

It wouldn't do Liam any good to feed into her panic. "It is possible," he said low. "For someone like me."

"What?" Devon asked on a bark of incredulous laughter. "An alien?"

Liam leveled his gaze. "A werewolf."

Devon's manic laughter rang out around him like a chorus

of angry bells. "You've got to be fucking kidding me." Tears trailed down her cheeks as she continued to laugh. "I mean, you're working some kind of angle, aren't you? You run out in front of a car in the middle of the night, fake some stupid amnesia routine, and then . . . what? Rob your victims blind or beat them to death before moving on to the next person?"

She didn't believe her own accusations. Liam knew it by her scent. It was a lot to take in: the knowledge that the world wasn't the place you thought it to be. He understood her shock. Her denial. It was easier for her to believe he was a lunatic than a supernatural creature. The human mind was a fragile thing. Liam needed to let her come around to the truth in her own time. If he tried to push her, she'd surely crack under the strain.

"I haven't lied to you, Devon. Couldn't even if I wanted to. I tried, and believe me, it wasn't pleasant." The mate bond made sure of that. "My name is Liam Murphy. I moved to Stanley four months ago. I am the Alpha of the newly appointed Sawtooth pack. We were ambushed while out on a hunt last night. That's all I remember." Thanks to his wolf. He needed those details back. As soon as fucking possible. It would be nice if the wily animal would stop with the stubborn routine and be a little more forthcoming.

"What do you mean you can't lie to me?"

Her words came softer. Calmer. Liam let out a slow sigh of relief. He was throwing her into the deep end of the pool, barely giving her time to tread water before he submerged her once again. She was strong, though. She could handle it. His wolf wouldn't have chosen her otherwise.

"Our senses are keener," he said. "We can smell a lie. See the imperceptible shifts in body language that a human can't see. We're faster, stronger, immune to human diseases. We heal almost instantaneously from most wounds. We are dual natured. Two halves of a whole. The wolf controls our instincts and impulses. Our wolves recognize their mates. Through sight, smell, all of those tiny perceptions that have been bred out of humanity over millennia. The mate bond is sacrosanct. Any lie I told to you would burn through me and cause me unbearable pain."

Liam wanted to close the distance between them. To comfort Devon. To allow himself some small physical contact with her in order to comfort himself. He craved that connection. His wolf demanded it. And yet, he held back. Held them both back. Liam would give her as much time as she needed.

Devon's head came up at his words. She searched his face, her own expression pinched. He saw the confusion in every groove cut into her fine features. Smelled the sharp tang of her doubt and worry. Beneath all of that, Liam sensed her curiosity. He hoped she held on to that and let it grow rather than quash it.

"You can't lie to me . . ." she began. "Because you're a werewolf and the animal part of you thinks I'm your mate."

Yes! Relief washed over him. It was a small victory, but a victory nonetheless. "I don't think, Devon," Liam said. "I *know*."

"Show me." Her jaw took a stubborn set and she crossed her arms over her chest. "If you're a werewolf, then prove it."

Liam raked his fingers through his hair. "It's not that simple, Devon."

Her hands went to her hips. "Why not?"

He admired her fire. "The transition is . . ."—living it was one thing, explaining it, another—"difficult."

"Uh-huh." Her doubt angered his wolf. The animal part of him surged to the forefront of his psyche, scratching to be let out.

"When the moon is full, the transition is as easy as slipping into a pool of warm water. I can initiate the transition if I'm under a great deal of stress, or if I allow the animal to take control. The transition is painful under those circumstances. And it's not something I'd want you to witness."

"How do I know you're not making excuses?" Devon was talking herself out of her belief and Liam couldn't afford for her to do that. He'd prove it to her if he had to, but it would be a gruesome sight. His bones would break and re-form. His body would obliterate and remake itself. Fur would sprout from his skin and the sounds he would make would undoubtedly frighten her.

She'd issued a challenge, though. And that very alpha part of him refused to back down. He wanted to teach her a lesson, one that she'd be wise to heed: don't tempt a werewolf unless you're ready to face the consequences.

Liam took a long step backward. The transition could sometimes be violent and he didn't want Devon to be unintentionally hurt. If she thought witnessing him heal before her eyes had been a shock, she hadn't seen anything yet.

The wolf grew anxious. Pinpricks of sensation danced over Liam's skin. His muscles tensed and his gums ached. He met Devon's gaze. Her jaw went slack and he knew that his own eyes were no longer deep brown, but had given way to feral gold. The shift had been initiated and there was no turning back now. It was going to hurt like a motherfucker and he would be weakened from this. But it would be worth it if it convinced Devon once and for all.

"Keep your distance." Liam's voice grated in his throat with the warning. "And don't make any sudden moves."

CHAPTER 7

Devon wondered if she'd made a mistake in goading Liam. But seriously, a werewolf? Even drunk, she wouldn't have bought that line. There was definitely some freaky shit going on that she had no logical explanation for, though. And she had a feeling things were about to get freakier still.

"Keep your distance. And don't make any sudden moves."

His voice was like gravel scraping against sandpaper. Bright gold sparked in his eyes with an otherworldly light that both frightened Devon and held her transfixed. Maybe she'd been a little too hasty with her mocking attitude.

Liam doubled over with a grunt of pain. As though she had no control over her own actions, she took a lurching step toward him, her own worry congealing in the pit of her stomach until it formed a tight knot.

"No!" His voice was even harsher with the barked command. "I told you to stay back."

Devon froze. Even her lungs seized up as Liam's knees buckled and slammed into the concrete floor beneath him. His palms slapped down in front of him and his back arched. Panting breaths grated in his chest and his jaw squared, cutting sharp angles into his finely chiseled features. The severity of pain in his expression made him look wild and the bright gold of his eyes made him appear anything but human.

Ho-ly shit.

Devon's limbs began to quake and her muscles tensed as she witnessed something right out of a damn movie. Liam didn't cry out. There were no shouts of pain or anguish. But Devon knew the pain was excruciating. She practically felt the snap and crack of her own bones as she watched Liam's bones break, shift, and re-form. The speed of her short breaths matched his and silent tears trickled down her cheeks. She'd done this to him. Forced his hand. He'd told her the transition would be difficult but he'd failed to properly convey to her what it would entail. Dear god. There was no way any man could survive this.

But he wasn't a man. Devon was forced to come to terms with the truth she'd refused to believe. Liam Murphy was a werewolf.

His face began to change. To elongate. Devon drew in a sharp gasp of breath and squeezed her eyes shut to spare herself the gruesome image. Her hands came up over her eyes and she forced her rapid breathing to slow before she started to hyperventilate. She listened to the sounds of Liam's distress, the scrape of his nails on the concrete floor, the grunts and moans that transformed into low growls and whines.

Devon's hands dropped from her face. She focused on deep, even breaths as she slowly let her eyes come open. Her heart hammered against her rib cage and her muscles ached from the rush of unspent adrenaline in her system. "Oh my god." The words were little more than a whisper.

The wolf nearly stood at eye level with her. Bigger even than the timber wolves the Department of Fish and Game had transplanted in the county over the past several years. It was absolutely massive with paws the size of dinner plates and a boxy head that could easily sweep Devon's whole body aside with nothing more than a nudge. Its hulking shoulders tapered down to a narrow waist and strong haunches. Its dark brown coat shone with veins of copper and its bushy tail swayed back and forth behind it.

"Liam?"

The wolf let out what she assumed was a bark of confirmation. She was having a hard time wrapping her mind around what she'd just witnessed. But unless he'd managed to slip her a hard-core hallucinogen without her knowing it, Devon had to believe.

Wow.

The world as she knew it evaporated around her and another one settled in to take its place. One where imaginary creatures existed and anything was possible. What else was out there? Devon reached out a hand and pulled it back. She wanted to touch his fur, see if it was as silky soft as it looked. But she had no idea what werewolf etiquette was in this sort of situation. Honestly, she wasn't sure she was ready for it. It felt too intimate.

"I'll give it to you," Devon remarked. "You're not a liar."

If he'd been telling the truth about being a werewolf, did that mean he'd been honest about everything? Including his inability to lie to her and the reason for it? The implications left her reeling. Seriously! His mate? The way he'd made it sound, Devon had no choice in the matter. She was his and that's the way it was. Devon had always believed the decisions she made in her life were *hers*. In a few short minutes, Liam had managed to steal that choice from her.

Devon's stomach lurched as a wave of panic stole over her. She rushed past the imposing wolf and pushed open the door. The midwinter wind hit her in the face and she took the cold air into her lungs in frantic gasps. It didn't even register when her knees hit the snow-covered ground. She didn't feel a thing as the wet and cold soaked into her jeans and chilled her skin. Life wasn't random. Not even close. Everything that had ever happened to her in her entire life—the months she'd wasted on Nate, their dysfunctional relationship, moving to a tiny town in the middle of nowhere to get away from him—had all led her to this moment. To Liam.

Nothing was in her control. Not a damn thing.

Devon's teeth began to chatter. She stared at the blank white of the snow and continued to breathe through the panic attack that threatened to take her down. Why even bother moving? If she wasn't the one in the driver's seat, why not just stay right here and wait until God, fate, or whatever told her what to do.

Warmth buffeted Devon's back and the tension in her muscles gave way to relaxation. Liam's presence behind her formed a wall of protection that she found much too comforting. She should have known last night when she touched Liam and found his skin hot despite the blizzard that raged around him, that there was something decidedly not human about him. His body temperature had to run at least thirty degrees warmer than a human's. The delicious warmth soaked into her and Devon allowed herself an indulgent moment to revel in that heat.

"I'll be okay," she said without turning around. "I just need a minute to process all of this."

A minute? Try a couple of years.

The wolf let out a low, disconcerted whine. A long, quiet moment passed before his comforting warmth disappeared. The sound of the animal's footsteps in the snow was almost imperceptible as he left Devon alone to her thoughts. She drew in a steadying breath and let it out in a cloud of steam that rose above her head toward the sky. From this point on, her life would never be the same. She wasn't sure if that warranted celebration or mourning.

At any rate, sitting in the snow catching hypothermia wasn't going to solve anything. The cold bit into her fingertips as Devon pushed herself up to stand. She turned toward the building, prepared to face whatever came next.

Transitioning so quickly from one form to another had depleted Liam's strength, but he hoped it would be worth the sacrifice. He'd erased any shred of doubt Devon might have had in her mind. Of course, he'd replaced that doubt with a crippling anxiety that Liam felt as though it was his own. His senses were awash with her distress, causing his stomach to tie into an unyielding knot. Human minds were fragile; he could only hope Devon was strong enough to bear the weight of what was to come.

The chill of the concrete floor soaked into Liam's skin. His arms trembled as he fought to push himself upright. Weakening himself when there was an unknown threat in the area wasn't a good idea. Especially now that he had Devon's safety to consider as well. What was done, was done, however, and he had no choice but to suck it up.

Devon's scent filled the building as the door swung wide and she walked inside. Liam held the sweet scent in his lungs. Her earlier distress seemed to have abated and a wave of relief washed over him. He knew she'd overcome her shock. Devon was the mate of an Alpha. His wolf would have chosen nothing less than their equal.

"Oh my God, Liam." The door slammed behind her as Devon rushed to his side. "Are you all right? That was—" She went silent as though at a loss for words. "How in the hell did you survive that?"

The transition could be brutal. It must have been a gruesome sight for her to watch. "I'm sorry you had to see it." Gods, it would have been so much easier had he more time to get her used to the concept of his world. "I'm fine. Just a little weak. It'll take me a while to recover, but it's nothing I haven't dealt with before."

Her scent soured slightly and Devon drew her bottom lip between her teeth. Indecision marred her beautiful features and Liam shoved his weight against the floor to push himself to his knees. "You never have to be afraid to ask me anything, Devon. What is it?"

"Did you kill that man at Kirkham hot springs last night?"

He knew it would be only a matter of time before she gave voice to her fears. He'd be more than happy to assuage them if his damn wolf wasn't selfishly guarding their memories of last night. He took a chance, knowing the loophole of his memory loss could allow him to lie to her. "No."

"But you said you can't remember what happened last night. How do you know the dead guy isn't the one who jumped you?"

She had a sharp mind. Liam admired that. "I told you I can't lie to you. I said the word easily enough. Believe me Devon, if I ever speak a single false word to you, you'll know it."

Her expression transformed from worry to that same daring curiosity. She wanted him to prove it to her. She hesitated to ask. Probably because he was kneeling on the floor, barely able to keep himself upright.

"I'll prove anything you want me to prove," he said after a moment. "All I ask is that you give me a breather first. I don't mind a little pain if I'm rewarded for it later, but the past twenty-four hours have kicked my ass."

Devon caught the innuendo. His mouth hitched in a half smile as her lips twitched with amusement. "I believe you," she said. You've proved enough to me. It's not fair to make you jump through any more hoops."

"I'll jump through anything you want me to, love," Liam replied. "Later."

Her mouth went slack at the endearment, as though no one had spoken something affectionate to her in quite some time. Liam wondered what had happened to her. What had driven her to this place, miles from anything and anyone? There would be time enough to learn her secrets. After he made some sense of the tailspin their lives had been thrown into.

"You're naked again."

Her voice went low and husky. There wasn't a bit of anxiety in her scent this time. Instead, it grew richer, sweeter with desire, and Liam's arms damn near gave out on him again. She wanted him, and that pleased both him and the wolf to no end.

"One of the pitfalls of being a werewolf," Liam replied.

"Sort of explains your lack of modesty," Devon said with a laugh.

"Werewolves have no time for modesty," he said. "Though I have to admit, in situations like this, it can be . . . problematic."

Her mouth softened and another bloom of her delicious scent hit his nostrils. "How so?"

"The way you're looking at me right now, for starters." Gods, how he wanted to crush his mouth to hers. Taste her, enjoy her, touch her . . . "It's not exactly easy to keep my desires discreet."

Her gaze dropped between his legs. His cock might as well have been a fucking flagpole the way it jutted from his hips. Not exactly subtle. Liam wasn't embarrassed, though. He had nothing to hide. By all rights, Devon was his. *His mate.* She was beautiful, intelligent, full of fire, and he wanted her.

Devon's eyes came up slowly to meet his. "We should go back to my place. We have a lot to talk about and I don't want to do it here."

Agreed. If Liam thought he could get her to drive to Stanley tonight he'd ask her. She'd be even better protected there. With the entire pack to watch over her. After they talked, he'd suggest it. And hopefully, she'd agree. "Let's go. We should probably beat the storm, anyway."

"Yeah." Devon cleared her throat. "It's moving in pretty fast. Wanna get your clothes back on, or were you planning on going commando?"

Liam curled his lip at the discarded sheet, T-shirt, and boots. "Those aren't clothes by any stretch of the imagination."

"Hey." Devon smiled. "Don't dis the shirt."

"I'll wear it," he replied. "But only because it smells like you. The sheet too."

The sweet scent of Devon's desire bloomed around him once again. They needed to get out of here all right. Before he locked the door and took her on the concrete floor.

"I'll go start the Jeep." The fire in her hazel eyes told him they were on the same page.

Gods, the mate bond was a beautiful thing.

CHAPTER 8

Devon didn't know what had gotten into her. She'd never been particularly brazen, but seeing Liam naked for the third time in twenty-four hours was a serious blow to her self-control. She'd never seen such a perfect specimen of masculinity. Liam Murphy made "tall, dark, and handsome" seem lacking in comparison.

And according to him, he was all hers.

She climbed into the Jeep and tried not to let her attention wander as he settled into the passenger seat beside her. The storm had moved in quicker than she'd expected and gusts of wind were already beginning to create snowdrifts across the highway. Not good. This storm was going to be bad one.

Goose bumps rose to the surface of her skin but Devon didn't turn the heater up. Liam's body temp ran way hotter than hers. He'd be sweating to death by the time they made it home. She could stick it out. Her coat was warm enough.

"Are you intentionally trying to freeze yourself to death?" Liam's chiding tone made Devon cringe.

"I just don't want you to get too hot, that's all." Liam reached to the console and turned the heat on full blast. Devon relaxed as the warm air hit her and her grip loosened on the steering wheel. So much better. "You can roll down the window if you want."

Liam let out an indignant chuff. He turned to face her, brows arched over his shrewd brown eyes. "A dog joke?"

"God no!" She'd never even considered how that might have come across. "Of course I didn't mean that . . . I mean, you don't think I'd . . ." He broke out into robust laughter that made Devon want to reach over and smack him. "I just know you'll be too hot with the heat on."

"My body temperature can regulate itself just fine," Liam assured her. "Yours can't. Your comfort comes first. Always."

A pleasant rush shot through Devon's body. Liam's words warmed her better than the Jeep's heater ever could. The more Devon thought about it, the more she marveled at how easy it was to be with Liam. From their first exchange of words, something had just . . . clicked. She didn't feel that instant connection with many people. With Liam it had been more than instant. Maybe there was something to this whole mate-bond thing.

"Why did you ask me about bears earlier?" The question had seemed strange at the time, but now Devon wondered.

"Something big ambushed our pack last night," Liam said.

"Bigger than you?" He was huge in his wolf form.

"Much bigger." A shiver of fear shook Devon's form. She couldn't believe any animal could be larger or scarier than Liam. "A bear shifter is the most likely candidate. And they have a wide territory, so it would have been nothing for one to drag me fifty or so miles from where we were attacked."

"Shifter?" Devon was going to have to take a crash course in supernatural terminology. "So they're not were-bears?"

Liam chuckled. "No."

"What's the difference?"

"Biology. Magic. Whatever it is that makes us what we are."

Liam reached for the heat control on the console at the same time Devon did. Their fingers brushed and a riot of butterflies took flight in her stomach. Warmth flooded her and she was more than happy to turn down the heater a notch. She felt like she might combust at any second. Liam's presence turned her body traitor and spun her world on its axis.

"I'm not cold," she said. "Promise."

Liam gave her a doubtful look but didn't try to turn the heat up any higher. "I'm not a shifter, so I can't say for sure. But from what I know, their dual natures are different from ours. The full moon triggers a transition whether we want to change or not. Stress or danger can trigger the change as well. Those of us strong enough—like me—can initiate the transition without any of those things, but it hurts like a son of a bitch. Shifters slide into their animal selves. It doesn't matter if it's day, night, full moon or waning. The shift is seamless. It doesn't deplete their strength. It's not as easy for a werewolf."

Devon could listen to him talk for hours. She eased her foot on the brake, pumping it slightly, as she rounded a particularly slick corner. It was tough to keep her focus on the treacherous snow-covered roads when all she wanted to do was to give Liam her undivided attention.

"Doesn't seem fair," Devon said.

"No," Liam remarked. "But when is life ever fair?"

True enough. She'd learned plenty of hard lessons over the course of her thirty-three years. The most important thing was to take one day at a time. Sometimes, that was all a person could do.

"Do bear shifters hate werewolves?" She figured there'd be prejudices in the supernatural world, just like anywhere else.

"Not as a general rule," Liam said. "But territorial squabbles break out. Bear shifters don't run in packs. They're loners, which can make them difficult to deal with. They tend to live in remote locations and are tough to police."

"Who polices them?" Devon was hungry for every bit of knowledge she could soak up.

"The supernatural community has its own justice system in place. It's broken up by territories and regions. Not much different than how the human world polices itself."

Everything Liam told her helped to shed a little more light on a world she never knew existed. But it still didn't explain why Liam had been attacked in the first place. "Do you really think a bear shifter would have attacked you just because it's territorial?" Good lord. She couldn't believe she was having a serious conversation about bear shifters. "It seems like there'd be more motivation behind an attack that would prompt him to drag you over fifty miles from home."

"I have a few theories," Liam replied. "But until I can remember exactly what happened, they're just that. Theories."

"Why can't you remember?"

Liam drummed a rhythm against his sheet-covered thigh with his fingers and Devon found her eyes drawn to the display of strength in the simple act.

"Do you black out when you, um, change?" Words like "transition" and "shift" might have been commonplace to Liam but it would be a while before Devon felt comfortable with the supernatural lexicon.

Liam gave her a soft smile that made Devon's stomach twist in on itself. "No. The wolf and I are two parts of a whole. But sometimes," he said ruefully, "the bastard thinks he knows better than me and goes out of his way to protect us."

"He's keeping the memory from you?"

"More or less."

"Okay then," Devon said. "What do we need to do to get it back?"

———

She'd gone from wary to defensive to frightened, shocked, resigned, aroused, and now determined, all in the space of twenty-four hours. As humans went, Devon was strong. Resilient. She was extraordinary. And Liam was proud to know she was his.

The storm intensified with every passing mile. Drifts piled up on the highway, nearly as tall as the grille of the Jeep, making it impossible to drive more than thirty or so miles per hour on the winding mountain road. It was enough to make Liam more than ready to be out of the Jeep and back in Devon's house where she'd be safe. Really, though, was anywhere safe?

"It's tough to find unity within myself when the moon is waning." There was so much he needed Devon to know. So much to teach her. He was giving her a crash course in Werewolf 101 and doing a right shitty job of it. He was all over the place, throwing out answers as she asked questions. "In a couple of weeks I'll be able to recall the memories, no problem."

Devon's eyes slid to him. "Something tells me we don't have a couple of weeks."

We. Did she even realize she'd used the word? Liam liked the way it rolled off her tongue. Sweet and sensual at the same time.

"No," he replied. "We don't."

The rest of the drive passed quickly despite the glacial pace at which they traveled. Liam was convinced a horse and sleigh could have gotten them to her cabin quicker. By the time they pulled in to her short driveway, the snow had begun to pile up. There was no evidence it had even been cleared away once already this morning. The wind whipped and howled, pushing the blanket of snowflakes through the air like tiny frozen needles.

They climbed out of the car and for the hundredth time

Liam wished he'd told Owen to drive down. If anything, to bring him some damned clothes. If he had to walk around in this gods-awful sheet and rubber boots for another second he was going to blow a gasket. The storm raged, drowning out any other sound. As Devon got out of the Jeep and waded through the snow toward the front door, the creak of a branch straining in the large pine tree next to the cabin drew his attention. The branch cracked under the weight of heavy snow and the force of the wind at the exact moment Devon walked beneath it.

Without thinking, Liam dove for her. He gathered her in his arms, turning in midair as he brought them both to the ground. His back took the brunt of the fall and the snow cushioned them. The limb crashed down where Devon had once been standing and she looked over Liam's shoulder, her eyes wide with shock.

"Holy shit!" Her voice barely carried over the din of the blizzard.

Liam held her close to his chest and scooped up her legs with his other arm. He was beginning to the think the universe was out to get him or at the very least, doing its damnedest to keep him on his toes. Her arms came around his neck and Liam's eyes threatened to drift shut from the sheer bliss of having her hands on any part of his body. He carried her up the steps onto the tiny covered porch, and paused only long enough to get the front door open before taking her into the house. Mac hopped up and down, circling them with excitement. Devon reached out to give him a scratch behind the ear and once he'd gotten a little affection, he settled down. Liam's eyes met Devon's as he kicked the door closed behind him. Her mouth parted, her lips full and inviting. He'd planned to put her down on her feet but instead, Liam gave in to his own desires and put his mouth to hers.

She was like a sip from an ice-cold mountain stream on a hot summer day. Clean, and sweet, the only thing that could adequately quench his thirst. He urged her lips to part and his tongue slid against hers. An indulgent moan worked its way up her throat and her arms tightened around his neck. He'd stand here all night. Hold her until his gods-damn legs went numb if he had to. Anything to prolong this moment between them. Their racing breaths mingled into one as the urgency of their kisses increased. Swept up in the frenzy, their mouths slanted, tongues darted, teeth nipped. Liam took a stumbling step backward, and then another until the backs of his legs met the small couch in the corner of her living room.

Liam cupped the back of her neck as he settled them down on the cushions. He'd thrown so much at her in the past twenty-four hours. Flipped her world upside down. Expected her to accept her fate as though she had no choice. She had to be exhausted. Mentally. Physically. Emotionally. And yet, she kissed him with a fervor that excited him to the point of combustion. Despite everything that no doubt weighed on her, she wanted him.

Devon repositioned herself so she straddled his hips. She brushed the hard length of his cock, barely covered by the thin cotton sheet, and he sucked in a sharp breath. Liam's fist wound into the hair at the nape of Devon's neck and he eased her head to one side so he could taste the flesh at her throat. Things moved quickly in Liam's world. Relationships included. He didn't want Devon to feel rushed into anything she wasn't ready for, but the sweet scent of her desire, the heat of her mouth against his ear, and the warmth of her body against his was about to snap the last fragile thread of his resolve.

"Liam . . ."

He loved the way she said his name. The way the sensual

sound of it was for his ears only. Still, he sensed her hesitation, the slightest doubt.

"Devon, we can stop." He needed to put her at ease. What Devon didn't understand was that to a werewolf, the safety of his mate was tantamount. He would sacrifice his life to protect her from any threat. Even if that threat was himself. "It's been a long day—"

"I don't want to stop." Her breathy response caused his gut to tighten and his cock to harden to stone. "I just . . . I can't even begin to describe how badly I want you right now. It's like nothing I've ever felt before. It doesn't make any sense."

Emotion welled in Liam's chest at her admission. The mate bond was a powerful thing. He often wondered if a human would feel it with the same intensity a werewolf did. Devon answered that question. It seemed they both had a lot to learn. He couldn't wait to experience all of it with her.

His teeth grazed the sensitive skin near the hollow of Devon's throat and she shuddered. The cold of the storm penetrated the interior of the dark cabin as the wind and snow continued to vent their rage outside. "I could build a fire," Liam said against her throat.

Devon's low laughter sent a lick of heat down his spine. "Are you kidding? You *are* a fire. I don't need anything but you to keep me warm."

Gods. That simple sentence knocked the air from Liam's lungs. "I want to take you upstairs." The last thing he needed was to behave like the animal he was and fuck her right there on the couch. Especially when she'd made it clear how she felt about being seen by her neighbors.

"I don't know if I'll make it upstairs. I want you right now."

She made it tough for him to be a gentleman. But truth be told, he doubted he'd make it the thirty or so feet from the couch, up the stairs to her bedroom, either. He'd only known her for twenty-four hours and yet, it felt as though he'd wanted her for centuries.

"I want you too." He crushed his mouth to hers for another urgent kiss before pulling away. "I can't go another second without you."

CHAPTER 9

Six months ago, that sort of intense admission from any man would have sent Devon into a panic. A PTSD reaction from having lived through a relationship with a man who'd disabled her car battery to keep her from leaving for the weekend because, "I have to be with you every second of every day." Nate hadn't wanted a relationship with her. He'd wanted to *own* her. And even after she'd managed to find a way out and file a restraining order, he'd tried to get her back. His relentless obsession had pushed Devon into the isolated Idaho wilderness where she'd assumed she'd never have a chance at a relationship again.

Guess that assumption turned out to be wrong.

Liam was the first man to ever make her feel safe. Which blew her mind since she'd known him for all of about a day. Wasn't a moment all it took, though? A moment to connect with someone. A moment to feel a kinship. A moment of interest, a moment to fall in love. . . . Devon had no idea what the future would hold. Could she love Liam? Maybe. Maybe not. But one thing was certain: she was going to ride the wave and see where it took her.

The heat of his mouth met her throat once again and Devon's bones went liquid. The glide of his fingertips against her skin, his grip on her hair, his lips on hers was an indulgence that only made her want more. Without a fire burning in the stove, it was cold enough to see her breath. Devon barely noticed the chill. Liam provided all the warmth she'd ever need.

She pulled away only long enough to shuck her puffy down coat. It fell to the floor somewhere behind her and she peeled off her T-shirt next. Liam's eyes sparked bright gold as his gaze devoured her. Devon's stomach did a backflip and floated down on a blissful cloud. Desire overwhelmed her. Her fingers shook as she reached back to unhook her bra. At this rate, she'd be lucky if she'd be able to get her own jeans unbuttoned.

Liam crossed his arms in front of him and stripped the shirt Devon had lent him from his chest. All thoughts of getting her bra the rest of the way off melted as her gaze met the bulging wall of muscle. She could safely say she now knew what zero percent body fat looked like. Her hands abandoned her bra as she reached out, desperate to press her palms against the definition of his pecs. Her hands hovered, unable to close the inch or so distance that separated their bare skin. Everything was happening so fast. Devon worried she'd get whiplash when the gravity of the situation finally hit her. Right now, she was too busy living in the moment. Would there be repercussions for her actions? Would she survive the emotional fallout?

"It's okay, Devon."

She cocked her head to one side as she studied the details of Liam's face. She couldn't hide anything from him, could she? There would never be an ounce of deception between them because the mystical biology of their relationship wouldn't allow for it. She still didn't understand any of it. Not really. She had to hope that somehow, everything would work out the way it was supposed to. Otherwise, she and Liam might both be ruined.

Her palms came down on his heated skin and she let out an indulgent sigh. "I still can't get over how warm you are."

"Werewolf metabolism," Liam replied proudly. "It's why we heal faster and are able to build the muscle mass necessary to withstand the stress that transitioning puts on our bodies."

Liam Murphy was a goddamn medical miracle and the world didn't even know he existed. Her hands moved over the hills of his pecs, across his wide collarbone and the strong curve of his shoulders. Every inch of him was chiseled from marble, smooth and unyielding. A fire burned beneath the surface of his skin and behind his eyes as she continued her exploration, letting her hands wander over his shoulders to his back, down around his biceps and powerful forearms, to his hands. Her fingers moved to the sheet that still circled his waist, skimming the edge of the fabric as she traced the skin below his belly button. His muscles flexed and tightened under her touch as she pushed her palms up the ridges of his abs and back to where she'd started.

"I don't know if this is something men like to hear," she said with a gentle laugh. "But you're absolutely beautiful."

His lips curved into a sardonic smile. "From you?" He traced her bottom lip with the pad of his thumb. "My mate? It's the best compliment I could ever receive."

Devon blew out a breath. A few hours with Liam had already surpassed each and every prior relationship she'd ever had. People talked about love at first sight, soul mates, and Devon had always turned her nose up at the notion. There was no such thing. You just muddled through it until you found someone you could tolerate on a daily basis. All of her bitter, cynical convictions had taken a permanent vacation the second she'd dragged Liam out of that snowy field. He was the game changer.

"Mate." The word was as foreign to her as he was.

His hands began a wandering path along her bare skin. Devon's lids drifted shut and her head rolled back on her shoulders as he began an unhurried exploration, his touch feather-light. Chills rose to the surface of her flesh. It was an indulgent moment. Luxurious. His hands found the straps of her bra and he dragged them down the length of her arms before he discarded the garment beside him.

"Beautiful doesn't even begin to describe you, Devon." He cupped her breasts, brushed his thumbs over her taut nipples. The heat of his fingertips provided a sharp contrast to the chilly air that permeated her skin. Ripples of sensation danced through her nerve endings, racing down the length of her torso and settling as a deep thrum between her legs. An urgent need rose up inside of her and Devon stood. She missed the skin-to-skin contact immediately and hastily fumbled with the button of her jeans as she fought to free her feet from her boots.

Without a word, Liam reached for her. His hands gripped her hips, and in a movement so fast it made her head spin, repositioned her so that she lay on the couch. "You're killing me." His voice was a low growl that only intensified the slow pulse of blood that rushed to her clit. "If you get undressed any slower, I'm going to explode."

She let out a nervous laugh. "I've never been wound up like this before." Funny, she wasn't a bit embarrassed by the admission. "I can't get my brain to work right. It's like I can't remember how a damn button works."

The feral gleam returned to Liam's eyes. Hungry. Intense. It burned through her and made her breath come in quick, desperate pants. He jerked at the laces, pulling them loose before he slid her boots from her feet. Her socks were next—a quick tug and they joined her shirt on the floor. Her stomach twitched as his fingertips skimmed the waistband of her jeans. He plucked the button loose with no effort, worked the zipper down, and with a wide sweep of his arms, divested her of the denim and underwear in a single, artful swoop.

She grinned. "I take it you've done this in a hurry before?"

His gaze grew serious. "No. Make no mistake Devon, I've lived long enough to sow my oats and then some. But no woman, no female, will *ever* compare to you. You have no equal. I am yours and yours alone. I need you to understand that and know that these words are my vow. You are my mate. The finality of that is sacred. Do you understand me?"

"Yes." Fear vibrated through her. Not a fear of Liam, though. Not a fear of that intensity or the sanctity of the words he spoke to her. What she feared was her own reaction to that vow. A wave of relief that washed over her. A release. As though she'd waited her entire life to hear those words spoken specifically from him. A wish fulfilled. An odd and foreign sensation, but the rightness of it left her shaken. "I understand it completely," she said with wonder. "And I feel the exact same way." She couldn't explain it, but there it was. She was Liam's. He was hers.

It was a truth that she felt in the very pit of her soul.

Liam guided one leg over the back of the couch. Anticipation rippled through her as a rush of wetness spread between her thighs. He stood only long enough to kick off the black boots and remove the sheet. That he'd been willing to wear that ridiculous getup was proof enough that their bond was a serious thing to him. She couldn't imagine any man agreeing to do that for her. Then again, Liam Murphy wasn't a man, was he? He was something else entirely. And he'd pledged himself to her in the quiet dark.

Even in the low light, Devon could make out every inch of his naked body in glorious detail. His erection jutted proudly from his hips, complementing the strength of his powerful thighs and trim waist. He rested one knee on the couch cushion as he lowered himself to her. She expected him to settle his hips between her legs, but as his head dipped to her pussy,

Devon sucked in a surprised breath. His tongue lashed out at her clit, searing like a brand. Blinding pleasure washed over her and she marveled that she hadn't come from that very first contact.

"Oh my god, Liam. Don't stop." The words left her mouth in a desperate rush. She was already mindless with want, her control hanging on by a thread. Her hips thrust up to meet his mouth as he latched on and she cried out with the first earnest pass of his slippery tongue. Devon's back arched off the couch, her eyes squeezed shut. His tongue swirled over her clit in a slow, deliberate circle. Tension built over every inch of her body, her stomach curled into a ball, and she felt as though her body shrunk inside of itself. The sensation of his hotter-than-normal mouth over her sensitive flesh was more than she could stand. And when he took her clit fully into his mouth and sucked gently, Devon came apart in an instant.

Deep vibrations spread outward from her convulsing sex, through her abdomen, and up her torso. Shock waves pulsed through her breasts, into her tight aching nipples, her arms and legs. Her fingertips tingled as did her toes, and her cries of passion echoed off the walls that closed them in.

Never in her entire life had she ever felt anything like this. Tears pricked at Devon's eyes but she held them in. She'd never believed in magic until today. The truth of everything Liam had ever said to her, the truth of her own feelings and her body's response to him, resonated through her. She was lost. Ruined. He'd staked a claim on her in that moment and she had become irrevocably his.

Liam's wolf howled with satisfaction. His mate's pleasure was his. Her desires were his to sate. The taste of her on his tongue drove him mad with want and his cock throbbed almost painfully as the desperate need to take her grew to the point that his mind gave way to the haze of lust that sought to master him.

The mating urge brought the two halves of Liam's nature together in the same way that the full moon did. Reason gave way to instinct and his only thought was to take her, to join their bodies and solidify through that pairing the bond of the vows he'd spoken. Devon belonged to him. *Mine.* The wolf knew their mate and from this moment on, he'd decimate anything that sought to come between them. He would protect her with a ferocity that would incite fear. He would defend her with a tenacity that would weary even the most stubborn. *Mine.* The word resounded in Liam's mind over and over again until it became a mantra. *Mine.* She was his world. His entire universe. His sustenance, the air he breathed. She was the moon and he would forever answer her call.

Mine.

He came up on his knees and grabbed her firmly by the hips. A desperate growl gathered in his throat as he lowered himself to her and her hips came up to meet his as he thrust home. The warm, silky glide of her sex against his rigid cock sent Liam's head back on his shoulders as he let out a grunt of pleasure. She was so tight she squeezed him like a fist, her inner walls contracting greedily against his shaft as he buried himself as deep as he could go.

"Gods, Devon." His words came between pants of breath as he put his mouth to her ear. It was damn near impossible to force himself to stillness but he gave her a moment to adjust to his girth. She was so tight. So gods-damn wet that it nearly stole his ability to form a coherent thought. A sense of urgency rose within him and his stomach twisted into an unyielding knot as he pulled out slowly to the tip and plunged back in.

Devon's gasp ended on an indulgent moan that vibrated

through him and settled in his sac. He pulled out again, slowly, and drove home with the same painful precision. It was a sweet torture to keep such an unhurried pace, but Liam wanted to draw out her pleasure, coax a second orgasm from her so he could feel the evidence of it around his shaft. He wanted her to bathe him in the wet rush of her pleasure. Fuck, he *demanded* it from her.

"Come for me." His need to please her surpassed his own need for release. He couldn't get enough of the sound of her voice, her sweet, mewling cries, the chills that broke out on her skin at the moment the orgasm swept her up in its storm. Wind and snow buffeted the house, but the blizzard's intensity was nothing compared to the tempest that raged between them now. "I need to feel it. Need to feel you." The rhythm of his thrusts increased in speed as he angled her hips up and ground against her. Every thrust coaxed a low moan from her lips that sent him closer to the edge. He refused to topple over until she did, though. "Let me feel you come, Devon." He drew her earlobe into his mouth and sucked.

Her back came off the couch and she bit down on his shoulder as she came. The animal part of him reveled in the act and his own jaw longed to clamp down on tender flesh. The walls of her pussy squeezed him tight as her racking sobs filled his ears. A rush of wet warmth cascaded over his cock and Liam let out a violent shout as his own orgasm drew him into a swirling whirlwind of sensation that left him panting and shaken. He thrust hard and deep. His jaw clamped down and his muscles went rigid. He continued to pump his hips until she'd milked him dry then collapsed on top of her with a shuddering breath.

He'd never known such a sense of completion. His wolf purred with satisfaction. Power vibrated through him, an ancient magic that only a mate bond could evoke. It fortified his strength, nourished him mind, body, and soul. It grounded him and at the same time left him with a buzzing high that rushed through him like quicksilver. Liam thought he'd known magic. Thought he'd felt power. He knew the draw of the moon and the sway of its hold. None of it held a candle to what Devon did to him. The mate bond was truly extraordinary. The rarest of gifts. And he would be sure to nurture it until the day he drew his last breath.

The couch was impossibly small. It was a wonder they'd managed so well. Liam's body was longer than the frame and his knees bunched up against the armrest as he laid his cheek against the perfect swells of Devon's breasts. Her heartbeat rushed in his ears and his own matched its pace in perfect synchronicity. Long, silent moments passed, the only sounds that of the storm outside and their mingled breaths. *Bliss. Peace. Home. Mine.* The words played a loop in the primitive part of Liam's mind. *Complete.* He was finally whole and he had this amazing, accepting, trusting woman to thank for it.

"I don't even know how we're still on this couch," Devon said with a laugh. Her voice was low and husky. A breathy caress that coaxed chills to the surface of Liam's skin. He brushed the hair away from her face and lost himself in the beautiful hazel depths of her eyes. "There's no possible way you're comfortable right now."

"I could fit into a much smaller space if you needed me to," Liam replied. He put his mouth to hers for a slow kiss. "Just say the word."

Her answering laughter was like warm rain in the summer. "Honestly, it's a wonder you even fit in this house."

A chill shook her and Liam's brow furrowed. "Are you cold?"

"Are you kidding?" Her lips twitched with amusement. "I meant what I said earlier. With you around, I don't even need to build a fire. You're like a personal electric blanket. What's your average body temperature, anyway?"

Liam gave an unconcerned shrug. "Around one-ten, one-fifteen I think."

"Good lord!" Devon's head came up from the armrest. "Do doctors lose their shit when you go in for a checkup?"

Liam smiled. "Werewolf, love. We don't generally have a need for doctors."

He loved the way her gaze went liquid when he said "love."

"Right." She let out a chuff of laughter. "I forgot. I have so many questions. Like, how long do werewolves live? Do you seriously never get sick? And what about that whole silver bullet legend? Were you born? Made? And—oh my god!" Her eyes went wide as she came up off the couch. "We didn't use a condom! What were we thinking?"

He smoothed her hair, letting his thumb brush against her temple. "It's all right, Devon. Werewolves don't contract human diseases."

Her brows gathered over her eyes. "Yeah, well, what about little werewolf babies?"

"Only fertile the week before the full moon."

Her expression turned dubious, but her lips curved into a smile. "That totally sounds like a line to me."

"Ah, but I can't lie to you, *mate*." Her smile widened. "So you know it's not a line."

"Oh, you're smooth," she purred.

A very smug sense of male satisfaction swelled in Liam's chest. "Only when it comes to you, love."

"Sounds like another line," she remarked playfully. "But I'll take it."

Mac gave a frightened bark followed by a whimper as he turned his attention to the living-room window.

A sense of worry crept up Liam's spine and left him feeling chilled despite the warmth of his mate's body. In the aftermath of their passion, the two parts of his nature had become one. And with that union, his memories of last night came back in a violent rush that compressed the air from his lungs. A dangerous predator stalked him, and by association now stalked Devon as well. Instinct scratched at the back of his mind and his wolf let out a disconcerted whine. Evil was coming for them, and it was close.

CHAPTER 10

Liam's expression changed from playful to concerned in a beat.

"Liam?"

He stared blankly past her at the far wall as he concentrated on who knew what. Even Mac was a little riled up, whimpering as he paced from the living room into the kitchen and back again. Liam's nostrils flared as he inhaled a careful breath. Devon's heart leapt up into her throat and her mouth went dry. "Liam?" she said again. "What is it?"

"We shouldn't have come back here," he said more to himself than to her. "My scent is everywhere."

"What do you mean?" If she didn't get some answers soon, she was going to blow a gasket. "Why does it matter if your scent is here? What's going on?"

"We need to get back to Stanley. Right now."

Leave? Right now? This was crazy. Liam pushed himself off the couch. He reached down to grab Devon's hand and pulled her up to stand with so much force, her feet actually left the ground for a second. There was no doubt Liam was strong. More than capable to deliver an ass kicking to anyone who might have plans to hurt him. Something had him spooked though, and Devon didn't like it one bit.

"Liam, I don't even think the roads are open. You saw the

drifts when we drove home. The highway is almost snowed shut."

"We'll drive as far as we can and walk the rest of the way." His eyes flashed feral gold, which Devon had quickly learned happened in relation to intense emotion. "Get dressed. Your best boots, long underwear, hat, gloves . . . whatever you're going to need to keep warm. We need to be out of here in less than fifteen minutes."

Devon jerked her hand from Liam's grip. She dug her toes into the thick pile of the throw rug, determined to hold her ground. "No."

Liam's gaze narrowed. A deep groove cut into his forehead and his lips thinned. Shadows played on the angles of his face, making him look harder—and decidedly more dangerous. Devon's pulse skittered in her veins. She'd yet to see him angry and it was truly a terrifying sight. "I'm not playing games. Get ready to leave. Now."

"No." She could be as stubborn as he was frightening. "I can't leave Mac and I'm not stepping foot out of this cabin, into what is no doubt the worst storm of the year on the worst highway in the county, until you give me some answers!"

Liam let out an exasperated huff of breath. "Mac will be safe in the house. Safer, in fact, if we're not here. We don't have time for this."

Well, he was going to damn well make time. "Look, Liam. I might be your"—the word was still difficult to utter—"mate, but that doesn't make me your property." She'd been through that bullshit once and she vowed it would never happen again. "If you want me to do something, you're going to give me a good reason as to why I should do it. Otherwise, you can take yourself to Stanley, because I'm staying right here."

Liam's jaw clenched and he bared his teeth. The words "big, bad, wolf" came to mind, and Devon was pretty damn sure that even burly tough guys cowered under that wither-ing stare. Good thing she wasn't a guy. "He's coming, Devon. Get a move on."

"Who's coming?" She refused to be kept in the dark.

A muscle in Liam's cheek began to tic. He stared her down, as though sheer intimidation could prompt her to action. She met him look for look. One thing Liam would have to learn about Devon was that she'd gotten to the point in her life where she didn't take shit from anyone. And that included a high-handed werewolf who thought because she was his mate, she would follow orders without question.

His shoulders hunched as his expression transformed from anger to resignation. "I moved the pack from Colorado six months ago because a shifter named Christoph declared war on the pack. Rather than risk the pack's safety, I took the high road and left. Apparently he held his grudge and tracked us, because he jumped the pack last night on our hunting grounds outside of Stanley and dragged me to Lowman to finish me off. He'd thrown me across the highway into that field last night right before you drove by and hit the brakes. It seems you saved my life. And now, Christoph is on his way to finish what he started."

Even with everything she'd learned today, that was a lot to process.

"Gods." Liam dragged his splayed fingers through his hair. "He could have killed you last night."

The realization sent a shock of adrenaline into Devon's sys-tem. She'd been out there in the blizzard, alone, wrestling with Liam as she tried to get him out of the nearly waist-deep snow. She'd felt a presence somewhere in the darkness. Felt the weight of eyes on her. Her knees nearly buckled under her weight. By her association with Liam, she'd inadvertently been immersed in a very dangerous world. One she knew very little about.

"What will he do if he finds you?"

"In the state I'm in now? Kill me. And then he'll kill you."

The air left Devon's lungs as though sucked through a vacuum. She'd seen him as the wolf. His sheer size had been astounding. But she'd also witnessed the toll the transformation had taken on him. He said his strength waned with the moon. If Christoph found them here, they were as good as dead.

"Okay, Liam." She wasn't about to argue. Devon might be stubborn, but she wasn't stupid. "I'll get ready. I'm not sure how far we'll get, though. The roads are *bad*. But what about you?" She had the snow gear necessary to stay warm in the storm, but Liam had nothing. "You can't go out in my T-shirt and a sheet."

"I'll be fine."

"You won't be fine!" He might be the big, strong, Alpha werewolf, but even supernatural creatures had to eventually feel the cold. "You'll freeze to death."

Liam grabbed Devon's hand and guided her palm to his chest. The heat of his body scorched her. Okay, so his internal body temp ran a little hot. But that wasn't enough to protect him.

"A blizzard isn't going to put me down."

She wondered if arrogance was a werewolf trait or if it was just Liam. "Maybe not, but if you're cold, it's going to slow your heart rate. If your arms and legs are numb, it's going to slow you down. If you're hypothermic, it's going to affect your brain, heart, lungs, everything."

"It's not, because I'm not going to be walking around on two legs."

Worry tugged at Devon's chest and she folded her arms across her torso as though to protect herself from it. "You said that forcing the transition made you weak. I saw what it did to you. And I won't be able to communicate with you. How am I supposed to know what to do?"

She wasn't equipped to deal with this sort of situation. She'd just found out about the supernatural world. What if they got into trouble? Or more to the point, what if trouble found them? She didn't have the necessary knowledge to make a snap decision.

"Liam." Devon's own voice sounded foreign in her ears, small. "We could die out there."

His grim expression confirmed what she already knew. "Yeah. We could. But I'm not going to let that happen. You're going to have to trust me, Devon. I won't let anything happen to you."

A mated werewolf was a dangerous creature. Devon might have accepted the fact that there was a connection between them that couldn't be explained, but she didn't understand it. Her world wasn't his and until she was immersed in it, had the necessary time to learn and adjust to it, she was going to have to trust him.

"I want to, Liam." Her doubt soured the air. It riled his wolf and a growl gathered in his chest that Liam forced away. "But we have no idea what's going to happen once we step foot out this door. I'm scared." Her doubt was natural. Expected. It wasn't a reflection of her opinion of his capability to protect her. It spurred that instinctual part of him to squash that doubt. To prove to her that she would never have a reason to feel that way again. It made him even more determined to get them back to Stanley before the shit hit the fan.

"I know you're afraid"—and gods how it rankled—"but we're running out of time. It's true that we won't be able to communicate, but this is going to be simple. We're going to get in your

Jeep and drive. If we can't drive, we'll walk. The closer we get to my pack, the better."

"It's fifty miles, Liam." Fear shone in Devon's eyes, and cut through her soft expression. "You might be able to walk that in a blizzard, but I can't."

"I'll carry you if I have to." She opened her mouth to protest but he cut her off. "I'm strong enough to carry double your weight and then some. Your arguments are only wasting time. I'm going to keep you safe, Devon. I promise. Go get dressed. Now."

His wolf grew more agitated by the second. The animal part of him wanted to stand and fight. To face their enemy head-on and settle this business between them once and for all. The wolf didn't run. He didn't cower. Fierce. Fearless. Predator.

Werewolf.

The wolf pushed and Liam's body responded. His skin tightened on his frame and his bones creaked and cracked with the impending transition. The animal wouldn't be denied. It didn't matter that the moon was no longer full. He wanted control and he'd press his case until Liam gave it to him. But first, he needed to know that Devon would cooperate.

"Devon?"

"Your eyes are bright gold," she replied. "You're going to change, aren't you?"

"Not until I know you're going to go upstairs and get ready to go," he said.

"All right." The words came slow, as though she fought to say them. She turned and headed toward the bedroom. Liam watched her go, and she paused as her foot hit the first step. Devon looked over her shoulder at him and said, "I trust you," before she climbed the rest of the stairs to her room.

Thank gods. One obstacle overcome, only a couple more to go. The wolf surged in his psyche, scratching to be let out.

Liam's jaw clamped down tight as his femur snapped. He went to his knees, his panting breaths the only sound in the quiet dark. He could protect Devon better this way. He could protect them both better this way. A fresh wave of pain crashed over him and stars swam in Liam's vision. He squeezed his lids shut and his mind went blank as he gave himself over to the change.

Christoph would regret following the pack here.

Liam woke to his second consciousness. His headspace was different in this body, his perception of the world around him changed by the wolf and the magic that allowed him to become one with his animal half. His eyes opened and the dark interior of Devon's cabin came sharply into focus. In this form, his senses became even sharper. The sweet scent of his mate hit his nostrils and he drew in a deep breath as he let out an approving growl. She was incredibly fragile. Human. Mortal. Fallible. Until Liam could change that, he would decimate anyone or anything that tried to harm her. The moment his wolf had claimed her, Devon became his top priority. The only other thing that mattered this much to him was the safety of the pack that had pledged their loyalty to him.

He let out an impatient whine as he waited at the foot of the stairs for her. The fine hairs on Liam's undercoat stood on end. His scent covered every inch of the cabin and Devon's scent covered every inch of him. Even with the heavy winds of the storm, Christoph would easily find them. Their only hope was to get to the protection of the pack, not because Liam couldn't take the bear shifter on. In a fight, his strength was nearly equally matched with Christoph's. Liam had only one disadvantage and that was Devon.

"Liam, I'm ready to go."

He looked up to see Devon standing on the landing at the top of the staircase just outside her bedroom door. She was dressed for the storm in head-to-toe snow gear. Her puffy down coat swallowed her slight form and as she came down the stairs, the swoosh of fabric from her insulated ski pants alternated with the thick clunk of her boots. The clothes would keep her warm, but they would slow her down, make her even more susceptible to attack. A rush of anxiety-infused adrenaline coursed through Liam's veins. It would be a mad dash from here to Stanley and at best they'd be traveling at half speed.

Devon's eyes met his as she hit the bottom stair. She reached out a hand and laid it atop his head. Liam leaned into the contact, canting to one side as he reveled in his mate's touch for an indulgent moment before turning and heading for the front door. No words would be spoken between them until they reached his pack. Liam prayed that the bond between them was strong enough that words wouldn't be necessary. Otherwise, it was bound to be a very long night.

He headed for the door and turned when he realized Devon wasn't following. She changed course and headed for the kitchen. She yanked open the drawer and pulled out the Beretta before sliding it into her coat. She took her safety seriously and Liam was glad for it. Because things were bound to get a hell of a lot worse before they made it to Stanley.

Heavy, wet snow pelted the thick fur of Liam's coat. He dropped his head to shield his eyes as he waded toward the Jeep that was already almost buried to the grille in the accumulating drift. If Devon's driveway was this bad, he could only imagine how treacherous the highway would be. But they had to give it a shot and put as much distance between them and Lowman as possible before they set out on foot. Devon went to the passenger side of the Jeep and opened the door. Liam moved to hop inside but she put a staying hand on his shoulder.

"Are you okay?"

He offered his reassurance by nuzzling her face. Her mouth puckered and her gaze narrowed in a rueful expression. "I think you're just trying to placate me with sweet talk, but for now I'll take it."

Liam let out a slow sigh of relief as he hopped into the passenger seat. He'd absolutely been trying to placate her. He'd been worried they wouldn't be able to communicate, but Devon proved he had nothing to fear. Their bond was strong. She was his mate. They belonged to each other and Liam was going to make sure they stayed together for a good long while.

CHAPTER 11

They were in deep shit and Liam knew it. Devon tried not to let her nerves get the best of her as she closed the passenger door and rounded the Jeep to get in. She pulled off her gloves and stuck them in the center console before buckling her seat belt. Her fingers shook as she inserted the key into the ignition and turned it. Chilly air blasted from the vents but she didn't have time to sit around and wait for the engine to warm up. They were racing against time, the winter's worst storm, and a bear shifter who could apparently easily tear them both to shreds.

"Hang on," she said. "We're out of here."

She might as well have been driving in waist-deep sand. There was no way the county plows would be able to keep up with the accumulation and they'd be lucky if they made it five miles down the road, let alone the fifty to Stanley. Devon pulled out onto the highway, a death grip on the steering wheel. This was going to be the sort of harrowing, ass-clenching drive that made your muscles ache like you'd been in the gym lifting weights all day. *Stay loose, Devon.* Tension wasn't going to do her a damn bit of good.

With four-wheel drive and excellent snow tires, the Jeep handled well enough in the deep snow. As long as she kept her speed below forty miles per hour, the sometimes squirrelly vehicle was sound. That's not to say their slow speed didn't crank Devon's nerves up to a nearly unmanageable level. She was pretty sure Liam could get out and run as fast as they were driving.

Beside her, the hulking werewolf remained calm. It was almost comical the way he was crammed into the front seat, his boxy head pushing against the soft top of the roof. He was much wider than the seat and his massive front paws rested against the dash to brace the bulk of his body.

Dusk gave way to dark, further hindering Devon's ability to see the road ahead. It was slow going, but the Jeep continued to eat up the miles as she plowed through the drifts that gathered on the highway. She eased her foot off the gas, slowing to a near crawl to ensure she wouldn't get too far over on the shoulder of the road. If she did, the heavy snow would suck them in and they'd inevitably roll down the hundred-foot embankment to the icy river below. Devon wasn't sure if what they were doing was incredibly brave or very, very dangerous.

Up ahead her headlights reflected off the road sign confirming what she'd already known. "Shit." The gate across the section of Highway 21 known as Avalanche Alley had been shut down over the highway, prohibiting traffic from driving through. Devon flipped on her emergency flashers and pulled the Jeep to as safe a spot as possible on the side of the road. She shifted into park and killed the engine before turning to Liam. "Looks like this is where we get out."

They were still a good thirty miles from Stanley and the storm showed no signs of letting up. She grabbed her gloves from the center console and pulled them on, prepared to walk all night if she had to. She opened her door and turned to Liam. "Ready?"

He let out a loud chuff of breath in response before he climbed out behind her. For the past year Devon had led a ridiculously routine life. From home to the bar and back again, over and over, day by day, until she'd been pretty sure her Jeep could make the trip on autopilot. If anything, she could thank Liam Murphy for bringing a little excitement into her dull and routine life. The past twenty-four hours had definitely been ones for the record books.

They trudged through the snow for what felt like hours and still Devon was convinced they'd yet to cover a solid mile. She looked over at Liam who walked patiently beside her. "You should've left me at home," she shouted over the din of the storm. "All I'm doing is slowing you down!"

He let out an obnoxious snort that let her know exactly how he felt about her statement. Without warning he sprung into the air, the maneuver so effortless and graceful it made Devon's jaw drop. He came down into the snow directly in front of her and leaned down on his haunches. His head jerked toward his back, and Devon gave a firm shake of her head.

"No. No way. I'm not riding you like you're some kind of horse." There was no freaking way she was going to climb on his back like that.

Liam's lip pulled back to reveal the sharp points of his canines and he let out a warning growl.

"Liam," Devon implored. "I'm already slowing you down. There's no way you can haul my big ass around on your back."

Another snort. Apparently he wasn't taking any lip from her and likewise, he wasn't moving until she did as he wanted. High-handed, stubborn werewolf. Did he not realize how humiliating this would be for the both of them? Ugh. At least there wouldn't be any witnesses around to see it.

"Fine." Devon let out an exasperated huff of breath. "Only because we're in a hurry, and only because I know you won't take no for an answer."

His lips pulled back again and this time she swore the wolf

smiled at her. She rolled her eyes and pulled her beanie down tighter over her head to shield her ears from the biting wind. She put her arms around his massive neck and swung one leg over his back. "I know you're exhausted," she chided. "You're putting me down the second you're too tired to carry me." Liam bucked his head in the air, which she took as an acknowledgment. "Good. You're not the only one who can be stubborn, you know."

He made a sound that she swore was laughter. At least one of them had kept their sense of humor in this otherwise grim situation.

Liam stood as though Devon weighed nothing at all and took off at a slow lope that not only proved she'd been slowing him down, but that she'd greatly underestimated his strength. She bent her head low, letting his broad shoulders shield her from the storm. That Liam had transformed into a wolf of such an impressive size still astounded Devon. It violated the laws of physics and everything she knew about the world. No wonder the timber wolves had been scarce lately. Liam's pack had no doubt scared them all deep into the Sawtooth wilderness.

From her right, a massive black form plowed through the deep snow. Before her brain could make sense of what her eyes saw, the giant black bear crashed into them, launching Devon into the air. Her breath stalled in her chest as her world turned on its axis. Down was up and up was down as she landed head-first into a deep drift of snow.

The force of her landing buried her to the waist in the drift. Her lungs fought for a pull of air under the crushing weight of snow but it was impossible to take a breath. It wasn't a pile of powdery fluff that had cushioned Devon's landing. The wet sticky mess she'd been deposited in closed in around her like a straitjacket. Avalanches were common in this area and Devon had heard the horror stories of people being buried alive and suffocating to death under the weight of heavy wet snow. The odd angle at which she landed made her arms practically useless. She kicked with her legs, squirming and flailing in an effort to loosen the snow's hold from around her. The muted sounds of angry snarls, an enraged bellow, and an equally frightening growl made their way to Devon's ears. She drew on every ounce of strength she had, doubling her efforts to free herself. Somewhere close, maybe a few yards away, Liam was fighting for his life. And you could damn well bet that Devon was going to do everything in her power to help him.

Christoph plowed into Liam with enough force to dislocate his right shoulder. The searing pain ripped through him but he pushed it to the back of his mind. Devon had been thrown from his back and luckily the snow had cushioned her fall. Liam's sole objective now was to keep Christoph occupied and the bear's attention as far from Devon as possible.

Liam brought his nose up and sniffed the air. They were still miles from Stanley but close enough to their territory that he picked up a faint trace of the pack's scent. He drew in a deep breath and let out a long and mournful howl that echoed off the surrounding mountains. Owen or any other member of the pack could easily hear his call and come to his aid. He just had to hope someone was close and listening.

The fur along Liam's back rippled in an undulating wave as Christoph lumbered close. There was no doubt the shifter was determined to pick Liam off while he was still separated from the safety of his pack. Liam shifted, walking a half circle and putting Christoph's back to Devon. The bear's lips twitched, pulling back from incisors the size of daggers and just as sharp. If Christoph managed to get his massive jaw locked around Liam's throat, he was as good as dead. Liam couldn't afford for his opponent to make a plan of attack, so he did the only thing he could do: charge.

The deep snow made it difficult to get his footing, but Liam managed to find the momentum he needed to launch his body into the air. The pads of his paws slammed into Christoph's head, knocking the bear off-kilter. Whip-quick, Liam's head came around and his jaw latched on to the skin near Christoph's jugular. The bear let loose an angry roar as he came up on his back paws and thrashed his head to shake Liam's hold. The coppery tang of blood scented the air, further awakening the instinct of Liam's inner predator. It was the same all-consuming bloodlust he experienced during a full moon hunt. Liam gave himself over to that part of his nature that wanted to hunt, to fight, to kill. He leapt again at the bear's throat, this time locking his jaw down tight as he bit. Christoph thrashed and swiped at Liam with one giant paw. The wicked tips of his claws sank past the protective layer of thick fur into flesh, piercing Liam's skin.

It would do him no good to blindly fight. All they'd manage to do is hack and slash each other to bloodied messes. There could be only one victor and Liam was bound and determined to make sure Christoph didn't walk away from this fight. But he was weakened from the stress of a forced transition twice in the same day. Liam gave a violent shake of his head to clear the cobwebs from his mind and the lethargy from his weary limbs. He looked up to find Christoph's gaze focused on something over Liam's left shoulder. Fear stabbed at Liam's chest, cutting through muscle and bone as the bear lunged to its right and darted past Liam at a full run.

Devon.

Liam swung around and gave chase. Christoph's legs were longer, his body wider. He cut through the snow like a giant plow whereas Liam was forced to navigate the drifts with wide leaps and bounds. Bears were always perceived as clumsy and slow, but in reality they were quick and agile despite their size. Christoph could easily kill Devon with a single bite or swipe of a massive paw. Urgency spurred Liam forward and he pushed himself faster, until his muscles burned from the effort and his heavy breaths fogged the air.

He surged forward and clamped his jaw around Christoph's back leg, severing the tendon with his bite. The bear threw his head back and bellowed to the sky. It was a temporary wound, one that would quickly mend. It offered a momentary distraction however, and that's what Liam needed. He gave a violent jerk of his head, further tearing into Christoph's flesh. Liam twisted as though the hulking bear was nothing more than a doe and this was nothing more than the standard hunt. His three-hundred-pound prey went to the ground, and Liam used the opportunity to hurdle over him and get to Devon.

He raced toward her and without stopping bent his head down to take the back of her coat between his teeth. She let out a squeal of surprise as he scooped her out of the snow bank and sprinted toward the nearest tree.

"Liam!" He wanted to roll his eyes at her indignant tone. "Goddamn it, put me down! You're going to hurt yourself!"

If he had a voice to give to his thoughts, he'd remind her once again that he was the supernatural creature and she was the delicate human. A violent bear shifter was about to make her his next meal and she was worried about him hurting himself in the course of carrying her to safety. Infuriating. A loud roar echoed behind them, and Liam picked up his pace. Thirty yards separated them from a towering Douglas fir. Twenty yards. Ten. Five. Liam came up on his hind legs as he braced his front paws against the trunk. He lifted Devon toward the nearest branch, urging her to climb. Her eyes met his and her brow furrowed. Liam let out a frustrated growl and pushed her once again to the branch. *Climb, damn it!*

Devon's eyes went wide and she reached up to wrap her arms around the branch at the exact moment Christoph's jaw locked around Liam's torso. He watched, unconcerned with the pain that ripped through him, as her legs dangled and she struggled to get her body up on the branch. Liam lurched forward and the motion caused Christoph's incisors to cut deeper as he nudged Devon's feet with his snout to give her a boost. She managed to swing up and get her belly over the branch before swinging one leg over to straddle it.

With Devon's safety at least temporarily secured, Liam threw himself back into the fight. He twisted in Christoph's strong grip and managed to break loose the hold of his jaw. Blood pumped from the wound and Liam became light-headed. The skin tugged as the punctures and tears in his flesh began to heal but the blood loss had taken a toll. He braced his legs wide, thrashed his head to clear the fog, and pulled his lips back in an enraged snarl as he charged the bear and attacked.

What came next had no finesse. No coordination, no reason nor rhyme, no tactical sense. The fight was wild, desperate, violent. Claws dug through fur and dove into flesh; jaws snapped and teeth tore. Skulls met in a violent crack that resounded around them and made Liam's ears ring from the impact. Years of hatred and Christoph's twisted need for revenge fueled the fight. His need to see Liam dead kept him going even as he began to tire and lose the upper hand. Liam had told Devon that in a dangerous situation compassion was a person's worst enemy. Without brutal conviction, a second of hesitation could be your undoing. So why then did it make his stomach sour to know that Devon would watch as he ended Christoph's life?

He recalled her earlier fear, her anxiety, her trepidation. Their mate bond was so new, he worried how this act of violence would affect her. How it would affect her opinion of him. She didn't know this life, didn't know the rules of the supernatural world. Would she understand? Or would she see him as a monster?

That single moment of hesitation was all Christoph needed to land a deadly blow.

His wide paw swept toward Liam. His claws tore into the flesh at Liam's throat, ripping open three wide gashes and barely missing his jugular. Blood spurted from the wounds, painting the pristine white snow a grisly shade of crimson. This time, he wasn't sure he'd heal before he bled to death.

"Liam!"

The sound of Devon's panicked shout came to his ears as though through a long tunnel. He took a lunging step forward but his legs refused to carry the weight of his body another step. The snow cradled him as he collapsed. Tiny clouds of steam rose into the air above him with every labored breath that rattled in his chest. He refused to die here. Refused to leave this earth so soon after finding his mate. Christoph loomed above him and let out an arrogant chuff of breath. He came up on his hind legs, prepared to deliver the killing blow, when the report of a gunshot rang out, slicing through the silence like a crack of thunder.

A succession of loud pops followed, peppering Liam's ears like firecrackers. The scent of gunpowder scorched his nostrils and Liam watched as Christoph's massive paws came down on the snowy ground beside him. His vision blurred and a gauzy haze stretched over his mind as myriad howls joined the echo of gunshots.

Reinforcements had arrived and now it was time for Christoph to be afraid.

CHAPTER 12

The gun shook in Devon's hand. She'd shot it hundreds of times but never at a living target and never in the dark. All she'd known was that Liam was in trouble. She didn't think, didn't consider her actions, didn't weigh her options. The only thing she'd been certain of was that if she didn't shoot, he'd die. She'd made the decision before she'd even pulled the gun from her coat pocket.

Her aim wasn't stellar but she'd managed to strike the bear with at least three of the six shots she fired. Fifty percent sucked, but at least she'd managed to buy Liam a little time. Over the din of the storm a chorus of howls could be heard. Devon's heart beat a wild rhythm in her chest as fear transformed to hope. She hopped down from her perch, the snow cushioning her fall. Liam was hurt. He needed help. And she'd be damned if she didn't go to him when he needed her.

A pack of wolves burst through the tree line. They kicked up snow as they ran, fanning out as they emerged onto open ground. They rivaled Liam in size, in speed, and in strength. A pack of werewolves had answered their Alpha's call. It was a mesmerizing sight Devon knew she would never forget.

The bear was wounded but not immobilized. It let out an enraged bellow that gave Devon a start and sent her heart up into her throat. She sensed the animal's hatred, its loathing, as well as its fear. The bear wanted to stand and fight, to finish Liam off, but saw the pack approaching and knew his odds. He was injured and had no choice but to retreat. A part of Devon wished her aim had been better. Rather than put an end to Liam's troubles, she had a feeling the turn of events had just made them worse.

The wolves broke off into two groups. Five ran straight for Liam while the other four veered off to chase the bear. Devon wasn't quite as agile or quick as she waded through the deep snow to Liam. Her breath sawed in and out of her chest and her heart beat painfully against her ribs from stress and exertion.

"Liam!" She fell to her knees beside him. Her arms went around his wide neck as she pressed her face into the warm fur. The scent of blood turned her stomach and she swallowed hard against the bile that rose in her throat. The snow that surrounded him was painted in hues of black, brown, and gray, the blood that he'd spilled distorted by the ever-darkening night. It was a scene out of a horror movie, and tears pricked at Devon's eyes as she realized she might lose Liam after having only just found him.

"Oh my god. Liam, please." A desperate sob built in Devon's chest. "Please don't die."

Several warning growls stole Devon's attention. She looked up to find herself surrounded by giant wolves. Her protective instinct kicked in and she brought up her arm to point the gun in a wide sweeping semicircle. She had no reason to doubt this was Liam's pack, but that didn't mean she was going to let her guard down.

"I-I'm his mate," she stammered. If they were werewolves they'd have to understand her, right? And they'd know the implication of her words. If they were enemies . . . well, they were probably both about to die. In which case, she knew she'd done everything she could.

One of the wolves leaned in toward her. Its snout wrinkled as it ran its nose from her head down her torso and sniffed. As though satisfied, it turned to the others in the group before letting out a low howl.

Devon's left hand dove into Liam's fur. She kept the Beretta firmly in her right, her wary gaze trained on the many sets of feral eyes watching her. The wolves showed no signs of aggression but neither did they back down. Likewise, Devon planned to stay by Liam's side until she could be assured of his safety.

This would all be so much easier—albeit a little creepier— if the wolves could talk.

The waning moon peeked out from behind a break in the clouds and the jagged crowns of the distant Sawtooths, illuminating the snowy ground with a silvery light. The storm's rage had begun to calm. The wind no longer howled in her ears and fluffy white snowflakes drifted around her like goose down. Her eyesight failed her in the darkness, a disadvantage she knew the wolves didn't share. Several yards away, footsteps crunched in the snow and Devon's muscles bunched with nervous energy. Whoever was coming had better be ready for confrontation, because she wasn't going down without a fight.

"Gotta love a tough girl," a sardonic voice spoke from the darkness. "But unless there's silver ammo in that clip, it's not going to do you a whole hell of a lot of good."

Whoever he was, he didn't sound hostile. That didn't mean Devon was about to let her guard down. She and Liam hadn't covered silver bullets yet. For all she knew, the guy could be lying. "Maybe," she said. "Maybe not. I'm not opposed to doing a little myth busting if you come any closer without telling me who you are."

His amused laughter reminded her of Liam's. The knot in her stomach loosened but she didn't lower the gun. "I can't wait to hear the story of how you two got together." Devon wished she could see through the dark to put a face with the voice that spoke to her with familiarity. His lighthearted amusement quickly vanished as he asked, "How bad is he?"

He could be an enemy. Trying to get Devon to reveal something, to confirm Liam's weakened state. Her gut instinct didn't think so though, and she knew that Liam would encourage her to trust that feeling. "He's bleeding badly." Devon choked on the words as a fresh wave of fear clogged her throat. "I can't see the wounds. I don't know if he's healing."

The crunch of footsteps came closer. "I'm coming to check him out," the disembodied voice said. "But I'd feel a hell of a lot less twitchy if you'd lower that gun."

"Who are you?" Devon thought it odd that he was the only man in a group of wolves. Then again, she was sitting smack dab in the middle of them, too. Maybe this guy was someone's mate?

"Owen Courtney," he said.

"You're Liam's cousin?"

He laughed. "Looks like Liam's been busy the past twenty-four hours. Yeah, I'm his cousin." A tall form stepped into view just behind the semicircle of wolves. It was too dark to make out his features, but his stature certainly reminded her of Liam. "And you are . . . ?"

"Devon Kincaid," she replied. A sense of pride swelled in her chest as she lowered the gun to her side and said, "I'm Liam's mate."

Owen let out a low whistle. "Damn. 'Busy' is an understatement."

Owen walked past the barrier of large wolves. He squatted down beside her, and in the low light Devon took in the man who bore a resemblance to Liam. A sense of kinship rose within her and once again she trusted that instinct. "Is he going to be okay?" She brought her gaze up to Owen's and held it for a brief moment.

Silence descended as Owen bent over Liam's massive form. Devon's breath raced in her chest and her heart beat a mad rhythm against her rib cage as she waited for Owen to inspect Liam's injuries. A year seemed to pass in a matter of minutes before Owen leaned back on his knees and turned his attention back to Devon.

"He'll live." Relief squeezed the air from Devon's chest and she swallowed down the sob that threatened to escape her lips. "Reinforcements are on the way with snowmobiles," Owen said. "You'd think the Alpha would be the one to stay out of trouble. But Liam's always been the exception to the rule."

Devon liked Owen. She brushed her fingers through Liam's silky fur and said a silent prayer of thanks. It had been one hell of a day and she hoped it was going to get easier from here. She heard the buzz of snowmobile engines in the distance. She was exhausted, freezing, and didn't think she could take another step if she wanted to. "Is there room for me on one of those sleds?" she asked Owen.

He flashed a mischievous smile. "Liam would have my hide if I left his mate behind," he said with a laugh. "Welcome to the family, Devon. Hope you're prepared for a wild ride."

She didn't know if she was prepared or not but she'd give it her best shot. She returned his smile and hoped it offered some small reassurance. She'd do whatever it took to adjust to this new life. Anything for Liam.

For the second time in forty-eight hours, Liam woke in a bed he didn't remember putting himself into. This time, however, he wasn't alone. A warm body pressed against his back, one slender leg slung over his calf. He reached back and slid his palm over his mate's silky, naked flesh. She'd stayed by his side. Protected him. Devon had gone through the wringer and proved that she was strong enough, stalwart enough, and stubborn enough for this life.

Liam couldn't be more pleased.

She stirred beside him. It had been one hell of a night and he knew she was exhausted. Careful not to wake her, Liam eased her leg from on top of his and slid out from between the sheets. Dawn hadn't yet broken but already he heard the stirrings of someone in the kitchen on the ground floor. Liam eased open a dresser drawer and pulled out a pair of workout pants that he slipped on before heading downstairs.

Owen sat at the island bar in the center of the gourmet kitchen, working on a cup of coffee. Liam went to the cupboard and grabbed a mug to pour himself a cup. "I'd say you look like shit, but that would be an insult to shit," Owen remarked.

Liam snorted. "You'd know. Since you regularly aspire to look like shit."

Owen gave a humorless laugh. "The tracking party lost Christoph's trail. We'll find him, though. He won't be able to hide for long."

"The Boise County Sheriff was alerted to a dead man at Kirkham hot springs in Lowman yesterday. Colorado plates on his car. I haven't had time to investigate, but I'm thinking it was someone from the Elk Mountains Range Territory. One of their Sentries who'd been sent to fetch him."

"Shit." Owen's disgusted tone echoed Liam's own feelings. "Christoph is definitely calling you out."

"He'll come to us." The grim reality of their situation settled on Liam's chest like a stone. He'd brought this trouble to the pack's door and it was time to face the music. "Or more to the point, he'll come to me."

"Not before he makes you suffer." Owen's gaze met Liam's. "And now he has a way to cut you deep."

Devon. If any harm came to Liam's mate it would cut him

to the quick. Christoph knew this and he wouldn't waste any time delivering the blow.

"This is a disaster," Owen said. "You know that, right?"

Liam raked his fingers through the length of his hair. He was still sore from the injuries he'd sustained last night but it was a drop in the bucket compared to what Christoph could do to him if he managed to get his hands on Devon. "She's safe here," Liam said. "We can protect her here."

Owen scoffed. "She's not safe anywhere and you know it."

It was a hard truth he didn't want to admit, but Owen was right. Until Christoph was dead, Devon would never be safe.

"She's tough, I'll give her that," Owen said. Liam took a seat on the bar stool next to his cousin and stared down into his cup. "She has no idea what you're going to ask of her, does she?"

"No." A human would never survive in their world. It was too wild. Too violent. And much too dangerous. The only way Devon would make it was to become a werewolf.

Owen's gaze slid to the side. "What if she chooses to remain human?"

Liam sipped from his mug. That choice had been taken from her the moment Liam's wolf recognized her as his mate. "She'll come around." Liam's eyes drifted shut for a moment. Hell, even he didn't believe Devon would ever come to terms with her inability to control her fate, despite the inevitability of it.

"You'd better hope so," Owen said. "And soon. I can guarantee you Christoph isn't going to give us much of a breather. And you can bet he's going to bring reinforcements next time."

Owen was right. The shifter wouldn't give them time to regroup or lick their wounds. There would be no grace period. No time for Devon to weigh and contemplate her decisions. She might grow to hate him for forcing this life on her, but it was a chance Liam had to take. He'd suffer her hatred. He'd suffer whatever the hell he had to in order to keep her alive.

"We'll be ready for him," Liam said. "No more running. No more hiding. This has to end."

"Finally." Owen held up his mug in a silent toast. "You're a shitty diplomat anyway, and a much better warrior."

It was an unfortunate truth. Liam had always thrived on the battlefield. He'd never been much of a negotiator, and Devon would soon learn that when Liam made a decision he expected his orders to be obeyed. He'd do what he could to convince her. To woo her. To assuage her fears. At least as a werewolf, Liam would be afforded the opportunity to wait out her anger whether it took years or decades. As a human, all Liam would be guaranteed was his mate's death.

The rest of the morning passed in silence, both Liam and Owen lost in their individual thoughts. It wouldn't be long before the rest of the pack began to stir for the day and the quiet calm he felt right now would evaporate under a flurry of activity.

"Good morning."

Liam looked up to find Devon standing at the edge of the kitchen. She wore her long underwear and a T-shirt. Her mahogany, sleep-tousled hair framed her face. She gave him a wan smile and her hazel eyes still bore a weary glaze. It was a good thing she was strong, because Devon's trials were only about to begin.

"And that's my cue to GTFO." Owen gave Liam a playful knock on the shoulder as he pushed out his bar stool. He crossed the expanse of the kitchen to where Devon stood. "Morning," he said with a wink as he walked out of the room and left Liam alone with his mate.

"He looks a little like you." Devon shuffled farther into the kitchen, her expression unsure. Liam left his perch to cross the kitchen and retrieve another mug from the cupboard. He poured Devon a cup of coffee and set it in front of her along with cream and sugar, much like she'd done for him just yesterday.

"Our fathers were brothers," Liam remarked. "I'm better-looking though, right?"

Devon smile didn't quite reach her eyes. "He got away, didn't he? Christoph."

Her fear soured the air and Liam's nose wrinkled. Making her a werewolf was the only option. There was no other way. "He did," Liam said. "But you have nothing to worry about, love. I promised you I'd keep you safe and I meant it."

Devon turned to face him. She reached up and cupped his cheek in her palm. Liam leaned into the contact and allowed the comfort of his mate's touch to wash over him. "Who's going to protect you?" she asked ruefully.

Liam reached up and placed his hand over hers before bringing her palm to his chest. He placed it over his heart and kept his gaze locked with hers. "You will," he assured her. "Has anyone ever told you you're a pretty good shot?"

A half smile flirted with her full lips. "You're trying to placate me again, aren't you?"

"That depends," Liam said. "Is it working?"

Devon smile grew. "For now," she replied. "But only because I'm too exhausted to argue."

Liam bent his head to hers and kissed her once. Slowly. He pulled away to find her expression soft and a spark of heat ignited in her hazel eyes. Their trials were only about to begin. Until then, Liam wanted Devon happy. "Let's go back to bed." His body responded to the sweet scent of her desire. "I want to show you my appreciation for saving my life last night."

Devon's hand fell from his chest to the waistband of his workout pants. Her fingers dipped below the fabric and Liam sucked in a breath. "This is becoming a habit, you know," she teased. "Me saving your life. If you're not careful you're going to be indentured to me."

Liam would take these pleasant, peaceful moments with her while he could. Soon enough, her affection would turn to anger. "I'm already yours," he replied. "Let me take you to bed and prove it to you, mate."

"Mmmmm." Devon's approving hum vibrated over Liam's skin. "I can't think of a better way to spend a morning."

Their lips met again, and Liam's tongue darted out to taste her. "Neither can I," he said against her mouth. "Or a better way to spend an afternoon."

Devon smiled. The expression was pure seduction. "Lofty goals," she said. "You had a rough night. Think you're up for it?"

He took her in his arms and she melted against him. He couldn't quash the fear that shot through his chest like the scorch of a silver bullet. He'd spend the day making love to her, solidifying their bond. The road ahead was a bumpy one and he needed every advantage he could get. "Oh, I'm up for it. I'm stronger than you think."

"Yes, you are," Devon said with a wicked grin. "Come on, werewolf. Take me back to bed and show me how strong you are."

She didn't have to ask twice. Devon squealed with delight as Liam scooped her up into his arms. His mouth met hers in a ravenous kiss. He'd spend today like tomorrow didn't exist. Today was for pleasure. For happiness. For the sheer joy of being alive. Tomorrow, they'd begin to face their trials. And Liam would make sure that they faced them together.

He'd do whatever it took to keep Devon.

He refused to let her go.

CHAPTER 13

"Well, that's one way to spend an afternoon."

Devon rolled to her side and molded her back to Liam's chest. His arms came around her, holding her tight, and she let out a contented sigh. They'd spent the rest of the morning and the entire afternoon in Liam's bed. His appetite for her was as voracious as hers was for him and it seemed that neither of them could get enough. She'd never wasted the day away with round after round of intense, passionate sex before. Being with a werewolf definitely had its merits. Still, she couldn't shake the feeling that Liam was somehow trying to distract her. They'd yet to talk about what had happened last night. One of them was going to have to broach the subject and she guessed it would have to be her.

"He got away. Christoph."

Devon wasn't so foolish as to believe that last night's attack would be the end of it. It was only a matter of time before shit hit the fan again and she wanted to be as prepared for it as possible.

Liam stiffened behind her and his arms tightened around her. He put his lips to the back of her head and whispered into her hair, "He did."

"He'll be back." It wasn't a question of if, but when.

"Yes."

"Why?" If Devon was a part of this now, she needed to know everything. "What happened between the two of you that he'd follow you across two states to keep his vendetta alive?"

Silence stretched between them. Tension thickened the air with every passing second and Devon fought to take a breath deep enough to calm her racing heart. Whatever had happened between them, it wasn't some petty thing. Devon didn't know how much more quiet she could take before she snapped.

"I killed his sister."

The admission hung in the air before settling its weight atop Devon's chest. Fear skittered along her spine and her muscles grew taut. She was perfectly aware of the fact that Liam could be formidable. But was he dangerous? The part of her that felt so at ease with him argued with that part of her brain fueled by the fear of her past experiences. She opened her mouth to speak, to try to further the conversation and get some answers, but the words froze on her tongue.

"It was an accident." Grief accented Liam's words and squeezed Devon's heart. "I'd been tasked with ousting a rogue werewolf that was stirring up trouble in the Elk Mountains Range Territory. Trisha had worked the territory in the past and was familiar with the area. I brought her along as a guide. We got sloppy and the rogue jumped us. He got Trisha with a silver bullet in the head. There wasn't anything I could do to save her."

Devon wrapped her hands around Liam's and squeezed. His entire existence was so foreign to her. So violent. She didn't know if it was the sort of life she could be a part of. "It was your job to get rid of him?"

"More or less. I was the Alpha of the designated territory. According to our law, it was my responsibility to take care of the encroachment. Trisha had no business being out there. But the rogue kept to the fringe of the pack's territory and I knew she hunted that area. I'm responsible for her death. Christoph's need for vengeance is certainly justified."

"It was an accident." Devon might not have understood his world, but she certainly understood the circumstances of what had happened. "You had no idea that would happen."

"No," Liam admitted. "But I knew the risks. I knew the rogue was dangerous and I put Trisha in that situation."

"You didn't." How long had he carried this burden of guilt? "You didn't force her to go with you. She went willingly. She obviously recognized the danger and the risk and made her decision anyway. That's not on you, Liam."

"I asked her to go."

"And she could have said no."

Devon turned in Liam's arms to face him. "Whatever happened, Christoph's sense of vengeance is misplaced. It wasn't an accident, but it was under no circumstances your fault."

"What you or I believe doesn't matter." Liam's gaze delved into hers. "Christoph won't stop until he's had his pound of flesh. If he can't get to me, he'll get to the next best thing."

Devon didn't have to guess what that was. "Me."

Liam's eyes burned with gold. "Exactly. Which is why . . ."

His pause sent a shiver down Devon's spine. "What, Liam?"

He let out a breath. "Why you need to become a werewolf."

Come again? Devon's breath stalled in her chest. She didn't even realize it was a possibility and certainly not an idea she'd entertained since meeting Liam. "No." The word burst from her lips before she could think better of it. "Liam." How could he possibly ask that of her? "No."

His brows gathered over his eyes, part frustration, part hurt. "It's the only way to ensure you're strong enough. It's the only way to protect you." Liam paused. "Is what I am so unsavory to you?"

"Of course not." Could he not understand the position he'd

just put her in? The decision he expected her to make on a moment's notice? "But Liam, you can't just expect me to jump in headfirst and agree to something I know nothing about. What you're talking about isn't something as simple as moving in together. You're suggesting I change not only who, but *what* I am."

"I would never ask you to do anything that would harm you or change *who* you are."

Devon swallowed against the lump in her throat. "How is it done?"

"A single bite is all it takes. I won't allow anyone but me to turn you and I'll see you through the transition. It'll be difficult at first, but I promise you, I would never ask this of you if I thought it would cause you prolonged pain or distress. It's a necessity, Devon. For our bond, for your safety." He gave a gentle laugh. "For my sanity."

Whatever this was—the bond or connection—between them had hit Devon so fast she hadn't really given herself time to contemplate what the dynamics of a relationship with Liam might be.

"How long have you been a werewolf?" There was so much she *didn't* know about him. How could she possibly agree to forever?

"Four hundred years."

The air left Devon's chest in a whoosh. "Four hundred years?" That sort of life span was incomprehensible to her. If she allowed Liam to do this to her, everyone she knew would be long dead while she lived on. "How can you possibly keep your existence a secret from the world?" People were bound to notice that he didn't age.

"We keep to ourselves, relocate when it becomes a necessity. We age, Devon, just slowly."

Relocate? She'd been reluctant to run from the life she'd

built for herself a year ago. It had taken months for her to make new friends and get comfortable in this tiny town. Now Liam was telling her that she'd be required to throw away any relationships she'd built and pull up camp every several years in order to keep the secret of their supernatural existence?

"I need to get out of here. I'm sorry, Liam, but I've got to go home."

Devon was on the verge of a full-on panic attack. Her heart raced in her chest, her breaths quickened. Her eyes went wide with distress and her skin became cold and clammy. His mate was in distress and he'd been the cause of it. Liam's wolf let out a warning snarl in the back of his mind. They couldn't control their mate any more than they could control the wind and it worried both of them. Liam had told Owen that Devon had no choice in the matter of her turning, but deep down, he knew that trying to force her would only drive her away. The logical part of his brain told him to trust in their bond and give her the time she needed to adjust. But the overprotective Alpha side of his nature urged him to keep her here and refuse to let her leave.

Making Devon a prisoner wouldn't do anything to foster trust between them. But letting her go when the very real threat of Christoph's presence still loomed only invited disaster. Gods. Liam had never felt so damn torn, and considering his dual nature, that was saying something.

"Christoph is unaccounted for. He could be anywhere. Devon please, reconsider—"

"No." Her firm response cut him off. "I need some time to think and I can't do that here. Not when being with you clouds my thoughts and influences my judgment."

It would kill him to let her go, but if he didn't give her a little space, it might cause irreparable damage between them. Liam wasn't simply going to put her in her Jeep and send her on her way, however. "Fine. But I'm sending Owen with you."

"Liam, I don't need a babysitter."

The hell she didn't. "I won't be moved on this, Devon. Your safety comes before even that of the pack. I appreciate your need for a little space and time to think, but I can't let you leave here unprotected. You saw Christoph with your own eyes last night. You know what he's capable of. Owen will go with you. Period."

"I don't like being told what to do." She looked away but he saw the resignation in her expression. He trusted Owen with his own life and could think of no one better to watch over his mate.

"You're mated to an Alpha werewolf," Liam replied. "I'm afraid you won't be able to avoid a little high-handedness now and then."

"Liam." Her voice trembled on the word. "You need to know something. I left Corvallis because I was in a relationship with someone who thought he could control every aspect of my life and treat me like property. I left my life behind to get away from him because he couldn't let me go. I can't live like that again. I won't."

Jesus. Liam's chest constricted and he resisted the urge to rub the tightness away. Her tone, demeanor, and scent told Liam everything he needed to know about that previous relationship. Whoever he was, he'd put her through hell. The wolf let out a warning growl. When they found out who he was, they'd make him pay.

Later. They had bigger problems to worry about right now. If Liam could eliminate the imminent threat of Christoph's revenge, he could give Devon more time to come to terms with what her life was about to become. Perhaps by sending her home with Owen to watch over her, it would give Liam the time he needed to track his prey. When this business with Christoph was settled, Liam could be afforded the opportunity to settle into his bond with Devon rather than force it.

"I understand." Liam held her close, knowing it would be the last time he felt his mate's naked skin against his until she returned to him of her own free will or Christoph was dead. His wolf let out a forlorn howl in the back of his mind. "And I promise you, Devon, I won't do anything to ever give you reason to think that I consider you nothing more than a possession. I'm sending Owen back with you because your safety is tantamount to my own sanity. Nothing more."

She gave a slight nod of her head. "I believe you."

"There's a break in the storm. The roads should be plowed by now. Owen can drive you to the Jeep and he'll follow you home from there." Gods, he didn't want to let her go. But their bond was fragile and Liam knew he had no choice. "When it's safe, and if you want me to, I'll come to you."

Devon tilted her head up to his and kissed him once. "Of course I do. I'm not trying to push you away. I just need some time."

Liam would do whatever was in his power to give her that. "Get dressed." Letting her leave was like ripping one of his limbs from its socket, but Liam had no choice but to give her what she needed. "I want you on the highway before the sun sets and I don't want you caught in another storm." His arms released their hold and it took a sheer act of will for Liam to turn away from her and get out of bed. "I need to get Owen situated before you leave. I'll meet you down in the kitchen in twenty minutes."

Liam quickly dressed, careful to keep his attention from Devon. If he allowed himself to turn and look at her, naked and tousled in his bed, he'd be tempted to go against his word and keep her here whether she wanted to stay or not.

He grabbed his phone and fired off a text to Owen and headed for the kitchen. Aside from the large main house, the property was dotted with many tiny cabins that housed pack members. They were a tight-knit group but there was definitely such a thing as too much togetherness. Owen was already waiting for him by the time he got to the bottom of the staircase.

"What's up?"

Liam rolled his shoulders to release some of the tension that pulled his muscles taut. "I need you to do something for me."

Owen pushed away from the counter, his posture ramrod straight and his expression serious. "Say the word and it's done."

One of the things Liam appreciated about Owen was that he didn't fuck around when it came to pack business. And as the Alpha's mate, Devon's safety was at the top of that list. "Good, because daylight's burning and I want you out of here in twenty minutes."

"All right." Owen folded his arms across his wide chest. "Where am I going?"

"Lowman. With Devon."

A mischievous light glinted in Owen's eyes. "Road trip," he said with a grin. "Excellent."

Liam sighed. Gods, he hoped this was a good idea.

CHAPTER 14

"So I take it Liam dropped the bomb, huh?"

Devon glanced at Owen from the corner of her eye. The Toyota pickup negotiated the snowy road with ease as they headed northeast on Highway 21 to where her Jeep was hopefully still parked at the gate to Avalanche Alley. He reminded her so much of Liam if maybe a little more . . . subdued. Easygoing. "I'm not sure I know what you mean." She knew exactly what he meant, but she wasn't sure she wanted to discuss the mandate Liam had given her with his cousin.

"Uh-huh." Owen's skeptical tone coaxed a smile to Devon's lips. "You're forgetting who you're sitting beside, tiny human." He tapped the side of his nose. "Superior werewolf senses. Insta-lie detector."

Tiny human? Devon snorted. "He dropped the bomb, all right."

"It's a lot to process," Owen said. "I can only imagine how well that conversation went."

"Trying to reason with someone who's used to being obeyed without question is a little frustrating," Devon replied.

"That's an understatement," Owen said with a laugh.

Devon cleared her throat and turned in her seat to face Owen. "What's it like?" Somehow, it was easier to talk to someone other than Liam about it. Owen was basically a stranger and she didn't feel as vulnerable and raw with him as she did with Liam. She could have a conversation that didn't devolve into a heated debate ruled by emotion.

"Honestly?" Owen gave her a quick glance before turning his attention back to the road. "It's fucking awesome."

Devon found herself wishing she possessed werewolf senses right about now so she'd know whether or not Owen was being truthful or trying to make the sale in order to help Liam. "Really? Because I saw Liam change and it didn't look like it felt very awesome."

Owen let out a slow sigh. A few quiet moments passed and Devon let him gather his thoughts. "Look, it's not a cakewalk. I won't lie to you. But we rarely transition outside of the full moon. A full moon transition is virtually painless. And it takes a while to get used to having a second consciousness, but after a while, you don't even notice it."

"Second consciousness?"

Owen tapped his forehead. "The wolf. It's invasive at first and the animal is pushy and insistent. But soon, you learn to communicate, to not fight each other. To cohabit the time and space you share without resistance. The wolf makes us stronger. We're resistant to disease, we age so slowly we might as well be immortal. The only thing that can kill us is silver or to take our heads from our bodies. Not a bad deal if you ask me."

"What about everyone you leave behind?" It had been the one aspect of Liam's mandate that had bothered Devon the most. "The people who grow old and die? Your family?"

"I won't sugarcoat it. It'll hurt like hell for the first hundred years or so. After that . . . your perception of time will change. Human lives are *so* short. They pass in the blink of an eye. Why do you think Liam is so anxious to turn you? The pack becomes your family and you learn not to form attachments to fragile things."

It made sense. Devon understood why Liam would want her to become a werewolf. She supposed in his position, she'd want the same.

"Think about a tiny house fly," Owen said. "It lives for what—a few weeks before it dies? Do you pay much attention to it? Does its existence weigh on you? Do you become attached to it?"

"No." Devon supposed she'd never really thought of it before. "I guess not."

"It's sort of the same concept with humans."

Not a very cheery thought. "I don't want to be like that." Devon turned her attention out the window. "I don't want to become callous or uncaring."

"You won't." Owen's reassuring tone didn't do much to assuage her fears. "You'll still care. But their short life spans won't trouble you. Their deaths won't weigh on you."

So much to think about.

"Devon." Owen's voice went low and serious. "The pack dynamic is like nothing you've ever experienced. It's powerful. The sense of belonging—of being a part of something bigger than you—it's amazing."

"So you're saying it's worth it?"

"It was for me," Owen replied. "But only you can determine if it's worth it to you."

The recently plowed roads made the drive from Stanley much quicker than it had been last night. They reached Avalanche Alley in under an hour and Devon's Jeep was still parked on the side of the road, thankfully not buried in snow thrown by the county plow. She said a silent thanks that when Kelly had plowed he hadn't buried her vehicle, but it also meant that he'd be wondering where she was and how her Jeep got there. She'd have to check in with him when she got a chance so he knew she was okay.

"Looks like that's your ride." Owen pulled over to the side of the road and brought his pickup to a stop. "I'll follow you back to your place."

Devon got out of the pickup. "Sounds good. My place isn't far from here, fifteen minutes or so."

Owen nodded and flashed a playful smile. "See ya at the homestead."

Devon's mouth formed a reluctant smile. She liked Owen. She had a feeling she'd like the rest of Liam's pack just as much.

She unlocked the Jeep and climbed into the chilly cab. Steamy clouds of breath fogged the interior as she started the engine and gave it a few minutes to warm up. When warm air finally rushed from the heater vents to thaw the windshield, Devon turned on her wipers and pulled out onto the highway. Next stop: home. She had *a lot* of thinking to do . . .

Devon's mind raced as the Jeep ate up the snow-covered pavement toward her cabin. She wanted Liam, no doubt about it. And she felt a connection to him that went way beyond casual interest. It was like they'd known each other for a lifetime. He could protect her. From anyone and anything. He'd said as much. She could be happy with Liam. She knew she could. All she had to do was agree to let him irrevocably change her . . .

A hulking black form darted across the highway and slammed into the passenger side of the Jeep. The vehicle lurched and Devon hit the brakes but it did little good as the boxy vehicle was pushed off the side of the road and down a narrow embankment. She braced herself as it rolled onto its side and then its roof before righting itself and stopping with a groan of metal. The radiator hissed and steam billowed from the hood.

Stunned and a little too dazed to form a coherent thought, it took three tries before Devon could unfasten her seat belt. The driver's side door was ripped from the hinges at the exact same moment and her vision was filled with a massive black head with powerful jaws and quivering lips that pulled back to reveal dagger-sharp teeth.

Christoph. Shit.

Running away from Liam was obviously the biggest mistake of her life.

Liam brought his truck to a skidding stop as he watched the massive bear push Devon's Jeep off the embankment. A scouting party had found Christoph's massive tracks in the fresh snow near the highway heading northeast not long after Devon and Owen had left. He'd wasted no time in jumping in his truck and racing toward Lowman. He never should have let her leave. He'd known Christoph would want to hit Liam where it hurt. An eye for an eye. Liam had gotten his sister killed. What better revenge than taking the life of Liam's mate?

"Liam!"

Owen jumped out of his own pickup and raced toward him, his eyes wide with alarm. He was ready to run headlong down the embankment when Liam reached out to snag his cousin by the coat to stop him.

"Don't!" Liam's own urgency to act warred with common sense. "We can't give him a reason to hurt her." The words soured in Liam's mouth. Hurt her? Christoph wanted to kill her.

A transition right now was out of the question. The time it would take to suffer through the painful shift would leave Devon unprotected for far too long. The Jeep rolled once down the short hill and came to a bouncing stop on its tires. Liam's wolf let out a mournful howl in his psyche as Christoph tore the driver's side door from the vehicle and locked his jaws around Devon's shoulder as he pulled her from the cab.

"Christoph!" The male's name was a battle cry as it tore from Liam's throat.

The giant bear dropped Devon in the snow and pinned her in place with one massive paw. Liam took a lurching step forward and froze. The animal's claws rested at Devon's throat. All he had to do was flex his paw and she'd be dead. Liam's wolf let out an enraged snarl in the back of his mind. Neither of them enjoyed feeling helpless. Inaction went against their very nature as Alpha.

With no effort, the bear shed its animal form to reveal the male who'd tracked Liam for months and across three states to seek his vengeance. Christoph grabbed Devon by the collar of her coat and hauled her against his naked body as though she was nothing more than a ragdoll. His lip curled back in a cruel sneer as he jerked his head toward Liam.

"I think I found something that belongs to you! You have a nasty habit of endangering those entrusted to your care!"

A growl built in Liam's chest. Blood trickled from a split at Devon's temple and the skin there was swollen and already beginning to bruise. The embankment was only thirty or so feet, but it was enough to have totaled her Jeep when it rolled. Liam could only imagine what damage had been done to his mate in the crash.

"What stands between us has nothing to do with you, Christoph!" Liam shouted. "Let her go and we'll settle this."

"There's nothing to settle." Christoph's voice grated with emotion as he wrapped his fingers around Devon's throat. Her eyes went wide with panic and Liam fought the urge to charge through the snow to her. "You killed my sister!" Christoph railed. "And as repayment, I'm going to kill this human who reeks of your scent."

Liam refused to stand by and watch Christoph snap Devon's neck. He launched himself down the embankment and crashed into Christoph's left shoulder taking him and Devon both down into the snow. They were both unarmed, but Christoph had the upper hand in that he could shift into his bear form at a moment's notice while Liam was confined to his human one. He'd last far longer in a fight than Devon would, however, and so he'd take the beating of his life if that's what would keep Christoph's attention from her.

Anything to ensure her safety.

Liam seized Christoph by the arms. He wedged his booted feet against the male's stomach and sent him flying into the air. Snow scattered in a white cloud as he landed a good twenty yards from Devon, giving Liam some much needed breathing room. He left his mate's care to Owen and focused his attention on Christoph who quickly abandoned his human form for the much larger and more formidable bear. Liam took a fighting stance. He was at a serious disadvantage. The odds were good that Christoph would kill him and all he could hope was that Owen would get Devon to safety before anything happened to her.

"I should have known you wouldn't fight me on equal footing!" Liam shouted at the bear. "You know I'd kick your ass hand-to-hand!"

It might have been stupid to goad him but Liam wanted his mind clouded with rage in order to help level the playing field. The bear let out an angry bellow that coaxed a territorial growl to Liam's chest. Christoph was entitled to his grief and need for revenge. Perhaps if Liam had nothing to live for, he would have let Christoph kill him. Now, though, it was different. He had everything to live for.

His wolf refused to bow.

Liam braced himself for impact as Christoph charged. Somewhere behind him, Devon shouted. A frightened, weary cry that speared his heart and threatened to steal his focus. "Liam! Run!"

Devon would see firsthand that he never backed down. It went against an Alpha's nature. He'd fight until he had nothing left to give. He didn't know how to quit. And now that he'd found his mate, Liam's tenacity only intensified.

Christoph barreled into him. Liam took the brunt of the attack with ease and managed to stay on his feet while avoiding the bear's massive snapping jaw. The bear had at least three feet of height and about two hundred pounds on him, but Liam's supernatural strength gave him an equal chance in the fight.

Ego convinced Liam he had a fighting chance against Christoph. Reality swooped in to give him the smackdown in the form of a serving platter–sized paw. White-hot pain shot through him as Christoph's dagger-like claws sank into Liam's torso. His back arched as the bear's weight overpowered him and they both tumbled down into the deep snow in a tangle of fur, claws, and thrown punches.

Liam was preternaturally strong. Fast. His wounds healed quickly and his body was stalwart enough to sustain massive amounts of damage. None of that mattered against a foe whose strength not only equaled, but in this case, surpassed his. Christoph's teeth broke the skin as he bit down on Liam's shoulder, and he let out a pained shout. The bear bellowed and swiped at him again with his paw, opening four deep gashes in Liam's chest. In the distance, Owen called out for Devon to keep moving while she argued, demanding that he let her help Liam. Gods, he hoped that Owen got her the hell out of here. Because he was pretty damned sure Christoph was about to get his revenge.

Myriad voices shouted from the highway drawing Christoph's attention. Liam used the distraction to his advantage and kicked the bulk of the bear's weight from his body so he could roll away. He came to his feet as a dozen Sentries rushed down the embankment toward them, weapons drawn and at the ready. The supernatural world's enforcement squad took justice seriously. Liam knew firsthand, since he'd once been a member of their ranks. They hit Christoph with stun guns designed to take a supernatural creature down. Fueled by rage and his need for revenge, the bear didn't go down easily. He let out a vicious bellow as he fought against the dozen Sentries who tried to subdue him. They hit him again and again until he came down onto all four legs and shed his animal form. Christoph writhed in pain. He let out an angered shout that echoed off the surrounding mountains as he was surrounded by Sentries on all sides.

"Christoph Martineau," one of the Sentries said. "You are remanded to the custody of the Sawtooth Territory Judiciary for extradition to Colorado." The supernatural world operated under different laws than that of humanity. Christoph wasn't read his rights. He had no rights. The Sentries bound him in silver shackles and without another word hauled him past Liam and up the embankment to where their vehicles were parked by the side of the road.

Liam's knees gave out and he collapsed into the snow. He looked up to see Devon break away from Owen's grip and he watched as she trudged through the deep snow toward him. A cry of relief escaped her lips as she collapsed into the snow beside him and threw her arms around him.

"Oh my god! Liam . . ." Her words died on a hitched sob. "I thought you—I thought he was going to—"

"Shhh." Liam held her tight against his chest as he ran his palm over her hair and soothed her. "It's all right. I'm fine. It's going to be okay."

"I never should have left. It was stupid."

"No." She'd needed space. Liam knew deep down that he'd done the right thing in letting her go. They'd never be able to have any kind of relationship if he couldn't give her freedom and offer his trust. "You were right to go. You need time. I'm never going to pressure you, Devon. I won't ever make another demand. I was wrong to pressure you into this world. This new life."

"We'll figure this out. Together," Devon said on a shaky breath. "Take me home."

"All right, love. I'll take you to your cabin."

"No." Her voice was muffled by his shirt but no less adamant. "*Your home.*"

Liam's chest swelled with tender emotion. "Our home."

Devon pulled back to look at him. A large circle darkened the skin under her eye and the blood that trickled down her forehead had dried to a dark crimson. Delicate. Human. So incredibly fragile. And Liam vowed that he'd let her remain that way for as long as she needed to. He'd never pressure her to bend to his will again. She was his mate. Nothing else mattered as long as she was at his side.

"Our home," he repeated. "Come on, let's go."

CHAPTER 15

Four months later . . .

The pool nearest the river at Kirkham hot springs under the nearly full moon was one of the most beautiful things Devon had ever seen. Hot water cascaded in a trickling waterfall, adding to the sound of the river as it rushed by. Devon shivered as the cool spring air kissed her naked flesh, coaxing goose bumps to the surface of her skin. She marveled over the events of the past several months that brought her to this moment. Her life had done a complete one-eighty. And she had a very sexy werewolf to thank for it.

The heat of Liam's body warmed her back before his bare chest even made contact with her skin. Devon's lips curled in an indulgent smile as she allowed her eyes to drift shut.

"Cold?"

The deep rumble of his voice resonated through her and she shivered for a completely different reason. "Not even a little bit."

"Liar." Liam chuckled. "You're covered in goose bumps."

Okay, so maybe she was a little cold. But Devon welcomed the chilling sensation. After tonight, Liam assured her that she'd never feel cold again—at least, not in the same way—and Devon wanted to commit the feeling to memory. Everything would change. She'd leave the life she knew behind. Four months ago, the prospect of change had terrified her. But Liam had given her the time and space she needed to make a decision on her own and she was ready now. She wanted this life. She wanted Liam.

Forever.

He took her by the hand and guided her into the shallow pool. Pins and needles pricked at her skin as the geothermally heated water made contact with her cooled skin. It only took a moment for her to adjust to the temperature as she settled down into the shallow pool. Liam settled down behind her and she let her back rest against his wide, muscular chest.

"Better?"

Devon let out an indulgent sigh. "Much better."

Last year, she would have balked at the prospect of skinny-dipping, even at night. But Liam assured her that modesty was something that a werewolf quickly learned to live without and she figured she might as well get used to running around outside without her clothes on. After all, she'd be doing it at least once per month for the rest of her existence.

Several quiet moments passed. Liam's hands roamed her body. His lips touched down on her bare shoulder, her throat, the nape of her neck. "You don't have to do this you know." When he finally broke the silence, Devon sensed the worry in his tone. "If you're not ready, if you need more time, I'll understand."

Of course he would. Liam's patience with her seemed to have no end. Since that day when Christoph had sent her car down the embankment, Liam had gone out of his way to be patient with her. To cater to her needs and be understanding. It hadn't all been smooth sailing since then. Adjusting to pack life was something of a culture shock. Sort of like living on a campus with fifteen rowdy brothers and a few sisters. Boundaries were often crossed, but Devon had come to learn that with such a tight-knit group as Liam's pack, boundaries were bound to blur. There wasn't a single member of Liam's pack that she didn't adore. She already considered them family. And after tomorrow, she'd truly be one of them.

"I don't need any more time." Devon turned and tilted her head up toward Liam. He leaned down for a quick kiss. "I'm ready. I've been ready for a while. It's time to move forward and get on with our lives."

"Hmmmm." The deep hum of his voice sent a fresh round of chills over Devon's skin. His eyes lit with gold as a wide smile spread across his full lips. "I like the sound of that."

He reached around to cup her breasts in his palms. Devon's head fell back on his shoulder and she let out a slow, contented breath. The pads of his thumbs brushed her pearled nipples and she shuddered. The simplest touch from Liam ignited a bright spark within her that quickly turned to a raging fire. Devon had never known true desire until Liam.

Devon loved Liam. The more she thought of it, the more she realized she'd been in love with him from the moment she'd laid eyes on him.

"Are you worried?" Liam had done his best to prepare her for what the transition would be like. She was beginning to think it bothered him a lot more than it bothered her.

"A little." There was no use lying to a werewolf. "But I know you're going to take care of me until I settle in to it."

Liam kissed the top of her head. He continued his slow exploration of her body that heated Devon's blood and quickened her breath. "You'll have nothing to fear," he murmured against her ear. "The pack will take care of you."

Devon's biggest concern had always been the prospect of losing herself. Of becoming someone else. Liam assured her that the changes she'd experience would be merely metaphysical in nature. That while her body would change, the essence of what made her unique would always remain the same. He'd also let them split their time between Stanley and Lowman and agreed to continue to do so after her transition so that Devon could run the bar and keep that part of her life intact. She knew there would come a time that she'd be forced to let it go, but Liam assured her that it would be years before that would happen. For now, very little had to change.

"I'm lucky to have you." Tender emotion swelled in Devon's chest. "I'm lucky to have all of you."

"I'm the one who's lucky." Liam's solemn tone only intensified the emotion that lodged itself in Devon's throat. "To have found my mate after believing I would never find her is a gift I will never take for granted."

Devon didn't speak. She couldn't. The words stalled on her tongue, stayed by unshed tears. She'd never felt for anyone what she felt for Liam. He was her heart, her soul, her comfort, her home. Words hadn't been invented that could properly describe what she felt for him. And by letting Liam bite her under the full moon tomorrow night, she would ensure that they would be together for as long as possible.

She turned in Liam's arms. Their mouths met, tongues danced, hands explored. Their breaths mingled into one. Time stood still while they enjoyed each other's bodies under the light of the full moon.

"I love you, Liam." Devon uttered the words against his mouth. She'd told him every day for months and would continue to do so until she didn't have breath to fill her lungs. "I love you so much."

"I love you, too." His mouth found hers again and the urgency of his kiss banished all further conversation. They didn't need words to convey how they felt. All they needed was each other.

Liam paced the confines of his bedroom. The moon would be up in less than a half hour and with his transition, he'd no longer be able to communicate with Devon. Tonight's full moon would be solemn for the pack. There would be no hunt. No running through the forest. No wild abandon. Tonight, the pack would stand watch over Devon as she recovered from the bite that Liam would deliver. He knew that she was strong enough. That she'd survive the transition. That her mind was sound and that duality wouldn't weigh on her. Still, he couldn't help but worry. Nothing mattered more than her safety. He'd never forgive himself if something happened to her.

"Relax." Devon's easy laughter released the tension in his muscles. "You're so nervous you'd think *you're* the one about to be bitten by a two-hundred-and-fifty-pound werewolf."

It would be only a nip. Just enough to break the skin. But Liam was reluctant to harm her, even if the result would help to strengthen their mate bond and ensure that they would be together for centuries to come.

"I don't want to hurt you." The admission made Liam's chest ache.

"You won't. Not enough for it to matter anyway."

Gods, she was strong. Brave. Fierce. She'd make a formidable werewolf, Liam had no doubt in his mind. "Are you sure you're ready . . . ?"

"Liam." Devon gave a rueful shake of her head. "We discussed this last night. I'm ready."

"Last night I was too distracted by your body to think clearly." He teased, but it wasn't far from the truth. Devon could easily distract him with nothing more than a heated glance.

Her husky laughter sent a delicious chill down Liam's spine. His wolf gave an anxious yip in the recess of his psyche. The animal was close to the forefront of his mind, ready to be let out and even more eager to make their mate truly theirs. As a werewolf, Devon would feel their mate bond in the same way Liam did. The wolf was as anxious for that connection between them as Liam was.

The past four months had been bliss. He didn't want to ruin a good thing. What if she had second thoughts, or regrets? What if he did something tonight that he couldn't take back that would cause her to resent him? To hate him? He'd shrivel up and die if that were to happen.

"Are all Alpha werewolves so broody and melodramatic, or is it just you?"

Her teasing tone did little to temper his anxiety. She smiled and the brilliance of it was like the sun, banishing the dark cloud he'd cast on his thoughts. Tonight was supposed to be a time to rejoice, not mourn. He wasn't killing her, he was giving her a new life. A life they could share. Devon was truly remarkable. That they'd managed to find each other in this sparsely populated wilderness still amazed him.

He supposed he had Christoph running him out of Colorado to thank for it.

Liam's skin tightened on his frame and the magic of his impending full-moon transition sparked the air. The wolf wouldn't be denied for much longer. As soon as the moon crested the horizon, he would have no choice but to succumb to the animal's—and the moon's—pull. Once he bowed to that instinct, there would be no going back for either of them. The wolf would follow through. Devon might not be afforded the opportunity to change her mind. The wolf was a high-handed bastard. Alpha logic.

"I just want to be sure." He needed Devon to know that his love for her wasn't conditional. That she didn't have to make any sacrifices for him or anyone else. "I love you, Devon. Just as you are. That's enough for me."

Devon crossed the room. She took Liam's hands in hers as

her gaze held him still. "I love you, too. And I've told you already, I'm not doing this for you. I'm doing it for *me*. I want this. I've been ready for weeks. Stop trying to talk me out of it. My mind's made up. I can be just as stubborn as you can, you know."

That was certainly the truth. She was the perfect mate for an equally stubborn Alpha. "You win." Liam allowed for a chuckle as he bent down and kissed her forehead. "No more arguing. No more trying to talk you out of anything."

"Damn straight!" Devon gave him a playful knock on the shoulder. "Now, let's get this show on the road. The buildup is driving me crazy."

Liam took her by the hand and led her out of their bedroom and down the stairs. After tonight, everything would be different, and at the same time, wouldn't change at all. Liam reminded himself as he walked ahead of Devon through the house to the back door that his bite would be a gift and not a curse. He'd never once thought of his existence as anything to regret or be ashamed of. He possessed power and strength, the ability to protect those he loved and were under his care. And now, he'd pass those traits to his mate.

They stepped out the back door to find every member of the pack waiting for them fifty or so yards from the main house in a large clearing. Devon gave Liam's hand a gentle squeeze and in the small gesture, he felt every ounce of love she had for him.

"So much pomp and circumstance," she teased. "I feel underdressed in jeans."

Liam laughed. Gods, how he loved her. "If you feel underdressed now, wait for the next full moon." She'd have to get used to a lot more unabashed nakedness than she was used to. Pack life always required a time of adjustment for newly turned werewolves, and Devon would be no exception.

"Oh, I know it." She walked beside him now, her hand still in his. "It'll be interesting, that's for sure."

An understatement. "For both of us." Whether it came with the territory or not, Liam wasn't sure he was ready for the pack to see his mate without her clothes. For the first few full moons, Liam thought it might be best for his own sanity if they ran separate from the pack. At least, until Devon became more comfortable with her newfound duality.

She turned to face him and her expression became mischievous. "Jealous?"

"Always." Liam doubted there would ever be a time that he didn't feel possessive of Devon.

"Good. I sort of like that." She leaned in for a quick kiss.

She drove him absolutely mad with want. Liam stopped and allowed the kiss to linger. The moon wasn't up yet. He'd take every spare moment he could get.

"Hey." Devon pulled away. "Are you trying to distract me?"

"That depends," Liam replied. "Is it working?"

"Nope." Devon flashed a wide smile. "The moon's on the horizon. Are you ready?"

Liam's skin tingled with the impending shift. It was time. He kissed her once more in farewell until the moon set and he could speak to her again. "Everything's going to be okay."

"I know." Her trust in him made his chest swell with pride and tender emotion. "As long as I have you, everything will always be okay."

He felt the exact same way. He couldn't wait to start this new chapter of their lives. Liam belonged to Devon and she belonged to him.

Forever.